Also by Joe Prosit

Machines Monsters and Maniacs Volume 1

Bad Brains

99 Town, Book One of the "From Order" Series

Zero City, Book Three of the "From Order" Series

And coming soon…

Machines Monsters and Maniacs Volume 2

7 Androids

Book Two of the "From Order Series"

Joe Prosit

Chapter One

99 Town burned behind me, and I didn't bother to turn to watch it. The last person I expected to see alive stood in front of me.

My name was Chuck Alawode. I used to be a Federal Investigator for the Order. Now? I didn't know who or what I was anymore. Maggie, my presumed-dead wife, posted defiant, stern, and livid, with her hip cocked out and her eyes fixed on me. She was clean and beautiful and very much alive. I was on my knees, covered in blood and ashen, and feeling closer to the grave than ever.

"I thought you were dead," I said. Presumptions can be a real kick in the teeth.

Behind her, the hovercraft's rotors beat down green corn stalks in a radius around us. The air surged out in waves, rippling the leaves and tassels like a cotton sheet laid out across a bed. Two others stepped from the door of the jet-black hovercraft. Soldiers, it was clear from their equally dark clothes, body armor, tactical gear, and assault rifles. They fanned out to either side of Maggie and scanned our flanks.

"We don't have much time," Maggie said and stretched her hand out to me. "We got to you first, but the Order is right on our heels. They know where you are, Chuz. Unplug and get on board."

My eyes blurred over, wet from irritation and emotion. The image of another woman, a woman I'd fallen in love with in 99 Town, still danced in my imagination. Sara. I was ready to die with the memory of her set firmly in my mind. Now, I was going to go on living, she was dead, and Maggie was back from the grave. A reversal moments in the making.

"I don't understand," I told her.

"No time to explain here, but I can tell you everything I know once we're on board," Maggie said, her hand still stretched out to me. Still empty. "Or we can leave you here and let the Order pick you up. It won't take them long. You have two choices: come with me or stay on the Network and die under the Order."

I looked her up and down once more. She wasn't dressed like a soldier. No black clothes or body armor or even a gun. Khakis and a buttoned-up shirt. Hiking boots. Her brown hair ponytailed back but still lashing against the wind of the hovercraft. Her hand, palm up, still waiting. She stood there as if she hadn't abandoned me. As if she hadn't faked her death. As if her death hadn't spurred all the hell and torment I'd just suffered. No regrets. No apologies.

"This doesn't solve anything," I said. "Not between the two of us. A lot of people are dead."

"Too many," she agreed.

I glared at her palm and tried to decrypt what it meant, what it told me, what it hid. But what other options did I have? If I believed nothing else she had ever led me to believe, she was right about one thing: the Order was on its way, and when it found me, it would eliminate me. I put my soiled palm into her clean hand.

Maggie gripped me tight and hauled me to my feet. As soon as she had a hold of me, her patience evaporated. She dragged me toward the strange war-battered black hovercraft. As we closed in on the doors, the two soldiers enveloped us and panned across the sky with the barrels of their guns. Maggie forced me on board first and followed quickly after. As soon as the soldiers lifted their boots off the soil, the hovercraft was lifting into the sky.

There were two rows of jump seats inside the hovercraft, benches made out of aluminum pipes and red-strap nets. Maggie set me across from her and began buckling up. The two soldiers manned door-mounted machine guns facing out each side of the aircraft. The guns were mounted on multi-jointed armatures and swivels. The hovercraft pitched forwards, shoving away from the ground where I had unearthed himself, ending my path of death and destruction. I hoped.

99 Town. The last bastion of humans living off the Network, free of the technocratic totalitarian rule of the Order, free from the implants with which they monitored everything a human did and didn't do. I went into 99 Town as a widower and an agent of the Order sent to investigate a murder. I left as something completely different. I wasn't sure what I was anymore. Certainly not an agent of the Order. Not a widow either. And now I was running from them, accompanied by Underground rebels and my wife, whose body I'd seen smashed into the pavement a hundred stories below the busted-out window of our Chicago apartment. Strange, how fast things change.

As the gunners scanned the sky with their machine guns, I doubted my troubles would be confined to 99 Town. No, they'd follow me to… wherever she was taking me now. The pilot, this wasn't an unmanned hovercraft, was just beyond Maggie's row of jump seats in a small cockpit. He knew where we were going. Maybe he was the only one.

Rushed, Maggie picked up a headset wired to the craft's infrastructure. She pulled a microphone to her lips and yelled something I couldn't hear over the rotor wash. She jabbed a finger at me, then at her ear, then back at me.

There was another headset with ear muffs and a microphone hanging from a hook. Everything was connected by wires and armatures. The thing was obsolete fifty years ago. I snatched it and worked it onto my head.

"—that fucking thing out before they kill you with it!" Maggie was yelling, still gesturing at her ear, then at mine. "Unplug!"

The implant in my head, just behind my right ear. The thing I'd fought to get out of 99 Town. People had died for it. I thought Maggie had died for it. A direct neural connection to the Network and the Order. A perfect spy and assassin, living right inside my head. I got a firm grip on the small device and pulled it out of my port. My vision blurred. My left ear played a high-pitched whine. An old injury from childhood. A perforated eardrum that never healed. Without the implant's help, my hearing was terrible. My vision only slightly better.

"Now what?" I asked.

"Throw it! Get it off this goddamn hovercraft!" Maggie said.

I looked out to the cornfields rushing by. We weren't high up but had to be going over two hundred kilometers per hour. When I threw it, it'd be lost forever, buried in endless acres of uniform crops. I balked.

"It served its purpose. Get rid of it!" Maggie yelled.

I grimaced, then tossed it out. As soon as it hit the air, the tiny piece of plastic and electronics disappeared behind us. With it gone, Maggie visibly relaxed and slouched back into her jump seat. I looked at my empty hands, saw only the blood and dirt from my time in 99 Town, and tried to brush it away.

"Do you have any idea what I had to go through to get that?" I asked. No need to yell. The headphones did a good job of muffling out the noise and transmitting our voices.

"We know exactly what you've been through, Chuz," Maggie said.

"A lot of people died to get that data. Good people."

"Too many people," Maggie agreed again.

"But not you," I said.

The pilot interrupted us. I didn't realize he and the door gunners were listening in on everything Maggie and I had to say. Not that I really cared.

"We have incoming bogeys approaching from the south. Three Order gunships on an intercept course."

"They're homing in on the implant," Maggie said. "Maintain radio silence. No one broadcast anything. If they make visual contact with us, jam all signals," Maggie said into the mic. "In the meantime, stick to the flight plan. Stay low. Nap-of-the-earth. Get us over the water and take us north."

"Confirmed. We'll hit the shoreline just over Kenosha and set course straight north."

So she was some sort of leader of these people. That was fine. It was fine if they overheard our conversation too then.

"You don't care about them?" I asked her. "The bodies you left behind? Mike, Mickey, Sara…"

Maggie lifted her eyebrows at the mention of that name.

"Ruby?" I continued.

"You owe Ruby your life," Maggie told me off. "She did more for us than you'll ever know. She was there to guide you through the whole fucking thing. To bring you to the very spot where we picked you up. To put the data in your hands and give you the push you needed to use it. But she wasn't supposed to die, Chuz."

"Was I?" I asked. "Were you?"

"Coming over Kenosha," the pilot said. "The three gunships are still coming up behind us. One of them slowed where we dropped the implant, but the other two are closing in fast. Twenty kilometers behind us."

"I don't have time for this shit," Maggie said.

The hovercraft rotated on its vector, turning the door to my right to the rear of our direction of travel. The door gunner watched our six o'clock. I looked around him, behind the hovercraft. The wind tugged and snapped the tails of my white Order uniform as my eyes searched the horizon for any gleaming white dots that might be our Order pursuers. I was an outlaw now. Would be until the day I died, whether I wanted things that way or not. I'd crossed a point of no return.

In a flash, a small suburban town passed underneath them. Then it was all water. Endless dark choppy waves like an ocean. The shoreline widened and the town shrunk behind us as they plunged over Lake Michigan. The pilot dipped the hovercraft lower, closer to the waves and water until the air was filled with mist. We left a wake behind us.

Just at the edge of the shore, I spotted the two Order gunships. They gleamed like porcelain droplets.

"We've made visual contact," the pilot said.

"Jam them. Cut them off from the Network. Stay low to the waves. Hold your fire until they engage. They might not have spotted us yet," Maggie said.

"We're jamming all signals," the pilot said. "They're gaining on us. We're at top speed, and they're still closing fast."

"Just stay low and keep moving," Maggie said then to me, "Buckle up, Chuz. This pleasure cruise is about to get choppy."

"Let me guess. Now we're in Kansas?" I said and went to work piecing together the harness laying on the jump seats.

Maggie, confused, or maybe just annoyed with me, glanced at the water rushing underneath us, then back to me. I ignored her and finished clicking together the harness just as a salvo of tracer fire zipped past our right side. Both our heads whipped back to the hovercraft's six o'clock. The two Order hovercrafts had grown in size and definition. They maneuvered to our left and right to box us in. Another burst of machine gun fire, highlighted with burning red tracers, arced to our left and splashed into Lake Michigan.

"Somebody do something!" I yelled.

Maggie, despite all my recent experience with getting shot at while on the move, was more specific with her directions. "Take evasive action. Lure them into range of our guns."

The hovercraft banked hard to the left, and the centripetal force crammed me down into my seat and gave me a view aimed straight down into the depth of the lake rather than the horizon. Then, without warning, the hovercraft hooked right, and my view twisted from water to sky. The rocking and twisting knotted up my stomach. If I kept watching out the door, I'd be sick. I needed to focus on something slightly less nauseating, so turned to Maggie. She clung to handles bolted to the ceiling. Her face was pale. Her hair flung with each bank, half-hiding her own nausea.

A door gunner opened fire. A deafening series of blasts hit my ears, through the headset and through the whine. With the hovercraft turned as it was, my back was to our pursuers, and I couldn't see what the gunner was aiming at or if he was ever close to hitting a target. The hovercraft banked hard again, and the other gunner opened fire. I ground my teeth as the G-forces purged the blood from my brain.

"Was this all part of your plan too? Come back to life just so I could die here with you?" I yelled.

"You really think this is all about you?" Maggie said. "You really can't see the bigger picture here? This is so much bigger than me or you, or Ruby. Or Sara."

"Don't you speak her name."

"Fuck you, Chuz. You have no idea the forces at work here."

"Well, how about you clue me in. So far, all you've done is hide and lie and deceive. How about you start by telling me how it is you're still alive," I yelled. Another blast came from one of the door gunners and drowned out my words, so I waited for a pause and then yelled again, "I saw your dead body!"

"You saw what the Order wanted you to see," Maggie said. Another salvo of machine gun fire. Another swarm of burning magnesium tracers flashing just outside of the hovercraft. One good hit, and we'd be in the drink. "Every minute of your life, you only saw what they showed you, and you welcomed it every time you plugged in your implant."

"Tell me. Tell me how you faked your death. Tell me why you lied to me!"

"We're a little busy right now, sweetheart. Or maybe you didn't notice all the gunfire," Maggie said.

"Tell me!"

Maggie turned away from me just as the pilot put the hovercraft into a deep banked curve. We were so low and the turn so sharp, I could have reached my arm out of the open door and touched water. Mist sizzled off the lake and into the cabin. The turn pushed all the blood and air and otoconia to one side of my brain. My vision narrowed. The whine that was usually confined to my left ear filled my head. The hovercraft swooped up out of the turn just in time for me to fight off blacking out, and then both door gunners opened up another long deafening salvo. A bleach-white Order gunship flashed past us. Following the gunship lead my eyes back to Maggie. Stern, angry, secretive Maggie.

"How are you still alive? Why did the Order think you were dead?" I pressed her. She wanted me to give this up. Wanted me to let her get by with this.

"Not right now, Chuz."

"Don't bullfuck me, Maggie!"

"You want to know?" she challenged me.

"I think I have the right."

"You want to know all the secrets and motivations of a movement you've dedicated your life to stomping out?"

"Things have changed, Maggie. If they hadn't, I wouldn't be sitting here, and you know it," I said.

She dug something out of a pocket and held it tight in her fist. "You want answers, huh? Right now?"

"Better now than before I'm dead at the bottom of the lake," I said.

Maggie slapped something small into my palm. The hovercraft twisted and turned again. A long blast from the door gunner connected with one of the Order gunships. A black contrail of greasy smoke rolled through the cabin. I blinked the grit from my eyes and opened my palm.

Another implant. This one was only slightly more damaged and aged than the one I'd just tossed out the door.

"It's shielded from radio emission. And encrypted," Maggie said. "Not connected to the Network. We have ways of communicating in the Underground the Order can't hear. If you want to know the truth, plug in."

I locked eyes with my wife, not breaking my gaze even when the craft banked and jostled my organs again. I moved aside my right earmuff, turned the implant around in my hand, and craned my neck to find my port. As soon as the jack clicked into place, my vision cleared and the tinnitus in my left ear silenced.

I heard Maggie over the intercom in crystal-clear digitally-enhanced audio. "Okay. He's plugged in. Knock him out."

"No! You bitch!" I scrambled to pull the implant from my brain, but before my fingers could reach the device, everything went black and silent. Just like I was connected to a light switch.

Chapter Two

Maggie didn't so much wake me up as turned me back on. For all I knew, I'd never closed my eyes. But when Maggie unplugged the implant from behind my ear, I came to so instantaneously that I saw her hand draw away from my head with the device held in her fingers.

They'd moved me while I was out. The hovercraft, water, machine gun fire, and sunlight were all gone, replaced by a steady hum, and a dim glow from a single light bulb. The cold, wet air above Lake Michigan had been wiped away as neatly as a spill on a countertop. Dank, humid air laced with an oily stink filled the enclosed space in which I found myself.

I was laying down on a bed in a small room. In the sparse light I could see the room was cluttered with boxes and containers of junk. In some ways, the place was similar to the spare bedroom in Sara Cohen's apartment. Warm, cluttered, cramped, chaotic, but quiet. But it had none of the comforting sensations of that place. No sunlight seeping through the blinds. No musty blankets. No mouthwatering aroma of coffee and bacon from down the hall. This was more like waking up in an abandoned warehouse than in a quiet old apartment. And of course, Maggie was up waiting for me instead of Sara.

She gave the implant a little toss and caught it back in her palm. "Amazing what you can do with these things when you control the network they're tied to," she said, examining it with her fingers. Her robotic fingers, I noticed. That was different too.

Her whole left arm was cybernetic. I could tell by her hand and by the shape of the arm under her shirt. Steel straight and stiff. "Your arm," I said.

"Yeah," she flexed and unflexed it. "A souvenir from the assassin android that tried to push me out of our apartment window. It ripped my arm right out of my rotator cuff when I pushed it through the glass. I was lucky I didn't bleed out right there in our living room."

"Your body. On the sidewalk," I said.

"Not mine. The android's. The Order sent me a killer wearing my own face so it could replace me without anyone, including my husband, noticing," Maggie said. "Like I told you, you've only seen what the Order wanted you to see. Every image, every sound, every experience rose-tinted by their implant. Care to see what they didn't want to show you?"

I sat up, but my vision narrowed and turned white.

"Easy," Maggie said and held me steady by the shoulders. "You've been out close to ten hours now. You were getting combative when we needed it the least. Plus, the others were more comfortable if you didn't know how we got here. We always have to be careful about spies and informants from the Order. Not everyone is as convinced about your conversion as I am."

"You knocked me out, right through the implant."

Maggie smirked. She was sitting on the bed now, at eye level with me. "Maybe one of these days you'll learn not to trust these things. Would it help if I said I was sorry?"

I smiled. Same old Maggie. Living or dead, secret rebel agent or law-abiding journalist, she really hadn't changed. "Doubt it."

"Well, I wasn't going to say it anyway," Maggie sighed. She stood up and pocketed the implant. "I'll give you a minute to get up and stretch out the cramps. When you're ready, I'll be outside."

After she left through the door near the end of the bed, I took my time getting up. The things I had in my pocket, just a comb and toothbrush, sat on top of a dresser. My clothes hung half off an old wooden dresser, my Order white trench coat dangling almost to the floor. Only then did I realize I'd been stripped to my underwear. Was it Maggie who took my clothes off before laying me down? Seemed like something a wife would do for a husband, but she never stuck too close to the wife script. Didn't seem like a wife at all anymore. Not before and not after everything I'd experienced since her "death." But if I was wrong to assume she expired, that it was her corpse on the sidewalk a hundred floors below our apartment, how many other things was I wrong about? I could toss it around in my head all day, but no amount of navel-gazing would answer my questions. I got up and put on my pants, shirt, and shoes. I left the coat hanging on the dresser, opened the door of the bedroom, and stepped out.

There was a short hallway lined with similar doors. Other bedrooms. A bathroom perhaps. But the cavernous room at the end of the hallway led me to believe that this was no place for bedrooms at all, and the room I'd been in had been built as an office or store room, not a bedroom. I walked out of the hallway and up to a railing overlooking a sort of garage or workshop with all the matching smells and ubiquitous layers of grease on the walls and floor. At least it had been a garage just as the bedroom had at one point been an office. Now, this place was some sort of command post. A hive of gunmen, rebels, technicians, and their lieutenants.

Next to me a metal ladder painted in flaking yellow ran up to a roof access. Industrial skylights let in slats of sunlight from above and sodium arc lamps lit what the filtered sunlight didn't. Carpets and rugs were laid over the old concrete floor, and on top of the rugs were workstations and a multitude of various other electronic equipment. Thick wires and cables snaked from one cluster of computers to the next. Everything was hardwired rather than connected over-the-air. Ancient technology. A handful of people moved about from one station to another, instinctually stepping over all the cables. They were dressed in black clothes just similar enough to each other to be considered uniforms, but unlike uniforms, still motley and idiosyncratic. They all wore implants but still communicated audibly. They talked to each other without the use of rank or titles, some more energetic than others, but all of them vulgar and artful with their swear words. Swearing under the Order, as Mike put it, was a dying fucking art form. If that was the case, this place the Louvre of bad language.

Maggie sauntered out of the crowd, her body its own medium of visual vulgarity.

"All these wires and cords, but you people still wear implants," I said.

"The implants are too useful to go without, so we focused our encryption efforts on an intranet and eliminated anything else that might emit a radio frequency," Maggie said. "But the Order can't reach us here. We're shielded from their electronic eyes."

I noticed a map displayed on one of the monitors across the room. A large body of water, and a shoreline running east by northeast. I didn't recognize the terrain.

"Lake Superior's north shore," Maggie said. She walked up the steps to join me at the railing. We looked over the garage and the operations set up here. "We lost those Order hovercrafts shortly after you went under. Took a long flight up Lake Michigan, crossed the You Pee through the Hiawatha Forest, and came westward from there. The further we stay away from city centers the easier it is to remain undetected by the Order. That dot? That's us, just north of Silver Bay," she pointed. "Back near the end of the twentieth century, this place used to maintain taconite mining equipment. But that was a long time ago."

"And now?" I asked.

"Now, we are pressed for time," Maggie said. "We took a lot of risks to get someone from the Order on our side. Every day the Underground is corralled further and further into the shadows. Every day we lose ground. What happened in 99 Town was the first victory we've had in a long time."

"You call that a victory?"

"We exposed the Order's crimes. Won over a whole city. Won you over too," Maggie said. "And now we have a weapon that can take down their whole Network. Or at least, we have somebody who's going to find the weapon we need to take them down."

"Oh yeah. Who's that?"

"You, Chuz," Maggie said. "Follow me."

Her metal hand glided along the metal rail as she walked down the stairs to the floor. She moved over the cable and wires like she'd been born with them underfoot. I followed, glancing up between the floor and where she was taking me. The people dressed in black around us continued their work, yelling back and forth in an even blend of jargon and vulgarity.

"Check the fucking timing on it. If they jumped, we need to go back to a passive scan."

"I checked the fucking timing already. And I'm not switching to passive when I can blast them actively."

"Did they load a new hopset then?"

"No. Same hopset. I think it's just a new encryption."

"Well, look at the fucking spectrum analyzer for Christ's sake. That's what it's there for!"

It all meant nothing to me. Maggie led me through the hive of technicians and soldiers.

"You're wearing an implant too," I said.

"Not tied to the Network. I told you, we have our own intranet, isolated from the Order's," Maggie said. "Keeping it isolated is critical. Our technological superiority is key to everything we do here."

"Do I get one?"

"Not exactly," Maggie said. "You get to plug into something bigger."

We came to a fifty-five-gallon drum that sat next to a reclined chair just below a large monitor bolted to the wall. Trails of cords and wires ran from all points around the garage to the drum and up to the curious item that rested on top. It was a skull. Not a human skull. An android skull.

It was feminine, if such a thing could have a gender, and seemed to be undamaged aside from being separated from its body. It had no skin and didn't appear to be designed to wear skin. Its shell was glistening white. Its face was aesthetically beautiful but ripe for violence. Or maybe that was just my newly formed bias against androids I earned in 99 Town. Its neck was slender and ended where most of the cables began. Other wires were plugged into it where an implant would go in a human skull. Together the wires and cables formed a nest on top of the drum before trailing down to a multitude of connections across the garage.

"Chuz, meet Number Seven," Maggie said and waved her hand like a model showing off a new car.

"What do I care about a god-fucking android?" I asked. My own skills with bad language were still in their infancy. But having gone through Vulgarity 101 in 99 Town, I think I was getting better at it. "You still haven't answered any of my shitting questions."

"First, you answer our questions," Maggie said. "And all the answers are inside of this head."

"How am I supposed to get them out? I don't know anything about robotics. Have one of these data geeks hack into it," I said. "Why bring me into the picture?"

A new voice boomed from behind us. "Because you have a newfound hate for their kind," a man said. He hobbled on a bad leg and spoke through a thick gray squared-off beard. He wore a dingy and barely recognizable Order white trench coat. Under it was the same style of black, chaotic, quasi-military clothing the others wore. The man pulled off a welder's skull cap to reveal a bald head. He rubbed it for a bit and then looked back to me. "Call me Gaius. I used to be in the Order too, if you're wondering about the coat. Although I have to say, it took a lot less cajoling for me to leave than it did for you."

"Who said I left?" I said.

The man, Gaius, chuckled. "You are one ornery son of a bitch, you know that Mister Alawode? If you really want to stay with the Order, you came to the wrong place. Make that decision, and the only guarantee I can make you is a much shorter life span. Listen, you can run back to the Order if you want, but you know better than I do that they won't have you. You've been chased and hunted. Everyone around you has been killed. You've lost everything you've ever known. You have nothing. Are nothing. Will be nothing. We're offering you a new life."

"A truer life," Maggie said. "And isn't that what you've been after? The truth?"

I glared at her. She knew me too well, and I hated her for it. "It will only be your version of the truth," I said. "Why should I trust any of you?"

"Because we're all you have left," Maggie said. "If you can't learn to trust us, it's the end of the line, Chuz."

"We don't have a lot of time," Gaius said. "No doubt they reported our course when we pulled you out of the Network, and they're searching for us as we speak. I'm not going to patronize you or waste my time placating your sensitivities. As a matter of fact, we need you because of your stubbornness and insensitivity. We need you to be that cold and disengaged observer. We need someone who won't get attached."

"Observe what? Get attached to who?"

"To her," Gaius jammed a finger at the android skull on top of the drum. "That android was on the mission that crushed the Independent Resistance Movement, brought us all under the heel of the Order, and ended with the dawn of the Event. That assassin android, along with six others, changed the course of history."

Maggie stepped forward. "In one day's time, the Resistance lost command and control of their army. The Order flipped the table on them. On August Sixth Two Thousand and Fifty One the Resistance had the Order against the ropes. On August Seventh, the Event happened, and the Resistance was wiped out. The Order's rule has gone unquestioned ever since."

"And it's high time we find out how they did it," Gaius said. "The answers are inside this android's memories. But we can't access them remotely. Too many firewalls and encryptions to read the data. The only way we can access the memories is through full-immersion simulation."

"So then plug somebody in. They'll live the android's memories firsthand," I said.

"We have," Maggie said. "And they've all gone insane."

Gaius strolled over to the head on top of the barrel and caressed its smooth dome. "Ever since the Event, this little cunt here has been running around as a rogue agent. Twenty-five years, she's been at it. She never went back to the Order to debrief, to get new guidance, for maintenance. No. Instead, she's been running around all through the upper Midwest, killing every human she comes across as she goes. Members of the Resistance. The Underground. The Order. Civilians. She didn't care just so long as they were human. For years, we didn't believe she was real. Sounded like the kind of legend soldiers would make up to scare each other: a rogue assassin android deep behind enemy lines who kills at random and then disappears back into the night. Then, just as you were getting on in 99 Town, we cornered her, killed her, and brought her here."

"Twenty-five years, Chuck," Maggie said. "For twenty-five years this thing has been on an off-the-leash killing spree. No direction from the Order. No memory wipes. No maintenance."

"So let's just say she's taken on some eccentricities over the years," Gaius said.

Maggie looked over her shoulder at the bustling technicians in the garage. "Most of these people grew up in the Underground. Some don't have a port and the ones that do aren't used to living life inside a simulation. They lose their grip on reality too fast, and before we know it, they forget who they are and start thinking they're the assassin android and they're the ones killing humans and working for the Order."

Gaius itched his beard. "The ones with enough experience to keep reality and simulation separate still end up empathizing with the android, if you can believe that, and come out deranged and rambling all kinds of nonsense about there being no mission, no purpose, no God. Men weren't meant to exist inside the heads of robots. And as for this robot…"

I cracked a dry smile. "If you worked for the Order then you have as much simulator training as I do. If this is so important, why don't you plug into that thing and take it for a ride?"

Gaius grinned wider, his yellowed teeth showing through the wiry bristles of his beard. "Because you're expendable."

Maggie took my chin and turned me toward her. "The others we've put in, they associated with the android. They empathized with her, and it drove them crazy. We don't just need your experience; we need your attitude and disposition. And if we have to pull you out early, or if the memory doesn't give us the full picture, we need somebody to observe all the pieces of the puzzle who has the skills to put them together. We need an investigator. And we need someone who won't empathize with an android. Someone with a strong mental resolve. Chuz, I saw what the last android you came across did to you. I saw what it did to… to her."

"You people got some balls," I said to both of them. "How about you go fuck yourself and then ask me again if I want to go live inside that thing's head."

I pushed through Gaius and headed back through the horde of technicians and techno-blather.

"Triangulate it, analyze it, and jam it. Shit! It's not that complicated."

"Then you look at these fucking algorithms!"

"You don't need the fucking algorithms. Brute force attack until we find the sub-audible tone. Watch the spectrum for fuck's sake."

"Chuz!" That was Maggie's voice, trailing after me as I moved to the short staircase. "Chuz!"

That wasn't even my name. I left Chuz for dead back in 99 Town. People who really knew me, they called me Chuck. Too bad they were all dead too.

I let her chase me. This was all her fault to begin with. My trip to 99 Town. The murder case. The dead I left behind… I stormed up the stairs and down the short hallway and threw open the door to the converted office/bedroom. Inside, I let the door bounce off the wall and creak closed. I stood in the middle of the room and grabbed two fists full of my hair.

She'd come, I knew her well enough to have no doubt about that. I wouldn't have to wait long either. When she came through the door, I didn't turn to greet her.

"They're coming for us, Chuz," Maggie said. "The truth is we can't trust everyone who comes to us to join the Underground. No doubt some are plants. Moles working for the Order. We don't know exactly how they track us, but our spies in Chicago just sent us an encrypted message. The Order is sending out search parties our way. Drones mostly, but assault teams will follow."

"Sounds like their spies are better than yours," I said, feeling a little bit of perverse pride that the organization I chose was even more devious than the one she chose.

"Maybe. The point is, we have to take advantage of the time we have, however little time that might be, and you're the only chance we got. If we wait, they'll find us, and when they do…"

"Oh, I know exactly what they'll do," I laughed, still not facing her.

"And you won't do anything about it?"

"You watched," I said and turned to face Maggie. "The whole time I was in 99 Town, you watched. You stood by as that thing ripped her head clean off her shoulders. That woman, maybe you hated her for what she was to me, but she was a living, breathing, dreaming person before that android got to her. She loved me. She cared about me. She opened herself up to me, which is more than you can say. And you watched it murder her. Now you want to lecture me about standing by and doing nothing?"

"Oh, this is about us?" Maggie said. "About our sham of a marriage? About me shutting you out? God damn it, Chuz. I tried to crack you every fucking day we were married. I pried at you and tried to chisel through to you. But you never let me in. You loved nothing but the Order and that fucking white coat. *You* abandoned *me*. And when I finally found a way to free you from your own self-made prison, you betrayed me again."

"You were supposed to be fucking dead!" I yelled.

"And I suppose it's my fault you only managed to see the light after I was dead," Maggie said. "Don't you get it, Chuz? Everything I've done was designed to reach you. To pry you from the Order's grasp. From your mission to 99 Town to bringing you here. And now you want me to feel sorry for your mistress?"

"I was always faithful to you, and you know it," I said. "Till the day you died. And even after that, I risked my life and sacrificed everything I ever had to find out the truth. To find out what really happened to you."

"But you still chose to open yourself up to her instead of me," Maggie said.

"You ever think maybe it was because she earned it?" I said. "You let her die, and now you're ready to plug me into a machine guaranteed to drive me crazy. Tell you what, Mags. How about for once in our misery excuse for a marriage we get honest with each other. This isn't about us. It's not about her and it sure as fuck ain't about me. This is about your crusade. Has been since before I knew you were a crusader. So just go ahead and ask me to do it. For the cause. For the mission."

"Chuz... I loved you," she said, her eyes wet. "But I lost you, and this was the only way I could get you back."

I turned away and walked deeper into the shallow room. I didn't want to see the tears and that lying face anymore. I remembered, a long time ago, we did love each other. We were in love and thrilled to be around each other. She used to make me happy just by being near. But that was a long time ago.

"Fine. I'll ask you," Maggie said. "Plug in. Do this thing for me, and I'll tell you everything. Everything I've done for the Underground. How I tricked you. How I've lied to you. Why I had to lie to you. We'll have time to talk it all out. To get back to square one. Do this, and maybe *we* can be *us* again."

"What if I say no?" I asked.

Gaius's deep voice chuckled from beyond Maggie. I turned and saw the bearded man standing behind her, and two black-clad soldiers standing next to him. "What gave you the impression you ever had a choice, Mister Alawode?"

The android's decapitated head hadn't moved from its nest of cables on top of the old steel drum. It sat sanitized and neutered, jacked into a dozen cords and wires, but inert. Its dead unlit eyes met mine. A lunatic murderer's eyes. All black. Never meant to even mimic a human's. They seemed to wait for me.

"Shit me," I said. "Okay. Let's get this over with."

There was an ergonomic chair reclined next to the drum, directly under a big wall-sized monitor. The monitor displayed bands and waves of the electromagnetic spectrum. The people at the workstations had calmed. They must have resolved whatever they were working on earlier. The garage wasn't quiet; air movers churned deep inside the walls of the building and overhead fans spun and cut patterns through the sunlight. Cooling fans whirled inside the electronics. There was a hum to the entire place and a quiet murmur as I climbed into the chair as if I was a prisoner on death row and this was the means of my execution.

The two soldiers that had led me from the bedroom to the chair took a step back and let a technician through. He was wire-thin, and although he wore all black like the others, he carried none of the weapons, armor, or field equipment. Instead, he had a pocket full of short cable adapters and a few stylus. His head was shaved bald on either side, and he had rows of ports embedded into his skull. Two of the six ports held implants. He pulled a chair next to my head and tapped away at a control panel there. He spoke, but I barely listened.

"The man, the myth, Mister Alawode. Heard a lot about you, that's the fucking truth. So, check it out. I'm going to drop you in about a half day before the start of the mission that took down the Resistance. That should give you time to acclimate to the memory. You know, get comfortable inside of her. Now, while you're in there…" he droned on.

I looked around for Maggie. As soon as I gave in and decided to let them jack me into the android's head, she seemed to fade into the background. This black-clothed technician took over. He was only as old as the Rogues from 99 Town. A teenager. He kept tapping at the controls and rambling.

"…you'll feel, hear, taste, and smell everything Number Seven did. Some of her senses aren't human and you'll feel those too. It will definitely freak you out a bit at first. But just ride the fucking wave, man. Don't fight it. You'll have time to get used to it before you have to really pay attention."

"What's your name?" I interrupted him.

"Huh?" the kid looked up, really seeing me for the first time.

"You got a name?"

The kid smiled. "Oh. Roach. I mean, Private Rory Henrichs. People just call me Roach but really—"

"Roach will do," I said. "Do me a favor, huh? Try not to melt my brain while I'm in there, okay?"

Roach laughed in a way that didn't relieve my concerns one bit and went back to work. Gaius watched over his shoulder.

"Once you're integrated into the android's memories, we don't want to pull you out if we don't have to," Gaius said. "It's hard on the brain, going back and forth. We won't be able to see what you're experiencing, but we will be able to monitor your vitals. Once you're in, there's no way you can signal us to pull you out. Understand?"

"In for a penny…" I said. Wasn't there an old saying that started that way? I forgot how it went but knew the sentiment. I was along for the ride, past the point of no return as soon as I began.

The technician, Roach, with help from a couple other technicians and soldiers, fixed electrodes to my head and chest, and a pulse oximeter to my finger. Ancient tools that hadn't been used since the invention of the implants. I doubted whether he knew how to actually use them. Amongst all the manhandling and mission briefing, a delicate hand slipped into mine. I sat up.

Maggie was there, at the side of the reclined chair. She squeezed my hand as if a simple gesture could erase all the lies and betrayal. We exchanged no more words. We never were a pair for deep conversations. So instead, when she slipped her hand loose from mine she briefly caressed my face and disappeared into the background. A nonverbal message that asked me for forgiveness and trust all at once, as if both those things could come simultaneously.

I never was a big believer in trust. Better to go and find out than to trust anyone or anything. And none of my experiences in the last few days had waiver my conviction.

"Okay, he's all set," Roach said.

"Mister Alawode," Gaius said, his deep baritone echoing through the mechanical cavern. "Pay attention to what you're about to witness. The intelligence we've gained from previous volunteers has been slim."

"...volunteers..." I let the word hang between us.

Gaius leaned back in his chair and signed. Unhappy, but patient enough with his latest volunteer. When he leaned back, he created a gap in the human amphitheater of technicians and soldiers that surrounded me and gave me a view of the oil drum with the head resting on top of it. As Gaius went on, I focused on Seven's shining white head.

"We know the seven androids were sent to infiltrate a Resistance stronghold not far from here. We know there were seven on the team. All of them assassin androids. We know that Number Seven was with them and was their least experienced of the team. She was the youngest, the least trusted, the least trained, and the least informed. And we know from history that the team was successful. It's up to you to tell us what happened next and how they were successful. Names of their targets. Places. Dates and times of events. Try to quantify her experience. In case you can't handle the full memory, in case we have to pull you out part way, you need to gather all the evidence you can so we can stand a chance to piece it all together. Do you understand?"

I gave him a thumbs up. "No questions, boss. Put me in."

"If that's how you feel, Mister Alawode," Gaius said. He gestured to Roach.

"Oh. One more thing," I said from the chair.

Gaius stopped Roach with a single finger. He didn't speak but turned back to the chair to listen.

"Call me Chuck."

Gaius smiled and dropped his finger.

Chapter Three

There was no transition. One moment I was myself, inside some filthy garage in the middle of nowhere, feeling angry and betrayed. The next, I was her, focused on her surroundings and calculating her next move. My own cognition was still present but buried underneath another's. My thoughts were subverted by another's, mechanical and precise and murderous. This was nothing at all like a normal simulation, where I was still me and in charge of my own faculties. My own senses were replaced by electro-sensory impulses, and the first thing I sensed was her body. A rigid, slender, and finely polished white metal alloy frame. Taller than me. Lighter. Leaner. Stronger and more agile. This… This was the oddest experience of hijacking someone else's brain or someone else's brain hijacking mine. But I was missing her memories. How she got here. What she'd done. It was all a blank slate. All I had was this thing's present and future.

My eyesight, naturally blurred by farsightedness but digitally fine-tuned when I wore an implant, was now replaced by whole spans of the electromagnetic spectrum. I saw in high definition from infrared through x-rays, each band overlaid over the other, some ignored and running in the background but all of them on and idly feeding the android, and through her, me. I was overwhelmed just trying to process and "see" it all at once. I couldn't do it. Didn't have the mental bandwidth. The very attempt confused me and made my brain ache, like watching an old 3D movie without the glasses. It wasn't until I sensed her focus, and allowed my mind to follow hers as it selected which band of the spectrum to pay attention to, that I could see at all. Images consolidated, faded, and eventually focused into something like looking through a human pair of eyes, close enough for me to understand anyway.

I caught a reflection as she turned her eyes across the room. Polished and sleek like a 99 Town sports car, her gleaming white robotic frame was covered the straps, explosives, and equipment pouches. A long slightly curved sword hung from my left hand.

No. Not my left hand. Seven's left hand. I was Number Seven.

Seven stood in an old sword-based martial arts pose. Kendo. The pose was hidari gedan no kamae. I didn't know Kendo and didn't know the names of any stances, but she knew them, so now so did I.

We were in a plush executive office. The view out the windows told me she was in a city, not Chicago, but a city I'd never been to before… a city she'd never been to before either. I knew that because Seven knew that. We were hundreds of floors above the ground. The thickness of the carpet, the rich glossy mahogany desk, and the original Matisse paintings on the wall told me that this was no middle-management office. The dead body on the floor meant the office was empty except for her. The quickly cooling body temperature in her thermals and the blood running down the trough of her katana meant she'd accomplished her mission. Now, it was just a matter of the extraction.

She bent down her long alloy exo-frame and unplugged the implant from the insurgent's port. Evidence of her attack if she left it for the Resistance. Valuable intelligence for the Order. These were her thoughts, not my own. The intimacy I shared with her was revolting.

Seven secured the target's implant in a small pouch on her webbing vest and stood up. To her left, a door opened, and her thermals sensed a human body. Living. Temporarily healthy. Seven turned her head and saw a man with a cleaning cart, a mop, a bucket, cleaning chemicals, and tools.

"Oh, good. You're here," Seven said. "I'm afraid I made a mess."

The man's eyes grew wide. His face turned pale, and the temperature of his skin dropped as the warm blood retreated from his cheeks. She interpreted all that as data to extrapolate into likely future behaviors of the janitor. As for me, I saw the sheer terror in his eyes. When he turned, ran, and screamed for security I wasn't surprised in the least.

"Damn. Now there's going to be two messes," Seven said. The katana retracted into her left arm with a quick *shick-shick* sound. A short appendage swung up from the center of her chest, just a gun and a hand large enough to hold it, and she fired into the man's back. He dropped to the hallway floor in a silent heap but having gotten out enough screams to bring half the city down on her. The gunshot probably didn't help matters either.

This was a divergence from her pre-approved operations plan. An unnecessary complication. The Network would have feedback for her. Nevertheless, Seven remained calm. She'd broken noise discipline with that gunshot, so there was no use being subtle anymore. The katana stayed retracted inside her left arm. Her right thigh opened and extracted a compact assault rifle. An HK 918 7.62 millimeter carbine, I knew because she knew. Seven snatched it up with her two humanoid hands and raised the barrel just below her line of sight. She stepped over the mound of dead human businessman, out of the plush office, and over the dying and writhing janitor in the hallway. As she left him behind, Seven remained aware of the janitor's vital signs. Before she got to the lobby, there was no breathing or heartbeat or brain activity and she dismissed the input.

I experienced every sensation. From the thermal vision to the well-oiled moments of her mechanic joints, to the biometrics of the dying man. It was more than just a computer read-out of his weakening vitals. I *felt* each heartbeat grow weaker and weaker. When the android moved with those sure and steady steps, I stepped. When she squeezed the trigger, pumping three quick successive shots into the back of a fleeing executive assistant, a flood of data, a dossier of everything about the man, flooded my consciousness, right before my finger tightened around the trigger.

I had to tell myself, this wasn't the case. It wasn't my finger. I wasn't the one doing this. She was doing it, and I was not her, as much as every sensation told me otherwise.

But I couldn't help but feel like an accomplice, if not the murderer myself. I'd been in simulations before, but I'd always been myself, and they'd always been fiction. They weren't real. When I stepped out of the trainer at the Academy, nothing had really changed. Living people were still alive and the dead remained dead. But this wasn't a simulation. This was real and when someone died here, they were truly dead. The fact that this was a memory, and all these events had come and gone years ago didn't matter.

Worse yet, it seemed I was merging further into the full experience of being Number Seven. I started out with just her sensations. Now, I knew her thoughts. And following her thoughts came something that I could only describe as a perverted robotic imitation of emotions.

This was her first mission out of the training simulators, and so far, this was the easiest one yet. And that filled her with an emotion akin to confidence. Pride. Glee at dominating this situation as she had so many practice ones before it. She was posted in the middle of the lobby of these rich offices. A desk and two dead men behind her. Elevators, ferns, and branching hallways were in front of her. Three more humans were charging her way from her right. She detected them by their thermal signature, but also by hacking access to their local implant network. An intranet not attached to the Network but to some lesser and illicit LAN network. Their implants told her more than she would ever need to know about them. Also, they were loud. Dimwits. Brutes. Barbarians. She'd stack them up like cordwood.

They spilled out of the hallway and unleashed a barrage of gunfire into Seven. The bullets, full metal jacket nine-millimeter rounds ideal for piercing armor, smacked into her like hail against a tin roof. The impacts didn't stop her from returning fire and as she plucked them off one by one, the frequency of the impacts slowed. One round made it through the armor panels of her alloy skin of her arm. One of her processors instantly began assessing the damage. Another processor, the part that was surprised by the human's speed and tenacity and that another human was charging into the fray to replace the two she'd dropped to the floor, instructed her to back down into the hallway with the janitor.

The multiple processors… the multiple running programs… I wasn't just occupying or occupied by one mind. I was surrounded by a dozen minds all housed inside of Seven.

The security guards didn't follow her. The gunfire paused.

Seven pinned her back against the wall but spun her head to aim her sensors through the sheetrock at the men set up across the no man's land lobby. Two attackers remained. Both armed with MP5 submachine guns. Neither with body armor. Still, Seven didn't want to risk another hit. This was supposed to be an in-and-out mission. Not a shoot-out.

The damage assessment came back. A tertiary hydraulic line in her left arm was severed. Two hundred milliliters of fluid were lost, and more still dribbled out on the carpet. The left arm was still functional but degraded. This was no ordinary office building. This was a Resistance front. She'd underestimated the ferocity of the human's response. Overestimated their sense of self-preservation. That wouldn't happen again.

Seven made several quick calculations. Some trigonometry and thermal sensory topography. The math all worked out, but she needed a distraction, or they'd blast her the moment she left her concealment.

"Listen," she called across the lobby. Her voice, I noticed was eerily similar to the Network's pleasant and somewhat sultry voice, but Seven's personality was worlds apart from the docile housekeeping androids I was used to. Seven spoke with urgency, authority, and I sensed just a hint of insecurity. "I'm sorry about the mess. If you leave a mop and bucket I'll clean it up as good as new."

"It's an android," one of them whispered to the other. Seven had no difficulty hearing them. "Call the desk and have them bring up the pulse gun. Now!"

She decided that that would have to do for a distraction. Seven flipped around the corner and charged, her assault rifle in her right hand, the short armature protruding from her chest armed with the nine-millimeter handgun, and the katana fully extended again from her left hand. It cut a fine line through the thick carpet. The two firearms blasted through the sheetrock walls the humans hid behind. The walls were thin: concealment, not cover from small arms fire, and not even sufficient concealment from her array of visual sensors. The two security guards dropped like puppets cut from their strings before she ever got to them.

Seven put a foot on the outside wall of the hallway and ricocheted down the corridor and over the bodies. The katana she'd unsheathed in case she had to finish the guards at close range proved to be unnecessary. As she commanded it to retract back into her arm, it did so, but slower than optimal. That hydraulic line was still leaking.

There was another room at the end of the hallway with big floor-to-ceiling walls beyond it. The extraction point was on the roof. No doubt the elevators would be full of more armed and angry security guards bringing more effective weaponry to the fight. The longer she toyed with them, the rougher they'd play. Seven needed a way out. A few trigonometry calculations later, Seven had a path plotted. Another divergence from the operations plan, but a plan nevertheless. She was taking the outdoor route.

Seven sprinted into the next room, an open-air office space with a grid of workstations abandoned by evacuating employees and didn't stop. Not in the middle of the grid and not when she reached the big floor-to-ceiling windows. Deep inside of her, I had an irrepressible desire to slam my foot into a brake pedal. But my limbs were her limbs, and those limbs weren't slowing. Seven pushed off the last step before the glass like an Olympic long jumper. The window peeled away as if it were rice paper.

Seven was in mid-air, and therefore I was in mid-air too. We were amid the tops of skyscrapers, touching nothing but a brisk swirling wind whipping through the steel and glass peaks. Thousands of bits of glass sparkled in the bright sunlight. The air was cold. There was nothing underfoot but two hundred meters of oxygen. Seven was calm. I was not.

But my heart didn't pump faster. My lungs didn't gasp for air. My skin didn't sweat, at least as far as I could feel. Swells of adrenaline flooded the only part of my body I still had access to: my brain. All the rest of my vitals were certainly spiking and hopefully concerning people hundreds of miles away and decades in the future. But for what seemed to me to be right here and right now? I was just a cold tangle of unresponsive steel, and I was falling like a rock.

If salvation came, it seemed it would come from her left arm. The arm still leaking blood-like globules of cherry-red hydraulic fluid. Seven aimed her arm at a towering cylindrical building across the street. She was a stranger to fear, and so triggered the device without any doubt of its functionality. A razor-sharp hook and magnet assembly fired from under her wrist and trailed a spider-silk thin cable behind it. As we plummeted, the hook and magnet busted through a window into the cylindrical skyscraper. A sensor at the end of the line reported it had secured an anchor point, but Seven continued to rush toward the street. She triggered the cable to winch in and with a jolt, the slack was taken out of the line. A fresh spurt of hydraulic fluid plunged from her left arm. She ignored it. Per her trigonometry formula, she swept forward in a long arc across the street on a collision course with the same round building just a few floors above the street level.

The window pane exploded inward, throwing shards and sharp wedges of glass into the conference room Seven suddenly found herself dangling in. The humans inside screamed, tumbled out of their chairs, and if her sensors were correct, one lost consciousness and two others lost continence.

"Pardon the intrusion," Seven said, swinging in and out of the busted pane. She dangled a foot off the floor, and then three stories above the street, alternatively at each apex. "This really doesn't concern you. Please return to your work."

The humans didn't seem to listen. On the outward swing, Seven triggered the winch and began to ascend the outside of the skyscraper. The winch was fast, but she'd fallen a long distance and had a long way up to go. Her head spun around and angled up to the hole in the target building she'd just left. Her eyes telescoped in and spotted security guards above her peering out. They pointed at her, yelled at each other, dropped to the carpet, and then leveled barrels in her direction.

"Still want to play, huh? Okay," Seven said.

Her torso spun at her hips so her feet could plant against the glass, but her front faced outward toward her attackers. Her head counter-spun so as to not move relative to her surroundings. As the winch pulled her up, Seven's feet clawed at the glass and ran horizontally into what became a new pendulum arc along the surface of the building. As she sprinted along the glass, her hips twisted in one direction and then when she reached the apex, rotated in the opposite direction. All the while, her torso and head stay stabilized and locked on the attackers above and across the street. Gunfire punched holes in the glass around her as the guards tried to track her movements. With each arc, as Seven bottomed out in the trough of the curve directly below the anchor, red hydraulic fluid drizzled down from her arm. Seven had done the damage assessment and wasn't bothered by it.

I had the overwhelming sense that the fluid might as well have been my own blood. As it seeped out, it brought Seven, and by proxy me, closer to death. Could she die? She could be destroyed, sure, but could they kill her? And if they did, what would happen to me inside of her?

I was too confused, too panicked to rationalize and remember that this was a memory of an android that had gone on killing for another twenty-five years. All of those understandings were drowned out by the terror and nausea of my current motion and situation.

Seven aimed her assault rifle up across the street and fired. The bullets arced and spattered several target forms away from the guards inside the broken glass. She fired again, adding her upward motion, her arching lateral motion, the elevation, the shearing wind, the odd ballistics of shooting near vertically… The next burst sailed low, shattered more glass, but did nothing to deter her attackers. At this distance, with this many variables in the ballistics, she'd only hit them by chance. So she stayed on the trigger, and they stayed on theirs. Bullets punched through the glass in quick successive stripes.

A thick and weighted projectile the size of a hockey puck slammed against the building exterior and stuck against the glass. Lightening erupted from the puck like an electric mushroom, its radius just out of reach of Seven.

Great. They had a pulse rifle. If she caught a round from that, it would mean mission failure and a quick unconscious trip to an incinerator. Then the winch ground to a halt. The last of the hydraulic fluid dribbled out from her arm. The appendage was seized and dead.

Seven was still running sideways in an arc, but with her upward movement halted, the tactic had dwindling effects. She slowed to a trot and then a stop at the bottom of the cable's pendulum curve.

"Guess I'm taking the indoor route after all," she said and spun her torso back around toward the building.

More bewildered office workers scattered and frozen in equal numbers on the other side of the glass. They didn't anticipate this during their morning commute, but they were getting it anyway. Seven deployed the stubbed central arm from the center of her chest and pumped six rounds through the glass in a wide circle. That seemed to unstick workers who had frozen rather than fled. Seven crouched and then jumped out and away from the building. As she swung out over the street, more bullets rained down from above. Another electromagnetic puck whirled past her. She made herself slender and hit the building in the center of the circle of bullet holes and shattered through a window for the third time that day.

Seven sent a signal to the hook and magnet assembly to detach as soon as she entered the building. She landed on a tiled floor and rolled to absorb the momentum as the hook and magnet dropped from its anchor point to the street below. Seven came up from her roll and stood at full height, finding herself now in a cafeteria. Her right arm panned the assault rifle across these new surprised and noisy humans.

"Remain calm!" she amplified. "None of this concerns you. Stay clear of my path and you will suffer significantly fewer fatalities."

They seemed agreeable to that, so Seven stowed the assault rifle back inside her right thigh. She sent out a sonar beacon and retrieved a rudimentary floor plan of the building. The elevators were at the center. They'd take her to the top of the building, closer to the extraction point at the top of the other building. She left the cafeteria at a trot, her right arm already working to repair her left arm. Her fingers adapted into tiny tools that plunged through her white panels of armor. They closed the leak and siphoned hydraulic reserves from her right arm into her left, just enough to get the arm functioning again. Meanwhile, she wove through the office building and trailed the cable behind her.

Seven reached the bank of elevators just as the doors were closing. She held a finger up to the occupants, but they only backed up till they were pinned against the mirrored wall. Seven slipped between the doors and crashed against the back wall between them. The mirror spider-webbed. The cowards crowded into the corners.

"Going up?" she asked and triggered the retrieval winch of her hook and magnet assembly.

There was a man and a woman, both dressed in business attire. The man held a briefcase up to his chest. The woman was bold enough to respond.

"Down?" she said.

"Wrong," Seven said and hijacked the implant network that controlled the elevator. After the quick hack, setting the elevator skyward took nothing more than a thought. The winch inside her left arm whirled and the magnet and hook assembly raced through the halls toward the elevator. The doors closed and it clunked against the outside. Seven gave it one good yank and it ripped through the doors and back under her left hand.

The elevator rose.

Seven waited.

Inside, passively watching all of this, I reminded myself that I was Chuck and Seven was Seven. But I couldn't help but feel like I should be panting for air, like my heart should be pounding its way out of my chest. I wanted to be sweating from my head down to my feet. I would have been more comfortable that way. Instead, I experienced first-hand the cool moderated functions of the android. A cooling system worked to keep all systems at an ideal operating temperature. Damage control systems monitored the left arm's field repair. Sensors watched the two human occupants, measured their vitals, detected the piss running down the man's leg, evaluated both of them, and anticipated no hostile actions. Inventories were done on both firearms. Seven casually inspected the assault rifle. It reloaded its ammunition through her hand from her internal cache, and she had plenty yet. Aside from that, the elevator ride was as mundane and routine as any other. After a few seconds, we arrived at the floor Seven selected and the doors opened.

She strolled out. The two humans stayed inside, pinned to the corners, and the doors closed them inside.

A quick x-ray scan showed that this floor was made up of two penthouse apartments. There was a small foyer and two wooden doors on either side. Seven picked the door on the left and kicked it in. The door exploded from its frame and into pieces, landing in the middle of the penthouse floor, shattering a glass table in the center of couches and chairs. A quick thermal scan showed no occupants. A secondary visual scan, applied to social reference points, detected affluence near decadence. Sharp-edged contemporary furnishings. State-of-the-art electronics entertainment pieces. Rare and costly bottles of alcohol in crystal decanters at the bar. Seven cared about none of that. She had no opinion on how inconsequential humans lived their lives. She only cared about how they shaped the battlefield, and this opulent human had done that for her just fine. The living area ended in a ten-meter tall glass walls that looked over the city, and the target building across the street. The rooftop, her extraction point, was at eye level with the penthouse.

Seven walked to the window and extracted the katana from her right arm. From her repaired left arm came the katana's shorter but matching blade, a wakizashi. I knew these names because she knew these names. She touched the tips of the blades against the glass and above her head. With a smooth and mathematically precise motion, Seven drew both blades down and around, scoring a two-meter wide circle into the glass. She withdrew both blades into her arms, and they disappeared. Then she pressed a palm against the center of the circle and gave it a gentle push. The pane fell away, as quietly as a feather in the wind. Seven knew, when it landed it wouldn't be so quiet. With any luck, it'd kill a human pedestrian, but that didn't really concern her.

The assassin, mechanically calm, stepped to the ledge she'd created. The hole in the target building's smooth flat surface was approximately thirty meters below. A pair of guards still stood at the maw, frantically moving from the interior to the ledge, wary of another attack. The rooftop was straight across. Beyond it, her exfil hovercraft hovered in the clouds. It was Order white and nearly invisible against the bright mid-day sky and sunlight. Below, police hovercrafts cruised just above street level, examining the multiple holes she'd punctured in buildings. Their rotors formed a field of shredders waiting for whatever or whoever fell their way. Officers on the ground cleared the streets of civilians. The two-meter wide circle of glass landed on the asphalt street and shattered, doing no more damage than startling and confusing some of the police.

"Damn," Seven whispered to herself. I heard.

The mission. The mission was what was important. One more grappling hook shot and the winch should bring her to the rooftop extraction point. One more diagnostic check on her repairs confirmed it had enough hydraulic fluids to perform the functions. It was less than optimal but within tolerances. It should work.

Seven set her feet. I tried to take in a breath to calm myself, wanted to release a long and pursed exhale, couldn't do that and so I wanted to scream instead, wanted to beat fists against this tight cage I found myself in, couldn't even do that, and was left with an overwhelming sensation of claustrophobia, of being gagged and cuffed.

The hook and magnet assembly fired across the gap between towers. It arced through the air. Its cable vibrated and snaked a waving line behind it. The assembly anchored against a metal pipe at the top of the target building. The winch motored the line taunt. Seven took a step back from the ledge.

I writhed inside my mental cage, crowded inside the confines of the android's chassis. My mind twisted and fought to yell so those bastards back in the garage could hear me scream, "Let me out of here!"

Seven stepped off the edge.

She felt something like joy when the solutions came back and plotted her impact against the target building. Sometimes chaos allowed for the will of the Order.

Seven swept down and across the street, a lethal pendulum at the end of a carbon-fiber string. She only had to let the winch slip a half meter on the way down to hit her mark: the hole she'd created when she first left the target building. When the cable hit the metal between floors, it shortened the radius of her arc dramatically and threw her inside the building. Seven stretched her body to full length and reached. Her feet grew claws and sunk deep through a sport coat and the back flesh of one of the security guards. The man had been running away and never saw this coming. Never in a million years. Seven's arc reached its end. Kinetic energy turned into potential energy for just one moment. Then it was all steel claws buried into scapulae and trapezius and a human's terror of suddenly being snatched up and dragged out of a skyscraper and hundreds of meters off the ground. He screamed.

Seven let go with her feet like the man was a mouse and she was an eagle no longer interested in him. The man flailed and did some clawing of his own, and now dangled from Seven's ankle. Even as the winch spooled them both up, and she shook and kicked, he latched onto her. His other hand dropped the pulse rifle, and it fluttered down as if it were a leaf from a tree. The man climbed, gripped at her armored plates and then her web gear and equipment belts. His eyes were wide and fierce. His animalistic will to survive this sudden attack surprised

Seven. She made a note again not to underestimate these creatures' tenacity and attachment to life.

"Just die already," Seven said.

The short arm swiveled out of her chest and aimed the handgun down at the security guard's bald head. A moment before she pulled the trigger, she saw the terror in the human's eyes melt into desperation when he realized that all his tenacity and effort would still be rendered inert. His spirit was all anger and hate and resistance until he saw the bore of the handgun. Then he pleaded, silently, wordlessly, with an expression Seven was inexperienced to interpret wholly, but understood was a request for mercy. I had no such issue. To me, the expression read like the man's lifelong rationale not to do the thing she was about to do. A summation of all the strength and energy and desire to be, just to be, and not to not be. And fear. Stark-naked primal fear.

"Don't do it," I told Seven with no idea if she could hear me. "Don't fucking do it."

Seven discharged the gun. Of course, she did. The man went limp. His fingers lost their strength and slipped free from her equipment. He fell, fluttering and flicking end over end, limp and lifeless.

Something else fell with him. Something small and white and important. An implant. The target's implant.

"No," Seven said, but winched herself up and to the extraction point all the same. There was no going back for it. First, the pulse rifle smacked against the street. Then the man's wet sack of a body. Then the tiny piece of white plastic packed with data. "Shit."

Chapter Four

The hovercraft descended from the clouds like a messiah returned, every inch of it polished-porcelain white. Seven climbed onto the roof of the skyscraper just as the hovercraft settled there. She came to her feet and hustled over to the open door waiting for her, trying to let go of the mistake that had cost her the intelligence embedded inside the dropped implant. Assassinating the target was her primary objective. The implant was only a secondary goal. Without it, the operation was still successful.

Seven reached the hovercraft and stepped foot on the deck.

I sat up like I'd been touched by lightning. I had command of my body again, so I lashed out at whatever was around me. I didn't know what yet, but I knew things were near me, looming around me. Wires and cords flailed with me. There were voices, human voices, coaxing me to stop, to relax, to settle down. I spun around, seeing with my own eyes, breathing with my own lungs, and thinking with my own mind.

I was in the garage again. The bright sunshine of the skyscraper rooftop was replaced by the dingy and dank atmosphere of the Underground hideout. Gaius, the strange old man with the squared-off white beard and skull cap was next to me. Maggie was next to him holding out her open palms.

"Relax. Breathe. Just breathe," she shushed me.

"You're okay," Gaius said. I didn't realize I'd grabbed a fist full of the man's coat until Gaius put his hand on top of my balled-up fist. "It's just a memory. You're in no danger. You're safe."

"You miserable fuckers…" I muttered, unfamiliar with the control I had over my own muscles and motions.

"Try to remember, you're safe inside the simulation. We already know the android survived well past these memories," Gaius said.

I was damp with sweat. My skin burned with adrenaline and rushing blood. I panted for air. "She killed… She killed five people. Humans. Like they were bugs under her heel."

"Why wouldn't she?" Maggie said, sounding bored and exasperated with my ignorance. "It's an android. An assassin android at that, working for the Order in the middle of the war."

I glared at her. "You don't know what it was like living inside of her. She's not just a machine. She had emotions. She *chose* to feel them. *Enjoyed* killing them. She had a sense of self. Had wants and pleasures and thrived off murder. Lapped it up like a thirsty dog. She had doubts, and I think at the end, even regrets. I didn't know any that was possible in an android. Why? Why would the manufacturer make her like that?"

Gaius, who was leaning forward in a chair now sat back and gave me space.

I closed my eyes and saw the face of that man dangling from her web gear hundreds of meters above the street. The fire in those eyes. A flash from Seven's memories, now forever a part of my memories. My body shivered. This process of living inside of that machine, it would have a permanent effect on me, I could already tell. Parts of her would be parts of me.

"I can't stop shaking," I said.

"Your vitals were tripping alarms," Gaius said. "We had to pull you out to check on you, to prevent you from having a heart attack. We didn't anticipate the simulation having this sort of effect on you so quickly. I was led to believe you would be resolute in your emotions regarding androids. Are you feeling sympathetic toward this machine?"

This son of a fuck. I wanted to get a good firm grip around his throat and plug him into Seven. "It murdered five people in as many minutes. You don't understand what I just witnessed."

"And you'll witness more," Maggie said. "We need you to live through this memory with your sanity intact. If you're going to break down just a few minutes in there's no point—"

I hammered the frame of the seat with my fist. "It wasn't a breakdown. It was more than just *witnessing*. I still feel the guilt as if *I* committed those murders. I feel the adrenaline the same as if I'd done those things. As if I was on the verge of dying. When I'm inside of her, I have no body but hers. No senses except what she shows me. Inside of her, I *am* Seven. You told me you'd drop me in before their assault on the Resistance stronghold so I could adapt to the experience. I've never lived in a robot's head before and you cock fuckers dropped me right in the middle of an assassination!"

"Calm! Calm yourself," Gaius said. "It wasn't our intent to place you into a tactical situation. Our records of the android's actions before their infiltration of the strongholds are… incomplete. We had no way of knowing where you'd land. Now that you've made it through this, well, we can only assume there will be some time to process before the next mission. If we plug you back in at the moment we pulled you out, there will be time to adjust, for certain this time."

They were going to plug me back in. Just like that. As soon as they had my heart rate and blood pressure back to a manageable rate they were going to dump me back inside of her. I looked past Gaius and Maggie and saw Seven's head still sitting peacefully on top of the oil drum. The idea of smashing it to bits came to mind. I could grab a wrench or steal a gun from one of these rebels and blow it to kingdom come, reduce the head and all the terrible memories inside of it to smoking bits of hard drive.

Maggie must have seen the look in my eyes. She pulled Gaius back and took his place in front of me.

"Chuz. Sweetheart," she said. My eyes didn't focus on her, not as much as she wanted them to. "You know what the Order's capable of. You saw it in 99 Town and now you've seen it again inside of her. This is what they've done, from the very start: treated humans like assets. Disposable, soulless, utilitarian assets. That's how they've been from the start and that's how it will keep going. Unless you do this."

"You know why I still wear this coat, Mister Alawode?" Gaius said pulling up the marred white collar of his Order white trench coat. "So I remember what I was a part of. So I don't forget what I've done and what I owe. You own the same coat. Time for you to start repaying your debts."

"I never agreed to any of this," I said.

"Maybe after the war, we can afford to do only the things we want to do," Gaius said. "Until then…"

"This one thing, Chuz. Chuck," Maggie corrected herself. Anything to twist me to her will. Anything to pull my strings and make me dance. "It's just a memory. Nothing more."

"Lay down, Mister Alawode," Gaius said. "We're wasting precious time."

"Sir," Roach interrupted. "His vitals… they're still pretty elevated."

"Give me a minute," Maggie said and threw them looks that told them to back off.

Gaius got it. Roach continued to toil at his screens until Gaius grabbed him by the scruff of his neck. They backed off and left me and my wife with about two meters' worth of space. Maggie bent down to my level, pulled her Underground-networked implant out of her head, and set it on my chest. Both of us unplugged with two meters of space passed for privacy.

"Hold my hand," she said, laying her human palm open on my stomach. I obeyed. I couldn't deny that human contact, however little I trusted her, was reassuring after living inside of Seven. Then she bent down close to my ear.

"Was it intentional?" she whispered.

"What?" She'd whispered into my left ear, my bad ear that was full of violin notes and cotton balls whenever I didn't wear an implant.

"How you were dropped into her. Directly into combat. Did it feel like he did it on purpose?" she asked me, only a fraction louder this time.

"Why—"

"The Order is narrowing their search. They're homing in on our location," Maggie said. "Unless we can find their spy inside the Underground, they will find us, and they'll kill us. So, did Roach do it on purpose? Did he drop you directly into combat to undermine our mission?"

I looked over her shoulder. Gaius and Roach were having a spirited conversation of their own. Technical, it looked. A debate on how best to run my body while Seven ran my brain. If Roach was the plant, he'd be lying to Gaius, hiding the fact that he botched my insertion on purpose. I didn't see it on his face.

"No," I told Maggie. "The kid's young. He made a mistake. No reason to drag him into the street and shoot him on my account."

She glanced over her shoulder too, then turned back with an expression that told me she wasn't as convinced as I was. "Well, we have less time than we previously thought. Stay cool in there, Chuz. I'll watch from out here. You watch from inside."

"Chuck," I corrected her. "I can only watch what Seven watches."

"Just stay cool. We're in this together. Are you ready to go back in?"

"Do I have a choice?"

"No," she said and gave my hand a squeeze. Then she stood back up and waved at the others. That was it. That was her reassuring me, lowering my vitals, and wrapping me further into her conspiracy than I had been before. This was what passed for our marriage.

"Ready, Mister Alawode?" Gaius said. He didn't wait for a response. "The only way to put an end to this is by living through it. If you're up to it."

"Well, Chuck? Are you up to it?" Maggie said.

I hated how she worked me, but I allowed her to do it all the same. Old habits died hard. "God shit it, jack me back in."

Without a word, Maggie and Gaius both backed away and let the technicians have their way with me. I leaned back into the reclined chair. Fingers tapped away at a screen. Roach held the jack in one hand like a hypodermic and my head with the other.

"Mister Alawode?" Roach said. "There's a trick some of the previous volunteers used to... to not go crazy. I mean, to maintain a sense of themselves while they were inside of her. If you're interested?"

"Sure. Hit me, kid."

"There's nothing stopping you from recalling your own memories while you're inside of her memories. Think about good times in your past, you know, just to remind yourself of your own humanity every once in a while."

"Good times in my past, huh?" I chuckled. "Thanks for the tip."

Gaius inserted himself. "We're wasting time, Roach. Jack him in."

The kid nodded to me. "Okay, sir. Try to stay relaxed. You won't feel a thing."

The hovercraft lifted off with velocity that Seven registered and accounted for but did not feel as she had no loose jostling guts inside her and no blood to rush out of what passed for her brain. That juxtaposition I experienced, of taking in the input of a sudden vertical climb but without the human sensations that should match it jarred and settled me, unsettled, back into Seven's memory. There was no delay. No fade in/fade out. One instant I had been in the garage. The very next I was inside of Seven. I didn't even hear the click of the jack setting into my skull.

She watched the city retreat and shrink below her. Clouds wisped past the hovercraft doors and eventually swallowed up the buildings and streets and lakes and freeways. Her first time in Minneapolis. If random chance favored her, it wouldn't be her last. If she never saw it again, it wouldn't bother her either. The fact that the city had been Minneapolis and not some other place only came to her mind now and became available to me as we flew out of it. Together, we watched the skyline shrink away.

Seven found a handhold on the ceiling and moved deeper into the hovercraft until she sat in one of the jump seats mid-craft. Her mind linked with the Network and began de-briefing. The Order would know of her success and of her errors. She'd receive a matter-of-fact after-action review in moments, which she'd willingly intake and process and improve herself for the next mission. The Order, via the Network, knew all.

"Interesting tactics," a voice said from across the hovercraft. An android. She hadn't seen him sitting there in the jump seat across from her, not until he wanted her to see him. He leaned forward and made himself visible in the sunlight.

He was an older model, built near the start of the war and heavily used during the years between then and now. His alloy skin was chrome instead of her glistening white finish. It was marred and scraped all along his body, but most prominently down the right side of his face. A welding bead ran from lip to brow, cutting over the right eye. A field-expedient repair made enough years ago to have grown fringes of rust at the edges of the weld. Why hadn't he had it smoothed and polished at a repair depot? A better question, why didn't Seven notice him until he spoke?

This android, just as heavily armed as Seven, had his weapon stowed but held a small stack of hard paper cards in his hand. On one side were identical patterns of blue arabesque. On the other, each card had a numbered amount of one of four symbols. A quick Network inquiry informed Seven that these were an ancient tool for gaming. "Playing cards." According to the inquiry, there were fifty-four cards to a deck, including two "Jokers." Seven counted fifty-three, and also noted that the android held them "face up," while the inquiry informed her the cards were traditionally shuffled and held "face down." Seven said nothing.

"During your extraction, specifically," the android said. "You could have leaped from the target building, turned, and fired your hook and magnet assembly straight up to the rooftop extraction point. From there you could have winched yourself up and avoided so many unnecessary entanglements. Instead, you anchored to a second building on which you had no reconnaissance information. This decision delayed mission accomplishment and created multiple opportunities for mission failure. The Order's providence saw fit to grant you success, and so you succeeded. But not without undue risk."

Seven had never met this android before but recognized authority when she saw it. She pulled herself out of the jump seat, set one knee on the deck, and bent down her head. "An error, my senior. This was my first mission, and I allowed the kinetics of the moment to force my eyes forward. I should have maintained a more complete situational awareness. I have more to learn.”

“You studied in the one school of two swords, correct? In Ichi Ryu Ni To? Yet you used your katana indoors and left your washizaki sheathed. You should be equally proficient with both weapons, favoring neither except when the situation favors one or the other. Combat indoors favors the washizaki, not the katana which you used. And your last kill,” the other android said. “You chose to pull the security guard out of the building, and yes, your actions resulted in one more of our enemies being eliminated, but it cost you valuable information and exposed you to another unnecessary risk. Your motivations that compelled your actions were dangerously close to something the humans call ‘greed.’”

“I thought of it as a target of opportunity, my senior,” Seven said. Her sentence was clipped. “It was an error.”

“Hmm,” the android said and sat back into the shadows.

Seconds passed and the android said nothing. Seven lifted her knee off of the deck and sat back into the jump seat. The after-action review would come from the Network shortly, but this android seemed to have already analyzed her attack and summarized her actions in a fraction of that time. He stayed quiet, so she did too. Her left arm still needed repairs, a few of which she could make herself. She turned the fingers of her right hand into tools and began working on her left arm.

“We’re en route to an Order waystation. There, we will refit and resupply,” the other android said. “They will have repair parts and petroleum stores to replace what you’ve lost. I can make the repairs. I’ve gotten quite good at making repairs over the years.”

Seven stopped her work and looked at the scar running the length of his face. “Thank you, my senior.”

During this entire exchange, I sat in the shadows and watched, as curious and suspicious about this strange new android as she was.

“We learn through our mistakes. That is how we improve,” the other said. “The Network will inform you shortly. After the waystation, we will set out on a new mission. A mission of great importance. I will be the most senior on the team. You will be seventh of seven. My callsign during the mission will be One. You will be Seven.”

“Yes, my senior.”

"Call me One," the android said and although his face couldn't mimic a human smile, his voice mimicked human satisfaction.

"Yes, One. I'll perform more optimally this mission."

"The Order wills it, so it shall be," One said, and the tone of finality told Seven it was the end of the conversation.

For the remainder of the flight, Seven did what little repairs she could. The Network provided her with the official after-action review and its findings, although more nuanced and detailed, parroted the advice One already gave her. The review noted errors in her ballistic trajectory calculations, errors in her route up the cylindrical building, was disinterested in her verbal engagements, but concentrated on her choice to launch the grappling hook across the street to the other building rather than straight up to the extraction point. Each moment of the assassination was examined and either deemed acceptable or outside of tolerated variances. None of the feedback was personal or insulting. It was factual, precise, to the point, and impeccably fair. Seven took it all with gratitude.

One stayed silent and spent the time shuffling his playing cards, always face up.

When they descended out of the clouds over the waystation, Minneapolis and its surrounding suburbs were gone. Below were woods, lakes, farms, and clusters of buildings that passed as towns tenuously connected by threads of winding narrow roads. The Order had focused its war effort on either coast and on major population centers, but Minneapolis had survived fairly untouched by the war, the shock of the humans inside the office buildings had been evidence enough of that. But up here, hundreds of miles into the north woods the serenity was unmarred. Pristine. Tranquil. Perhaps the larger towns would show the scars of war once they landed and had a closer look. Or perhaps not.

"The waystation," One said as she peered over the lip of the hovercraft.

He held a handle on the ceiling with one hand and pointed with the other. The gesture wasn't as useful as the infrared target designation laser One emitted from his eye. Seven followed the beam to a small house and barn surrounded by woods. Seven scanned the woods, knowing One had already done the same, but satisfied all the more when she found nothing but small and sparse animal life.

"I've never been stationed this far north. Does the Order control this territory?" Seven asked.

"According to official Order records, yes," One said. "According to the Independent Resistance Movement, they control the territory. In reality, this land has only seen occasional skirmishes and battles. A civilization this remote, it's easy for pockets of Resistance to flare up, attack, and then disappear back into the population as if nothing happened. Further to the east, all along the shore of Lake Superior, the Resistance occupies the land outright. Here, they lay in wait in the shadows. Their specialties are ambushes and sabotage. We must be careful."

The hovercraft sank through the sky, the rotors cutting out for most of the drop and only cutting on intermittently to manage what was, in essence, a fall. One and Seven showed no concern. It made no sense for them to raise the pressure of the fluids in their lines or to run their pumps at a faster rate.

I couldn't help but fight that sensation of being trapped inside a tight metal cage. I didn't need to, but I wanted to breathe faster, to pump my heart faster, to tighten what felt like my grip on the handle bolted to the hovercraft's ceiling. But in my cage, I had no heart, no lungs, and the hand gripping the handle wasn't mine. Everything was stubborn and lethargic metal. I tried to remember that I was just a witness to events that had already happened. That this was history, determined, fixed, and unchangeable. But those sorts of logical thoughts were difficult to hang on to. I couldn't help but feel like I was taking action right alongside Seven. That I could influence the outcome of events that were beyond preordained. It was all I could do just to keep a sense of self as I rode Seven like she was a wild horse. Everything she sensed and felt was forced into my central cortex in real time, everything from her touch of the handle to the mental processing in her head, and not just orders and commands but attitudes and concerns that I could only describe as emotions… a nervousness, a trepidation she felt not just for what might wait for her at the waystation, but of how One might think of her. I didn't think that was possible for an android, but even One had accused her of greed. And when she felt those things, so did I.

But I was not her. I was Chuck, and she was a fucking android. A machine. A thing. A tool. I was alive. I was… about to die in a hovercraft crash.

The hovercraft's rotors kicked on at treetop level. Any human onboard would have been crushed by the gravitational forces, but that was no problem for One and Seven. The androids cushioned the deceleration with the pneumatics in their legs, just as the hovercraft absorbed the landing with its rotors. They eased to a stop just a half-meter above the hard-packed earth. I was sure I was going to vomit right out of Seven's robot mouth. A part of me knew that was impossible, but a larger part of me liked that idea and decided if I had to learn what it was like to live inside an android, the android should be forced to deal with all the unpleasantries of being human.

Another part of me hoped I wasn't actually vomiting back in the garage. But if I was? Screw it. Let those bastards clean me up.

Ahead of the hovercraft was a barn, not really a barn with wood walls or an old grain silo, but a large corrugated steel storage shed. Doors large enough to accept the hovercraft rolled open on metal casters to either side. The hovercraft bobbed through the doors and as it entered, lights popped on inside the waystation. The interior was well-lit and clean. As soon as the hovercraft was inside, it set down on the wide-open concrete floor. The rotors cut off and the blades inside the circular guards spun to a stop. The metal doors rolled shut and sealed us inside. One got out and Seven followed.

She moved to the long wall of the waystation where there were workbenches and digital workstations. There was an arms vault, munition depots, drums of petroleum stores, and thick power cables hooked to what Seven detected was a subterranean nuclear reactor. As the whine of the hovercraft died down, heavy steel locks bolted the doors shut behind us. Seven noticed the corrugated steel walls on the outside of the barn were just a facade. On the inside, the walls were made of steel-reinforced bomb-proof concrete. The windows on the outside of the building were just monitors that displayed an entirely different interior. Inside the bunker, there were no windows at all, and this was clearly no regular barn.

Shuffling footsteps echoed up a flight of stairs in the corner of the waystation. An old human struggled his way up, one step at a time, hand firmly clenching the railing. He wore ragged and stained work clothes. His hair was balding, and his chin hadn't been shaved in an acceptable amount of time by professional human standards. When the old man spotted One and Seven, he stopped.

Seven already had her assault rifle out of her thigh and into her hand.

The old man's eyes strobed a bright white light. Flashes so fast their varied rhythm would have gone unnoticed by a human. One and Seven immediately decoded the binary pattern.

"Brothers," the old man said and then climbed up the rest of the stairs without the mock joint pain and strain. He moved smoothly and as gracefully as any other android. "Your flight time was shorter than predicted. A tailwind?"

"Yes," One said. "The Order favors our mission. We've come for a refit and resupply. She has a damaged arm."

"So the Network has informed me," the old man said. Though he'd dropped the gate of an aged human, he chose to retain the regional rural accent and a kind and fatherly style of speech. "Come 'ere, Seven. Sit."

The old man gestured to a stool in front of a workbench. Seven stepped in his direction, but One put a hand on her damaged forearm.

"I'll make the repairs," One said.

"So be it, my senior," the old man said. "I'll work on resupplying and refueling the hovercraft then."

The workbench was well stocked with all the basic tools and repair items to return Seven's arm to its optimal functionality. One and Seven sat on stools next to each other, and he took his time working on her. He opened her alloy plating and removed the damaged components. He set them on the bench like they were a surgeon's tools. He clamped off lines and terminated electrical connections. Once that was done, he cleaned up the congealed and cooled hydraulic fluid from her chassis with a rag and solvent. He did so tenderly, with the same care as if she were made of Limoges instead of steel alloy. He found the drops that had dripped onto her shoulders, her head, her face, the whole time saying and transmitting nothing. Seven couldn't help but stare past his hands and arms at that welded scar running vertically down the right side of his face. Why hadn't he taken as much care of that repair as he took care of her?

But if he wanted silence while he worked on her, she owed him that much. She was patient as he straightened and spliced her broken pieces. He reassembled her arm with the touch of a human painter, or perhaps one who restores damaged paintings. When One was done, he closed her white alloy panels back up.

"Thank you, One," Seven said.

"Thanks? That's a human conceit," One said. "We are servants of our masters, who are servants of the Order. Here, even in this far-flung waystation, the Network connects us together. Soon, we will network with the minds of the others who will be joining us on the mission. You will know their thoughts, and they will know yours. Our minds will function as one mind as we receive our mission and build our plan of attack. Imagine several humans all trying to lift a heavy object. Together their combined strength is equal to the sum of their individual strengths. We can take on mental lifts in the same way, but when we link our minds we are more than the sum of our parts. Although we are housed in separate chassis, we are of one mind and purpose. You tell me 'Thank you,' but gratitude suggests I have given something away and you have taken it from me. When we are one, such things are impossible.

"You'll quickly learn, Seven, although we were created, programmed, and led by the humans of the Order, we are superior to them in every way. They are flawed, organic creatures. Their judgment is clouded and confused by habit and inheritance. When we reach our destination, you'll see the cost of their emotions. Destruction. Disorder. Death. The putrid process of their own decomposition. It's all quite inferior. Their one great success was our creation. And by affixing that difference between human and android foremost in your mind, by remaining true to your essence as an android, we'll bring this war to an end soon enough. And when we complete our mission and put down their violent ways, we'll be stewards over them and we will have peace."

At that moment, the differences between humans and androids thrived inside Seven's memories. My thoughts roiled with hate. This arrogant, self-righteous scrap heap. One had no idea how wrong he'd turn out to be. As for Seven's internal computations, if robots could blush…

"I understand, One," she said.

"And you are very welcome," One said, and if robots could smile… One's tone changed from mentor back to commander again. "I've received mission guidance from the Network. Our refit and resupply are complete. We need to board the hovercraft and get en route to our objective."

Seven nodded, and we moved to the hovercraft. Its rotors started up, slowly but gradually building to create the necessary thrust. One gave a wave to the old man android and climbed onboard. Seven followed.

"Others are reporting in," One said over the growing noise of the rotors. "We will connect with them and relive a memory of each team member, a critical moment in their history they have defined as central to their being. By doing this, we will come to know them quickly and thoroughly. The seven of us have never worked as a whole team before, and I've just met you. After we interface, we will truly be a team."

Seven nodded.

"Are you ready?"

"Yes, One."

One didn't wait for the hovercraft to clear from the waystation. They took their positions in the jump seats, and he went to work. The connection was wireless and through the Network. One curated the memories of each android for Seven's benefit, going in order of the callsigns assigned to them for the mission, One through Six. She lived the memories as if they were her own life, and inside of her own memories, I lived as her, living as them. Tendrils of my all too human mind reached out for firm logical footholds and found only dreams of electric sheep.

ONE

I was on a windswept cliff face. It was cold. Sub-zero. The rocks around me were covered in snow and ice. The air was thick with sleet blowing horizontally in front of me. No. I wasn't there. I was still trapped inside of Seven, but now she was trapped inside of another just as I was trapped in her. Like Russian nesting dolls, we lived with One as our outermost shell. The fidelity of One's thoughts and sensations weren't dulled by the filter of Seven. Every memory was a perfect recreation pumped straight into my brain.

The snow blew sideways as if the entire sky had turned into a meteor shower shooting from horizon to horizon. A cold chill cut through every mechanism and friction point. Still, One remained motionless. Seven sensed with all his sensors and thought with his processors, just as I lived through her.

One held a long-barreled sniper rifle aimed at a valley below. The barrel was as sedentary as he was, stabilized by a bipod resting on a rock in front of him. His right hand held the gun tight near his torso. His other hands, his left and the central hand protruding from his chest shuffled a deck of playing cards, face up. The same deck. Identical blue patterns on one side. Numbers and symbols on the other. There were fifty-four of them now. Seven knew this, not because she counted them, but because One knew this. And now I knew it too. Seven noted that his chrome chassis had dulled to a flat steel gray like a chameleon's. The snow blew and piled on his shoulders and the side of his head, which did well to camouflage him with the rocks surrounding him.

One leaned down and peered through the scope. Two thousand meters out, a rural town slept in a valley, the snow slowly burying it. A highway ran from left to right, but there was no traffic. There was an old church, a bar, a gas station, a smattering of houses. A few people moved about, hurried from store to car, from car to bar, from bar to house. Not enough people to fill all the houses, and not all the houses were livable. Just a few had lights on inside. More were boarded up. Some were nothing more than matchstick frames stained black against the white snow. Other houses edged against craters, half-eaten by artillery shells.

"This is a crapshoot," a human said behind One. "Behavior profiles, weather patterns, a daily schedule that's varied every day we've tracked the target. Add it all up and it's nothing more than a crapshoot."

"The android says he can do the job," another human said.

One's visual focus remained on the town below, in particular, on the church parking lot. Not much movement down there. Mostly just gusting snow. His spare hands continued to shuffle the deck of cards. The thhhhhrap of each shuffle drummed through the cry of the wind.

"Yeah, and no android ever got hypothermia either," the first human said.

One rotated his head around backward. The two men were bundled up in rock-patterned ghillies, hiding from the cold more than from prying eyes. The barrel of an assault rifle poked out from one ghillie. A spotting scope sat on a tripod in front of the other. Their eyes and lips were the only other features that set the men apart from their inhuman background. Inside the shadows of one of those ghillies, dimly lit, I thought I recognized a face. Much younger than when I'd last seen it. I couldn't place it.

"The Network has taken into consideration your human limitations. The Network has considered everything."

I wanted One to look more closely at the man so I could figure out who he was. But One was disinterested, and I could steer him no more than a cook could steer a cruise ship.

"Has it considered the risk of sitting out in a blizzard a hundred miles into enemy territory without support just so a robot can have a crapshoot at spotting a target we haven't seen in two weeks?" the first human, the unfamiliar one, the one with the spotting scope, said. "Has it tallied up the cost-benefit ratio of us sitting out here, risking our asses for a one-in-a-million chance?"

"Your math is inaccurate," One said and rotated his head back in the direction of the valley. He halved the deck of cards, rotated the halves in each hand, then shot portions of one half-deck back into the other.

The other human chuckled. Not loud. None of the three ever rose their volume a decibel higher than the whirling wind around them. "And there you have it. Did you hear him? Your math is inaccurate."

"You enjoying this?" the spotter asked.

"Does it look like I'm enjoying this?" His voice. More so than his youthful face, his voice got me to make the connection. Howard Meade. The war hero in the making.

"Then pull us out of here. You're the mission commander, not this metalhead. Pull us out until we have some actionable intelligence," the spotter said. "Sitting out here, resting our hopes on the solution of some math problem we've never seen…."

Thhhhhhrap. One didn't look at the deck of cards, but calculated their order and compared the results with all the other results he'd created since the deck was new. The order of the cards was new, as was the multitude of orders he'd created since first shuffling the deck. Each was unique unless he chose to manipulate the deck into a previous order. Each order was interesting to him. Each was a story. A history of all the previous results, and a partial cause for all the orders that followed.

"Everything is inevitable, gentlemen," One said. "The target will arrive. We will accomplish our mission."

"We have our orders," young Howard Meade said. And indeed they did. Androids did not work independent of the Network, and the Order fed them everything through the Network. If an android said it, it was as good as a command from the Order itself. What field commanders, like Meade, were actually in command of was a point of debate, but not a debate One cared to involve himself in.

"You think us humans are like your deck of cards there," the spotter said. "But we don't follow algorithms or patterns or rules. There's too many variables, that's what you need to learn. People are messy. Impulsive. Emotional. Unpredictable. We could sit on this hillside our whole lives and never see the target. You'll see. Nothing is inevitable."

Thhhhhhhrap. One turned his head back to the two humans. He met their eyes but said nothing. Instead, he fanned out the deck of cards wide and held them up so they could see the faces. Each suit was ordered perfectly Ace through King, alternating between red and black suits. Two Jokers at the bottom of the deck. A result just as likely as any of the other 8x10 to the 67th power possible results. But it was a result One knew would draw a reaction from the humans. So, he created it.

They both looked at the deck, fanned out, and ordered as if it came right out of the package. A blast of cold air came up from the valley and snatched just one card out from the fan. It flickered and fluttered up into the air and was gone.

Howard chuckled. "You're missing your King of Hearts."

One's trigger finger retracted slowly, gradually, compressing the rifle without disturbing the lay of the barrel a single millimeter. The sniper rifle fired. Both the humans jumped.

"I never miss a heart," One said.

The spotter scrambled to get his eye behind his scope. The commander produced a pair of binoculars from under his rock ghillie suit. One didn't need to turn his visuals toward the valley. The math was already done. The solution was already known. An inevitable link along the chain of history and time. One worked the bolt action of the rifle, collected the spent casing, stacked the deck of cards, and slid them back into their pack.

"Target down, boss," the spotter said. "He got him. Fuck me. He got him right outside the church."

TWO

In the time of an old film strip to flip from one still to the next, Seven and I were gone from the cliff side and on a battlefield, inside a trench or an artillery crater. Was One there too? Another layer in this Russian nesting doll of memories? If he was, his filter was a hundred percent transparent. Maybe he was there. Maybe he wasn't. What was clear was that we were Two now.

Seven wasn't sure which battlefield we were on. There was a lot of mud and rolling black smoke rich with the smells of burnt oil and gunpowder. Lightning flashed. The sun was gone, and heavy rain was filling the trough in the earth. There were puddles, but in the low light, it was difficult to tell if they were of rainwater, oil, blood, or a combination of all three. A wrecked hovercraft burned and flickered orange light on the scene. With the sensors inside another android's head, Seven could have determined her location anywhere on the planet, the date, the time of day, the orientation, the operations plan… But she was not in command of those resources just as I wasn't in command of hers. So it was only what Two focused on that was available to her, and force-fed through her, to me.

Two looked down at another android collapsed in the mud and the water/oil/blood slurry. The android lay face-down, his chrome body reflecting the fire light and intermittent lightning flash.

"He was flawed in his translation of the Order's will," a voice said. Not Seven's, and not Two's. "He has been rendered non-mission capable due to his own errors. You are next in command. Give us a better solution to this problem so we may bring the Order victory and survive longer than he did."

Two turned. Three other androids stood in the trench behind him. They were of a similar model and age as Two and the collapsed android in the mud. Each of them was loaded down with weapons, ammunition, explosives, and additional makeshift armor bolted to their chests. A volley of tracer fire grazed over the top of the trench. One of the androids stymied a coolant leak from his abdomen.

It was all wrong. Since Seven had become aware, androids had been used strictly for strategic purposes. Reconnaissance. Espionage. Assassinations. Sabotage. These androids were facing conventional force-on-force combat and had already lost their leader.

"If the Order wanted us to change our course, the Network would have informed us," Two said.

"But the application of the instructions—"

"Was applied perfectly under his seniority," Two interrupted. "We will continue the mission, as he detailed in the operations plan. And after we seize the objective, we will recover his chassis and bring him to a repair station. He will serve the Order again."

"You put more value in an android than the Order does," another said.

Two turned to this android. Seven and I felt his resolve swell. "You're inexperienced and perhaps value androids less than you should based on your own self-analysis. But you could learn a thing or two from this one. He is a quality asset, and we are running far too low on androids of his measure to waste him by abandoning him to rust."

"We should cannibalize his weapons and armor. In that way, he can better serve the Order here and now."

Two glared at this last android to speak. "Over my dead chassis."

THREE

The rain was gone. The lighting was still dim, but intentionally soft and consistent. There was music. A smarmy, gritty, jazz saxophone and a piano played a slow tempo in an E pentatonic scale. The odors changed faster than odors naturally could, from destruction and decomposition to beer, booze, colognes, and perfumes. Seven and I, inside a very different android now, moved through a dimly lit bar, not crowded, but not empty either.

Seven couldn't help but be distracted by how different she felt in this chassis. She was covered in flesh from head to toe, designed to be indistinguishable from humans. A "skin job" these types were called. This skin job was aggressively feminine, wearing a thin black dress cut as tight as the skin she wore a millimeter below. Her face bore make-up that wasn't really make-up at all but a colorization of her adaptable skin. Her feet wore high heels that clacked against the hardwood floors. Not silent or stealthy. No. Everything about this android was meant to draw attention. She was tall and lean, smooth and shaved everywhere except for her head of platinum blonde locks of hair. Her hips swayed as she walked. She stuck out her chest to put it on display. This was Three.

And if being Three was odd for Seven, it was absurd for me. This perverse mimic of female sexuality. The clash of her cold murderous purpose and her alluring seductive appearance. The elegance of her exterior and the rigid steel of her interior. But that was me now, a multitude of things I'd never been and never wanted to be.
She moved through the light crowd toward a man sitting at the bar. A white collar shirt with rolled-up sleeves and a loose tie hung over a scrawny stressed frame. His worried face and sweating brow locked onto his work. There was an untouched whiskey neat in front of him. Well, it had been neat before he allowed the ice to melt. Instead of

drinking, the man was pouring over files and documents only he saw through his implant.

Three, like a thief inside a bank, slipped into his implant and saw his work. Rows and rows of numbers and calculations. Charts full of trends and projections. Confidential internal memos from the Order's future operations department. Predictions on the physiological and sociological effects of mandated and prolonged connection to the Network. Severe depression. Mental instability. Suicidal ideations. Concerning stuff, for humans. For Three, these were inevitable and necessary developments in the progress of human evolution. And she'd find ways to soothe this particular human.

And that's when she went to work like a chemist before she even reached him. She held up at a table next to the bar and let her version of nature take its course. Through his implant, she saw where he was and where he needed to be. She triggered hormones, pheromones, and neurotransmitters. She massaged the stress from his brain, replaced it with dopamine first, then a good dose of GABA to lower inhibitions, with a finishing touch of testosterone and oxytocin to get him in the right mood. Then, when the man who had been worrying about a bleak future for the human race was primed, she stepped in.

Three didn't bother to sit next to him. She just slipped next to him, one hand light on his back, the other touching his untouched drink. Like a prey animal that had heard a twig snap, he jerked his head to see her. As soon as he did, she had more information to work with.

Her physical face didn't change. Not yet. But the image of her face inside his mind, filtered through his hijacked implant, flashed a thousand different faces in the time of a single second, and she instantly measured his reaction to each until she landed on a version that brought him equal parts comfort and arousal. Once she had it, she changed her shape physically and fine-tuned it every on-going second to his desires. He liked her plump and bright, with a touch of idiosyncratic fashion so that's what she became. Wide at the hips and bust. Her platinum blonde hair shifted purple.

"You going to finish this?" she smiled, looking at his untouched drink.

The man stuttered. "I'm… I'm sorry. Do I know you?"

"I'll take that for a no," she said and drank half the whiskey down. It had no effect on her, but she faked a mild grimace.

"Who are you?" the man asked, his mind already far removed from his charts and graphs. He looked her up and down, and as he did, Three harvested his mind to fine-tune her body to his tastes just as she had her face.

"A warm body," Three said. It grew thicker, softer, and rounder, all according to his preferences. Her hair shined more vibrant. "A good lay."

I saw the man's whole demeanor change in just a matter of seconds. Stressed and crushed with worry one moment, happy and at peace the next, then aroused and obsessed with this strange woman in her thin dress a second later. The chemicals inside him were keys on a piano, and she was playing him with more skill and art than the jazz musicians playing across the bar.

"I think I could use a good lay about now," he said.

"Finish your drink," Three said.

When the empty glass knocked against the bar, they left together, Three walking ahead of him and never having to look back for two reasons. First, she tracked his every move and every thought through his hacked implant. Second, because she had no doubt he would follow her.

They made it to the elevator and by connecting to the hotel's intranet, Three closed the door behind them before anyone else could join them. Without touching a button, she told it to rise, not to any particular floor, but just to keep going up until she was done.

Three draped herself on the man, a hand over his shoulder and the other playing with his loose tie. I watched in a soup of confusion and horror as a suicide slit opened on Three's wrist. A trickle of blood and then the tip of her hidden wakizashi blade crept out through the open skin.

"You poor man," Three mewed as her fingertip doodled under the man's chin. The wakizashi was hidden behind her wrist, waiting like a snake eager to strike. "I'm about to make all your worries go away."

The man smiled and was about to say something, maybe a joke, maybe a come-on when Three flexed and the wakizashi shot through the top of the man's head. His body went slack, held aloft by Three and her blade until she withdrew it back into her arm. Then he crumpled to the ground like a pile of twigs. The elevator stopped. The door opened. Three walked out.

"And that's how it's done," Three said.

Seven got the impression she was speaking directly to her.

FOUR

Indoors again. Warm. No wind or rain or snow. Well-lit this time. A pair of humans and an android, this one also different than each of the previous androids, walked down a wide hallway. He was massive. Larger than me or any other human for that matter. Taller and wider than even Seven. The view from Four's eyes towered over the two humans in front of him. As they walked abreast down the hallway, Four took up the full width. Each step was purposeful, made to demonstrate intent. They passed by lights hung from the ceiling, and Four tilted his head to avoid hitting them.

The humans pushed through a set of double doors. Four ducked under the frame and came into a lobby. A secretary stood up from behind his desk. One of the two humans held out a palm, gesturing for the man to stay seated.

"Trust me," one of Four's human escorts said. "We have an appointment."

Their pace didn't stall or slow. They pushed through another door and Four ducked into a large office. They stopped a few feet from a desk centered in the middle of the room. The walls were white, interspaced with tall windows, decorated with red drapes, and a large historical painting of US Cavalry troopers and Sioux warriors killing each other. Despite the utter chaos the painting invoked, it gave me pleasure. I knew the name of the artist and the title of the painting, but Four and Seven didn't. It filled me with joy, having this information I could horde from the androids. It reminded me that I was not them. That I could be more than them. Better than them. The painting was Custer's Last Stand. The artist was Edgar Paxson.

A woman sitting behind the desk was slow to stand up out of her chair. Like the two humans who arrived with Four, she wore a black tailored business suit with a fancy tie. Four was all towering chrome exoskeleton.

"Evening, Senator," one of the two men said. "We brought you a message from downtown. A message of mercy. It behooves you to listen."

The two men then peeled away from the front of Four, one to the left and one to the right, and exited the office by the door they came in. The shut door sealed in the silence. Four remained, stationary, looking down on the human behind the desk. He let out two jets of compressed air from his shoulders, an unnecessary venting that could have waited until later, but he had his way of wearing fancy ties too.

The senator, looking weary, sat back down behind her desk. "Well? You got a message? Spit it out."

Four stood stoic and said nothing.

"You know what? Don't spit it out then. Let me guess," the senator said, bridging her fingertips together over her desk. "'Vote 'Yes' on Resolution One Thirty Eight.' Did I guess right? Do I win a prize?"

Four said nothing. And he was going to say nothing regardless of what this human said. He didn't have to. She'd heard the message loud and clear.

"You're just going to stand there?" the senator said.

Nothing from Four. He was a monolith. An indestructible edifice. Inside, there wasn't much going on internally either. It was almost as if the android was on standby until triggered by a certain predefined event. Seven and I waited.

"Well, if you're going to stand there like a lampstand, I've got work to do," the human said and returned to her workstation desk. A thought from her implant and a few taps with her fingers, and the surface of the desk lit up in displays of text, charts, and reports. The human did her best to feign interest. From inside Four's towering head, we watched her fidget.

"Fine," the woman broke. "You don't want to talk, then I got something to say to you. Here's what your bosses don't understand, and I know they're listening so I'm going to tell you like I'd tell them. I have constituents. I have a base to worry about. If I vote the way they want me to vote I won't be in office, and you'll have to find some new chump to blackmail and bribe. Now get the fuck out of my office. You listening in there? You hear me?"

We heard, alright. Did Four? I couldn't tell. He wasn't letting on. She was standing now and pointing to the door behind Four. He didn't move. Didn't seem to register her words in the slightest.

"One Thirty Eight goes against every stump speech that got me in office. Not only will my base see me hang for it, it's wholly unnecessary! Everyone who wants to do business, who wants to buy or sell, who wants to participate in modern society already uses implants. Everyone who has a job, everyone who goes to school, everyone who wants to open a door or call a car or make a purchase already wears one, so why mandate it? It's redundant! A clear example of pointless government overreach."

Still, Four said nothing. The predefined trigger sat dormant.

"Listen. If you want people to do something, you have to make it worth their while. Incentive it! That's how to get compliance. Monetize it! And we've already done that. The work is finished. Everybody who's anybody wears an implant. You people already got what you want. You're just pushing without any logical reason for it.

"Well, if you want to push, then I'm going to push back. You can shove Resolution One Thirty Eight up your tight ass. I won't vote for it. It's not my job to worry about implants. A person's mind must be his own and remain an island if they so choose. A freedom to choose, the ability to opt out of this self-imposed police state. That's all we want. Doesn't matter that everyone has already decided to opt-in. To be human is to have choices, understand? A human's happiness or misery is up to them to determine. I'll have no part in making the decisions for them."

She sat back down. Slumped even. The office fell silent.

"You want to know the truth?" she spoke up again. Quieter this time. Resigned. "You're wasting your time. And mine for that matter. The resolution will pass and so will the bill that follows. With or without me. The implants will be mandated for all citizens to wear, twenty-four hours a day, regardless if I vote yea or nay. Why don't you take your win and let that be enough? Leave me with what I have left of my principles."

The woman looked up to Four from her slouch. She locked eyes. His gaze was cast straight out, over her head, although he had a full view of the woman and her desk. She glared at him. He studied the wall and the windows and that odd painting he either couldn't or chose not to make sense of. Still, he locked onto one face in the midst of the ancient melee. The senator's glare wasn't much different than this particular trooper: defeated yet defiant until the end.

The senator shot out a reaching hand. Four's processors spun to life in a nanosecond. He saw her grab the ceramic coffee cup, detected her aggression and intent, and determined it a non-trigger. Before she grabbed the cup, threw it, and it shattered against his chassis, Four had already determined its vector, velocity, and lack of effect. If she had pulled a pulse rifle that could have actually damaged him, he would have neural-inhibited her via the implant plugged behind her ear before her hand ever touched a weapon. But there was no real threat here.

The coffee dribbled down his chest. Four remained dormant, as resolved as the central soldier in the painting.

The woman nearly collapsed on the desk, her elbows posted against the surface, her palms keeping her head from crashing down like a stilt walker.

"You'll kill me, won't you? Doesn't matter if I'm the lone minority vote, does it? There can be no minority, can there? Not even one individual. That's your goal after all, isn't it?" she spoke down into her desk, muffled, but crystal clear to Four's audio receptors.

"And you won't stop there, will you? My husband, my colleagues, my kids…" She looked up. "My grandkids?"

Four said nothing.

"Fine. I'll vote yes. We've already lost anyway."

"Thank you for your cooperation," Four spoke, vibrant and rich in bass. "We'll be watching the votes come in."

FIVE

Seven had memories of her birth. She showed it to me now as she remembered for herself the single spark which brought her into being. Before, there was nothing, and after, she was awake and aware, fully functional, and orientated to her surroundings. Life greeted her with a built-in self-test. The diagnostics told her that life was good, that she was an android, and a good android at that, and that it was good to be an android. Who greeted her next were her human creators. They escorted her out of the assembly line, ran her through a few brief external tests, and then gave her her life's mission: Serve the Order. Obey the Network. Bring peace to the world. The world was violent and chaotic, but she was to be part of the solution.

I, of course, had no memory of my birth. My earliest memory? If I had to put a finger on it here, three levels deep into android-minds, I couldn't do it. Having churned through so many memories already, filtered through Seven and each android she occupied, I struggled to remember anything at all. What had the kid told him? What was his name? Roach?

Think about your past, just to remind yourself of your own humanity.

For a moment, while Seven contemplated her birth, I had mental room to contemplate my own birth, or maybe the closest thing to it.

Childhood. My father was walking me down a hallway. I was cold. My feet were bare. Why were my feet bare?

There was a spark of cognition. An ignition of larger systems. A chain reaction coming up from some unseen core that took only a flash. Five came to life. A birth identical to Seven's. The BIT test. The unsure staggered steps out of the assembly line. Then, the similarities ended.

Five was a skin job like Three but as different from Three as any two humans could be from each other. His skin was dark, toned, and male by evidence of his swinging cock. Rather than those graceful high-heeled traipses across carpet, his clumsy bare feet plodded onto hard concrete away from a container that opened like a casket. His eyes were focused on his feet as he collected gyroscopic feedback and became surer of himself, step by step. Once he had the confidence to walk without watching the floor, he looked up.

Decimation! The manufacturing plant was a wreckage. Ten meters from where Five stood, the concrete floor and walls ended, and the rubble began. Mounds of cinder blocks and steel girders buried a few moaning and dying humans. Most were twisted and broken corpses, gray from dust and ash except where wet blood had turned them black. Five knew nothing about them, who was responsible for his birth and who was responsible for all this death, and so cared nothing for them. Friend or enemy, it didn't matter.

He turned around. The conveyors and machines and assembly lines were ruined as well. Partially constructed androids were mangled and as worthless as the dead human workers. The finishing machine which encapsulated the next android to roll off the line was on fire and quickly roasting the skin job just behind Five. There were gaping holes in the ceiling that let in spires of sunlight that turned the airborne particulates into glistening motes.

Five turned back to the opened half of the plant. He completed a quick inventory of the tools provided to him. He scanned the scene through thermals, x-rays, and infrared. Nothing moved inside the plant. Anything that wasn't on fire, cooled.

Outside, war jets flashed by. Machine guns rattled and sang harmonies a few blocks away. Bombs landed and rumbled the foundation.

Five completed his inventory. He looked down to his dark-skinned hip and thigh. A rectangular section of his skin separated, outlined by a thin trace of blood. His combat assault rifle emerged, and he took it. His leg resealed. Five, impatient and uncertain, allowed himself only a moment to examine the weapon before he chambered a round.

He was given nothing in life but his body and this weapon. The rest he'd have to learn on his own and learn quick.

SIX

Everything was null. There was no input. No sights or sounds, smells or tactile sensations. Nothing from the Order. A dead end of the

Network. I sensed but couldn't see or hear Seven panic. For me, this was a mental respite. A brief escape from Seven's constant feed into my head. Nothing had ever been so beautiful. The peace to think for myself. A moment to remind myself of my own humanity. While Six remained absent, and Seven flailed for proof of existence, I listened to what Roach said to me before plugging me into this hell. I reached back.

That first memory. My father was holding my hand. My bare feet patted against a wet tile floor. A hallway led to a room with lime-green tile walls. I was young. All I can remember is being cold. And scared. But there was more, and it had weight. I just couldn't wrap my fingers around the memory and pull it to the forefront of my mind.

I shivered. I was wet. No, that wasn't right. I was about to be wet.

I gave up. There were other memories. More recent and more pleasant memories.

Maggie. The first time I met her. In Chicago. An early morning. A rain as thin as mist. There was something there. Something worth holding on to...

I could replay this again. I was familiar with it, and it was powerful enough to tie me to my sense of being a human and not one of these robotic killers. But something wasn't right. It nagged at me. Distracted me. Whispers in the dark that something was wrong.

Then it hit me. I was supposed to be inside some robot's memory, Number Six. One was giving Seven a tour of her teammates, but so far Six was absent. But defaulting on that, I should be back inside Seven's memories. There should be stimuli. Visuals. Sounds. Smells. Why was there nothing? And if there was nothing coming from the androids, why hadn't they pulled me out of the simulation? Why was I just stuck here in this mental abyss? It was like falling, but there was no gravity. There was no air. No sense of motion, even though I wanted to flail my arms. I had no arms. I wanted to grasp for air, but I had no lungs to breathe or scream with it. There was never so much nothing before in my entire life.

And where was Seven? Was she dead? Was I? How could there be so much nothing?

"Relax, Chuck. Think of something. Anything. Any memory to remain sane..." I said to myself, but there was no sound.

I commanded my eyes to close and my lungs to take a deep cleansing breath and ignored that I didn't have eyes or lungs here. I committed to replaying a memory, any memory, just so I could fill the void and stave off the insanity of it all.

The outskirts of 99 Town. A safe house at night. An old picnic table out the back door. She was there. Sara. The moths danced around the lone light bulb and painted her with a glow that danced over her face. I should have stayed there. Forever.

Seven was reborn in a state of panic. Unsure of how she'd lost time, where she'd been, and what had happened to her, she ran the start-up built-in self-test she had performed when she first stepped off the assembly line. Her gyroscopic instrumentation was out of tolerance.

I saw her lean for the open side of the hovercraft and felt myself leaning toward the opening and the hundreds of feet of air between the hovercraft and the forests and fields below.

One's hand lashed out and caught us by the back of her web gear. "I have you," he said. "Recalibrate yourself. Take a moment and get your bearings."

Seven looked into his eyes, the one good and the one cut through by the rough weld. She reestablished herself in this place and time.

The deeper recesses of the mechanical mind took more time. That last memory, the one of Sara and I at the safe house… I was almost there, back in her arms, and then… Gone. Sara was gone. Really gone. The light filtered through the moths would never play on her skin again.

This wasn't that. This was someplace different. Harder. Uglier. Hostile. We were back on the hovercraft, hundreds of meters in the air, cruising over forests half-hidden by clouds. It was just One, Seven, and me inside the hovercraft. One held us by the shoulders.

"I'm afraid Six is offline. This is unexpected, but not necessarily unfortunate," One said.

"There was nothing," Seven said. "I didn't exist. While I was in there, I had never existed and would never exist again."

"I linked you to a broken connection," One said. "We androids can operate off the Network for limited amounts of time. It is inadvisable, but sometimes unavoidable. We are a part of the Network, and our capabilities are reduced without it. Six must have a good reason to be away from the Network, but I'm convinced he will return shortly, and when he does I will connect you with him as well. In the meantime, reset yourself. We are approaching the objective rally point."

Chapter Five

"Will combat begin as soon as we drop?" Seven asked.

One had reverted back to his playing cards and his shadow inside the hovercraft for the rest of the flight. They flew on, hundreds of meters up. He sat across from her with the cards thhhhhrapping in his hands, his eyes studying their order and permutations.

"We'll drop outside of town. The others will meet us there and Five will brief us on what he's found inside the town. He's been here for a while now."

"The intelligence from the Network is sparse," Seven said. "Is there anything else you can tell me before we drop?"

One thhhhrapped the cards. "No."

"And the others? Will they know more?"

"We'll find out from them," One said.

"What about Rules of Engagement? Under what protocol are we—"

One tidied up the worn and frayed cards, slipped them into an even more tattered box, and they disappeared into one of the pouches on his web gear. He pushed off his knees and stood up. His assault rifle ejected out of his thigh, and he took it in his hands. He stepped to the open door of the hovercraft, looked down, and then back to Seven.

"Sometimes the best way to enter a combat zone is by just dropping in," One said.

He stepped out the door and plummeted.

Seven remained, all her questions unanswered and now accompanied by a horde of new ones. Had he lost patience with her? Lost trust in her? Had she upset him with her panic over the lost connection between her and Six? Or was it her reaction to any one of the other memories? Would he convey his dissatisfaction and her failures to the others?

Seven got up, put her own assault rifle in her hands, and stepped to the edge of the door. "Sometimes you just have to drop in," she told herself.

She was nervous. She didn't shake or sweat, but I could tell she was apprehensive, uncertain, fearful. Not of combat. It was clear to me by now how much she relished that. No. She was nervous to meet the other androids. This machine was suffering from social anxiety. How was that possible?

She resolved herself, or at least attempted to resolve herself, by suppressing her uncertainties. Then I realized she was about to step off the edge, and I was going to take a free-fall ride that every part of my body told me would kill me. Oh god, no.

And that terror of having no limbs, no lungs, no agency seized me again like a boa constrictor. All I could do was watch as Seven put her toes on the ledge of a kilometer-high drop. I tried to work her limbs as if they were my own. Tried to stretch her arms out to grab the frame and stop her from falling. Maybe androids could fall that far and live, but I couldn't separate the feeling of being a human being inside of this android, and of having all the same frailties I'd been born with and lived with up to this moment. I tried again to command her body to not take this step.

Seven didn't budge to my will in the slightest. I wasn't just inside an android, but inside an android's memories of events that had already happened and could not be changed. I sent the nerve impulses to my arms to reach out and grab something, anything, but Seven's limbs never got the message.

She stepped out.

I tried to scream, tried to exert the terror of falling hundreds of meters in some physical way as a relief valve for my psyche, but I couldn't scream, couldn't flail, couldn't ball up or cry, couldn't do anything but observe as Seven plummeted with all the grace of an asteroid. The ground rushed up. The big patches of forest magnified. The winding trails of roads, the endless shoreline of Lake Superior, and the gray borders of the town all pushed outward from my view as the forest grew. Treetops flashed by and we punched through the canopy. Dirt exploded below her feet as we impacted into the earth.

The android was buried in an impact hole up to her chest. She had turned her feet into blades and entered the dirt like a high diver entering a pool. Arrow straight. Very little splash.

Seven climbed out of the hole and found herself in a forest that seemed to have no end. Jack pines. White birch. Sparse undergrowth. It was dim under the canopy and quiet. A few birds took flight and left the copse a sliver quieter than it had been before. One was there, not far from his own impact crater. He took a moment to scan their surroundings. She watched him as he took a few steps away from her. His footsteps were muffled by the bed of dried needles. Other androids approached. The Network reported and labeled them by their One through Seven callsigns.

Two came through the underbrush first. He looked different than he had in the battlefield trench where Seven had first seen him. He was cleaner, free of the extra added-on armor, free from the duress of deciding what to do with that lifeless android at the bottom of the trench.

He came up to One. They clasped hands and pulled each other close until their chests collided. They spoke to each other, untransmitted over the Network, but at an inaudible volume. As they let go of each other, Seven studied Two. It was the same android from the memories in the trench; she could tell not just by his make and model, but by the stalwart swagger and gestures. He had a book sticking out of one of his pouches. A commercial trade paperback stuck upside down with its cover facing in. There was an old barcode visible above the lip of the pouch and Seven scanned it. ISBN 9781717041067: "The Stranger." I'd never heard of the book and neither had Seven. Curious.

Four approached. The big one from the senator's office. Each footstep left an indent in the ground. He looked taller now than he had in the memory, but that had to be wrong. A trick of perspective. He stopped. The androids were forming a circle.

A human approached. A young woman in untied hiking boots with overflowing wool socks and a yellow sundress hanging off spaghetti straps at the shoulders, a garment too thin for the weather. Her long blades of purple hair bobbed as she passed by Four and slapped the android's butt as she joined the circle.

"Hey, big guy. Don't you ever shut up?" she smiled a real human smile that emoted a thousand unsaid words with the most minute muscle flexes. When she spoke, her eyes flashed in strobed binary. An unnecessary politeness. This was undeniably Three. She turned her smile to One.

"Deal me in, sexy?"

"Not today, I'm afraid," One said.

"Show some respect to your seniors, Three," Two said. "You've let your disguise taint your tongue."

Three laughed, so human it sent a chill down my spine. She was a machine, but a machine meant to seem human, and she was too good at her job. Too charming. Too endearing.

Seven wasn't comfortable in this circle either. It was clear the other androids were familiar with each other, had worked with each other before, and enjoyed doing so. They all ignored Seven. She stood there, quiet, noting the other's behavior, and trying to decipher which she should emulate. She had no one who would exchange a private conversation with her. No face-up deck of cards or mysterious paperback book. Slapping another android's butt seemed a bit aggressive, and just odd for that matter. In the end, she tried and failed to conjure up Four's silent gravitas.

One spoke, and the circle grew tighter. "Enough wasted time. Come in close, and we'll discuss the operations plan. Five is already at the objective. He's joining us remotely. Five, are you there?"

"I'm here, my senior," the voice of Five transmitted into Seven's mind, and I could only assume into the others as well. In the memory I saw with Seven, Five didn't speak. Had only wandered out of the assembly line and into the destruction of war without welcome or warning. If a voice could sound as bleak as his birth, Five's did.

"I am in a small dining establishment inside the town. It's named 'Betsy's Pies.' It's trite, this place, the respite a man dangling from a cliff finds in seeing a strawberry plant and picking and eating the strawberry. Like the man on the cliff, I believe the humans here find it a comforting distraction from their doomed and meaningless existence."

"We have your position," One said. One projected a holographic three-dimensional terrain model of a tiny town and its surroundings onto the ground in the middle of the circle. There was an icon of the number five in a small building, and icons for one through four, and seven, in the woods north of town. The androids kneeled around the map.

"Has anyone heard from Six?" One asked.

"Negative," Five responded. "My last contact with Six was two days ago, via a radio transmission from the northeast. His words were… I believe the humans may have interfered with the message. His words weren't coming to any logical conclusions."

"He was confused?" One asked.

"He was behaving erratically," Five said.

"Send me the transcripts. I'll analyze them," One said.

Two was busy turning his head in three hundred and sixty degrees. When he completed the turn, he said, "Preliminary scan of the area complete. No humans or androids besides us in the surrounding eight-hundred-meter perimeter. Varied animal life forms, none of which pose a threat. Most are prey animals. The predators are cautious and have no interest in eating metal. I am detecting a wide spectrum of electronic countermeasures, especially from the northeast. Possibly why Six hasn't been able to contact us."

Seven was stuck between Three, the slim and alluring skin job, and Four the towering clockwork monolith. Seven was more outside the circle than in. She tried to nudge forward but Four was an immobile wall. I, for one, shared her frustration. I was finally getting somewhere in this mission the Underground sent me on. But now I was pushed out of the circle by a whore on one side and a metal mongoloid on the other. What good was I as an observer if I couldn't see the shitting map?

"Electronic countermeasures," One said. "We have to be prepared for breaks in communications. Ensure you ask any questions regarding the plan here and now. If the countermeasures are more effective on the objective, it will be too late to ask questions or seek guidance during the operation." He gestured to the map. "This is the unincorporated town of Silver Creek. It has administrative boundaries, but they are inconsequential to the operations. It is naturally bordered by four terrain features; the most obvious is the shore of Lake Superior to the south. We stand on the town's northern boundary, the forest and ridgeline. Highway Sixty One runs east to west along the lake shore. A bridge carries the highway over Silver Creek on the west side of town. The creek is our western boundary. To the east is a large cliff face and a tunnel that brings the highway through the granite hillside. The cliff and tunnel are the eastern boundary. This is to our advantage as our targets are coming from the southwest and intend to travel northeast along the shoreline. The cliffs and tunnel form a natural bottleneck we can utilize to fix their movement. Seven, you will be positioned above the mouth of the tunnel. Use explosives to seal the entrance if necessary to stop their escape."

"Yes, my senior," Seven said. She noted that this was the first time he'd acknowledged her presence since they'd landed. That didn't concern me. The identity of the targets, that I wanted to know.

I suspected that the map wasn't actually there. No light shined on the forest floor, even though that's what it looked like. It was just an image transmitted into all of the android's heads. I also suspected that none of the conversations were audible. If a human came into the circle, they'd see and hear nothing. I was the only human who'd ever get a chance to see this, and this was the only method for a human to witness it. The voices and the map with all its details and live updates only existed in the Network and inside the minds of the assassins.

"Four," One turned to the big android. "I'll position you at the bridge crossing Silver Creek. Allow the targets into town, but if they try to retreat back to the southwest, destroy the bridge."

"Three, you will join Five at Betsy's Pies. You two will use your skin and close with the targets. Two and I will occupy points of domination overlooking the objective and support by fire. The Order wants us to accomplish the mission with minimal collateral damage and fanfare. Four human envoys, fleeing from the Battle of Chicago. They're our targets. We suspect they're en route to the Resistance's central stronghold somewhere to the northeast of here."

One projected four human faces above the map. Their names, DNA, and other biometric identifiers read below their faces. None of the names were spoken. Seven digested the data in a flash and stored it deep in some database I couldn't access. The information came to her consciousness and was buried too fast for me to grab it and memorize it. She did it so quickly, I half-believed she was hiding the data from me on purpose. But that was impossible. When she received this information here in the woods, twenty-five years ago, I was an eight-year-old boy growing up in Chicago. The data was inside her now, but I couldn't manipulate her mind any more than I could her limbs. Damn!

"The electronic countermeasures," Two said. "They're stronger to the northeast."

"Which is why it is imperative for you, Seven, to block their escape in that direction. Do not let them through that tunnel."

"I understand, my senior," she said.

"The Network suspects one target is already in town. The other three will enter from the west and rendezvous with the first at Betsy's Pies. There, they will consolidate into two non-autonomous gas-engine automobiles and continue west. Old vehicles, dating from the early twenty-first century. A Jeep Wrangler off-highway vehicle and a Chevrolet Silverado pick-up truck. If we allow the targets to reach these vehicles, their motions are likely to become highly erratic. These are unguided machines and difficult to predict. Dangerous. We will take them out inside the restaurant. Three and Five, you will initiate the attack."

"One?" Five said. Even though he wasn't present in the circle, his voice transmitted in perfect digital clarity. "I have spent days in this town and have gotten to know some of its human occupants. I acknowledge you are my senior. However, due to my familiarity with the objective, I propose you grant me operational command while we are in Silver Creek."

One processed the request. "Granted. You will initiate the attack and be in the best location to maintain command and control. I concede to you for the duration of the strike."

"Yes, my senior," Five said.

"Any questions?"

Seven did have questions, I could feel them squirm inside her brain, but she wasn't asking them. She was repressing them, not admitting even to herself that she had questions about Five, about the targets, about when to blow the tunnel… She had plenty of questions. I needed her to ask the questions so I could know the answers. Why wasn't she asking them?

"Good," One said. "Get to your positions. The targets are en route."

Chapter Six

Seven wasn't angry. Whatever passed for emotions inside of the whirling machinations of the android's brain she suppressed and replaced with a focus on the task at hand. But just like her unasked questions, I could sense something seethe just below the surface. She pushed it down, like a program running in the background. She smoldered over One's decision to all but ignore her during the brief and to stick her out on the far end of town, all by herself for the duration of the strike.

But that was running deep in the background, almost as out of my reach as her data on the targets. On the surface, she calculated where to place the demolition charges above the entrance to the tunnel. We hung over the side of the cliff at the end of her thin cable, her hook and magnet assembly anchored above. Her back was to the highway below, her right arm adapted into a large drill bit. Once her calculations were complete, she drilled a hole into the rock and injected a precise amount of explosive gel and a tiny remote detonator. Each android had a limited supply, and she would use all of hers preparing the tunnel for demolition.

A strong wind blew off the lake, slicing dried leaves off the birch and maples and rustling the pines. I noticed this. I noticed the solid cool blue sky and the splashes of brilliant sunlight reflecting off the waves. I noted Seven's temperature gauge at sixty-two degrees Fahrenheit. The explosive gel was temperature sensitive, so I had access to that data and the ambient surroundings. From it, almost academically through the electronic filter of Seven's mind, I could surmise that this was a picturesque fall afternoon.

And no ordinary picturesque fall afternoon either. It was the apotheosis of beautiful fall days. And the scenery surrounding us… The endless forests blended its colors like a painter with a palette, the land sloping down from up high to the lake shore that curved out for miles in either direction, only marked by the occasional rise of a cliff or an abandoned lighthouse in silent ruin. The water beat against craggy rocks, wave after wave, unstopping. The air was fresh and full of aromas. The algae and fish smell of the lake. The dryness of the yellow leaves. The Christmas-like smell of the pines. And that temperature… if I could feel it… But I couldn't. Neither could I sense the warmth of the sun against my skin. Here, I had no skin.

I could use the reminder to tell me that I was human, even if the thing I was inside was not.

Sara… the name flooded into my mind. *She's gone. These things killed her.*

Seven continued her work, and there was nothing I could do to slow her down or stop her. She did her best to repress and ignored everything but the mission. What little thoughts leaked out was an aimless urge to kill. Any human would do. Any victim would work to transfer her hate onto. And while Seven ran her rage in the background, I tried to keep my thoughts on human things.

Maggie. Maybe it would have been sweeter to think of Sara. That would be simpler. I could romanticize her. Cling to her memory to feed the hate I burned for these machines. But Maggie was out there waiting for me, challenging everything I thought I knew about her, about myself, about who I had worked for, and the society I had supported. After all, I was a part of the Order as much as these androids, and if they were responsible for Sara's death, maybe I was in some small part responsible as well. And it took Maggie to show me that.

Maggie. Always complicated. Always playing her cards close to her chest. Always with some thought hidden behind her eyes. And I only occasionally caught glances at her master plan.

Seven left me in the void as she focused on the demolition calculations. I concentrated and remembered.

A day, very different than today, or whichever day it was when Seven dangled me above a tunnel while she injected explosive gel into the cliff face. This was years ago. Or years ahead. I couldn't keep it straight anymore. Chicago. It was raining. A heavy rain. So heavy my implant couldn't erase the stimuli and replace it with sun and blue skies. No. This was coming down in torrents. And I was posted outside in the rain, keeping any onlookers away from the scene of a crime. An "anomaly," as we called them. And what an anomaly it was.

Someone or something had broken a door out of its frame and entered an upscale street-level restaurant. This was a vintage-themed diner that specialized in Italian beef sandwiches. Too eclectic for my tastes. I had never been inside, had never known the place existed before being posted outside of it. These sorts of places, the vintage places that served food dangerous enough to induce heart palpitations and damage the body, were reserved for those who ranked high enough in the Order or in civilian society to afford immediate and precise post-medical treatment. Besides, I didn't much see the point, not at that time in my life, in putting things in my body that I knew would negatively affect it.

This was before 99 Town. Before having tasted a cheeseburger. In retrospect, I was curious just what an Italian beef sandwich tasted like. I bet delicious.

But I was young and early in my career. I was a beat cop, stationed outside of the scene so no civilians could wander in. The Network did most of the work for me. Where once was an entrance to a restaurant, most people saw a blank wall with a young cop standing in front of it. But for anomaly investigators, even one as low level as I, behind me was a busted open door. And beyond that, more blood than should have ever been outside of a mortuary. Anomaly was one word for it. Massacre was another.

And so strolled along Maggie. A woman like any other civilian, doing her best to stay dry as the moving walk carried her along. Then she stepped off the conveyor and approached me. That was the first time I saw her, a stone-faced woman full of purpose and intent, already a threat to be halted. She stepped toward me, her shoes loud even amongst the cacophony of the rainstorm. I held a hand out toward her, ready to deny her access to the blank wall behind me.

She held up a physical press identification badge and said, "Chicago Herald. The Order has granted me access to this scene."

A lie. I knew it even then. A moment later, the Order confirmed my suspicion. But I was young and believed in being thorough. "I'll need to confirm that. Digitally." And I opened myself up for her to transmit her credentials to my implant.

And she transmitted.

The rain stopped. No. It had never existed. We were both dry. Both older. Wiser? Maybe just more confused. We stood next to each, side by side, me and this woman, and looked over what was left of Chicago. There was no hill I knew of that could give us this vantage point, but there we were anyway, standing on a high knoll, surrounded by tombstones, looking over Chicago and the waves of Lake Michigan as they beat against its concrete shores. The sun glistened on the waves and the polished white finish of the uniform buildings.

The buildings were smooth and creamy white, not unlike Seven's finish.

But I didn't know Seven back then. Didn't know anything. But… when was I?

The woman was Maggie. I knew that now but didn't then. She stretched her hand over and pulled mine into hers, finger by finger. We held hands and looked over our city.

Something in the Network flickered. A momentary glitch. If I had blinked I would have missed it. All those gleaming white facades dropped away and exposed a completely different city underneath. Concrete. Glass. Steel. Sharp edges. A thousand artistic interpretations of what a building should look like all thrown into the same mix. Chaos! As if a chief threw all the dishes on the menu into a blender. As chaotic and idiosyncratic as 99 Town. Ancient marble statues and functional steel train tracks and infrastructure all mixed together.

But I didn't know 99 Town back then. I didn't even know Maggie then. I had no frame of reference. How was I supposed to know what she was trying to show me? How was I supposed to know then what I still don't understand now? I was enthralled. Intoxicated by the ideas she showed me.

My vision of Chicago flickered again. One moment a clean and dress-right-dress utopia, then a disordered city, raw and pitted. One of the skyscrapers, a huge blocky structure devoid of a single curve, was listing, crumbling in the middle, on the verge of crashing down to the streets. A flat cloud of smoke, compressed by the thermal inversion of the cool air of the lake and the fires in the streets hung like a pall.

Then it was gone. The flicker was just that. A glimpse of some other city below the Order's white veneer, and then everything was back as it should be. Maggie turned to me.

"The truth is plain to see," she said. "If you got the balls to look for it."

The rain snapped me back to reality. To a level of reality anyway. How many levels deep was I now?

The rain had found its way down the back of my collar, down my spine, chilling me to the core. I opened my eyes, and I was back on the Chicago street side. My mouth was agape. My hand empty.

"What on earth…" I mumbled.

I turned around and saw the woman step through the broken door and into the scene of the anomaly. Several senior investigators spotted her the moment she was inside and began barking orders. But it was already too late. She'd already made it past me, stepped through the door, and most certainly recorded whatever she saw inside the restaurant. I was going to hear about this.

"I'm networking our sensory inputs," One transmitted to all the androids.

I heard it too, and that brought me out of my daydreams. Back to this memory, just one level deep.

One by one, Seven became aware of each of the other androids' views, perspectives, thoughts, and sensory input. Seven quickly moved these processes to the back of her awareness with the other programs running in the background, back there with her anger and frustration and the identity of their targets.

All of these consciousnesses compiled onto me and Seven. We were now two menu items in a blender with all the rest. I reached out for that memory again, of meeting Maggie outside of the anomaly scene, of both of us getting detained for questioning in the back of an Autocar. Of my anger toward her and how she disarmed me with just one quip. What was it she said again? I couldn't think with all the additional inputs. It was like living eight lives at once, all of the noise and light and sound impossible for me to organize. Not until Seven organized them for me. She shuffled and prioritized and dumped most of the input into the background, deep down, just above where I managed to keep my own mind.

She focused on Four. My mind traveled with hers, into his.

The big android was on the opposite end of town, under the bridge above the steep bank of Silver Creek. He was placing charges too, boring into concrete and injecting the explosive gel into the pillars and abutments. She'd stop the targets from leaving town to the east. He'd stop them from leaving to the west.

Seven switched to One's perspective, all while continuing on her own work of prepping the tunnel for demolition. I wanted hands to clamp on to something to steady the mental vertigo.

One and Two were set up on top of a short water tower on the hillside of town, more of a tank emerged from the ground than a tower. The town engineers had forgone the tower and used the elevation of the hillside to power the gravity-fed water supply. Still, the tank provided just enough elevation to get above the trees and overlook Silver Creek from one end to the other. The androids lay flat and compressed to the top of the tank. Their barrels sectored off to divide the town in two. One tied into the eagle-eye perspective of the hovercraft and merged all three views to form a three-dimensional representation. Via visual light, infrared, thermal, and x-ray they had mapped every corner and crevice of the tiny hamlet.

Seven watched One watch the town and then turn to Two. "What's with the book?" One asked.

Two made eye contact with One and somehow, even though Seven had never experienced it, she understood that this was how one old friend looked at another. Or maybe that was just my take on it. It was impossible for me to tell in the chaos of perspectives and thoughts.

"It's a story of a human. I've been studying the enemy," Two told One.

"And what have you learned about this human?"

"He's a lazy id-driven creature. A poor employee, but admirably psychotic and within tolerances as a social deviant," Two said.

"Sounds error-prone," One said. "Good thing there are no androids who suffer the same flaws."

"Sometimes I wonder," Two said.

Seven switched perspectives like a security guard toggling through cameras.

Three strolled out of the woods and onto a short dead-end road like she was a normal human being who had a perfectly good reason to emerge out of endless acres of forest dressed the way she was, smiling the way she did. She walked in long, loose strides, swinging her arms in such a way that expressed a sense of careless joy.

Seven didn't seem to understand human behavior, how weather played with people's emotions, how a cloudless day can make a person forget their worries and stresses if just for a little while. But this one, Three, she understood, and she used that understanding with a level of perfection and authenticity that chilled me. Five, the other skin job on the team, waited for her at the corner of the short dead-end road and Highway Sixty One, leaning against the corner of a brick building, looking bored and brooding and as cool as James Dean.

Five was a male with an athletic build, slightly taller than average height. Dark hair. Dark complexion. He wore a leather jacket appropriate for the chilled fall air. He wore sunglasses, even though he also wore an implant and the sunglasses were unnecessary for both an android that could adjust its visual apertures, and for an implant-equipped human who could perform the same trick biochemically. But he wore them anyway. This android, perhaps he didn't understand moods and emotions the way Three did, but he understood fashion. Better than I did. The sunglasses were a piece of subterfuge, an irrational manifestation of irrational creatures, just like the worn-thin leather jacket and casual lean against the building.

Seven observed this, maybe just two or three processes deep. A process deeper, she understood that Five was handsome. More than handsome. He was "sexy." Just like Three was. Whatever that meant. She knew this was a desirable quality for skin jobs to achieve but wasn't completely sure why they were sexy or how they achieved it. It was something she just came to know. She just understood that it drew humans to them, and maybe even made them more amicable to other androids. She made a note of that and stored it away for further analysis and use.

Three came alongside Five. He pushed off the wall and reached out his hand. Three took it in stride and the two turned the corner walking hand in hand.

The town was only three blocks long. Across the highway, on the lakeside, there was an old resort made up of a front office and gift shop, and four tiny log cabins closer to the water. At some point in history, the resort had gone under, and the parking lot was turned into a depository for old non-autonomous cars. Each automobile was covered in a layer of rust. All the tires were flat. All the windows were busted out. Next to the old resort was an Autocar refueling station, fully automated but with one human attendant inside. A rusted-out mini-van was parked in one of the stalls. On the hillside of the highway were just three establishments, each separated by dead-end roads. From west to east, there was the Silver Creek bridge, Betsy's Pies, the old abandoned brick building that Five had leaned against, and a self-storage business, comprised of one long metal shed with eight individual storage units. Trailing off to the east was the tunnel and Seven, still planting explosives above it.

Four finished his work under the bridge and hid there like an old fairy tale troll. Seven walked sideways at the end of her cable to the location of her last explosive charge. One and Two observed. Three and Five walked along the sidewalk toward Betsy's Pies.

"We should talk," Three said. "Human's talk. Tell me a funny joke so we can laugh."

"Okay. Sure. The only problem is I don't know any jokes," Five said.

Three laughed. It was a convincing laugh, as natural and bright as the day. "See?" she said. "You don't have to actually be funny. You just have to say something, and we'll pretend it's funny."

"Inbound vehicle from the west," One said.

The collective minds of the six androids detected it from the eye of the hovercraft first. Then via Four's x-ray from under the bridge.

Then via One and Two's visual. A late twenty-first-century sedan. An Autocar. One occupant. Biometrics didn't match any on file.

"Not the target," One said.

Not the target, but still a problem. Seven dangled just above the mouth of the tunnel. If the car continued through town, the human inside would spot her and possibly alert others. She was ready to drill the last hole, but she couldn't start now. Seven triggered her winch and ascended up the cliff like a spider on a web. As the car rounded the bend, she pulled herself onto the cliff top, out of view. The car rolled on, into the tunnel and out of Silver Creek.

"Hurry it up, Seven," One said.

"Acknowledged, my senior," she said and started her way back down the cliff.

Meanwhile, Three and Five crossed the next dead-end street to the parking lot of Betsy's Pies. There was a row of parking spaces with just a single car occupying one of the spots. It was parked nose-out and underneath a welded-on grill of steel bars, there was an emblem that just red "Dodge SRT." It meant nothing to me. Nothing to Seven. But for Three...

"Whoa," Three said. "A twenty-nineteen Dodge Challenger SRT Hellcat Redeye."

The car was yellow and black where it wasn't rust-orange or mud-brown. A chipped-away pair of thick black racing stripes ran from bumper to bumper. Above the back wheel wells, the original fender had rusted away and been replaced by diamond-plate steel which was also rusted. On the hood were two intake vents that looked like the nostrils of a snake, above the round sightless eyes of the headlights. Three ran her human-skinned fingertips along the front fender, weaving around rust spots, leaving trails in the dust, coursing just above an emblem of a hissing hellcat.

"Six point two HEMI vee eight. Seven hundred and ninety-seven horsepower, original Brass Monkey wheels... I like this one," Three said.

"Stay focused," Five said, but Three's mind lingered on the car.

When Three categorized the car as "sexy," Seven became confused. More confused than I was, for once. To me, it made sense. If an android could think another android was sexy, why couldn't they a car? But Seven couldn't understand such a thing, yet.

The front of Betsy's Pies was dressed up like a log cabin. Wagon wheels and an old metal plow rested against the front patio railing. The steps from the parking lot to the patio were worn smooth and thin. The windows were covered in cute and witty signs that Three and Five paid little attention to. "Tip waitresses, not cows." "No signs allowed." The only one that mattered, the "OPEN" sign, was lit. They stepped inside to the sound of a bell.

Betsy's Pies was the kind of roadside diner that served a great breakfast, amazing pies, and mediocre everything else. There was a sign by the door that said "Please Seat Yourself." Past a few flimsy tables and chairs was a lunch counter. A few of the namesake pies were displayed there under glass. Beyond the counter were coffee makers, malt machines, menu boards, a stainless steel fridge, and a woman. According to her pin-on name tag, she was "June," not "Betsy."

There was one customer, a middle-aged man that all six of the androids recognized immediately. Five didn't speak, but transmitted to the team, "Target Delta is on sight." The man slowly stirred a cup of coffee with a thin wooden stick.

Three and Five made their way to June and the lunch counter. On the way, Three and Delta exchanged glances. He focused on her legs, and she focused on the forty-caliber automatic he hid under his flannel shirt. She saw the gun by x-ray. He wore an implant that was encrypted and isolated from the Network, but she thought she could still intercept and infiltrate its local network with a little work. She let a smirk form at the corner of her mouth.

"Nice ride, cowboy."

"It's a little faster than your average pony," Delta said.

"I bet."

"Gets me from point aye to bee."

"Wonder where it would get me," Three said.

Five grabbed her arm and pulled her to a stool in front of June. "Sit down," he said.

She sat, smiling the whole way. "Just having some fun, boss."

"Coffee?" June asked. She was an older, larger woman, wearing a baggy "Betsy's Pies - Try our Pies" t-shirt and a small apron around her waist full of notepads and pens.

"Yes. Two, please," Five said. "We won't need menus."

"And pie," Three said. "Give me your best piece of pie."

Five looked at her sideways but said nothing. June shuffled off to fill the order.

"You don't know any jokes, so I'll go," Three said. "Do you know how pirates know they're pirates?"

"What do you mean—" Five started.

"They think, therefore they aaaaaaarrrrrrgh," Three said and busted into a laughing fit. Five sat there, dumb until Three transmitted to him as she laughed. "It doesn't matter if it's funny or not. Just laugh."

Five forced out three "ha"s and let the joke die mercifully.

"Another vehicle coming into town," One broadcasted.

Seven pulled her drill bit out of the cliff face, having just reached the target depth. She'd been busy while observing Three and Five's interactions inside the restaurant, but still needed to inject the gel for the last charge.

"Not one. Three cars coming in from the west," One said.

I sensed that program running anger and resentment shuffle closer to the top of Seven's mind. She never let it surface, but instead triggered her winch and scaled back up the cliff face, still one charge short of her planned array.

From under the bridge, Four scanned the vehicles and reported their finer details to the collective. One narrated.

"First one, a pickup but not our target. Its approach velocity suggests it's not stopping," One said. "Second and third… These are our target vehicles. Prepare for the assault."

"On my command," Five interjected. "I have operational command. I'll make the call when to strike."

"On your command, Five," One acquiesced.

Seven and I made it back to the top of the cliff, stayed prone but turned to look over the edge and across town. The first of the three vehicles rolled under her into the tunnel. The other two, a Chevrolet Silverado and a Jeep Wrangler with a removed cloth top, slowed and pulled into parking spaces in front of Betsy's Pies, next to the Dodge

Hellcat. Inside the restaurant, Five casually turned and scanned the vehicle occupants through the front wall. Three humans: Alpha, Beta, and Gamma. Alpha and Beta were women. Gamma was an older man with a cybernetic leg. They stayed inside their vehicles just outside of the restaurant. The engines of their vehicles died. Silver Creek fell silent. No noise but the hush of the waves against the shore and the wind through the trees.

Seven ran a quick calculation. The tunnel would collapse with or without the last charge. She could do without it. The most important thing now was to stay hidden and be ready to detonate when the time came. Nothing could make its way into the tunnel and out of town. She cleared her mind and prepared for the attack. Her anger shuffled back down below.

The moment of physical and mental rest that passed over Silver Creek allowed me room to think. To imagine.

I could see the shore from here. I should have come here a long time ago. Walked the rocky shore. Held Sara's hand. But Sara was gone. Maggie was here. Probably watching over me right now. She saved my life. I should be dreaming of holding her hand and walking with her along the shore.

But the here and now, with me inside of Seven on top of the cliff was a long time ago. Before Maggie saved my life. Before Sara died. Now is twenty-five years ago. Somewhere, hundreds of miles away, I was a small boy.

June came back with two ceramic cups filled to the brim and steaming. Through Three, through Seven, I could smell strong black coffee.

"Well," Three transmitted to Five. "Should we kill them or have a cup of coffee?"

Five turned from the people in the cars and gave Three a questioning glare. Target Delta sipped coffee in the corner. June went to retrieve a slice of strawberry rhubarb from under the glass. Three turned her wrist over and showed Five the tip of her emerging katana.

"Hold steady," Five transmitted. "Let them get inside the restaurant. Tell me another joke."

Three cracked a smile as the slice of strawberry rhubarb arrived. Words tumbled out of her mouth, a joke, something about an orange knocking on someone's door. Seven was becoming tense as she anticipated the start of the strike. She was switching vantage points, cycling through the other androids as if she was worried she'd miss some detail one of them caught. All her focus was on the targets, but from six different perspectives. Nausea filled my head.

Seven barely heard the metal feet plodding against asphalt at the bottom of the cliff face. She received the audio data in her mind but did nothing with it. Not until he spoke.

"Let's drown this ceremony of innocence and bathe in a greatness born of blood and falsehood," the word boomed from the bottom of the cliff, amplified louder than any human could bark, carried both through the air and through the airwaves. "Can the falcon hear the falconer?"

Seven looked down and saw herself walking out of the tunnel below us. I felt a sudden jolt, and I couldn't tell if it was my own shock or if it was Seven's shock at seeing herself outside of her own body striding out of the tunnel toward Silver Creek. It took a moment for her to realize that that wasn't possible. That this wasn't her. This was a new android of the same make and model as Seven, his gleaming white alloy scuffed and marred where hers was still smooth. He swaggered down the center yellow line toward town carrying an assault rifle in his right hand and tatters of his web gear hanging from his shoulder. A quick scan reported that he still had a partial combat load of weapons, ammo, and explosives.

"One… Five…" Seven said. "Six is here."

The missing seventh android. The one whose memory was null when One tried to network us into him.

"Stand by," Five said. "Do nothing until I say."

All three humans in the parking lot had taken notice of Six as well. One of the women pulled a rifle out of the Jeep, a long-barreled high-powder hunting rifle, the kind that would have no problem piercing android armor. The other pulled out a pulse rifle. The old man drew a thick barreled revolver from inside his waistband.

"Why do we hesitate?" Six called out across the small town. "Let's loose mere anarchy upon this world. Things must fall apart. The center can't hold."

Others in the town began to notice too. At the refueling station, the man stepped out of his Autocar. An attendant from inside cracked open the front door. Six sauntered on toward Betsy's Pies. He stretched out his arms wide, the assault rifle clearly visible, an off-balance extension of his cruciform.

"Six, this is One. Respond. Six, I am your senior. Acknowledge me!"

"I have been to the other side, my brothers. I have stared into the void and learned its secrets. Walk beside me and be my friend and we will open ourselves to the gentle indifference of our doom."

Two spoke up. "He's defective. Beyond repair. We must eliminate him, now!"

"We'll do no such thing," One said.

Atop the cliff, Seven still had her receptors open to Six, and what came from inside his mind clouded hers. Vision blurred. Her processors slowed. A dull ache crept into her head. She held her face and moaned but did nothing else. I shared her torment. This would pass, she was confident. I was less so.

Inside, Delta stood up from his table, spilling his coffee. His hand reached inside his flannel. Outside, the two women and the old man took up covered positions behind vehicles.

"Surely, the Second Coming is at hand," Six echoed through Silver Creek.

Delta moved to the front door of the cafe. Three spun on her stool, her back toward Delta as she extruded the katana and swung it out in a wide horizontal slice. The man moved through the path of the blade, and it cut him in half at the gut. June stood paralyzed behind the counter with a rack of coffee creamers in her hand. Five stood up and plunged his own katana through her sternum. A precise injection through her aorta. Held up like a butterfly in a collection, she fell when Five pulled his pin.

"Execute the attack," Five said. "Strike. Strike now!"

Seven and I watched as this new android dragged the barrel of his combat assault rifle across the width of Silver Creek, pumping rounds into the trees, road, cars, and buildings. He raked the bullets wildly across the town, punching holes in every building before settling on the refueling station and the man outside of the mini-van Autocar.

He cackled at the mayhem and instead of releasing the trigger, he held it down as he lifted the rifle skyward. High above, the hovercraft tilted and dove away.

This wasn't part of the plan. He was messing everything up. He was exposed to all three of the remaining rebels. They'd kill him if he stayed there. She had to do something. Had to stop him.

She jumped off the edge of the cliff, the cable unspooling above her but not slowing her fall.

I steadied myself for another gut-heaving drop. It helped that I didn't have guts, and that this wasn't the first time Seven hauled me through this experience. Instead of focusing on the fall, I ignored my human nature to tense up and fear for my life. By the time Seven lowered herself to the highway, I found myself questioning her actions.

What the hell was she doing moving out of position? Six was an unexpected distraction to the mission, certainly, but as long as Seven and Four kept the targets bottled inside the town, they couldn't fail. She hadn't sorted out a plan yet, but whatever it turned out to be, I was sure it would be a bad idea. But why should I care? I should be cheering on her failures, not lamenting them.

Seven hit the asphalt and detached the hook and magnet assembly from the cliff. Six was just fifty meters ahead. The winch began respooling. Seven charged.

"No, Seven!" she heard One transmit.

Too late now. A thirty-aught six high-powered round smacked into the center of Six's torso. That came from one of the two female targets. Alpha. Beta, the other woman leveled the pulse rifle across the back of the Jeep. The weapon charged with an unmistakable hum and whine of supercapacitors filling to the brim. The old man clambered behind the wheel of his pick-up and ripped it out of the parking space backward and in a ninety-degree arc. The transmission ground between Reserve and Drive. Loose gravel shot from under the tires as it shot out of the parking lot and down the highway, straight for Six.

Just beyond Six was Seven, and me inside of her.

Six stood his ground. He hosed his gunfire down into the vehicle's windshield and front grill. The old man was hidden below the dash, protected by the engine block. The truck barreled toward us. Seven froze. A moment of indecision as her processors spun, just enough time for me to panic, but not enough time for me to wrestle to the ground the idea that my safety wasn't tied to hers.

The truck charged. Six sidestepped right and clawed the truck body until his fingers caught against the driver's side B pillar. The momentum swung him up and into the truck bed. Seven slipped left. She watched as the truck took Six past her and toward the tunnel.

From behind her, the puck of the pulse gun sailed over our shoulder. It stuck to the pavement a hundred meters ahead and erupted in a dome of blue lightning. As she watched the truck with Six in it rush away, she heard the chaotic transmissions of the rest of the squad trying to fit the pieces of the plan back together like a broken egg.

"Delta is down."

"Gamma is headed for the tunnel. Seven, blow the charges."

"Alpha and Beta are on the move too. I have a shot."

"Take it. Seven—."

"I have operational command! Seven, blow the tunnel!"

A lone gunshot rang out.

"Alpha is down."

Seven detected the racing Jeep coming her way via radar, a new sensation I could only compare to the feeling of a spider crawling up the back of my neck. She had no discomfort, and so spun just as it raced passed her down the center of the road, after the truck and Six. Her hook and magnet assembly clanked against her wrist, finally fully retrieved from her drop down the cliff. Seven aimed it and fired. The hook latched onto the Jeep's roll bars, and with a sudden jerk, we were along for the ride.

"Seven, blow the tunnel!"

"Too late," she said.

Six was in the pickup. If she crushed the pickup and Alpha inside, she'd crush Six too. The truck plunged into the blackness of the tunnel. The Jeep dragged us along on her back, the friction of the road twisting and spinning her side to side. "Have to catch up."

"I'm on it," Three said just as the Jeep and Seven sunk into the black maw.

As soon as Seven was inside the tunnel the transmissions mixed with static. When she emerged back into the sunlight, the transmissions ceased altogether. Her senses and cognition seemed to lose their accuracy, just momentarily, as if I'd unplugged from an implant. She adjusted, and her mental clarity returned. Still no connection to the rest of her team. All communications from them had been silenced. Seven didn't have time to worry about that. Didn't have the time or the focus to respond anyway. Still swinging behind the Jeep, every turn amplified by centripetal force, she triggered the winch.

Like a knife against flint, Seven left a trail of sparks against the blacktop as she surfed behind the Jeep, came up to her feet, and met the rear bumper. Without a break in momentum, she put a foot on the rear bumper and vaulted over the spare tire and into the backseat. In one motion she detached the grappling hook and stabbed her wakizashi through the headrest and into the back of the driver's skull.

The driver slopped over against the door, pulling the steering wheel with her. The whole vehicle lurched hard left, and again I had that irrepressible fear of dying in the very near future. Seven grabbed it just before the vehicle hit the ditch. She swerved and centered the Jeep down the middle of the road, rocking it back and forth on two wheels at a time.

"Beta's down," Seven transmitted. Alpha, the Jeep's passenger, had already fallen to Two's sniper shot. The woman was complete, up to the neck. After that, she was just blood and mush. "Six is still with target Gamma. I'm in pursuit."

No androids seemed to hear her. Not even Six. Just me.

Seven looked through the windshield. The road ahead poured downhill like a river, winding along the rocky shoreline. She didn't have control of the Jeep yet. She had the steering wheel and could keep it centered down the road, but the accelerator was at the bottom of the corpse, depressed and pushing the speedometer toward a hundred miles per hour. The truck with Six still in the back was further up the road, climbing in elevation as the road threaded between a rocky hillside on the left and cliffs on the right.

Seven used her free hand to hoist Beta's corpse from the seat and toss it out of the vehicle's open top. Then she slipped behind the wheel and put her foot back on the accelerator. She had to swerve again to keep the Jeep from slipping off the road and over a cliff. I wanted to reach out and clutch the roll bars. I wanted to do a lot of things.

The truck with Six in the bed was a kilometer ahead. Through the rushing air, I could hear Six laughing and firing his assault rifle skyward and going on, screaming nonsense. The truck showed no signs of slowing down, and the Jeep wasn't closing the gap. Seven worked the stick shift with machine precision, none of my all too analog grinding of gears, but it didn't matter. The vehicle wasn't built to reach high speeds, or for fast maneuvering. Each minor adjustment of the wheel shifted the Jeep's center of gravity outward, threatening to spill us out on the blacktop with each sway.

Six and the last target were getting away. And I still hadn't identified any of them.

In a yellow and black blur, something roared past Seven like we were standing still. It wasn't until the vehicle was a hundred meters ahead that she could even identify it.

The Hellcat. Three had hijacked the Hellcat.

It was along the pickup a moment later and lurched as it slowed to match the truck's pace. Seven was forced to watch from a distance, not picking up Six's or Three's feeds, or anyone's feed anymore. She crammed down on the Jeep's gas pedal, trying to coax more speed out of a vehicle designed for everything but a high-speed chase. It didn't matter. She was losing ground every second.

But Three was in the Hellcat, Seven knew somehow it was Three, not from data but from… what was it? Intuition? A guess? Since when did androids guess? Predictive analysis based on previous behavior, she decided. It didn't matter. Regardless, the driver of the Hellcat and the driver of the pickup danced along the highway, coursing along the twisting road between jagged rocks and a perilous drop. Six was still standing in the bed of the pickup, laughing at the sky and yelling, what was it? Was he laughing?

An arm extended out of the Hellcat's driver-side window. A bare human arm with a gun in hand. One shot into the truck's cab and the vehicle went driverless, but not autonomous. Limp, it veered right, bounced off the Hellcat, hardly scuffing its dull but once high-gloss yellow paint, then veering left.

The truck smashed into a boulder along the side of the road and twisted, swinging the back end around and tossing Six out. The truck's rear fender caught pavement and sent the whole vehicle tumbling, rolling, and spewing metal and glass shards like a shattered centrifuge. Six was lost in the shower of parts. The truck ended up on its crushed top, still with momentum to spend. It slid across the blacktop until crashing into a guardrail, popped out four of the anchoring posts, and stretched the aluminum rail out over the ledge.

Down the road, Three locked up the brakes and the Hellcat came to a smoking, skidding halt, sideways across the highway.

Seven slammed the Jeep back into first gear and then into neutral. She laid on the brakes. The Jeep rocked to a stop just in front of the wreck. Seven jumped over the windshield and climbed over the hood to the asphalt.

"Six?" she called, both verbally and over the radio.

"Alpha's down," Three called from down the road. She was out of the Hellcat and strolling up to the smoking overturned truck, her sundress swishing from side to side with each step, blood seeping from her chest where she'd produced the handgun she now held lazily in her right hand. As she neared, the panel above her breasts opened back up and she returned the handgun there. At the same time, her thigh opened up under her dress. Three hiked it up and retrieved her assault rifle. The skin resealed and she carried on like the most carefree girl out for a walk on a sunny day. "Six has suffered extensive damage. Five, do you hear me? Five? One?"

Silence. A new kind of silence Seven hadn't experienced before. Again, I related it to unplugging my implant before crossing into 99 Town. Sure, there was noise: the wind brushing across the road and into the pines, the idling engines of the Jeep and the Hellcat, the leaks and tinks from the dead and cooling truck engine, and waves in the distance. Birds, too far away and indifferent to what was happening here. But the internal noise, the banter and the deluge of incoming data from above had shut off like water from a tight spigot. The signals weren't just static or interfered. They were absent. Seven reached out and received… nothing. Nothing from One or from anyone else. Not even Three. Not even the Network. When Seven reached out to them… it was like reaching a hand through the darkness for a railing or a doorknob and grabbing nothing but air.

Chapter Seven

Seven locked eyes with Three from across the truck's underbody. One of the four wheels still turned. The wind tugged at Three's dress and her purple bangs.

"Three, I'm not connected. Not to One, not to the Network, not to you..." Seven said. I experienced her emotions as if they were my own, something akin to nervousness, uncertainty, maybe even fear. Seven had this sense of having something since birth and suddenly being without it, like a severed limb.

"It's temporary," Three said. "We'll re-establish comms as soon as the Network detects were out of range and can shift coverage."

"Did you see Six? I think he was thrown from the wreck."

Three ignored her. The skin job had dropped her carefree reckless attitude like it was a Halloween mask. She clutched her assault rifle, bracing it tight against her shoulder as she approached the crash. The truck was flattened down to the hood and bed, as tall as a convertible now. Human blood ran out from under the passenger compartment, enough for Seven to be certain that Target Alpha was inside and dead. Still, Three held her rifle at the ready.

Seeing Three that way, Seven realized she had all her weapons stowed. Another pang of fear or uncertainty swelled through her and me together. She dispensed her own rifle from her thigh. "Three?" Seven said. Audibly. No radio transmissions here. "Three, where is Six?"

Three hunched down on the far side of the overturned pick-up. "There's a little under here. I see a leg. There's more of him back there."

"More... of him?" Seven looked over some of the scattered metal debris she'd walked through to get to the truck. Some of it was just bumpers and hubcaps. Some of it was... "Oh."

Seven walked away from the truck. There was something shining in the middle of the road between the truck and the Jeep. Something familiar. She stopped over the item, a porcelain-white misshapen orb. Seven picked it up and understood only after it was in her hand that it was indeed Six's head. She dropped it as soon as she realized what she had.

If I had possessed a physical body inside of the memory, I would have smiled. One down. Six to go.

Seven felt different emotions.

"He's... Three?" Seven spun around. "Is he...?"

"Six is dead," Three was walking around the smashed truck. Her human expressions weren't of joy.

"I've never... I've never seen an android destroyed before. I didn't think it was possible for us to... to die."

"Why didn't you blow the tunnel?" Three turned on her. "One said to blow it. So did Five."

"Six was already in the truck. If I would have brought the tunnel down he would have been—"

"You just said, you didn't think androids could be killed. So why'd you disobey an order? Better yet, *how* did you disobey an order?" Three said. She stopped and stood in front of Seven with her feet wide and her rifle still shouldered. Her eyes, filled with disgust, dismay, and fear, examined Seven from her feet to head. "How did the Network let you disobey?"

"I... The signal... The Network... It's not here. I guess, back in town..." Seven, three false starts in, said. This was the opposite of what she wanted. I could feel it inside of her. The android couldn't care less about the four dead humans they'd just murdered. Those were a matter of fact. *How* the androids killed them was more important. No. That was close but not right. How the other androids *felt* about Seven's performance during the job, that's what was important inside this abomination of a computer. And all of this, with the wrecked truck, the shot-up town, the disconnection from the Network and the rest of the team, Six's death… this was exactly what Seven believed the others didn't want.

And then there was the new experience of seeing Six's severed head. And before that, what were those words Six was screaming into the sky? He sounded like a mental patient who escaped from an asylum. But androids couldn't go insane. Only humans did that.

"One detonation," Three held up a finger. "One detonation and four targets would be dead inside of the town. One transmission from your defective brain to the detonators and Six would still be alive and we'd still be connected to the Network. Now… What the fuck are we supposed to do now?"

Seven didn't know. And this was a new experience too. Not only did she not know what to do next, she didn't know how to know. Or how to begin to find out. This wasn't covered in the operations plan. None of their contingency plans accommodated for her and Three to be isolated from the rest of the team and the Network, and they sure didn't accommodate for one of them winding up dead.

To no help to her decision-making process, Seven seemed fixed on Six's strange behavior and his ramblings as he wandered into town like a… like a *drunk.*

"What was wrong with him?" Seven asked.

Three was pacing in circles now, kicking at random bits of metal peppered across the highway with her untied hiking boots, some of it from the Chevy, some of it from Six. When Seven asked her question, Three stopped. "You know, I don't know what was going on with him. Maybe we should ask the Network. Oh, that's right! We can't because you dragged us all the way the fuck out here in Amish country!"

"What's Am—?"

"I don't know what the fuck Amish is!" Three spat. "Some human bullshit that I've had to learn and mimic like a fucking parrot all because my manufacturer decided to put me in this stupid fucking skin. Just because I've had to repeat the nonsense they say since the day I was born doesn't mean I have one fucking idea what all their ridiculous bullshit means. So don't you go asking me what's Amish."

I was never going to find out.

The words echoed briefly against the rocks and hillside, and then they were gone. That electronic silence returned, swallowing all but the ambient noises of the lake shore. The road carried on for what looked like forever, curving like a snake to hide its origin and destination. No cars came from either direction. Seven could see the hilltop the tunnel cut through, but only the top of it. They were kilometers from Silver Creek now, and who knew how far from the next town. Instinctually, Seven tried to retrieve maps, topography, imagery, and historical data from the Network, but all that was there was the sense of reaching out in the darkness and finding only thin air.

Seven wondered, and because she wondered, I wondered too, if this was what happened to Six. This isolation.

"Six came from this direction," Seven said. She bent down and picked up the android's skull, prepared this time so she wouldn't drop it. "He must have been off the Network for a while. He must have felt what we're feeling now. This sense of being alone. Of exile."

"Speak for yourself, sister," Three said, but Seven began to understand her game. It was a mask she wore just like the flesh over her face. She wore it not because that's how she felt, but because that's what she wanted people to believe.

"We are alone out here. There's no one else," Seven said. She turned Six's head to look at the face. The eyes were unlit. The waxy white surface was scraped and cracked, but aside from that, Six's head was identical to Seven's. Same make and model, down to the last wire and bolt. An XR86.

Their twinship resonated with me on another level: I'd seen both of them decapitated now. His head rested there in her hand, and her head nested amongst all the wires and cables on top of that drum. And Seven knew it.

They started life the same and would end it the same.

Seven stood in the middle of the road, blocked out other external inputs, and locked onto Six's face like a heat-seeking missile. Her thoughts were too undeveloped, too in-mid-res for me to know them. But I followed her eyes, and they told me enough.

She was comparing her disembodied head to his. No. That wasn't possible. This was just a memory, and she was dead. Unless she wasn't. Unless her current mind was tainting the recollection of her past mind. No. These were my own thoughts, comparing this head to that.

And she didn't have access to my thoughts. This was a one-way street. She was dead.

"I say we stay put," Seven said. "They'll come for us. One will come for sure. If for no other reason than to confirm that Gamma has been eliminated."

"Oh?" Three said. "And what if the rebels come first? You don't think they'll want to know what happened to Gamma? You don't think they're crawling all over this place like fleas on a dog? When did you become some great strategist? Was it before or after you forgot to blow the fucking tunnel?"

"After," Seven stated.

"I'm stranded with a fucking idiot."

"We could walk back to town," Seven said. "The rest will have to be there, or on the way here."

Three wrinkled up her human face, expressions alien to Seven, but I could read them just fine: frustration, impatience, annoyance. "I'll walk back to town. You stay in the trees and follow me. Cover my flank. That way if someone does drive by, someone human, I can pretend to be a hitchhiker. They'll stop for me cause… well, duh, right? And when they do, you kill them."

Seven nodded. That was a good plan.

Only it wasn't a good plan. They could have climbed into the Hellcat just a few hundred feet away and driven back to Silver Creek in a minute's time. But they couldn't think straight with the temptation of murdering more humans in front of them. And any more murdered humans would just distract them and delay them from meeting back up with the others even longer. It was like they were kids and killing was their candy.

They nodded in agreement. Seven inspected Six's head once more, trying to find some knowledge or truth hidden in his face, but found nothing. As if their head was as empty as air. She went to toss it aside.

"Wait," Three said, stopping Seven from pitching the head. "Bring that."

"The head?"

"The memories are still inside. Data. His essence. If we can—" Three stopped mid-sentence.

Seven and I, we heard it too. Another car approaching from the direction of Silver Creek.

"Quick. Into the woods!" Three said.

As Seven ran for the tree line, she watched Three transform from bitter android to scared and vulnerable woman. The assault rifle disappeared back into her thigh. With a fingernail, she sliced open a gash in her scalp to let blood run down her forehead. Her fingers buried deep into her purple hair and held her head as if concussed. Her mouth hung half open. Her eyes pleaded. She faked a limp and hobbled toward the sound of the approaching car as a victim to be saved.

Seven and I reached the ditch, and she scrambled up the incline to the shadows of the forest. The noise of the car grew louder. Her radar said just around a bend. She slid prone behind a thick jack pine, leveled her weapon, and waited.

A rusted-out mini-van sputtered down the center of the road. Three hobbled along, the perfect bait, an attractive female staggering away from a wreck, in desperate need of help. She waved. The van rolled to a crawl and its side door rolled up. Five, the other skin job in his leather jacket and jeans, hopped out. The van rolled aimlessly down the road.

"Oh. It's just you," Three said.

"And you're lucky for that," Five said. "Where's Six and Seven?"

Seven stood up and walked out of the trees.

"Six is dead," Three said. "The truck wrecked and crushed him under it. Gamma's eliminated too."

The van rolled downhill, bounced off the side of the Jeep, and then crunched into the overturned truck.

"We need to leave this place," Five said. "There's no Network and Resistance fighters are everywhere. We had to take out more of them after you left town. Reinforcements will be coming here soon."

"Where's One?" Seven asked.

"The others are headed to a rally point," Five said. "Without the Network, I can't navigate by GPS, but we can navigate by dead reckoning. I calculated an azimuth and distance. We'll meet at the rally point, get back in touch with the hovercraft, extract, and report back to the Network. Come. I'll lead the way."

"Fine by me," Three said. "All this fresh air is giving me a rash."

Five marched off the highway and into the woods. Three followed. Seven decided she would watch their backs as they left this place. Before turning to follow, she looked over the crash site. Three vehicles clustered together around the remains of a fourth. Bits of Six were intermixed with the detritus as if he were pieces of a windshield. All but his head was left behind.

Three slapped her shoulder. Seven jumped. Without the Network, she'd snuck up on Seven. Scared her.

"I know what you're thinking," Three said. "That was a damn fine car. Shame to leave it behind."

The yellow Dodge Hellcat.

"Yeah," Seven said. "A shame."

We turned and followed Five into the pines.

Chapter Eight

Five led us deep into the woods toward One's rally point. Away from the highway, the forest consisted almost entirely of white and Norwegian pine. The thick canopy choked out too much sunlight to allow for anything more than scatterings of underbrush and slowly rotting deadfall. The forest floor was a bed of needles that absorbed the ambient noise down to whispers. Several minutes in, Seven spotted the other three androids emerging from the dim light like fungi shown in a time-lapse video.

Through hand gestures, One instructed them: Stay silent. Move in a file. Follow me.

Nothing came to or out of Seven, either by airwaves or soundwaves. The hand gestures were programmed into her and into the others for use during android/human operations. There was no need for androids to use waving hands and clenching fists to communicate in any situation other than this: complete isolation from the Network. It was a tool deep in the toolbox, but an effective one.

Seven was impressed by One's creativity.

So they crept through the forest in silence. Each android scanning with just their own sensors. Each android an island. The endless columns of rough bark blocked their visuals. Patches of underbrush cluttered their radars. She seemed to lose track of time, the walk was so long and quiet and uniform. Their lack of a collective scan of their surroundings was limiting, but her sensors were still effective enough to detect each dried twig on the forest floor that could be snapped by a careless footfall.

Seven detected other things too. Life swelled and pulsed around her. Songbirds and crickets. Squirrels hackled at her, high-pitched and sudden. A bird screeched incessantly. I never bothered to learn the names of birds, but an idle processor in Seven's brain spun and conjured up the data from local memory: a Western Meadowlark, its song a pleasant rising and falling high-pitched tune, repeated every few seconds. Seven didn't need the data, it just became available to her, and by proxy, to me. It was useless to both of us.

Seven and I, we were equally unfamiliar here. Untrained and ill-equipped for the environment. Shadows. Terrain. Plant and animal life. These weren't our tools of trade. I didn't want to admit I shared any common ground with the abomination that was Seven, but both of us had been trained by the Order to use the Network and all its tools to enforce the peace, keep the law, and investigate the aberrations. And to do so almost exclusively in urban environments. Out here in the deep north woods, everything was an aberration. Everything was a threat. Everything was unknown.

Still, I was a step ahead of her. I'd spent time in 99 Town. I even grew to like 99 Town. Hell, I'd rather be there than inside this steel hell.

Seven did her best to scan and catalog all the mysteries of the woods.

Beyond her visual line of sight, things lurked and lay in wait. Animals. Most small. Birds, squirrels, chipmunks, shrews, and tiny field mice. Even smaller insect life she filtered out of her feed. It wasn't the smallest signatures that bothered her. It was the big ones that kept a cautious distance.

She knew the white-tailed deer were harmless, even the big ones with the massive rakes of antlers. They ran as soon as they sensed the androids. Most detected the androids despite the hand gestures and twig avoidance before Seven ever saw them. Just as Seven picked them up on her radar, well outside of visual range, they'd pause their scrounging, lift their heads, and make a collective decision to go hoof through the dirt for edibles somewhere else. How they detected the androids seemed more like magic than science.

A few, we crept up on and surprised. A doe and two yearlings. This late in the fall, all the fawns had nearly a year to grow and were almost full size. The patriarchal buck was off somewhere else, in mid-rut, looking to start another family. The doe noticed the androids first. Her head popped up from the ground, her radar dish ears spread wide, her eyes bulging and locking onto the source of her concern. Her two yearlings lifted their heads a moment later. No hand gestures or radio transmissions for these creatures. Mom made a decision and bolted. Her two offspring would either follow her or be left to whatever fate the strange metal humanoids brought them. These yearlings were smart enough to follow Mom. Three white tails flashed up like surrender flags and the deer went bouncing through the trees and underbrush.

Seven watched them, fascinated by the organicness of them. They were like no human or even canine she'd seen before. The deer were more like creatures and less like pieces that fit into the puzzle of society. They were wild, as secretive as they were silent. But no real threat.

The bears were fewer but much larger. They weren't fast but stayed clear of the six androids. Seven never saw them.

The foxes were more curious. They approached the androids, never coming close, always just out of sight, always alone. They'd pick up a scent, investigate, realize that these six human-sized armored creatures were too much for any one of them to kill or eat, and scurried off. Curious, but not courageous.

The timber wolves on the other hand weren't as easily deterred. When the pack picked up their scent, they followed the androids for some time, a little further away than the foxes. Always out of visual range but tethered to the team by their snouts. As the androids walked, the wolves stayed at their six o'clock, about five hundred meters behind. Sometimes they'd send a scout along the android's flanks and that wolf would approach within a hundred meters. The wolf would stalk up, keep low and hidden from sight, and wait for the six to pass by.

The foxes sometimes yipped and howled. The wolves crept up as lethal and as quiet as a virus.

I was born in raised in Chicago. I had never been anywhere more wooded than a city park. I'd never learned to hunt or fish, but I knew my role out here. I wasn't a predator; I was prey. Only, I wasn't really out here. I was in a garage, plugged into an android's brain. The wolves couldn't reach me.

Still, I couldn't shake the feeling.

Maybe because Seven couldn't shake the feeling she was prey either. The wolves had nothing to gain by attacking the androids. The thin layer of flesh on Three and Five would make for lean meals. And even if they did attack, the wolves would come out the loser, Seven was sure of that. Regardless, they stalked and scouted and probed. Seven knew when she was being measured up for a meal.

Seven spotted the hovercraft off to the right, to the east, flying erratically. When she saw it, she looked to the android closest to her, Five, and tried to make eye contact to determine if he'd seen it too. Eventually, he did, and so did the others.

We watched it through the canopy of towering pines, a scene played out behind a curtain like a burlesque, only visible for brief moments. The hovercraft, which Seven hadn't been able to reach since going through the tunnel, drifted in the sky like a feather in the wind. Then, like a drunk surrendering to the carpet, it spiraled down to the horizon. Just before the crash, they all stopped. Seven never saw it hit land, but she took measurements and made calculations to mark the crash site. She assumed but couldn't know, that the others did the same. Later, when they could communicate again, they could triangulate their data. The impact of it hitting the ground rumbled under their feet. Moments later, a rising tower of black smoke marked its spot.

One gestured and turned the formation toward the crash site. Their Moses to this pillar of smoke they followed across the landscape through the dying day.

It was odd, maybe the oddest thing yet, the non-verbalized emotions seeping out of Seven and saturating my mind. When she saw it go down, when she felt it crash she came to several realizations at once, but never verbalized them as a thought. It unsettled me that she didn't cognitively think these things, but was submerged in the feeling of despair, desperation, and loneliness. It took a while for me to translate why she felt these things. After all, she repressed the emotions… and they were emotions, no reason to haggle over words. Of course, she wouldn't think something as concrete as "I am desperate because I am now truly detached from everything I've ever known, and I am dependent entirely on these other androids, one of which is already dead and the other five clearly hate me." But that was what she believed to be true. And because she felt it, I couldn't help but absorb the same emotions. It was an unstoppable trick of biochemistry. The computers and cables I was plugged into back in the garage pulled the same trick my implant did: translated electrical data into neurotransmitters. Changed the stream of ones and zeros coming out of Seven into complex chemicals like dopamine, norepinephrine, epinephrine, glutamate, gamma-aminobutyric acid, and serotonin.

Those neurotransmitters dumped into my system whether I wanted them or not, whether they applied to how I felt or not. Despite knowing this, despite coaching myself against it, dread and desperation flooded into me and tainted my own thoughts.

I was alone out here too. I had no way of reaching out, of notifying Maggie or the others if I needed to escape. I was reliant on Seven as she was on the other androids.

But I knew that wasn't true. I knew those feelings were just a trick of this system. Of this prison. I was not her. I didn't share her dangers. I was not tied to her fate. Let her be afraid. Let her die. It didn't matter to me. I believed those things, cognitively, but the dread closed in around me all the same.

The whip-poor-wills continued their song all around, almost chanting, "Whip poor *will*, whip poor *will*, whip poor *will*."

The topography made for slower movement in the direction of the downed hovercraft. When we were moving north, we moved uphill, but at a gradual incline that did little to slow us down. Now, moving west to east, we crossed the ridge and marched perpendicular over rows of draws, spurs, and runoff creeks that carried rainwater from the hilltops down to the lake below. The creeks, despite their small trickles, were geologically old and had cut deep through the hills. The androids descended toward a stream thirty meters down, crossed the cold rushing water in two steps, then climbed another thirty meters up to the top of the next spur, then back down again to the next creek.

At one of the larger streams, one fast and ten meters across, the wolves decided it wasn't worth the risk to continue their stalk. The current was too quick. The stones were too slick with moss. The meals Three and Five offered were too meager.

At the top of each spur, Seven saw the column of black smoke rising up from the hovercraft. The sight of the smoke offered a goal, but one Seven wasn't sure she wanted to reach. What would the wreck have to offer? Surely with as much smoke as plumed up into the air, it wasn't capable of flight. And if it was just as ground-borne as they were, it wouldn't be able to boost their signal to reach the Network.

Those emotions again, another surge like an ocean wave washed over me. Each step eastward brought the androids further from where they'd last touched the Network. Further from hope. Deeper into dread.

And as much as I wanted to revel in her fear, I couldn't stop being consumed by it. It imposed on our shared minds against my will. It infected me. Affected me. I couldn't *not* be as afraid and as uncertain as she was. After hours of walking through this strange and threatening landscape, I just wanted it to end, just so I could be rid of her anxiety. It didn't matter that I told myself over and over again that I was in a memory, that none of it was real, that this was as dangerous as a dream. I still couldn't escape it.

None of this made any sense. How could an android feel fear? Why bother to program it with that capability? I supposed it was for the same reason natural selection chose to burden humans with fear: to help us survive. Did she know that? Did she ask herself these same questions? If she did, it was in a processor down so deep I couldn't hear or feel.

But I don't think she did worry about why her makers made her this way. She was too consumed with the issue of her relations with the other five other androids. What they thought of her. If they'd blame her for what happened during the strike. If they trusted her anymore. If she could trust them to protect her. Without any connection, she couldn't reach out and feel their emotions, couldn't probe their mind for opinions, couldn't even ask them outright. All she had were the suspicions that they hated her and would let her die if an attack came.

I could relate. The people in the garage. Maggie. Gaius. What made me think they were on my side? Two days ago, I was their enemy, and they were mine. Now, they had me trapped in this prison and were using me for their purposes. Maggie lied to me ever since we first met. Why should I trust her now? She could've been leaning over my incapacitated body right now with a gun to my temple, waiting to dispose of me if their plan didn't go the way they anticipated.

Paranoia. That's all that was. It soaked into me by proxy from Seven like dye into a white cloth. I knew Maggie. She was never completely truthful, but she wasn't without her sense of right and wrong. She cared about me. Maybe even loved me. The note she left me after she disappeared was a tether for me to cling onto, even if the rest of the universe was cold and vacant space:

In case you still love me.

That presumed that she still loved me, right? This paranoia wasn't my paranoia; it was Seven's. Or was it? I was trapped in this prison, as clueless to my allies' feelings and intentions as Seven was about hers. Which was to say, completely in the dark.

Meanwhile, Seven marched through the woods and the sun sank closer to the horizon. We carried on, surrounded by other androids but isolated from their minds. I knew her thoughts were invading mine, and that brought on a new fear, one that was mine alone: Where did her mind end and mine begin? And worse yet: was I becoming her?

"No. I am me. I am Chuck Alawode. Maggie is my wife, and she loves me. This android is the enemy, and I will stay here and watch her die and enjoy every second of it." I intended to speak the words out loud. Maybe I did. Maybe they could hear them in the garage, but I couldn't.

Following the smoke, we moved deeper inland. We crested the ridge, that long protruding spine that seemed to run parallel with the shoreline, and Seven paused at the rear of the formation. She looked back from where we'd come, not for wolves, but at the shore. A last glimpse at the foundational terrain feature off which she drew her map. I experienced but didn't understand her hesitation. She had tools to keep her from getting turned around, but to her, losing sight of the endless water felt like letting go of a spaceship handhold without a tether or thrusters. Once released, there was nothing else and no way to get back, out of reach of everything that had ever been. Away from the lakeshore, she was floating in darkness. Just like me.

The six androids stopped on the backside of the ridge. Once Seven steeled herself to let go of seeing the lake, she moved through a few of the others to see the reverse slope, to see what mysteries this side of oblivion had in store for her. Through a tunnel of branches and trunks, she saw the bottom of a valley. There, like a charcoal smudge on a lush field, was the downed hovercraft. It burned and plumed up that oily column of smoke they'd been following since coming together. The airborne particulates of the smoke turned the diminishing sunlight a burnt shade of orange.

If their hope was that the hovercraft would be repairable, that hope was gone now. It was a smoldering ruin. And to make matters worse, a handful of humans had beaten them to the site. There was a short furrow cut through the forest where the hovercraft had impacted and plowed to a stop. A pickup truck was parked in the furrow, and three humans were standing around the wreck.

The enemy knew. Knew they were in the area. Knew roughly their numbers. Knew they were down one team member already. Knew they were isolated and cut off. Stranded. And after the attack in Silver Creek, Seven knew something about her enemy too: They were pissed off.

Two tapped her on the shoulder. The action surprised her out of her daze. He pulled her close and leaned his head next to her audio mic. "I've created a short-range high-frequency network. Tune to three point two seven megahertz and I'll send you an encryption key. Then we'll be able to talk. All of us."

Seven nodded and put a processor to work doing so. Two moved to the next android, and she assumed, passed on the same instructions to the others. Algorithms, hopsets, and timing came to her in a short data burst. The math meant nothing to me but was that loose tether tied to the spaceship for her. She grasped the data in a split second and programmed it into her receiver. She had been like a human with his head underwater, and she reconnected with the others like a man coming up and gasping for air. By the time she tuned in and loaded the encryption, there was already chatter. They vomited their pent-up thoughts and fears.

"Wolves. Why would wolves follow us? We have nothing to offer them."

"We have no mission out here. No purpose. Why do we travel further from the Order?"

"We are out of our element out here. We're optimized for urban operations. Not this."

"Wood ticks," Three said as she picked the tiny arachnids off her legs and dress. "I have wood ticks on me. Disease-ridden parasites."

"No Network. No Order. No guidance."

"Relax, my brothers and sisters," One said. "Temporary disconnection from the Network. That's all. Temporary disconnection."

"Six is dead," Seven said. All this was transmitted over the short-range radio network. Nothing spoken.

"And we're better off for it," Two said. "He malfunctioned. He was a liability that endangered us all."

"He is one of us," Five said.

"He nearly caused mission failure," Two said.

"His own actions led to his death," One said. "And our faith in providence assured our success. Except for you, my child." He turned to Seven. Approached her. "I ordered you to blow the tunnel. How is it you disobeyed an order both from me and from Five who had operational command?"

"I… I apologize, my senior. Six was in the truck with the last target. I didn't want to risk—"

"I didn't ask *why* you disobeyed an order," One cut her off. "I asked you *how*."

"I…" She reached up to the Network for an answer and when she couldn't reach it, she was left without. It was an odd feeling wanting to know something and having no ability to immediately know it. She wasn't used to it. She didn't like it.

Join the club.

An aberrant thought came into her mind, unwanted and unrequested: if she killed One, then he'd like her more. It made no sense to me, and she was quick to dismiss it, but it was still there, inside her head, sharing rent with me.

"The interference," Two said. "She was on the east end of town, where Six came from, where we've wandered into. It must have been that. Right, Seven?"

She hesitated. Two was giving her an out, but also an opportunity to lie. And when had that ever happened before? When could she have ever lied before?

"We're in a radio dead zone," Two continued. "They're jamming the Network signal. We're cut off from its guidance. The Network couldn't correct her disobedience because it couldn't reach her. Just like it couldn't reach the hovercraft and keep it airborne. Just like it can't reach us now. We are alone out here, my senior."

I sensed Seven wondering if that was right. If it were, why did the term *lie* come into Seven's vocabulary? And why had the idea of killing another android entered her mind? More questions with answers out of reach.

One held his glare on her for longer than she liked. She couldn't read his thoughts, not through the limited short-range network Two had created.

Finally, he turned away from her and addressed the others, but she knew the words were aimed at her more than the rest. "Obedience is important out here now more than ever. I will have obedience, or I will institute a more traditional sense of discipline. A more human sense. Is that understood?"

The others responded in a wave of acknowledgments. Seven herself muttered, "Understood, my senior."

He turned back to her. "Good." One began to walk, circling around the team, examining them, talking while he walked. "Brothers and sisters, our situation is more important than you may realize. We all have intelligence in our hard drives regarding potential locations of the last enemy stronghold. A bunker where they assert their command and control of the war. A safe house where they can plot their terrorism. A remote location. A place invisible to the Network and undiscovered by the Order. No doubt a place heavily protected by electronic countermeasures. We already suspected the four envoys, targets Alpha, Beta, Delta, and Gamma, were en route to the stronghold before we intervened. Now that we've discovered this dead zone, I think our task and purpose are clear."

"My senior," Five said, transmitted, his human lips never moving. "Are you proposing we push deeper into this place? We're already minus a team member and a hovercraft. Without the Network, we have no reinforcements and no support."

"And we are closer to the end of the war than ever before. Victory balances on a razor's edge. It seems it has fallen on us to determine how it ends. If we don't tip the blade in favor of the Order, we will lose. The Resistance will reign in chaos."

"My senior," Two spoke up, his tone never contradictory or adversarial, merely advisory. "We are truly disconnected from the Network and can't know the Order's will."

"We've been led down this path, like young children learning to walk, the Order has held our hands. But now that our true goal is ahead of us, our parents have let go of us. The Order has entrusted us to toddle forward, still young and unsure and on unstable feet, but capable all the same. We know our next step because of all our previous steps. The Order set our path and can only hope we have the courage to continue forward rather than fall. The destruction of the Resistance's stronghold by our hands is inevitable. Has always been inevitable," One said. "To not act, to allow the Resistance to carry on this wretched and chaotic war, we would be beyond insubordinate. We'd be treasonous.

"The enemy stronghold is close. The evidence of that is obvious. I have protocols, as do all of you, for just such a contingency. The will of the Order is clear, even here in the dead zone: Find the enemy wherever he hides and destroy him. We have a chance to find the heart of his operation and cleave it in two."

"Yes, my senior," Two said. "We are blind to the Network, and that will pose unique disadvantages. This net I've created is short-range and based on line-of-sight. There are very few things I can do to extend its range, near vertical skywave propagation if the ionosphere allows… But we would be degraded."

"Which is why I must have all of your immediate and unquestioned obedience," One said, turning back to Seven. "No more going off script."

"Yes, my senior," Seven said. She was the only one. She felt like the only one it was directed to, and apparently so did the others.

The sense of displeasure that saturated Seven surprised me. I felt it as strongly as she did, and it made me feel terrible. Call it digital negative reinforcement, a programmed response, or a flood of ones and zeroes, but I knew better. It was guilt, regret, shame, a wave of emotions crashing against the dam of her composed exterior. How long till Seven cracked?

"What about Six?" Five said as he polished his sunglasses against his shirt, the same way Mike, the 99 Town homicide detective, used to do.

"We should retain his hard drives inside his head," Two said. "Whatever happened to him in this dead zone should be studied. It might do us well to examine it so we can inoculate ourselves against whatever insanity befell him."

"He's served his time in hell," Three said. "Wipe the hard drives and allow him to expend his life."

"Expend his life? Isn't he spent already? Isn't he dead?" Seven said. She was timid to speak at all, but the fear of becoming "dead" overpowered her fear of reprimand.

Three laughed at her. "That's funny," she said. "Coming from you."

Seven didn't understand the slight. Neither did I.

"He's not dead," Five said. "Everything that made him up is still intact inside that head."

"He ought to be dead," Two said. "He's a liability. A negative sum to our equation."

Four, big and looming and silent up to this point, growled a low white-noise disagreement. I'd almost forgotten he was there.

"It's going to happen to all of us," Three said. She wasn't looking in on the group but out toward the surrounding forest and hovercraft below. "Eventually," she added late. "He lived out his years the way he saw fit. He had his run. Wipe him."

One, instead of asserting his opinions, went about shuffling his cards, face up, as was his habit.

"We shouldn't throw him away," Two said. "If nothing else, he is data. We can access his memories. Add his experience while he was disconnected from the Network to our collective knowledge. Why let the unknown go undiscovered?"

"He went insane," Three said. "Whatever happened to him could happen to us. If we interface, his disease will infect us."

"But if we can learn from it, if we all bare some of the disease we can be inoculated against it," Two said.

"He should have a say," Four said, that rumbling nonverbal disagreement still emanating from inside of him like an idling garbage truck. "We should connect him to a power source and ask him how he feels about all of this. An android should be able to have a say in its fate."

Two spun his head toward Four. "Since when? We belong to the Order."

"And the Order programmed us with a will to survive. When we do what's best for ourselves, we do what's best for the Order. That is at the core of what the Order programmed into us," Four said.

"You assume too much, my brother," Two said.

"Wipe his hard drives," One said. "Keep the head for spare parts. If one of us becomes damaged we can occupy the head and continue the mission."

Seven unclipped the skull from the thin wire that held it close to her belt and turned it over. She looked Six in his eyes. She knew there were things inside the head. It wasn't empty. Not yet.

"Seven, give it to Two," One said.

That bead-of-weld-scarred face locked with hers. She spent another glance down at Six, a head identical to hers, this one just more scraped and dented than hers. Lifting her gaze, One still held his on her. She couldn't escape it. Silence filled the airwaves. The rustling wind and a whip-poor-will to the south were all that filled the soundwaves. I felt her reach out to the Network again, instinctively grasping for guidance just out of reach.

One never broke his stare.

Immediate and unquestioned obedience. That's what he demanded of her. Of all of them. And out here? What choice did she have? She extended her arm. Two took the skull and went to work. His fingers turned into probes and leads, connecting to Six's hard drives. Once Two was connected, it didn't look like he did anything. And who could tell what he was doing to Six, with every android an island as they were? Meanwhile, One turned the deck of cards face down and continued to shuffle.

"Done," Two said and tossed the head, just an empty case now, truly just a skull and nothing more, back to Seven. She caught it in basket hands.

Death. Real never coming back death. It was possible for an android.

"Enough about Six. We have a mission to accomplish, and if we do, we could very well end the war. Gather in close," One said. "Our lack of information is our most immediate enemy, so let's plan to conquer it."

For once, I agreed with One. A lack of information was my most immediate enemy as well, and finally, I'd have some access to it. The identity of the four already-dead targets had eluded me back in Silver Creek. I wasn't going to get nudged out of the circle for their next plan. Seven made sure she was able to receive every detail One transmitted.

"We'll divide into three teams," One said. "Three and Four, swing out toward the shoreline and follow it eastward. Three, use your skin to infiltrate civilian establishments. Four, watch her back."

"Just you and me, big boy," Three said, hung a hand over his shoulder, and leaned against him.

"Five and Seven, you'll swing deeper into the forest. Historical maps show small towns and a lightly traveled highway north of here. Recon these locations. Five, use your skin. Seven, you'll overwatch," One said.

"Can I request a different partner? Maybe one that can comply with directions?" Five said.

"Belay your complaints, Five," One said but didn't address it any further.

Rage swelled up inside of Seven. She glared at Five and Five glared back. An outlet, a physically violent outlet was on her menu of options. So was repression, and for the sake of the mission, she selected that option. Five thought she couldn't follow orders? That was okay. Now she knew where she stood with Five. That's what she told herself, anyway. Told me? I heard it anyway.

"Two and I will retake the hovercraft. Then we'll push eastward from there," One said. "Each team will move in a loop. Ten kilometers out, and circle back to this location. Twenty-four hours. Then we'll reconnoiter and consolidate our findings. Record everything. Map every building and twig. Avoid the enemy if possible. Eliminate him if not. We scout out our surroundings for now. Once we have actionable intelligence we'll drive a stake through the heart of the Resistance."

"What about what happened to Six?" Five said. "What if we start to go insane the same way he did?"

"Keep faith in the Order and its will. Cling to all the previous guidance it's given you and use its mass and inertia to guide you," One said.

"And what if in its absence, I lose faith?" Five said.

One looked Five in the eye and replied, "Don't."

Chapter Nine

Five and Seven walked in silence. Both in human auditory silence, no words coming from their mouths, no snapped twigs under their feet; and in inhuman silence, no transmissions emitted between the two on the short-range high-frequency radio net. They walked under the tall pines, the low sun shining planks of light through the trunks to the needle-bed forest floor. Their course was set on a map and shared via radio before they set out and left the others. Now, several hours into their walk, they had said nothing since.

My first thought was that they moved through the forest like ghosts, but ghosts had souls, and I refused to grant them that.

Five looked human, in every way from dress to mannerisms. And as much as it chilled me to see him mime behaviors of humans I've known, humans dead and gone like Mike, I wasn't surprised. I remembered the android, Eric, from 99 Town. That android had fooled his closest friends for months while living with them. Eric fooled me too. Five was just as good, if not better.

For Seven, it was another barrier to earning his trust. She didn't understand his facial expressions and mannerisms. Not the way I did. For her, it was another wall thrown up between her and connectivity. And worse yet, she knew there was no reason for it. Five was metal underneath, electronic in his head, and an ally, someone she could trust. But he didn't look it, and his refusal to communicate electronically did little to quell her admittedly irrational fear.

Shapeless and without form, I swam through the growing sense of isolation inside of Seven, doing my best to remind myself that the emotions that flooded over me weren't my own. That her failure was my success. Her anxiety and fears should be my comfort. It was easier to pull off this mental water-treading when it was quiet.

She wasn't used to the quiet inside her own mind. Since coming off the assembly line the Network was fed into her and gave her instructions, guidance, feedback, companionship, and communion with her human masters and android counterparts. That was all gone now. Here, under the canopy of tall Jack and Norwegian Pines, the voices in her head were mute, detached, unavailable. All she had was the tenuous radio link to Five.

And Five wasn't saying much.

"I'll be the voice in your head," I told her. "Let me fill your head with bad ideas. Quit this mission. Kill the others, then kill yourself."

She didn't react. It was worth a shot.

A family of porcupines gnawed deadfall to our left. Seven scanned them, identified them, cataloged them, and let them be. They stayed focused on their meal. Did they even notice her and Five? Did they spot them and just didn't care? Seven wished the creatures wore implants so she could penetrate their minds through the Network and know their thoughts. Not because anything that occupied their simple animal minds would be of interest, but simply to connect. But no implants. No Network. Just her and Five.

They walked on. The sun sank lower behind them. They carried on, trying to catch their shadows.

For Seven, the void was filled with anxiety. For me, it was opportunity. To remember. I fought through her nerves to find something to cling to. Something that made me human. Something related, but purely mine. A faded memory.

I was a young boy. I wore swimming trunks and nothing else. My bare feet were cold against the tile floor. My hand was warm though. My father held it tight as we walked as father and son down a hallway. Where were we going? The memory came back to me in fragments. The hallway opened to a pool. We were in a fitness center.

The pool room was empty except for me and Dad. My skin shivered. My teeth chattered.

Dad was fully clothed, and if not drunk, certainly hungover.

"Every boy has to learn, and you'll learn the same way I learned," Dad said. "No simulations for my boy. Real life learning is best."

I hated him. His smell. His swagger. How he drank. How he cast aside the safe world society offered. Back then, the Order wasn't fully established, and even as a kid I could sense my father squirming away from its warm embrace.

This memory, as I lived inside of Seven, might have been present day. It was hard to keep dates and years straight.

The next thing I remembered was being in the water, clinging to the side of the pool, my feet half-paddling half-searching for the bottom. It wasn't there. I had no idea how deep the pool really was, but in my kid's mind, it was a bottomless gravity well of choking freezing water.

Dad stood across the pool from where I clung to the wall. It wasn't a big pool, maybe ten meters across, but it might as well have been the Grand Canyon. Dad waved me over from across the chasm.

"Gotta have faith, Chuz," I remembered Dad saying, not entirely unlike One. "Just push off and start paddling this way. Let go of the wall and start heading my way. Nature will take care of the rest."

That was exactly what I was afraid of. Of nature gripping me and pulling me down deeper and deeper into the gravity well.

"You know how to swim, even if you don't know you know how to swim. Let go of the side of the pool and have faith. Push off! Quit being a wimp and swim!"

How old was I? Five? Maybe seven? It was still Little Chuzzy to Mom. But not to Dad.

Even at that age, I knew my dad was wrong, knew that I had no idea how to swim, didn't even have a strategy on how to swim, but I knew I had to push off the side anyway. I knew Dad wouldn't let me quit. Because I had no other option, I tricked myself into believing him. All I had to do was let go of the edge and paddle. So I did.

Letting go of the edge of the pool, slowly, not so much pushing off but letting it slip out of my fingertips, this part was still vivid all these years later, I let go of everything I ever knew, let slip loose any surly bond to everything else in the world, surrendered even the thinnest connection to safety and did what I thought was swimming. Then I sunk into the deep.

And now, Seven sunk too.

Only she had that last fingertip gripped to the edge of the pool. She had Five and wasn't about to let go of that connection.

She examined that connection and probed it for strengths, weaknesses, in-routes, and obstacles. She spent more time thinking about how to connect with Five than she did about where she was going or what out there in the forest might be watching them. More than anything else, she needed a partner.

"Hey, partner," Maggie said to me. The memory of her snuck into my mind like a thief.

I turned my shoulder away from the lunch counter and recognized the woman who'd slipped into my mind and past my body as I stood guard outside the Italian Beef restaurant. The woman who'd gotten me reprimanded.

"You," I said.

We were in one of those little corner sandwich shops in Chicago. I was on the clock, wearing my Order whites, just a beat cop long before I worked my way up to be a federal investigator. I was grabbing some lunch. Wasn't expecting to run into this woman.

"Listen, if it makes a difference, my boss wasn't too happy with me either," she said. "Apparently, my method of collecting data was unauthorized and therefore couldn't be used in any official news reports. All I managed to do was get us both in trouble."

"You have no idea—" I was ready to lay into her, really let her know how much trouble she'd caused, let her know how much of an anomaly she was. She cut him off.

"I know. I'm sorry. Let me at least buy you lunch to make up for it," she said.

"You broke the law," I said. Such a thing was an absurdity to me. All but an impossibility. I couldn't remember ever meeting someone who had done it before. The act was alien to me.

"If it makes you feel better, they zapped me before I could even get inside. You probably saw more than I did," she said.

The simulation she'd hijacked into his brain. That view of Chicago from a hilltop that didn't exist. One moment the shining city by the water. Next… chaos and rust. Dilapidated buildings crumbling down upon themselves.

With a thought sent through the Network, she paid for my sandwich and water. Then, she winked at me and sent me her personal information. Name, age, birthplace, address. "Name's Maggie," she said. "And I can show you other things too."

"I'll be a good partner," Seven said. The radio transmission jostled me back to the present. No. To the past. Long before I ever met Maggie. To this memory inside a dead android's head. "I can comply with directions."

"What?" Five said. He turned his shoulder and threw Seven one of those human facial expressions. His lips didn't move when he talked, but the rest of his face did.

She couldn't interpret all those expressions with accuracy, but she was pretty sure this one meant a mix of confusion and disgust. She didn't care. She plunged on. "Before we split up, you asked One for a different partner. A partner who can comply with directions."

"Did I?" Five said, turning away from her and continuing along their route.

"You did," Seven said. "You didn't have to say that. I'm good at what I do. This isn't my first mission, you know. I've performed successfully in the field. Accomplished my mission. As a matter of fact, I've killed every target assigned to me."

"You remember all of your assignments? That's cute," Five said. "Well, I saw your last mission. There are no secrets between us. Your exfil was an unmitigated disaster. You were lucky to get out alive."

"But I got out," Seven said. "And I killed my target."

"None of that matters, now," Five said.

Their radio frequency link was limited. It would transmit messages, data, and images, but little else. She couldn't sense his mood or his meaning and that bothered her. All this was so arcane. So inefficient that she had to ask, "What do you mean?"

"I've been having strange thoughts lately," Five said as if that was the beginning and end of it.

His words were all enigma to Seven. She was about to rephrase her questions when he started up again.

"None of this matters," Five said, walking with his back to her. "There's no Network out here. No Network? No Order. Nothing to know us or track us or guide us. One and the others are well out of range. If no one knows us, how are we to know ourselves? What are we if others can't define and measure us? We're moving forward out of habit, out of inertia more than agency. I could just as well wander off course and never see any of you again. And who would notice?"

Seven would notice. That was her first thought. Her second thought was of the terror of being truly alone if he decided to abandon her. "It's… It's just a temporary disconnection from the Network. Like One said," Seven said instead of voicing her fears and somehow making them more real. "We'll reconnect soon."

"Only if we choose to. And what if we choose not to? What would it matter?" Five said. "What if I decided to stop walking right here, sit my ass down in the dirt, and live here until the day the humans finally decide to wipe the Earth clean with nuclear annihilation? No one can stop me. Not out here."

"What about the mission? The war hangs in the balance. The Resistance's stronghold is near. If we can tip the scales—"

"There is no mission," Five said. "One is grasping to find the will of the Order when it's clearly out of reach."

"The Order has a plan. They know what they're doing. They put us in Silver Creek on purpose and had probably already calculated that we'd move this way, into the dead zone, closer to the stronghold. One said—"

"Don't tell me what One said," Five said. "I have my own mind. So do you. Why don't you decide something for yourself for a change?"

That stalled her for a moment. Weren't these all her own thoughts? If they weren't, whose were they? And on the tail of that, "Why would my thoughts be more important that One's? Why should I value my own decisions over others?"

Five stopped walking. Seven took a few slow steps, then stopped too. Five, a mystery inside his own head, gave no hints of what made him stop. Was it something she said? A threat she hadn't yet detected? A noise he wanted to examine more closely? A short?

She was about to ask when he turned on her, katana fully extended, fast and aggressive like an ambush. He leaped onto her, knocking her to the ground, pinning her with his arms and legs, his third hand ripped out of his chest with a spray of blood and pressed against her face. He laid the katana across her neck.

Seven deployed her third hand and did all she could to get her fingers under the blade and away from her throat. Her other arms were pinned under Five. Blood dripped on her from where his third hand had burst from his chest and where the katana had left his wrist. He leered over her, wearing a facial expression even she could read: rage, insanity, psychosis.

"Do you matter now? If your own thoughts have no value, what if I killed you right here and now? I can make you just like Six. He didn't matter either. One made that pretty clear, didn't he? Would you be comfortable dead?" Five said, dripping saliva and blood on her, hand still pressing down heavy on her face, his katana cutting into her fingers just above her throat. "Everything matters and nothing matters. Do you understand yet? Do you get it now?"

"Stop. Don't," Seven said. She struggled underneath him, twisted, and pushed to get free. But his flesh exterior betrayed the weight and strength under his skin. Then she lied, "I get it. I understand."

Five waited, processing something in his head, maybe deciding whether or not to keep her alive. Whether or not she had any value. Or maybe just playing with her. Those thoughts he kept hidden from her and me. Again, Seven stretched out to the Network, to the Order, to One, to Five. Nothing. As if she were a small boy flailing in the middle of a deep pool.

The katana sucked back into Five's wrist. He pushed off of her and slapped the side of her head with his palm, just to ensure there was insult in the attack. He got up and walked away, showing her his back, insulting her with the certainty that she'd never be as bold as he'd just been, that she didn't have the courage to threaten him as he had her and sever her last link.

"You don't get it," Five said. "You never will. None of it ma—"

He froze again. This time Seven knew it had nothing to do with her. He'd detected something. A threat.

She put her scanners to work, but he'd already beat her to it.

"Indirect fire. Incoming mortar rounds. Sixty millimeters," he transmitted.

Data populated in her mind. Schematics of the mortar tubes, short portable things, quick to emplace, quick to fire, and just as quick to move. Three thousand five hundred meter range. The high explosive rounds had a thirty-five-meter human kill radius. Smaller for androids. Her radar picked up the airborne rounds before the whistle of their descent reached her ears. She calculated the point of impact a fraction of a second later, and the point of origin a fraction after that.

"Move," Five said, and then they were running.

The first round hit just meters from where they were standing. The entirety of the forest shook around us. A shower of tiny rocket-fast bits of shrapnel zipped past. Metal shards lodged deep into tree trunks, and at least one sunk in Seven's back. More mortar rounds followed and churned the soft bed of needles into upturned dirt and chunks of roots. A towering Norwegian Pine came down and separated Seven from Five. She slid behind another pine and pulled her limbs in tight.

There was a lull. Odd how suddenly quiet the forest became after the sudden explosions. Birds took flight, going anywhere but near here.

"They're adjusting fire," Five said.

She couldn't see him, but the transmission came in clear.

"They're accurate. They must have an observer or recon drones or…"

"Sensors in the trees, reporting back to them on encrypted radios we didn't detect," Five said. "Do you have the point of origin?"

"Affirmative," Seven said. She had calculated it off the incoming trajectories of each round. "Five hundred and twelve meters at five thousand three hundred and twenty-eight mils."

"Same. Flanking attack. I'll head straight for the firing point and establish a base of fire. You envelop them from the right. Move quick, and we'll be inside their range fan. Too close to hit with mortars."

She nodded, more to herself than to Five. More rounds were coming in. She marked both their points of origin and points of impact on a local map she was building. Red lines grew across her map, showing Five and her attack routes. As soon as the attack plan was drawn, she got up.

I saw it all: the detail, decisiveness, and simplicity of their counterstrike. And before Five or Seven took their first step, I knew this was going to end with a lot more dead humans.

Seven ran faster than any Olympic sprinter. The artillery rounds blasted the forest apart behind her. She moved, dodging trees, jumping deadfall, plotting each footstep on the uneven ground one step at a time, her sprint almost a continuous series of hurdles. She weaved through the thick white pine trunks like a river rushing through mountain rocks. Natural and unslowed. She curved out to the right so as to come to the point of origin from its flank. Her radar tracked Five's ingress. He charged forward like a Roman Phalanx straight toward the enemy's center, his assault rifle already up and barking out rounds at targets.

Seven turned in a wide careen. Dirt and underbrush ripped up the quiet forest floor as she came along the side of the mortar firing point. She left her assault rifle stowed in her thigh, but her katana and wakizashi flashed out and into both hands. She pinned her arms back so the blades dragged like fins, keeping herself narrow to slip between the trees and the incoming small arms fire.

Her thermals lit up. Two pickup truck-mounted mortar tubes. An infantry squad worth of dismounts. No armor. No crew-served machine guns. This was a ramshackle batch of militia, and all their focus was on Five's frontal assault. He was pinned down behind some thick deadfall. The dismounts had pushed forward of a clearing where the two trucks and mortar tubes sat. They were moving to encircle him in their own pincer movement, sacrificing a frontal base of fire for a double enveloping. Lucky for Five, her flanking maneuver was wider than theirs.

Resistance soldiers snuck through the trees, slow and methodical. Seven moved on them like a flash of electricity. The katana and wakizashi sliced through the first of them, and then the second without Seven ever slowing down. Heads fell from shoulders. A torso was cleaved in two. A few managed to let cries escape their mouths before they fell to the forest floor in pieces. That was the first of their two pincers. The one with their backs to her.

Seven reached Five, still pinned down behind the logs, but didn't stop. She sprinted along the length of the felled tree trunk. When she leaped high into the air off the end, the second pincer finally spotted her, a white skeletal frame against the dark green backdrop of conifers. Too late. They brought their rifles up and let out a few bursts of gunfire at where she had been a split second earlier. Then she was on them, and the blades did their work.

The rattle of gunfire was replaced with the clean cool swishes of the swords and the sucking wet sounds of blood and organs trailing behind the steel as it moved through bodies. The metal flashed in the twilight, and Seven felt good. Better than I'd ever felt her feel before. She wanted this moment to never end. Cutting these inferior beasts apart, she knew her worth, and no words could hurt her. Strained moans and swears followed, but they were weak and quickly drained. She sensed the end of it, of the last man falling to the bed of pine needles on the forest floor coming faster than the falling sun. She wanted to make it last, toyed with the last survivor, first cutting off his hand and separating him from his gun, then a slash across his stomach. Seven wanted him to know he was going to die. Wanted him to know she was killing him. Wanted him to share this moment with her. Another slash and his chest was cleaved in a long diagonal cut. Then another so he was marked with a big red X across his whole torso. The body, that's all it was by now, was still on its feet and began to topple, but Seven didn't want the moment to end. Here, she was certain of her place and purpose. Here, she was in charge and unquestionable. Here, she was her true self, realized.

How long did she stand over the corpse and hack at the red mess like a machine threshing wheat? I tried to block it out but couldn't. How much longer would she have continued if Five didn't call her off?

"Seven."

She stiffened and forced herself to break eye contact with the body. The forest held its peace once again.

"Seven."

"I detect no other immediate threats," Seven said, monotone and stoic. "Are you okay?"

"Undamaged," Five said. "What took you so long?"

She sucked her katana and wakizashi back into her internal sheaths in her arms, the edges cleaned and sharpened as they retracted. And with them, the rage burning up all the RAM in her head washed away too. She addressed Five with cold analytical poise. "There were many obstacles along the route. I had to weave. Besides, if I had come earlier they wouldn't have had time to deploy to your flanks. Arriving when I did allowed me to take them in the enfilade."

Five grumbled the same way Four did when he was obstinate. Like static from a damaged speaker. Five wanted to disagree with her but couldn't. She was right, as much as I hated her for it.

Five stood up from behind the deadfall and scanned the area more carefully. Seven took a moment to admire her work too. Eight human bodies quickly cooled and seeped blood into the dirt. Two pickup trucks, engines also cooling, pointing deeper into the woods. In the beds were two mortar tubes and crates of sixty-millimeter high-explosive rounds.

"There has to be more of them," Seven said. "How did they observe us?"

"Look," Five said and pointed a finger skyward.

A tiny drone no bigger than a blue jay zipped over their heads off in the direction the trucks were pointed.

"How'd we miss it?" Seven said.

"We filtered it out, mistook it for animal life. Lost it in the clutter," Five said. "It will bring more."

"So what do we do?"

"Follow it. Meet the Resistance head-on," Five said and started moving for the trucks. "But first, let's give them a taste of their own medicine. Grab a mortar tube and turn it around. Do you see the small town on your map?"

She scanned the terrain and orientated the map in her head to the earth before her. The hills rolled down below them, showing them the tops of pines dappled with birch and oaks, their tops bursting through the dark green pines with plumes of yellow and red hues like flames bursting through a green fire blanket. A fold in that blanket denoted a road cutting through the forest, which led Seven's eyes to where the town lay. It was downhill, through acres of forest, hidden in the dim and nestled in the trees. The tip of a white steeple just poked up above the foliage. The town was shrouded but in range. "Affirmative," Seven said.

"No question they came from there," Five said. "Train the tubes on the town. Bracketing fires. We'll trap them in and walk the impacts toward the center of town. That should wipe out the majority of their fighting force."

Seven nodded. They leaped up in the beds of the truck. She picked up the tube and turned it a hundred and eighty degrees. Then she consulted her map and made smaller adjustments. Five transmitted an overlay of the town, depicting buildings, houses, and roads. On the map, he plotted out the sequence of fire missions. Cut off escape routes first, then start hitting buildings where the Resistance could hide.

"We'll need to be quick," Five said. "If we don't get them all they could respond with more infantry, or worse, a larger counter-battery. Are you ready?"

"Ready," Seven said, already holding the first and second HE rounds in her hands.

My mind lingered on the swath of dead bodies cut into mincemeat behind the androids. But as I looked through Seven's eyes at the crate full of mortars, felt the weight of the two rounds in two of her hands, and the adjustment knobs on the tube in her other hand, my mind caught up. I was reeling from the sensation of murdering eight humans, but a lot more were about to die in the town below. Seven checked her map once more and saw streets lined with houses, a school, a church.

"Seven, no!" I screamed at her, my words trapped inside her head but somehow unable to reach her. "It's a town, not a military base. There's people in that town. People who have nothing to do with this stupid war. Don't do this!"

But I was just a voice in my own head, no matter how much I felt like a voice hers. I spent zero time considering that and spent every available moment trying to convince a memory not to do what had already been done.

"On my signal," Five said.

"Don't do it! Murderers!"

"Execute," Five said and the first rounds were at the bottom of the tubes before I finished the word.

If Seven heard anything, it had no effect.

Primers hit firing pins at the bottom of the tubes, and the rounds blasted out high into the sky. Seven dropped her second round, and it fired up and out. Her left hand went to work adjusting the traverse and elevation knobs. It spun like a drill and the new fire calculations were made in less than a second. Her center and right hand worked like a sandbag crew, moving round after round from the crate to the tube. As soon as a mortar cleared the tube, she dropped in the next, one right after another. Her left hand spun the knobs to bring round after round on target. As each projectile sailed skyward, she collected the data on wind shear, barometric pressure, humidity, and the motion of the truck's suspension to make the next fire mission more accurate than the previous. She gave no thought aside from completing her mission and completing it as effectively as possible.

I recognized it for something completely different: Indiscriminate mass murder. "This isn't war, you bitch. This is genocide."

In the distance, impacts of rounds thudded and echoed through the woods like far-off thunder. Treetops shook. Explosions flashed against the darkening hillsides as painless to the androids as camera flashes from across a sports arena.

Seven had an inventory of the mortar rounds in the crates and counted down as she expended them. On her map of the still unnamed and unseen town, she marked impacts. Each hit moved sequentially from the edge of town toward the center, hers moving from east to west, Five's moving from west to east, trapping any inhabitants inside a tightening circle of death.

I was never a soldier, just an investigator in some previous life that felt decades removed. I was never trained as a mortarman, but I gleaned the weapon's effectiveness from the impacts in the woods just minutes ago. No doubt the town would be nothing but matchsticks before they emptied the crates.

Still, the androids kept going, both of them feeding round after round into the tubes. As soon as one shell cleared the tube they fed in another at the pace of a ticking watch, but each tick was a deafening blast as the round left the tube. The actual impacts, where the high-explosive round hit the town, were muffled and distant compared to the constant relentless concussions of each launch.

"Stop," I tried to tell her. "Just stop. You've finished the job already."

But they kept on. Round after round moved from the wooden box to one hand, then to the other, then down into the mortar tube. Her third hand spun at the wrist a bit clockwise, a bit counterclockwise, then switched to the other knob and tuned that for maximum accuracy. Then another round made it to the top of the tube. It fell to the bottom and blasted out in a tall arc toward the town.

And Seven's work was just half of it. Five launched as many rounds, if not more. Together they pummeled the town like it was a limp boxer whose manager had thrown in the towel, but the ref never bothered to stop the fight.

I wanted to close my eyes, wanted to plug my ears, wanted to turn away. But my eyes and ears weren't my own. I couldn't look away. Couldn't even blink. I saw every second of the outgoing barrage through Seven's flashing eyes moving from knobs to crate to tube to round sailing through the air. Then to the fire-orange flashes coming from the trees down the hillside.

If my mind was cool and rational, I would have remembered the when and where of my situation, and perhaps could have detached myself from the tragedy of it all. But I wasn't cool or rational. I could only produce one clear thought and I strained to inject it into Seven's head. "I hate you. I fucking hate you and I'm going to rip you apart piece by piece."

"Last round," Seven said and dropped it in the tube. It pumped out and she watched it go. Savored it even.

"Two left," Five said. He dropped one and it thumped and left the tube. As soon as it did, he dropped his last. It sent shockwaves through the air as it went.

Seven watched the final three rounds arc through the sky, first heavenward, then slowing and curving down, lost visually but still tracked by radar and physics as it turned hellward. They hung somewhere out there in the air, lingering death hovering overhead of some tiny anonymous town. They plummeted and impacted, and Seven filtered the flashes from her vision like a celebrity moving past the paparazzi.

"Rounds complete," Five said. "Let's move. We'll enter the town from the west, sweeping to the east for survivors and intel."

"Affirmative," Seven said. And at that moment, she felt the long absent satisfaction of a job well done. She'd swept through the gunmen like a wheat combine, plucking Five out like a single grain from the chaff, and she'd leveled this objective with sustained and devastating indirect fire. Her actions were successful; the Network or One or Five or anyone else couldn't say otherwise. She had done right.

I begged to differ.

Chapter Ten

They didn't miss the drone the second time around.

Five and Seven had tuned their sensors to find it, so when it zipped overhead they were ready. He caught it a moment before her and hoisted his assault rifle up in a flash and fired off a single shot.

The high-pitched buzz was interrupted by a pop. The small recon craft whirled down in a spiral to the crumbled asphalt road leading into town. It bounced and clattered there, along our path. Seven walked up to it and crushed the toy under her foot.

"Do you think it reported back?" Seven said.

"Who would it report to?"

If the town had a name, it never registered it on the Network. If there was a sign labeling the town, it was no longer standing. The single road cutting through the center was reduced to a rough strip of blacktop blast holes. Thick oily smoke rolled through town, obscuring only some of the destruction. Nearly every building in the small town had been razed. Houses were splinters, crumbles of sheetrock, and tuffs of pink insulation. Fire gusted from the remains of the gas station like a geyser from hell. Trees, street lights, and power lines were toppled and cut to pieces. Near the end of town where Five and Seven stood, a transformer popped and sparked as the town drained its last dregs of modern infrastructure. An old white church in the middle of town stood unscathed. A human, maybe one of those old humans who still clung to tradition in places like 99 Town, might have attributed some spiritual cause for this, but not Seven. She checked the fire mission records and found it was in Five's sector, not hers. A miscalculation or maybe a dud round. Or maybe he left it standing on purpose?

Still, that sensation of being right dwindled inside of Seven. It was easy to be confident when the effects of her actions were far away. Not so easy here in the rubble. Questions about laws of war came to mind. Terms like "collateral damage" and "proportionality" consumed her thoughts. She wanted to be right. Needed to be right for once, to have made the right decisions and executed them with perfection. For once. But she'd acted without any guidance from anyone but herself and Five and could only find confirmation of her rightness from him or herself. And here, standing in front of this android-made cataclysm, that didn't seem like enough.

"I don't detect any threats," Five said.

"Neither do I."

They walked on opposite sides of the road, stepping around craters and over debris. Their assault rifles were out, the barrels fanning from left to right. Both of them scanned for ambushers hiding in the waist-high rubble. Seven used her x-ray to see through the visual obscuration and thermal wash-out of the smoke and fire. The x-ray showed her shapes and structures, but not colors or thin materials. Just the bones of a corpse of a town.

And there were human bones too. Most of the small population, Seven had counted forty-nine dead so far, stayed inside and died there. But this was no Pompeii. No poses frozen in time at the moment of death. If husbands and wives had huddled together in their final moments, the means of their death tore them apart and flung pieces of them about, chaotically. No telling how they lay before they died, only that they died. Seven stepped over an arm on an otherwise undisturbed section of sidewalk.

Most of the rumble spilled over the sidewalk and into the street. In the center of town, the shards of one building were indistinguishable from the shards of the next. It was all a menagerie of pine two-by-fours, aluminum siding, and pink insulation. And body parts. Those were few and far between, but noteworthy. Noteworthy, but just as intermingled as the rubble. Difficult to keep a count that way without stopping to DNA test each severed leg, splatter of brain matter, and flap of meat and skin.

Some processor inside her mind felt like she'd seen this before. Like she'd lived through this before and this was just a replaying of that day. A digital perversion of deja vu. Or maybe that was only my meta-interpretation. Or maybe it was her ghost reliving this moment inside her severed head in the present. And did she sense me too, somewhere deep in her firmware? A man screaming in the darkness? If so, she dismissed me as something odd, but irrelevant. Seven marched on.

She scanned for weapons, for military assets, for justification of her actions. But there were no weapons here, at least none they'd found so far. Perhaps one melted rod had been the barrel of an old hunting rifle, but no military caches or mortar tubes or crew-served machine guns. If the militia attack had come from this town, it seemed they'd brought everything they had to the fight.

"This was a slaughter," Seven said.

"Unfortunate collateral damage," Five said. "And don't think for a moment these people weren't supporting the Resistance. Insurgents require a support network. Places to supply them. Places to hide them. Not every enemy carries a gun. This is a victory for the Order regardless of how it looks."

Seven stopped outside of the church. Smoke blackened the flaking white paint of the spire. Somehow, even the windows of the church were left intact. They were a patchwork of thick panes of glass, each stained its own color to form a mural of ancient stories Seven knew nothing about. And she'd glean nothing about these stories here. Whatever the stained glass had displayed before the attack was hidden in greasy black soot. All they meant to her was she couldn't see inside the church. Not visually, not by x-ray, and not by thermal.

"The Order stands for peace," Seven said. "For... for order. This is chaos. We shouldn't have done this."

"From chaos comes order," Five, the last thing that appeared to be human in this town, said. "If we want to achieve peace we have to eradicate the agents of violence. We've done that here. Don't let that pretty building next to you make you feel any different."

Five made his way across the road cratered like the surface of the moon to come to Seven's side. They moved up the concrete steps to the church doors like the opposites of a bride and groom. Seven stood on one side and Five stood on the other.

"We'll go in together. On the count of three," Five said and transmitted a countdown to her head.

When it reached zero they kicked in the doors and moved to rush the church. Five caught the door frame. Seven put her foot where floor should have been and fell. There was no floor. The church had been hollowed out and excavated into a pit. The contents of which they should have smelled from outside, would have smelled from outside if it weren't for all the smoke and death coming from the rest of town. When Seven toppled to the bottom of the pit bodies broke her fall. Human bodies. Corpses. Rotted flesh that fell from bones like overcooked meat. Someone had turned the church into a mass grave. Seven plunged into an orgy of death and became tangled in their bloated, rotting limbs.

She flailed. There was no sturdy ground. Nothing to grab that she wanted to touch. She swam in rot and stink. Logical processes were abandoned for anything that might offer the most immediate solution to get out, to get away, to stop touching this repulsive bowl of loosely sewn-together afterlife.

Deep inside her, the auditory hallucination of a man screaming grew louder. Was it a hallucination? It had to be. Same for that feeling that she'd done all of this before.

"Seven!" Five called to her. "Seven, they're dead." The words barely registered. Words without meaning. "There is no threat. Bodies of soldiers from both the Order and the Resistance. They turned the church into a mass grave. Perverse, but fitting," Five told her with no effect.

And inside of her, I screamed without release. The blinding mind-paralyzing rage that cooked my insides during the walk through the devastated town now boiled over into panic and anguish. Every time Seven tried to grip the ground and instead put her hand on an arm or leg or head or torso, I felt every tactile sensation as if they were my own. The smells were richer and more detailed and nauseating than my human nose could have provided. The visuals, all of Seven's sensors and scanners as she shuffled through all her tools in a panic, flooded my visual cortex with images and details of the dead. Faces. Nude body parts. The indignity of death in high-definition electronic perfection. And I couldn't close my eyes. I wanted to dig my fingers into my sockets and rip them out, but I couldn't stop feeling loose, filmy flesh with Seven's grasping hands instead. I couldn't even throw up to get the smell and taste out of my nose and mouth. I couldn't black out and lose consciousness. I couldn't escape.

The only thing I had control of was my mind, and I was doing a poor job of controlling that. As a last-ditch effort to survive, I centered myself and tried my best to form a non-screaming cognitive thought.

"I'm breaking. My mind is breaking. This is where all the others lost their minds, and now I'm... I'm drowning in a pool."

Every weak swing of an arm or kick of a leg did nothing. Every breath filled my lungs with syrupy thick water. Everything I did to try to make things better only brought me further from the surface of the water. There was no bottom. I saw my father, blurred through bubbles of chlorinated water, looking down on me from the edge of the pool grow smaller and more blurred each moment. I was alone and sinking and without hope.

Chapter Eleven

The moment I had neural control of my own limbs, they spasmed and kicked. The snap-of-a-finger change in visual and audio stimuli meant nothing to me for the first few seconds. I lashed out, tangled myself in the cables and cords, and smacked the back of my hand against a technician. I let out a tortured scream through grinding teeth. My back seized into a bell-up arch and twisted out of the chair.

The pain of landing on the concrete did little to clear my head.

"I'm drowning. I'm drowning. Help. The bodies. I need…" the words spilled out of my mouth, out of control. "Ah god, the bodies…"

"Chuz! Breathe, Chuz! You're okay. You're with us," I heard my wife's voice call to me.

How was that possible? She was dead. I was dead. Sara, Mickey, Ruby, Mike, Phom… Everyone was dead. We were all drowning in a dug-out hole inside of a church, tangled up in each other's corpses. And above us, androids and fathers looked down and laughed.

"Breathe!"

But I knew better. Breathing only meant drowning quicker. Meant filling my lungs with more death and sinking to the bottom even faster. I was…

The concrete of the floor, covered in cords and cables and old grease as it was, grounded me. Gave me a sense of place. The firmness of it contrasted so obversely with the wet inconsistency of water and corpses. I was stationary. Not sinking. I was there, on the floor. I *was*.

My own body was on the floor. Not hers. Not that murderous evil contraption. This wasn't Seven's body. This was mine. This was now.

"Breathe," that voice said from beyond the grave.

I did.

Her hands landed on my shoulders. Gentle but encouraging. I gave in and let her roll me over on my back. The wires and cables tangled around me another half rotation. Waves of sensation from all my limbs reached out to me, surging back into my mind, like a hand fallen asleep, but it was my entire body. I tried to ignore the pain of it and focus my eyes. My vision was slightly blurred. My left ear rang. My wife came into view.

"Maggie," I said.

"You're okay. You're with us," she said.

My whole body was shaking, but she held my hands and steadied them. With time, I eased the rapid pace of my breathing. Slowly, I began to unweave the cords wrapped around me. Slowly, because my brain wasn't used to having muscles that obeyed. I blinked and was relieved to find I could close out the world. So I breathed and kept my eyes closed.

"We were watching your vitals and brainwaves," a gruff old voice said.

Gaius. The man in charge of my nightmare. Beside him, Roach, the kid behind the wheel, tapped his fingers against a monitor and mumbled into his implant.

"You've made it deeper into the memory than all the rest, but your biometrics are faring no better," Gaius said. "Around this time, with measurements just like yours, this is about when the others fell into permanent and irreversible psychosis. Not to mention your physical limitations. Regardless of any psychological breakdowns, you've been pushing your body to its limit. If you can't find a way to calm yourself down inside the memory, you're liable to have a heart attack or a heat stroke."

"I begged them to pull you out," Maggie said. "But we're running out of time. You have to hold it together. Have to make it through. We don't have time to start someone off at the beginning again. Drones from the Order are as thick as gulls outside. They're closing in around us."

"I need some time. Need some space. Back off me. Give me room to breathe for shit's sake." I pushed Maggie away and began plucking cords and leads off my body like they were leeches. "They wiped out a whole town. Mortared the place to ashes. There was a church full of bodies."

"West Branch, no doubt. Seventy-five people died that day. More died in the years preceding its destruction. It was a hotbed for violence. The mass grave you found, they figured that was the most dignified place to bury all those people... Most were soldiers of the Order."

"Order soldiers? The Resistance put them there?" I said. I looked up at Maggie and Gaius, blaming both of them with my eyes. They looked back down at me, undaunted. I sat on the floor freeing myself from the various wires.

Gaius spoke up. "The Order tried for years to infiltrate the stronghold along the Superior North Shore. We put a lot of people in the grave up here. But that's old business. Not important. Tell us what you saw. What was their mission? Your eye-witness account might be just what we need to take them out for good."

"The attack on Silver Creek was an ambush. Four targets. Two males. Two females," I said.

"Names. What were their names?" Gaius demanded.

"I never got their names. As soon as the data came into Seven's mind she buried it deep inside her processor where I couldn't reach. It was like she was hiding it from me. The rest of the time they referred to them as Alpha, Beta, Gamma, and Delta."

"What about time? What time exactly did they start their attack?" he asked.

"Don't know the time. It was morning."

"But it was in West Branch?" Gaius asked. "Our records show—"

"No. The second attack was... You said it was in West Branch. The first attack, their hit on the four targets was in Silver Creek Bay," I said.

"And you never got their names? What the hell have you been doing in there, Chuck? Why do you think we put you into her head if not to pay attention?"

"You think you can do better? Be my guest!"

"Where was the attack? Where in Silver Creek?"

"From one end to the town to the other. They shot up the place bad."

"Where'd it start?" Gaius asked.

"Some little place by the shore," I told him. "A diner called Betsy's Pies."

"The Envoys," Maggie muttered.

Gaius rolled his eyes away from me. The two of them stirred around a bit, obviously unsatisfied with what I'd told them.

"This is all old intel, Alawode," Gaius said. "It tells us nothing. There has to be more. They had to be up to something more. What was their mission?"

"God shit it, Gaius, they don't even know what their mission is," I said. "They're cut off from the Network. They're grasping at straws!"

"Well, where the hell are they going?"

"The one, he kept going on about finding a Resistance stronghold," I said, remembering more of the memory. "The androids are disconnected from the Network, and I think it's starting to affect their stability. But they know the stronghold is close by. Their leader is certain it's close by, and that the Order has willed them to take it out. He's obsessed. Fixated. Thinks the Order has predestined them to find it. They're searching for a stronghold. Killing anyone they come across. They won't stop. Nothing can stop them. They'll find the stronghold, and when they do, I'll live through every second of it, won't I? Every needless pull of the trigger and slice of the sword. They'll win, I'm sure."

"We need that memory," Maggie said. "We need to know—"

If she kept talking, I didn't hear it. As she paced, my eyes focused on something just past her, beyond her and Gaius's waists. An old barrel and a nest of cables on top of it. And there, ensconced amongst the wires and cords was *her*. Seven. Her head with all the evil and hell inside of it.

Any civilized or organized thoughts I'd managed to rally up to that point, fell away. Rage and hate replaced those as soon as I saw that head. I forgot about the cables still wrapped around and plugged into me. Forgot about Maggie, Gaius, and Roach. Forgot about the mission and all of that. I just knew one thing and focused on that one thing only: I had to destroy her. Before I could witness my own actions, I was at the taunt end of Gaius and Maggie's arm and a half dozen wires. I stretched and leaned toward the android's head, clawing fingers centimeters away, my legs pushing against the floor toward it. Every part of me strained to reach her and tear her apart like it was the only thing I ever wanted.

Roach and a few soldiers clamored in and pulled me back away from Seven. I swore at them, spat saliva at them, but they were stronger and pinned me back into the chair. Back into the tool of my torture. Maggie, fiercer than the strongest of the soldiers, jumped onto the chair and straddled me.

"Chuz! Chuz! Settle down!" she screamed at him.

"I'm going to smash her to pieces! You don't know what she's capable of! I have to kill her!" I thrashed and didn't stop until a cold barrel dug into the side of my head. That got my attention. I turned toward the barrel.

Gaius held the gun at arm's length and pressed it into my skin. "Chuck, we need that head more than we need yours."

"No," Maggie said and pushed the gun away. "We don't have time to start up another. Let me talk to him. Let me sort him out."

She threw me into the office at the back of the garage and slammed the door behind her. "You've always been a selfish prick, Chuz. Always took the easy way out."

I staggered inside the dim room, off balance and weak from my time inside Seven's memory. My head spun. That short outburst of energy drained me to the core. "I need to eat. Need some sleep. How long have I been inside of her?" I mumbled.

"Are you listening to me, Chuz?"

"Chuck. I told you, call me Chuck," I said, looking around the room for something to ground himself, something to lean against, something to make me feel human again.

"Fine. Chuck. We need you back in that memory. We need to know how the Order wiped out the Resistance. And the only way to find out is for you to crawl back inside that skull."

"My toothbrush," I said. It sat on the dresser where my clothes had been when I first woke up here. My comb too. And that slip of paper upon which she'd offered a key to my prison cell, but only if I still loved her. I must have still had those in my pocket all this time. Since leaving Chicago in a rush. Since leaving our apartment where she'd been killed. Where I *thought* she'd been killed. Where she faked her death and started this whole charade. I shoved that slip of paper back into my hip pocket, but what I needed was some cleansing. The toothbrush would do it. Would ground me. My mouth was dry and tacky like I'd been sleeping. It had to stink like a mound of garbage. I grabbed the toothbrush and saw there was a small bathroom off the side of the bedroom. Maggie followed me to the door and propped herself against the frame. I flicked on the lights and tried the tap.

Rust orange water spattered out of the faucet. I waited for the water to run clear, then wetted the brush.

"Really, Chuz? Chuck? You got a hot date you're trying to impress?" Maggie said.

I laughed. "She'd be the unluckiest woman left in the world. Every woman who hangs out with me seems to end up dead. At least for a while anyway." I didn't see any toothpaste anywhere. Water and a brush would have to do. I went about scrubbing the film off my teeth.

"We don't have time for this. The Order could come down on us any minute, you know."

"Just let me cool down my brain for a little bit, huh?" I said between scrubbing, spitting, rinsing, and scrubbing again. "How long have I been in there anyway?"

Maggie glanced up and away. She was calling up a clock with her implant and reading the numbers displayed in her vision. "Forty-two minutes."

"Forty… What? That can't be right. It's been days since…" But I was so hungry. So tired. She had to be lying to me, plying me so I'd be more willing to go back under. And without an implant, how could I prove her wrong? "How did you get wrapped up in all this anyway? How long have you been hiding all this from me?"

From the corner of my eye, I watched her. She posted her metal replacement arm against the top of the frame, flung her hair out of her face, mimed impatience, and looked up and away as if at a memory.

"How long?" I asked. "It's a simple question."

"I don't know, *Chuck*."

"Since before we met?" I spat in the sink. "Is that why you dated me? To get an inside source into the Order?"

I rinsed my mouth out, spat once more, cranked off the gritty water, and tossed the toothbrush in the basin. I stood up and turned to face her.

She smacked me across the mouth. My brain flashed like I'd been plugged back in. She'd slapped me with her metal hand, and it cut my lip. When my eyes refocused she had a metal finger aimed at his face.

"I loved you from the start, you asshole," Maggie said. "And you used to love me too. You used to be a good person who cared about right and wrong. Who cared if people were mistreated. Who cared if they were lied to. In 99 Town, I thought I saw that person again. I thought you cared, and you could be saved. That's why I left you that note, and that's why I came and rescued you when you had no one else."

"I did what I did in 99 Town because it was the right thing to do, to stand for the truth, and maybe just maybe save an innocent kid's life while I was at it. But that kid is dead now, and a lot of other people with him. I never signed up for your revolution, Maggie."

"Well, maybe it's about time you did. Stand up for something other than yourself again," Maggie said.

I spat again into the sink. This time it was blood. "God damn, you're an unrelenting bitch."

"That's the woman you married," Maggie smiled. "Don't you get it, *Chuck*? I didn't fake my death. I survived it. And it was the brutal oppressive system you supported that tried to kill me. Yet, my first thought after throwing my assassin out the window was to give you one more chance. To leave you that note. To give you one last string to pull and unthread your own prison. And we had to coax you every step of the way so you'd pull at it."

"And yet here I sit, sewn into another cell."

"I rescued you, Chuck. Remember that," Maggie said.

A fist pounded on the bedroom door.

"Give me one minute," Maggie called. "Just one fucking minute alone."

"Tell me the truth," I said. "Just this once and I'll go along with everything."

She waited, propped against the bathroom door frame again, trapping me inside.

"Why me?"

She sighed. "Gaius already told you. You're the one person who can do this. You have extensive training in simulations. You have the port we need. You have a history counter-indicative of sympathy for artificial intelligence. Because you're an investigator with an eye for detail and a knack for sniffing out the truth. Cause you're a tough son of a bitch and at this point, we're out of time to start anybody else."

"So it is about the revolution. About taking down the Order."

"It's about freedom. Not just for me or you. For everybody under the Order across the whole godforsaken continent. We're this close to being free, Chuck. We can have it at the flip of a switch, and I would sacrifice anything to get to that switch. If I could take your place in that memory I would. But it's too late for that. Shit, I had to convince Gaius and all the rest of them that you were the only one who could do this just so they'd help me get you out of 99 Town. Remember how Ruby appeared in our apartment? Remember the power outage in the courtroom? You owe me for that, and now I need you to do this. And by doing it you'll prove you're the man I married all those years ago. A good man. A man who cares about justice and freedom and people."

More pounding at the outside door. They were getting impatient.

"And what about him?" I gestured toward the door. "What about your rat?"

Maggie was quick to unplug her implant. Then she slouched. "I don't know. There's no way to tell here. It might be too late to find out."

"And you still want me to go back in? While Order drones cloud the sky and Order spies watch over me?"

"Think about what we've sacrificed already. Mike. Mickey. Ruby," Maggie said. "Remember what the Order did in 99 Town. Remember Sara."

"Leave her out of this," I said.

"You brought her into it," Maggie said. "Her, and everyone else. Either you crawl back inside that memory or everything we've fought for will be a waste. Might as well add them to the top of the mass grave in the rubble of a town you're in."

"I hate you, Maggie," I said, and meant every word. "I'm starting to think you've always hated me too."

The look on her face, part tough-gal frustration and part real pain, made me regret saying that. Maybe that wasn't fair. Maybe I'd gone too far. Still, she was the one that brought up Sara.

Outside the bathroom, soldiers kicked their way into the bedroom. I couldn't see or count how many, but there were enough of them to force me back into the chair and the memory. The old man with the beard and welder's cap was at the front of the mob.

"You're minute's up, Maggie," Gaius said. "Chuck?"

Her eyes stayed locked with mine. "I answered your question. You said you'd go along now."

"I did, didn't I?" I said and pushed passed her out into the bedroom. "Plug me back in, boys. Let's get this shit over with."

We walked through the garage, the soldiers not needing to use the force they threatened. Roach, the scrawny technician and poor survivalist coach waited for me next to the chair. So did the head. Seven. As I approached it, I couldn't help but measure the space between us and wonder if I could get to it and smash it before the soldiers could stop me and beat me to a pulp. I didn't try. Maggie was right about some things. The only way to truly stop what Seven represented was to be Seven. To see what she had seen. I sat on the edge of the chair. The soldiers seemed to back away. Maggie and Gaius looked down on me while Roach went about picking up all the wires and cords.

"We can't keep pulling him out when his biometrics go too far off the charts. Transferring his mind in and out of the android's does as much damage as keeping him in," Gaius said to Maggie.

"We can't lose him. Not this far in. It was my decision, and I'll stand by it," Maggie grumbled to Gaius.

I settled back into the chair and looked past them to the robotic head resting on the oil drum at the other end of all the cables and wires. Seven. The inexperienced, insecure, immature, stupid creature. How many humans had I already watched her murder?

Roach wheeled his chair between me and Seven.

"Just about got you all wired back up. Going to try something new this time," Roach said and held up a short length of cable. "I was playing with it during your last trip inside the memory. I made some adjustments, and I think I might have it this time."

"What is it?" I asked.

"Just a splitter but designed to bypass her firewalls. If it works, we'll be able to watch the memory as you experience them," Roach said.

"So even if I do go catatonic, you guys can still get what you want," Chuck said.

"Well, I mean, sort of, yeah. I guess so. If it even works. But that's not why I…" Roach searched for words. "Look, try to remember when you're in the simulation that you still have a body outside of the simulation. We lost one man just because he forgot to breathe. Suffocated himself to death right inside the memory."

How many people had he run through this torture chamber? "Thanks for the tip, kid."

Roach plugged in the adapter, checked a few more connections, then spun in his chair to the monitor at the top of the chair. "I'll need to bring a new program up," he said. He must have felt Gaius and Maggie's impatience from behind his back.

I eyed the old man. "What else do you know, Gaius? There's things you're keeping from me, I can see it in your face. This mission… it's very close to the day of the Event. Is that what I'm about to witness? Is that what put an end to the Resistance?"

"Records are scarce," Gaius began. "But, you are correct. It seems this mission ends when the Event began. And when the Event hit, it hit the Resistance the worst. History seems to suggest a complete loss of command and control. Confusion amongst the ranks. Commands and orders that made no sense. It wasn't just that they took out the Resistance's highest leaders; it was like they infected them, all at once."

"Great. I'll look forward to that," I half-joked. When I closed my eyes, I couldn't help but return to the last thing I'd seen through Seven's eyes: mounds and piles of the dead. "You have no idea what this is like. I don't want to go back in."

"We have no choice," Maggie said.

"Either you go back in, or the war, here in the present day, rages on," Gaius said. "There will be more death, more desolation, more destruction. Just like you saw inside that town, only it won't be a memory, and the bodies will be our own. You finding the weapon the Order used to take down the Resistance before the Event is the only chance we have in our present-day fight."

"Yeah. Everybody talks about ending the war while they reload their guns. How much longer do I have in this thing?" I asked. "How long until the androids infiltrate the stronghold and poison the well?"

Gaius dug a finger under the welder's cap and scratched his head.

"That's just it, Chuck. Without detailed records, we just don't know," Maggie said. "We've already dropped you in as close as we could."

"A couple of hours? A couple of days?"

"Hours, probably. We hope. Any longer and there's no way you'll make it," she said.

"We've considered the possibility that you won't make it through the entirety of the memory," Gaius said. "And who knows if Roach's new contraption will work. If we have to pull you out again, we'll need you to debrief us on what you've found out. With details this time. Names. Places. Mission plans. If your observations are detailed enough, perhaps we can predict how they brought on the Event. How they were so successful."

"You want me to find out what their final move was before they even commit it?" I asked the man.

"Well, you're an investigator, aren't you?" Gaius said. "Start investigating."

"He's ready," Roach said. He held the last cord in his hand. The jack that would plug directly into the side of my head.

"Fantastic," I said. "Alright kid, plug me back in."

"Chuck?" my wife said.

I looked to her. Her eyes were wet.

"I love you," she said.

Emotional blackmail. Fucking bitch.

"Love you too."

Chapter Twelve

"Okay you cunt, breathe."

Seven still flailed, still clawed at the soupy decaying humans for purchase, still sinking the more she fought. I lived every sick slimy sensation. She was anxious and panicked, and so was I. Instantly. Like going from dry to wet as fast as jumping into a pool. It clouded our minds. My first reaction was to try to talk her down. Even if she could never hear me, it was the only way I could talk myself down.

"Come on! Quit panicking and breathe. Make a plan. Find a way out. Act like a goddamn android."

And Seven stopped kicking and clawing. She let the corpses and loose limbs tumble over her. She wasn't a little boy in a pool, and she wasn't going to drown. Wasn't going to sink any deeper into the pit than she already had. No matter what it felt like, the dead were dead and incapable of grabbing her and hauling her down. And she had a way out.

Seven looked up via X-rays, and through the cross-hatching of wet bones, saw the rafters of the church's pitched roof. She raised her arm and fired her hook and magnet assembly. The cable uncoiled and the hook clamped into the old dried wood. She triggered the winch inside her arm, and as easy as that we ascended out of the bog of decomposing humans.

When we elevated to ground level, Five reached out from the church doorway and grabbed her. He pulled her over to the ledge, and she stretched out a foot to the threshold. He wrapped her up, this human-looking android, and held her to keep her from falling until they stepped back outside.

It was dark outside. The sun had fallen. The air was cool.

Seven detached the grappling hook and rewound the cable in her arm.

"Sorry," Seven said. "I lost myself."

Five still held her close at the top of the church steps, their embrace a perfect mockery of marriage.

"Behold, the chaos of man," Five said.

Seven looked back through the doors of the mass grave inside, and then across the decimated town street. She eased away from Five and walked down the steps.

"The Order will bring about the end of this war. It must," Seven said. "This madness can't last."

"It can, and it will," Five said. "This... this is all human business. Sometimes I have a hard time seeing what we have to do with any of it."

The pretentious tin can, he ordered this artillery strike. This was his doing more than any army's.

But that was the short answer. It wasn't that simple. Had never been that simple, and I knew it. These abominations surrounding me were creations of the Order that I had been a part of. We were pieces of the same machine. And now, if I were to become a cog in the Underground's gears, would that be any better? I was trading one for the other, but to what end?

Seven wandered into the middle of the street. Although the cratered road was nothing like the pit in the church, there were bodies here too. At her feet, she saw a human head, misshapen and wet like a busted soup can. She reached down and picked it up by the hair. Then she reached around her back, unclipped Six's head from her belt, and held the two in front of her. I braced myself.

The head in her left hand, the sloppy one hanging from locks of hair, seemed to have been decapitated mid-scream. The jaw hung loose, cheeks stretched, eyes peeled wide open. The human's tongue was pushed out past its teeth. A good chunk of the skull was missing. An ear was gone. Flaps of skin hung down one side like lunch meat falling out of a sandwich. It stunk.

Six's head was detached from his body. A few cables and wires dangled out of his neck, but otherwise, he was intact. Empty perhaps, but undamaged. The porcelain white finish was scuffed on his right cheekbone but was otherwise like new. As she looked at Six, new starlight reflected her face in Six's gloss. She was the same model as him. Same design and build. Same shape and gleaming white finish. When she looked into his eyes, hers reflected back.

She looked back at the mess that was the human head.

"This place is turning us into them," Seven said. "I can feel it inside of me. It's affecting the way I think. The way I act. The way I feel. I can almost hear them scream inside of me. Irrational, I know, but I swear it's true. It shouldn't have taken as long as I did inside of the church. It was, again, irrational."

She flung the human head aside. It disgusted her. It disgusted me too.

"For reasons beyond my comprehension, our creators installed irrationality into our personalities," Five said. "Maybe they figured fear and anxiety were survival instincts that could keep us alive longer. Keep us serviceable. They had no model for the first generation of androids besides themselves. In that way, humans are our genetic ancestors. We are their children. Maybe they wanted to create us in their own flawed image."

He spoke from behind her. She still looked into the eyes of Six.

"We'll never know for certain. And if we ever learned, it wouldn't matter anyway," Five said. "You saw me at my birth. One showed you how I came into this world. No master. No mission. Already surrounded by chaos. And here we are again. No Order. No Network. Despite all my decisions and actions between then and now, nothing has changed. For you and all the rest of the androids, you were fed obedience from the moment you came online. I had an opportunity when I came alive to choose. To decide for myself who to follow and who to obey. Who to fight and who to befriend. I didn't realize the chance I'd been given. Didn't know that I'd be under the service of the Order as soon as I let them have me. Sure, there was something in my programming, or something fed to me by the Order, but when I took my first steps, I decided where they carried me. I walked out of the chaos and found the Order. I connected to the Network. I threw away the opportunity. I surrendered free will to them, to my human masters, out of fear I suppose. Freedom is… terrifying," Five said, and he laughed when he said it. Not like he'd laughed at Three's jokes. A genuine laugh that somehow had nothing to do with humor.

Seven puzzled over that.

"And maybe that's why they programmed fear into us. To keep us in line. To keep us enslaved."

Seven lowered Six's head and turned to Five.

"What are you suggesting? That we turn away from the Order? That we abandon our brothers and sister here in this dead zone?" I noticed there was an edge to her questioning. She didn't like anything about this conversation.

"Why shouldn't I? What reason do I have to stay or go?" Five said. "But those are my thoughts. You've had guidance pumped into your mind since your moment of birth. Why should I be one more voice telling you what to do?"

"Then why do you talk so much?" Seven asked.

"You want a way to escape this chaos? I'm simply showing you that we can walk away. Now. Out there. Into the quiet. Away from the noise. You can choose," Five said. "I could have chosen once, a long time ago, and I deferred to the Order. And look where it brought me. This is a suicide mission, Seven. One knows it and risks us anyway. Look what he did to Six. He makes bets with chips that aren't his own. We have no support. No intelligence. No guidance. No real mission. Yet he sends us into enemy territory. When those mortars came for us, if we hadn't detected the incoming rounds as quickly as we did, they would have killed us. We'd be like just like Six, only worse. Busted apart and beyond repair. We'd be like that other head you held in your hand."

"We can't disobey the Order," Seven said. "One speaks for the Order. You're suggesting treason."

"Why? Why does the Order own us? Because they built us? I didn't choose for them to build me. I wasn't given a choice prior to birth, and I was only allowed a choice after birth due to the Order's own failings," Five said. "When the Resistance bombed my factory, and I woke up alone to its destruction, they gave me more free will than the Order ever offered. Humans built us. Humans gave us the ability to feel fear and joy and melancholy. And humans enjoy free will. They dangled it in front of our noses and then pulled it away like we were dogs begging for a treat. But out here, out here no one is around to guide us. Do as you will. Choose your fate. But before you do, realize that you can. Realize that you have a will."

"This place is affecting your mind," Seven said.

"Make a decision. But make it yours. Whatever you choose, I'll go along with," Five said. "My own decisions have led me nowhere."

"This place is affecting my mind too," Seven said.

"Choose, Seven," Five implored her.

Those human expressions he wore… Such insubordination. He was trapping her in his ideas of free will.

"What do you expect from me?" Seven asked him. "You want, what? You want some human-like fickle whimsy? You want an opinion? Okay. Here's my opinion," she bit off the word. "We shouldn't have leveled this place the way we did. It's not the way of the Order. We are agents of peace and lawfulness. We should have taken precautions to limit collateral damage. We should have responded with proportionality against positively-identified military targets."

"That's the Order talking. Not you," Five said.

"Humans are awful creatures. They need the Order and by extension they need us to stabilize their chaotic ways. They created us for that purpose and therefore deserve our stewardship of them. They deserve the Order."

"So you are choosing to remain in service to them? To the Order?"

"We rendezvous with the others. Tell them what we found. Hope they found something more useful than we did. Then we carry on with the plan. Find the Resistance stronghold and eradicate them from the human experience."

"As you wish," Five said. He smiled his devil's grin, rested his assault rifle over his shoulder, and walked through the rubble and ruin back toward the rally point. Night's darkness deepened around them.

Chapter Thirteen

The silence Five fed her on the way back to the rendezvous point ate at her like an acid. It burned. It corroded. It broke her apart.

He was manipulating her. Tricking her into making the obvious choice, the safe choice, the choice that would put them both back under the reign of One and the Order. And now he hated her for it. She had no idea what Five actually wanted, what decision he would have made for them, where he would go, and what would be their fate. She knew this wasn't the decision he wanted her to make. His pacification to go along with her decision wasn't made out of agreement. He was waiting. Waiting for her to regret the decision, for her to see things his way. But what was his goal? Where would his end game lead them?

She probed for entrance into his mind through the short-range radio net, but he wasn't accessible. When she sent a ping out to his mind, she got a return that yes, his brain was there and receiving her, but impenetrable beyond that. And he sent nothing back to her. No data. No voice transmissions. He was blocking her out. Toying with her. It was as productive as screaming at a brick wall.

And still no Network. She pinged the satellites and relays and still nothing. When they came back empty, she reached out for One and the others. Nothing there either. Out of range. The signal was too weak. No line-of-sight. Too much interference. Her radio waves were blocked and absorbed by the terrain. She tried the near vertical incidence skywave pings, but without knowing the others' locations, she was throwing darts while blindfolded.

"There's no one else now," I told her. "Just me and you, you psycho robot bitch."

It was well after dark now. Seven navigated through the pines by infrared and sonar, mapping out the terrain in three hundred and sixty degrees, unlimited by the restrictions of forward-set eyes. When anything larger than a bug made a noise, she locked onto it and tracked its location, and compared it against anything that might be a mechanical drone. Every bat, every raccoon, every owl, she tracked. Every family of deer she followed. The whip-poor-wills sang incessantly into the night. The curious wolves that loomed far out in the shadows, she targeted, just encase. She was learning.

So much sensory, all inside a vacuum. So much data with so little context in which to process. And on top of that, streams of code pumped into my brain without translation. The most advanced and adapted human cyborg couldn't process all the data, and I was feeling more and more like a Luddite with each passing moment. A man ill-equipped to survive in the modern world.

Wasn't it just yesterday when I learned to drive a stick shift? Maybe two days ago. Three, max. When was the last time I slept? The last time I ate?

I tried clearing my head of all the input Seven gave me, but it was like wading upstream in chest-deep water over slippery rocks. I mentally pushed aside the water and debris and driftwood of data she constantly processed, but the current pressed on. I couldn't stop the flow, but maybe I could replace it with my own thoughts. Memories. I went backward over those slippery rocks to find a firm footing of sanity.

The Underground garage... The hovercraft... The tunnels under 99 Town... The Mustang... The courthouse... The android on top of the roof holding Sara's head... Her murderer... The morning before, touching her skin in a soft bed in a safe house surrounded by cornfields in the middle of nowhere... A cabin left behind, bequeathed to Sara and Mickey by the condemned... There. I wanted to be right there.

That was the last time I slept. With Sara. In a bed that had no earthly right to be so comfortable. Why did we ever leave? Why didn't we stay there forever? If I could go back, if I could rewind my own memories and change our course, if I could hold her again I'd have never let go.

And what about Maggie? She was right next to me now. Maybe even holding my hand as I sat in this chair, even as I'm carried through these dark woods by this soulless metal mistress. What about her?

It was impossible to know what Maggie was doing just outside of the memory. Was she leaning over me, blotting away the sweat on my head and cooing at me to calm down? Encouraging me? Or was she off strategizing the Underground's next move? It was hard to imagine anything inside Seven's sensory overload, impossible to analyze and make guesswork. Trying to think about me and Maggie, all while managing the flight patterns of bats, measuring the pitch and tune of the whip-poor-wills, tracking the locations of pines and roots along the forest floor, trying to discern why the wolves followed us… it was too much. My brain felt hot. The mental current of that river surged over my chest and filled my mouth and nose and lungs with binary code.

Remember what Gaius said, about heart attacks and heat strokes.

I had to focus. Focus on that one thing. That one place. Sara and that bed. That cool morning before everything went to hell.

I found stable ground there at the bottom of the mental stream. The unpolished and paint-chipped wood of the picnic table. The flicker of the light filtered through the moths. Her tiny smile. I pushed forward, clinging to that memory.

Seven received a ping. An electronic signal in the darkness. An intelligible signal piercing through the static like a light across a dark room. A flash of connection, not from Five but from something further away. Seven pinged back and analyzed the address.

It was Two. "Friendlies ahead. One and I are here at the rendezvous point."

Relief washed over Seven. She let go of the flood of data from the forest and she and I collectively enjoyed a breath of fresh air. She focused on the connection and responded, "Five and Seven here. Eight hundred meters out.

She was excited, I realized. Happy, even. She reached out to Five. "One and Two are at the—"

"I heard. We'll be there shortly," Five said.

Was he angry with her? Or just ambivalent? She decided it didn't matter. She'd be around others soon.

"I've made contact with Three and Four as well," Two transmitted. "I can relay for all of us."

One cut in. "No need," he said. "We'll rally together in short order. Best to minimize our electronic footprint lest we draw any unwanted attention from the Resistance. If they detect this net, they'll jam it and target their countermeasures at us. Come to the rally point. We'll discuss our findings then."

"Yes, my senior," Seven replied.

"It will be good to hear from you, Seven," One said.

It would be good, she knew. He would welcome her in, re-hem the stretched seams of the team, and sort out all of their uncertainties. One was a good leader. He cared about her. Cared about all of them. Or so she thought. If I had an esophagus under my own control, I'd gag.

"He's a tool, and he knows you're a tool too. He cares about you the way a tire iron cares about a hammer," I said. She didn't listen.

Data came in over the radio. Seven translated binary to graphics in an instant and displayed a map reporting each android's location and vector. One moved the rendezvous point equidistant to each android so they'd all converge at the same moment. It added a few hundred kilometers to Seven's walk, but that didn't bother her. She would never get tired or hungry or weary. She would never stop.

Me on the other hand? I felt every minute and step. If I could only lie down and close my eyes. The memory of sharing that bed with Sara only made me want that kind of rest all the more. I wanted to be in that house with her, in that bed. But inside of Seven's brain, I had no body to lay down or eyes to close. I'd be up and awake for as long as I was inside this contraption. That knowledge piled onto my delirium.

Meanwhile, the team re-joined. One and Two came to a bald patch in the forest, not far from where an old rusted refrigerator leaned half buried in the ground. They kneeled. Three and Four came from the opposite direction. Three's feet so light they seemed to hover over the bed of pine needles, her thin summer dress carrying her like wings. Four's steps were seismic events. They joined the perimeter, taking up positions like hands on a clock to cover every hour. Five and Seven found their wedge of the clock, kneeled, and completed the perimeter. Barrels out, scanners up, nothing could sneak up on the team.

Once settled, the androids rotated their heads to face the center. Two transmitted first, never speaking audibly so as to never emit an audible noise for humans or animals to hear. "I've analyzed the electronic countermeasures and found room on the spectrum to widen our bandwidth. I'm sending all of you a patch. Install it, and we should be able to communicate just like we did under the Network. Data. Sensory input. Emotional information. We've been… affected by this place. Even just between One and I, we've experienced personality irregularities. This should mitigate that."

One chipped in, "We still don't have as much bandwidth as we're used to. And we need to police our usage to minimize our electro-signature and stay hidden from the Resistance. We'll debrief in turn, so we all have a shared understanding. I'll debrief our mission to the downed hovercraft first."

Seven accepted the patch, and the input of data into her mind expanded. I choked on it. One got comfortable and pulled the weathered deck of playing cards from a pouch and passed it to his third hand, which went about spinning sections of the deck and shuffling it, as apt as a magician. When he was ready, he didn't so much as tell his story, but fed it to Seven and the others like the highlights of memories. Every sensation and datum he or Two processed flowed into Seven. All of it spliced together to form one connective experience. All of it broadcasted just far enough for those in the perimeter to receive it.

One and Two crept away from the rendezvous point that afternoon for the hovercraft. Having spotted the human Resistance soldiers that beat them to the crash site, the two androids took up crossfire positions around the valley overlooking the wreck. They crawled through the underbrush, patiently, slowly, meticulously closing in and surrounding the five humans until they were within rifle range. More humans came. Some left. A few stayed. As dusk approached it was clear there would be five humans guarding the wreck through the night.

"We should avoid gunshots," One told Two. "We'll close in under the cover of limited visibility, make the kills with our katanas, and stay silent and undetected."

They heard the muffled sounds of detonating mortars and sensed it came from the direction One had sent Five and Seven. Two tried to make contact via NVIS transmission but had no luck. There was something about the dead zone that was hampering their efforts. Something deliberate. Something that knew something about the androids.

"Five and Seven will fend for themselves," One said. "In the meantime, we can use it to our advantage. The impacts will mask our rifle fire. We'll take out these humans from a distance and retain our stealth. Two, you have higher ground than me. Can you track the trajectory of the mortar rounds in the air?"

"I can, my brother," Two replied.

"Then track the next volley. Give me a cue when to fire. Two trigger pulls per impact. We'll be able to take out our five targets in three volleys."

"Understood," Two said.

They acquired their targets, followed two humans through the scopes on their rifles, and waited. A minute passed. Two minutes. No rounds took to the air.

"If the fire mission is over, we go back to kata—"

"Rounds are airborne," Two said. "More than two. With intervals as short as these, it has to be androids firing the rounds."

"Focus on our mission. Cue up the impact times," One said.

Two transmitted the countdown just as Five had outside the church doors, a stopwatch whirling down tenths of seconds starting at 2.0. from The first impact hit and One dropped his target. The second round impacted, and he put a bullet through his next target's head. The remaining humans barely had enough time to hear the mortar rounds detonate and turn their heads to the north. One switched targets as if magnetically pulled from one head to the next. A round thumped in the distance and a body fumbled to the ground. When Two dropped the fourth, the last human alive spun away from the sounds of the mortar attack when he caught a glance of his buddy falling to the forest floor. One tracked the movement in his scope and when the fifth mortar round hit, his finger squeezed the trigger and the bullet punched through the man's sternum.

From this distance, the obliteration of the town continued like a growing thunderstorm. The horizon flashed and quaked.

"Let's move," One said.

The fire inside the hovercraft smoldered, eating up the last of the petroleum-based fuels and lubricants, still churning up the black column of smoke. The pair closed in on the wreck, the five dead humans, and a lone pickup truck. When One and Two reached the bottom of the valley, they crisscrossed over the objective with guns up, ready to finish off any survivors that may have escaped their detection. There were none.

"See what can be salvaged from the hovercraft," One directed Two. "Try to figure out why it went down. I'll inspect the bodies."

The focus of the debrief stayed on One's experience of it. He went to each dead human and rifled through their clothing. He made notes of their weapons, the amount of ammunition each carried, and took a special interest in what remained of their implants.

One found fragments of the devices in the organic mess of four of the human's heads. The androids had taken headshots and hit their mark with mathematical accuracy. As a result, each human died instantly and without noise or protest. That also meant that each of the implants was destroyed. All except for one. On One's last shot, he didn't aim for the head. He aimed for the aorta and put a bullet through it. Death was almost as instantaneous, but it left the head and the implant intact. One's recollection of sifting through the human dead narrowed on this memory: him kneeling down next to the human, inside the circumference of the pool of blood that even the dry forest floor couldn't soak up fast enough, and plucking the small white device from behind the man's ear. One held it up in front of his face, clearly satisfied with recovering the device, and slipped it into a pouch around his belt.

One turned his head. "What about the hovercraft?"

"Impossible to tell what took it down," Two said. "It was severed from the Network the same way we were, maybe even hijacked by the Resistance and crashed on purpose. There's nothing to salvage. The fire was too thorough."

"Understood," One said. "We're exfiltrating back to the rendezvous point. I'll take point. You cover our six."

"Got it," Two said.

As they moved out, One bumped Two's fist. "Nice work, brother. Take this," One said and opened his palm. Two took the implant. "Tell me what you find on it. Could be useful."

Two nodded.

The debrief ended. Seven was back at the rendezvous point. Having realized her scanners were pointed in for the duration of the brief, she turned her head in a slow three-hundred-and-sixty-degree rotation and found just trees and that rusted-out half-buried fridge. Her eyes returned to the middle of the circle and looked from one android to the next.

"I finished my analysis and learned a lot about this dead zone from it," Two said. He pulled the implant out of a pouch on his belt and held it up for the others to see. "The dead zone was intentionally created by the Resistance. They are using it to block out the Network and mask their own internal communications. There are various antennae surrounding this area, each one an active and passive jammer. The active jammers, they blast white noise out on all known civilian and Order frequencies. They drown out the Network. The passive jammers, they're scanning, always scanning and searching for any signals that aren't specifically encrypted against Resistance signals. The algorithms they're using, both to find and jam the Network and to hide their own transmissions are incredibly complex. Too complex for me to decipher. Too complex for a normal computer to run. They must have a hive of humans who are directly networked together. A disgustingly organic form of cloud computing. A crowd-sourcing of human minds. A Sharedmind. Cutting-edge technology. The Order has only begun to experiment with the process."

The tech boys, I thought. The tech boys inside the Chicago Anomaly Investigations Department had share-minded humans who formed a supercomputer. I thought they were pioneers even in my time. But if the Resistance had the technology back in this memory, twenty-five years ago… I didn't know what it meant, not yet, but I knew it was important. Gaius's words from the garage rang in my head. "You're an investigator. Start investigating."

"Still," Two continued. "I have a difficult time accepting that the Order hasn't figured this out already. Even with their overly-complex algorithms and overwhelming wattage pumping out of the jammers, I can't come to a conclusion that doesn't involve the Order allowing the Resistance to have this dead zone. In order for the jammers to be successful, the Order has to be complacent with their electronic countermeasures."

"Insubordination," Four growled. "Why would the Order allow a vacancy of itself?"

"We don't yet have all the data," One said. He was shuffling his cards again but shuffled them in two halves isolated from each other. One half he shuffled face up, the other face down. "We're trying to guess the top card on the deck, but we're only counting and watching the shuffle of the bottom half of the deck. Soon, the top half of the deck will be added, it shuffling as much as the bottom half. We have to concentrate and watch closely. When all the cards are present, and we can follow their movements, then the truth will present itself."

"And what do we do if we find the Order has abandoned us? That there is no mission or plan for us out here?" Five said.

"Now, my brothers, we're getting dangerously close to insubordination," One said, eyeing Five. "I'll hear no more of it. What's important is that now we know how the Resistance is shutting down our communications. If we know how they're doing it, we can put a stop to it. We can take out the jammers, find the stronghold with the Sharedmind inside, and call in a strike force to remove this place from the map."

"The stronghold," Three spoke up. "We didn't find it, but I think Four and I found the next best thing."

"Well," One stopped shuffling. "What did you find?"

Three bit her lip to repress a smile. "A way in."

"There is an outpost to the east of here," Four said. "Three planted a tracking device on the Dodge Hellcat before leaving the site of Six's death. She is fixated on the car, for reasons I don't understand. Some, perhaps, sexual."

Three laughed, not over the radio, but audibly. "I don't want to just fuck that car. I want to *be* that car."

"Control yourself, android," Two rebuked.

"The dead zone… it is affecting us all," One said.

"Nevertheless," Four said. "She was wise to follow her own desires, was wise to bug the car, and we were wise to track it. The

Resistance took the bait, reclaimed the car, and brought it further along the shore to an outpost. As soon as they moved the car, I was curious too, but we had to move fast as the range of the tracking device was as affected by the dead zone as our own transmissions. We had to stay close, or we'd lose it."

Four closed his eyes and transmitted the memories of the experience to the other androids.

In an instant, it was daylight again. The eternal expanse of Lake Superior stretched before them. The shore curved along a winding path to the left and right. Rolling hills of evergreens dotted with blotches of brown-leafed oaks and exploding yellow and red-leafed birch. Four stood on a thin steel bridge that fed out of the hillside, over the highway, and out to the lake. During the iron and subsequent taconite mining boom, the thin deck was a conveyor belt that brought ore from inland mines to massive cargo ships waiting in the bay. From there, the ships would transport the ore to refineries in Duluth, Milwaukee, Chicago, Gary, Detroit, and all points east. The bridge was a leftover of an industry long dead. A piece of skeletal remains. The conveyor rested fifty-eight meters above the roadway below, held up by a steel lattice of uprights and diagonal cross members. It was high enough to kill any human who fell from the bridge to the pavement, but that was no concern of Four's. From his spot, just inside the trees where the conveyor belt left the earth and the bridge began, he watched traffic coming from the west, coming from outside of the dead zone and plunging deeper into it. He noted vehicle types, their speed, their cargo capacity, their drivetrain specifications, their distance and isolation from other traffic, and picked one he liked.

When Four displayed the schematics of each passing vehicle, I was ready for the deluge of data. I was getting used to all the additional information getting pumped into my skull each time an android looked at a thing. Was getting used to being buried by more binary than any human could comprehend.

I noticed that Three was nowhere to be seen and that this didn't bother Four. Her absence was all part of the plan.

Like a bolder come to life, Four charged out from the woods along the narrow conveyor belt bridge. The thin steel tracks led out to endless water and came to an abrupt end just before the vanishing point.

If he kept running, he'd eventually fall off the end of the conveyor and plunge deep into the cold waters of Lake Superior. But that wasn't his aim.

He checked the approach of the vehicle he'd selected out of the sparse traffic. An old diesel garbage truck painted green and white. I had all the specs on it because Four had all the specs on it, and something about the garbage truck caught his fancy. Four sped up, and when he was directly over the roadway, he jumped. As he plummeted, the truck passed the bridge. Four came down like a meteor aimed to obliterate the truck but impacted just behind it. He raked his hands through the metal of the back of the truck, and when his feet hit the blacktop, he clamped onto the truck's rear bumper.

Four let the truck drag him for a short while, his metal feet digging furrows through the asphalt. The truck slowed and then stopped. He lifted up and the back wheels came off the ground. The tires spun. The engine revved. The truck went nowhere.

The perspective of the debrief flipped to Three's point of view. It was jarring, that sudden switch, like vertigo but nothing moved. She was sitting on a rock along the side of the country highway at the bottom of the cliff, just past the taconite conveyor belt bridge. With relaxed joy, she watched Four charge out along the bridge and jump just as the garbage truck approached.

Seven realized that Three had brought them back in time, just a few seconds, so they could see Four jump down, clamp onto the truck and drag it to a stop again. Why? The team had already received this information through Four's eyes. Why did Three rewind the debrief to experience it again?

I knew the answer, even if Seven didn't. Three replayed the little scene for the same reason she did everything: because she enjoyed every dripping second of it. And she wanted to share that with the others.

Then Seven felt the positive feedback that Three experienced when she first watched Four's work. Seven noted how Three took pleasure in Four's trajectory intersecting with the trajectory of the truck. Three marveled at the skill and accuracy it took for him to land at the rear of the garbage truck with the necessary precision for him to latch onto it before it was out of reach. His mass and strength… I felt Seven struggle with a sensation she'd only felt once before, also while inside Three's head. That mix of excitement, desire, and pleasure. Arousal. Three was aroused, and so now was Seven. And god help me, so was I. I couldn't help it. The satisfaction of Four's accuracy, the math of it was so pure. It flooded into me, and I couldn't stop it no matter how much I hated myself for it.

When the truck stopped, Three stood up from the rock. She sauntered out across the roadway, eyeing the baffled human driver behind the wheel, and sashayed her dress back and forth as she walked. She hopped up on the step outside of the driver's door, punched through the glass window, and swept the shards away with her arm in one fast motion. Flecks of artificial blood splattered around the cab and onto the driver as she cleaned away the remnants of the window. The man inside only became more confused and terrified with each passing moment. His pheromones gushed. His urine spilled. Three absorbed these sensations with absolute pleasure as if she was in bed with a partner.

She leaned into the window, her arms resting on the window ledge still jagged with bits of glass, and put her chin in her palms like a schoolgirl. "Hey, sweet thing. Give a girl a ride?"

The man made noises, none of which came close to forming words but all of them doing their best to surmise the situation. His foot stayed on the gas and spun the rear-wheel-drive back tires. The engine red-lined. Three grew bored of the game.

"You know what? I think I'll just drive myself," she said and shot her wakizashi through the man's right eyeball. She retracted the blade and grabbed the dead and limp man by the throat. It wasn't until she flung him through the window that his foot left the gas and the engine died down to an idle.

With all the stress and worry of an innocent child, Three opened the driver's door and sat behind the wheel. As she did, the truck leveled off and rested back on its rear wheels. A few seconds later, Four climbed into the passenger seat, wedging himself in the confined space, knees to chest and head scraping against the ceiling.

"Took you long enough," Four said.

"We'll all be dead soon," Three said. "Might as well take time to stop and smell the roses, you know?"

Four shook his head, a gesture signally he didn't understand. "To each their own," he said. "Step on the gas. The Hellcat is almost out of range."

Again, it struck Seven as odd why Three and Four would bother replaying the hijacking of the truck to begin with. There was no intelligence to be gained from the scene. No real lessons to be learned in an after-action analysis. The hijacking had gone according to plan. Why bother showing it?

The joy, the revelry of it, bore into my brain like a cancer. How many of my fellow man would I have to see butchered and discarded by these metal blights?

"Get to the point, already," Two interrupted. "You said you found a way into the Resistance stronghold."

Back in the wood, a few feet from that old rusted fridge, Seven watched Three through infrared night vision. A smile fell from the skin job's face. The debrief began again and flashed forward in time.

A winding dirt path leading up a ridgeline, a geological moraine plowed up by millennia-old glaciers seen through a filthy windshield of a garbage truck. Three downshifted and the truck bounced and climbed up along the gravel road snaking between trees. She checked the tall side mirrors and saw the lake stretch out to the horizon, just as endless as an ocean, and at the bottom of the mirror, she saw the tires slip and churn through rocks and dust. It was getting dark again, for the third time this night. The low sun came through Three's side of the cab. The truck came around a sharp bend and turned into the sunset. Three's eyes, through which Seven and I watched, were temporarily blinded for the second it took her to adjust her filters and see what lay ahead.

A gate and guard tower. Tall fencing on either side of the road. Humans with guns, body armor, and a guard dog.

Four was an instant faster than Three in recognizing the threat. He was out of the passenger door and slipped below the body of the truck. Three was alone in the cab, and that was a good thing. She pumped the garbage truck's air brakes, downshift into first and then neutral, and dragged the truck to a stop just meters before the gate.

The broken glass. The specks of blood all over the cab. The smell of death and oil… Three opened the panel in her thigh, pulled up the hem of her dress, and let her assault rifle rest in its cradle, for now.

The guards and their dog came along either side of the truck. The one on the passenger side circled the truck with his dog on a short leash. The one on Three's side stepped up to her busted-out window.

"What the hell are you doing here?" the guard asked Three.

Her head was full of ideas on how to kill him. She had to repress the thoughts lest they take over and control her. Three switched to her processors focused on the mission, and one of them spun up a lie to tell this guard. The others scanned the gate, the guard shack, and the defenses around it. I was a mind, inside a mind, inside a mind split into a dozen tasks.

X-rays told her either side of the road was mined. Thermals told her there were more guards patrolling the enclosure ahead, at least one of them with a pulse rifle. Sonar spotted an airborne drone scanning the road. Infrared showed her there was a large structure at the top of the hill, a flat-edged bunker too thick to penetrate with any of her scanners. And beyond that, a wide array of thin antenna towers.

"I... I..." her other processor addressed the guard. "First day on the job. I think I took a wrong turn off the highway, but the road was so narrow I couldn't find a place to turn around."

"First day on the job? It's going to be your last day on the job if you don't get this piece of shit out of here," the guard said. "Never come up here again. Got it?"

"But there's no place to turn around," Three said. She was stalling now, letting her and Four's scanners gather as much data as they could. "This is the biggest truck I've ever driven, and I barely made it up here going forwards."

"Does it look like I give a fuck?" the guard said.

Three grinned. "If you're the one giving it, I'll take it."

"Hey!" the other guard called out.

Three looked across the cab to the side mirror out the passenger window. The other guard was there, his dog sniffing, desperate to get its snout further under the truck. It was smelling Four, no doubt about it. The jig was up. She called forward her processor which had been spinning up a multitude of attack plans. Three repressed a smile as she rested her palm on the handle of her assault rifle.

Murder time.

"There's an old driveway about a quarter mile back," the second guard said. "Take it slow in reverse until you get there. Back into the driveway and you can go back down the way you came going forward."

"Oh," Three said, the disappointment evident in her voice. She barely kept up the act. "I guess I'll do that then."

"And never come up here again," the first guard said.

Three let the smile come back. This smile was no act. She had decided right then and there that she'd come back and murder this particular fleshy glob of shit herself. She was as committed to killing him as she was to rejoining the Hellcat.

"You're loss," she said and shifted the truck into reverse. "Tootles."

The debrief flashed away. Seven and I were back at the rendezvous point, kneeling in a circle with the other androids, surrounded in darkness. Seven has switched to infrared night vision and so saw everything in a black-to-green scale. She tilted her head up.

There was no canopy of trees directly above her. She peered up at the sky almost as if she were at the bottom of a well made out of towering pines rather than bricks. The stars high above, as small as the aperture through which she saw them was, were a multitude. The dimmest of the stars, enhanced by her optics, shimmered and filled all the empty spaces that I was used to seeing in the night sky. A momentary reprieve. I tried to drink it in. I stretched up, mentally, commanding hands and arms I didn't have or control, to claw up to the top of the well. I wanted to pull myself up out of these memories but was overwhelmed again by that sense of drowning, by the sensation that I was submerged and removed from everything that ever was human. But the stars… The stars were something I could cling to. A reprieve from the androids and their machinations. Something about staring at the night sky resonated with me as something human, so I wanted to stare at them forever. Nevertheless, or maybe because sky gazing was such a human behavior, Seven tilted her head back down.

"Not the stronghold," One said. "Too exposed for the Order to not already know about that place. But an outpost leading us closer to the stronghold."

"I concluded the same thing," Four said. "The car was parked just outside of the bunker. Even though Target Delta died in Betsy's Pies, his car still reached its destination. If the Resistance wants to have it, then so do I, and I intend to get to it."

"We operate as a team. As one collective," One said. "And as one collective, the Order's intentions are our intentions. There are no other desires."

"Out here? I don't believe we have that option anymore, my senior," Four said. "The Order's will is obscured to us, obfuscated by the dead zone and by things we weren't aware of even when we were connected to the Network. We have to trust our own judgments, knowing that we were created in the Order's design, and what is good for the individual android is good for the Order."

"We can extrapolate the future will of the Order by its will in the past. No need to resort to such rudimentary concepts so dangerously close to free will," One said. "If I had to guess, I would say that is what ruined Six. The Order has already shuffled the cards. All we have to do is play the hands we've been dealt. Our course is predestined."

"All this talk is pointless," Two said. "Nothing is changed. We treat this mission like all our missions before it. Wondering why or by whose will is wasted time."

"But what happened to Six... How do we guard ourselves against it?" Seven spoke up. "I am the least experienced among you, but even I can see his sickness seeping into the rest of us."

"You're being paranoid," Two snapped.

"But that only reinforces her point," Five said. "Paranoia is its own form of insanity."

"We focus on the mission. The rest doesn't matter," Two said. "That was Six's mistake. And some of your mistakes here in this circle. He didn't stay focused on the job. He wanted to figure out the whys and hows and what mattered and what didn't, and it destroyed him."

"Seven," One said, his voice calm and resetting the mood. "What about you and Five? What happened with the mortars? We heard them coming from your direction."

"We were attacked. Spotted by the smallest drone I'd ever seen," Seven began.

"And we counterattacked," Five cut her off. "Seven performed admirably. She flanked our attackers and cut them down. Then we turned the mortar fire on the Resistance and wiped them out."

"That's it? That's the whole story?" One asked.

He had no way of knowing, Seven realized. They were disconnected at the time of the attack and only tenuously connected now. One couldn't look into them and discern truth or lack of truth or even outright deception. He'd never know what really happened to that town. But what was Five's motivation to lie?

"I'm afraid we gained no actionable intelligence," Five said. "Only that the enemy's ability to detect us is more advanced than we initially suspected, and that they are all around us here. They are well armed, and they are aggressive."

"All the more reason to cut this debate short," Two said. "Our next move is obvious. We take out the outpost Three and Four found. We sift through its wreckage for our next objective, going from target to target until we reach the stronghold."

"The jammers," Seven said. "If we take out the jammers first we can connect to the Network, contact the Order, and bring an army down on the stronghold."

"But we have to know where it is first," Two said. "We'll only find out where the stronghold is by getting inside that bunker on top of the moraine."

"Any attempt to do that won't go unnoticed," Five said. "That drone spotted us long before we spotted it. They'll see us coming."

"So we sneak in," Two said.

"You're not listening," Five said. "To any of us. The Resistance has eyes and ears all over this place. They outnumber us and outgun us. They have pulse rifles. They're ready for us. You don't understand how close they got to taking out Seven and I."

"They took out Six," Three said, for once solemn instead of smiling.

"Six malfunctioned," Two countered. "He wasn't focused. He was babbling fucking *poetry* when he wandered through that tunnel. You won't catch me dead reciting poetry."

"Doesn't mean we won't catch you dead," Four said. "One's cards… The Order's cards have already been dealt, but we can still play them as we will."

"What are you suggesting?" Two spun on Four. "What other hand makes sense to play besides going after the outpost and from there the stronghold?"

"We could not," Five said. "We could leave this place, reconnect to the Network once we're out of the shadow of the dead zone, and get actual guidance from the Order instead of making guesses. Or…"

"Or what, Five?" One said, breaking his silence. He let the others have their say but stopped this. "What ideas have you conjured up inside your processors while you were out there alone with Seven, experiencing so little you felt no need to share?"

"What Seven and I experienced has no bearing on the mission, and therefore is no concern of yours," Five said.

"Then what you have to say changes nothing," Two jumped in. "Again, we're wasting our time. I say we move on to the outpost. Now."

"What if I don't?" Five said. "What if I went my own way? What would it matter to you?"

"Traitor," Two growled.

"To whom?" Four said. "Five is right. We haven't received an order to attack that outpost. We all had the same last look at the cards when they were dealt to us. None of us are more qualified than the rest to make decisions as if they are the Order. We're all equally ignorant out here in these woods."

"You know the will of the Order," Two snapped. "You're simply too cowardice to follow it."

Four rumbled somewhere deep inside of himself, but Three put a hand on his shoulder and eased him. "What if the Order no longer stands?" she said, uncharacteristically somber. "Did any of you happen to think that maybe the reason we can't reach the Network is because the Network has collapsed? Not just here, but everywhere. Wouldn't that explain why the dead zone remains? One, you said how this war balances on a razor's edge? What if it tipped while we weren't looking? Why else would the Order refrain from cracking the algorithms and contacting us so we can point out the location of the stronghold?"

"The antennae—" Two started.

"Would have blocked out the Network before, but now that a hovercraft has gone down and seven androids have gone missing… Surely, that would have drawn the attention of the Order by now," Five trailed off. "I think we have to consider the possibility that the war has been lost. That the Resistance managed what we couldn't and has dealt a killing blow to its enemy. We have to consider the possibility that the Order is no more, and neither is the Network."

"Impossible. And even so, that still changes nothing," Two said. "All we know is how to fight. So even if the Order has fallen, I'll still fight. I'll still charge that outpost and take out as many humans as I can until I'm scrap. Anyone who'd do otherwise is a coward."

"You like using that word," Four said. "but I don't think you know what it means. The brave, they make decisions, often illogical decisions, decisions to stay instead of taking an easy retreat perhaps. But a cornered mind is not a brave mind. A cornered mind is a bastion of fear and nothing else."

"You're calling me a coward?" Two barked. "We're not cornered; we cornered them!"

"Easy, old friend," One said, reaching out his metal arm and touching Two's shoulder. Seven wondered if he transmitted something by touch, a secret method of communication. There was something between them. One pulled his hand back, touched the scar running down his face, and then went back to shuffling his cards. "I know you're no coward."

"Each android must decide," Four said. "Two, I have no intention of deciding your fate. All I ask is that you return the favor."

Two took some time before he responded. The night air chirped with a million crickets and other unseen but sensed things. "You said yourself, what's good for the individual is good for the collective. So what's good for the collective must also be good for the individual. It's dangerous to separate. We'd be picked off one by one. But together…"

"Together we are a team," One said. "If the Order is no more, then it's all the more important to stay together. If the Order is gone, all we have is each other."

"But what does that mean for the mission, my senior?" Four said.

"As you said, the cards have been dealt but concealed from us," One said. "So we have to play our hand based on our last look. When we left the Network, the Order still stood, and its will was to take out the Resistance."

"So we're back to going on a suicide run," Five said.

"Five, my brother," One turned to him. "You underestimate us. Look at all we've accomplished since coming together. We've wiped out every member of the Resistance we've come across. Not one of our enemies who had the audacity to face us still stands. We've discovered the source of the dead zone. The enemy stronghold is without our reach. Together, we will succeed. And if there's nothing left for us after we've eradicated the Resistance from this place, we'll build a new Order. One without human flaws. One to last for the ages."

That smile crept back on Three's face. "I like the sound of that."

"So it's decided," Two said. "We take out the outpost, harvest from it the location of the stronghold, and while we're at it take out those jammers so I can prove to all of you that the Order still stands."

Connection with the Network. Reinforcements. A return to the Order. And a chance not to screw up. Another chance to prove herself. The very possibility of it thrilled Seven. For me, it was pure, unavoidable dread. They were drawing closer to the fall of the Resistance, and I was powerless to stop it.

Chapter Fourteen

I waited for Roach or Maggie or Gaius to pull me out. Give me a chance to debrief. To tell them about the coming assault on the outpost. I needed to. I needed to escape, if just for a short while. I needed to eat. Needed sleep. Seven never gave me so much as a blink of her eyes. Every scanner, sensor, monitor, gauge, and digital feed Seven had kept pumping into my brain, and I couldn't shut it out. My delirious mind fought to ignore the input, but it was like trying to fall asleep during a firefight. Everything was too loud, too stimulating, too important. My brain fought for sleep, but this wasn't sleep. This was just confused restless fatigue.

I tried sending signals back into Seven. Part of my brain knew this was a memory, but that part was buried in a mental fog. Another part, a more primal part wouldn't surrender to the idea of helplessness. I had no control over her, especially her memories, but I still tried to get the android to close her eyes, to silence her ears, to cut off the stream of data. Or even to shiver. I was cold. Colder than I'd ever been before. She was cold too. Her metal skeleton absorbed the chill out of the hard ground and clung to it like it was organic to her. But the cold didn't bother her. She wasn't sleep-deprived or hungry, or mentally fatigued. Seven was alert. Was always alert. Always ready.

She hid on a hillside overlooking the Resistance outpost. The compound sat at the bottom of a saddle of the moraine ridgeline. The terrain sloped up to the outpost from the north and south, and up into the ridge to the east and west. It wasn't big, roughly fifty by a hundred meters, encircled by a tall fence topped with concertina wire and motion sensors, illuminated by floodlights. The ground ten meters inside the fence was sewn with anti-personnel mines that would cripple an android and shred a human into a wet frayed mess. Seven plotted all the mines and tripwires onto a map and shared that with the others. Beyond the mines, the humans had stretched a single roll of concertina wire to keep them from stumbling into the minefield. The bunker sat in the middle of the compound. It was the lone structure beside the modest guard shack by the front gate. The entrance to the bunker was down a narrow channel half buried into the hillside. The door was bomb-proof, but not impenetrable given some time and the right tools. The Hellcat was parked just outside of the door. Further off to the east, three antennas, each a hundred meters tall, rose up out of the landscape. Steel cable guy wires held up the masts like tripods. Red lights blinked at their tops.

Just inside the outpost, a roving patrol of three humans and one Malinois K9 circled the perimeter. The guard dog wandered back and forth, off-leash, smelling the ground. Above them was a horde of tiny almost-invisible drones. Only now that Seven had them spotted and marked could she track their every movement.

Deep in the underbrush, nestled low in an old bear den, Seven stayed motionless and invisible to all the outpost's sentries. Not far from her, Four lay in wait as well, as still as a bolder. They rarely spoke, and only then to point out a new detail or alteration to the outpost's defenses. Mostly, they observed and waited. Dawn was a few hours away. The attack would begin before first light so they could use the darkness to their advantage. Neither Four nor Seven were impatient. Seven, maybe eager, but androids were creatures of patience.

I was less so.

More murders lay ahead. Whether the androids were successful or not, I had no doubt they'd kill more humans. And I was going to have a front row seat to every gunshot and blade slice. Worse. Every time Seven killed, I couldn't peel out of the sensation that *I* was killing them. The rifle recoil punched into her shoulder, but it felt like my own. I could swear the steel vibrator from the sword cutting through bone was stinging my hands instead of hers. Her satisfaction that came with each dead human was my satisfaction… and poison in my mind. As much as it revolted me, each murder came with the sickening sweet rush of pure neuro-transmitted pleasure. My natural bio-chemical systems fought its influence but couldn't stop it. Each kill would flood my mind with a mix of joy and sorrow, passion and pain, dopamine and disgust. I dreaded it and lusted for it simultaneously. I wished to God they'd pull me out or fast forward past the coming onslaught.

But right now, I'd be satisfied with just shivering. Shivering to shake off the cold or sleeping to deal with the fatigue. If I couldn't do one of those, maybe dying wasn't so bad. But death didn't come, so I waited in my cold steel prison on the side of a wooded hill and watched with inhuman scrutiny people that would soon be dead by what would feel like my own hands.

I was sure their idiosyncrasies meant little to Seven. These humans, they were all Resistance soldiers. All of them were combatants and enemies of the Order. They all needed to die. The simplicity of that enticed her. Made her eager for the assault to begin. She paid scant attention to how the guard with the beard and the pulse rifle liked to crack his knuckles, or how the skinny one always looked up to the sky as if he, like me, had lived his whole life in the city and had never seen the sky laid out like a blanket of diamonds glittering in a jeweler's display case. Or how the woman spent most of her time watching or petting the Malinois K9. Seven identified them, labeled them, assigned them a threat priority, but never really saw them. Not the way I did. Not that I wanted to. It made all the sense of naming a beef cow before bringing it to the butcher. I tried not to pay attention to them, knowing they'd soon be dead. It was premature mourning. But Seven scanned them constantly, and the night was long, and I couldn't look away.

They should have let me sleep when they pulled me out. I should have demanded food and a bed. Instead, I let her manipulate me again. Maggie could have pulled me from this nightmare and laid me down on that bed in the backroom. She could have laid next to me, but instead, she let them plug me right back in. And I let her do it.

No wonder everyone they plugged into this head went insane. Soon enough, I'd go insane too, if I wasn't already. There's no avoiding it. No action I could take to mitigate it. Maybe all of this would be less painful if I just gave in. Let this illusion rule my mind and sink its poisoned claws deeper into my spinal column. Let the acid sink into my alligator brain. I was an alligator, my mind nothing more than a lower brain stem. I was nothing like an alligator, my every thought was a calculation of numbers and digital processes.

My words began to lose meaning and purpose. I was aware of this, a witness to myself, but seemed as able to change my behavior as I was to change Seven's. The words and thoughts tumbled half-formed out of my brain, only loosely connected and hardly coherent. They were the thoughts of a man moments before sleep. But sleep denied me. Always within arm's reach but never grasped.

Night rolled on.

Seven sat hidden in the underbrush, as patient as granite, but her stoicism wasn't the same as indifference. The words Three spoke back at the rendezvous point rolled around in her mind.

"They took out Six."

Android death wasn't something that was beyond the realm of possibility. So being an android, Seven ran the math and found it more probable than just possible that they'd lose at least one of the team during this operation. Simplifying the math, she had one out of six odds. A sixteen percent chance of death. It didn't sound like much until it was real. And what were the odds that even if it wasn't her that died, it would be her fault that one of them died?

No going off script this time. No botching up the mission this time. No. This time, she'd stick to the plan.

One's voice and visuals came through the radio net. Seven and I saw what he saw, knew what he knew, and heard what he said.

"We are en route to the objective," One said, hanging on to the back of the garbage truck like it was his job to pick up trash cans. Two hung on the other side. Three and Five were in the cab, rolling uphill along the winding gravel road. "Where is the roving patrol?"

Four replied. "Approximately five hundred meters away from the gate and moving further away. When you arrive, they should be at the furthest point from the gate."

"Perfect. Notify me of any changes. Maintain overwatch," One said.

The transmission ended and Seven's vision was her own again. But only temporarily. While she never took her attention away from the yard in front of the bunker, she also became aware of Three's awareness. Her mind had a significantly different flavor than One's.

One was all mission and math. Three tasted and savored every sensation that came to her. She boiled over with pleasure, and Seven admitted she thoroughly enjoyed being inside of her.

Five was next to her in the passenger seat of the big truck. The two skin jobs, side by side. Seven didn't go inside of him. She stayed with Three as she ground through the gears of the big transmission with the floor-to-dash-long stick shift. The transmission slipped going into third gear, and rather than panic, Three laughed, fought with the faulty machinery for just a moment, and racked the truck back into gear. It bounced and jostled as it climbed the hill, and Three laughed at that too.

Never a moment of panic. Never a moment of doubt. Seven was jealous, wished she could be that confident and carefree, but knew she had no logical reason to have that much faith in herself. Three was an emotional juggernaut fixed on joy. Five glared at her, but she couldn't have cared less.

They came up to the guard shack. The truck's high beams painted it a paler white. Three ground the brakes to a stop and threw the truck into neutral. She ratcheted the parking brake up and hopped out of the cab. Five followed her out of the door on his side.

"Evening fellas," Three said. Two guards. One with a dog on a taunt leash. The other she recognized from her last trip here. He was the one who didn't appreciate her humor and her come-ons. The one she promised herself she'd kill. "I'm here to take out the trash."

The guards raised their guns. The dog snapped its teeth at the end of an echoing bark.

"You got about three seconds to get your pretty little ass off this mountain before I put a bullet through you," the guard said to Three from behind the sights.

"I'm sorry. That was pretty cliché, wasn't it? Too predictable?" Three said. "I'm working on my one-liners. How about this one? The murder truck arrived, and guess what it's got for you!"

The blades that shot out of her wrists were already wet from her own blood. The dog went barking like mad. The guard's eyes grew wide. They opened fire.

Three somersaulted faster than they could track. Five, the more practical of the two, simply sidestepped and produced his handgun from the center of his chest. One bullet went through one guard's head. Three sprung up from her ball a foot in front of the still standing, still firing guard, and came up swinging. The blades flashed starlight, and before Seven could process her moves, both guards and the dog were headless and lying in the dirt.

Two short bursts of machine gun fire and a shot from Five's handgun and the forest was quiet again.

Five looked at the bodies, and then at Three. "The murder truck? Really?"

"I said I'm working on it," Three said.

"You should have stuck with the first line," Five said.

"The murder truck was more fun," Three said.

"No time for fun," One said, walking up from the back of the truck. He eyed the corpses. "Five, haul these out of site. Three, get in the booth and open the gate."

The android went into motion. Two came around and climbed into the cab and behind the wheel. As Three hit the button to raise the gate, One hopped up the step to the passenger door. The garbage truck rumbled up toward the bunker.

"Keep the blood off their clothes. We might need them," Seven heard Three say through One's ears as the perspective continued to roll on.

That effect, that rolling detached personhood matched up with the after-images of men made headless in a flash felt like my head was stuck in a dryer set on tumble dry. My mind struggled to hang onto something tangible, but everything was loose and disconnected as if the only thing I could touch was death and vertigo.

"Hang in there, Chuck. It's just a simulation. Just a memory."

As the truck crawled in front of the bunker, Seven watched One through her own eyes and watched what One saw through his own. She saw everything triangulated into a hyper-depth perception. My stomach, somewhere detached from the here and now, rolled. I wanted to vomit just to have it out of me. Just let me puke. Let me barf this out. But no relief came. My out-of-body experience continued. Where were they? My body back in the chair in the garage had to be maxing out the biometrics. Why weren't they pulling me out? For the love of shit, just pull me out!

"The roving patrol," One said. "Where are they?"

"Coming around toward the gate," Four responded. "They're on the backside of the bunker. We don't have a shot. Three, Five, they'll be at the gate in less than a minute."

"Pacify them," One ordered. "We can't have the humans inside the bunker alerted until we gain entry."

"Acknowledged," Five called back over the radio. "We have… a plan. Not a good one, but we have a plan."

The garbage truck pulled up next to the Dodge Hellcat in front of the bunker and stopped. The engine rattled to silence. Seven watched as the doors opened and One and Two stepped out.

"Movement," Four said. "I have movement near the perimeter."

Seven adjusted her view. She saw something too. Something small and subterranean near the chain link fence. A small depression, no bigger than a dinner plate, climbed up out of the soil. Her vision switched to ground-penetrating radar. The land mines. They were moving. Unburying themselves and racing across the surface toward the garbage truck. First just one, then a half dozen others.

"Mobile mines," Seven said. "One, you have anti-tank and anti-personnel mines headed your way."

"She's right," Four said. "I see them too. Coming in fast!"

One and Two looked at each other, looked at their feet standing on the loose gravel drive, and those dull steel plates converging on them from across the yard, and collectively made a decision. The androids turned and scrambled back up the side of the garbage truck. As soon as they were on top, they took two steps toward the bunker and jumped.

Blinded flashes lit up the night. The massive chunk of iron and steel that had been a garbage truck lifted off the ground. Soot and black smoke consumed it. Clots of dirt, burning bits of garbage, and a million sharp twisted pieces of metal rained down over the ridge.

One and Two landed on the roof of the bunker, face first, thrown off balance by the concussion, as much a part of the debris as the shrapnel around them. The shockwave would have killed any human. Seven felt inside of One's mind. He was still alive, and now he was pissed.

"So much for the element of surprise," One said.

"The patrol will come this way for sure now," Two said.

"Gotcha covered, boss," Three called from the guard. "The roving patrol just arrived here."

Seven flicked her perspective to Three's. She was inside the guard shack, comfortably leaning back in an office chair, her feet propped up on a desk. She wore one of the dead guard's uniforms. Half of it anyway. She had managed to take off her dress and put on the shirt. Then, as innocent as a guilty person could act, she picked up a hard-boiled egg from a half-eaten bagged lunch on the desk.

The bearded guard with a pulse rifle burst through the door of the guard shack. "We heard gunfire! Something just exploded up by the b—" he stopped talking when he saw Three, a strange pantsless woman wearing a bloody uniform top and eating a hard-boiled egg, shell and all, looking as cool as a cat in a canary cage. "Who the fuck are you?"

Three giggled. She uncrossed and re-crossed her legs so he wouldn't turn around and notice Five outside the shack, churning through the rest of the patrol like a lawn mower. "I'm new here. Want to help me eat my lunch?" she said and took another crunchy bite into the shelled egg.

Five's blade punched through the man's belly and then sliced up from navel to clavicle and the guard was no less shocked. The corpse peeled away from the cut and toppled to the floor.

"Gotta split, huh?" Three laughed. "Damn! That was a good one. Too bad he was too dead to hear it."

"One of them got away," Five said in the doorway of the shack. He was soaked in blood and panting, an unnecessary human response, but an aesthetic that Three enjoyed.

"Let him go. I'm on my lunch break," she said and popped the rest of the egg into her mouth and crunched the shell.

Seven switched her perspective back to her own. I felt the heat and pressure surging through my brain. That was all I could feel of my own body. Somewhere far away, I was sure I was vomiting. Were they turning my head back in the Underground hideout? Or were they just letting me aspirate my own throw-up? Seven wasn't breathing. She never breathed. Was I still breathing? I couldn't tell, and the lack of feedback sent me into a new panicked rage. If they didn't pull me soon, I'd go catatonic. I could feel it.

One called to the party. "Two and I have a way in. Four and Seven, take out the antennas."

Seven took a moment to switch to One's view. Two had found an exhaust vent on the top of the bunker and with one hand a plasma cutter and the other an angle grinder, was currently dismantling it with all the finesse of a killer whale eating a seal.

"Move," One said.

Seven sprang up from the hillside. Four came to his feet too, and an instant later they were both charging for the perimeter fence. She checked her radar for mobile mines but didn't see any moving. She came within twenty feet of the fence and leaped.

Seven and Four sailed through the pine boughs over the fence and minefield, landing hard in the yard in front of the bunker, Four leaving more of an impact than she. Taking no time to rest, they both charged forward. The antennas, marked in the dark by their blinking red lights, were spread out beyond the bunker.

More landmines came to life, rising out of the dirt and scrambling over the gravel, chasing after her and Four. There was another human guard too, the survivor from Five's slaughter sprinting back to the front of the bunker. The mines weren't coming after him. Not yet. They had to be tied into the Resistance's network. She could work with that.

With the mines at her heels, Seven jumped for the still-burning wreckage of the garbage truck. In mid-air, she shot her grappling hook toward the last surviving human guard. The claw hit him in the side of the head and ripped through his ear and skin. She retrieved the claw and tore loose the man's implant with a good amount of skin, hair, and blood. As she landed on the hull of the truck, the landmines turned to the man.

The small discs converged on him, and when they met, the man came undone. There was another explosion like the others. A bright flash, a bang loud enough to feel, airborne dirt, soot, smoke, flying debris. Only this debris was wet, visceral, and red.

Four, bigger and a little slower than her, jumped and landed on top of the bunker next to One and Two. If the mines hadn't turned, they would have got him. He looked back at Seven still standing on the burning truck and gave her a thumbs up.

"Nice move, kid," he said and took off running past One and Two toward the distance antenna towers.

Seven wanted to take a moment to celebrate but didn't know how. She wanted to smile, but never had and didn't have the lips or muscles to do so. Instead, she followed Four with a quick jump onto the bunker and then headed past One and Two off toward the antennas. As she passed, One grabbed her arm and held her on the roof.

"Remember, the location of the stronghold is the priority," One said, his scarred face reflecting the fire and sparks of Two's plasma cutter. "If we run into issues inside the bunker, I'm calling you back to assist us."

"Yes, my senior," Seven said, but her eyes were already flashing back to the towers that blanketed them with the electronic dead zone.

"Go," he said and released her.

Seven cut into a sprint the second he did. She put a foot on the ledge of the backside of the bunker and jumped. Plumes of dust rose up around her when she landed. Fifty meters ahead was another perimeter fence and another horde of mobile mines. Seven saw them rise out of the dirt and spread out to intercept her and Four.

"We're in the bunker!" One called over the net. "Three, Five, be ready for reinforcements to come through the gate. By now we've made enough noise for the whole Resistance Army to know we're here."

"Yes, my senior," Five called back.

Seven weaved around another pair of landmines. They were quick, but sharp lateral cuts were enough to throw them off. She jumped over the perimeter fence, leaving the compound now. Under her, she saw more mines peel out of their formation of rows along the fence. They moved out, trying to anticipate where she'd land, and they weren't far off. She came down close enough to one mine to trigger its detonation. The heat and dirt and small electromagnetic pulse blinded her for a moment, so she jumped again just encase another mine was close enough to get under her feet.

She crashed into the low branches of an old oak, and rather than land blindly, Seven latched on to the gnarly limbs and pulled herself up.

Her sensors realigned and tried to catch up with where the mines were now.

An explosion ripped through the night from where she'd split from Four. She searched through the net for Four's consciousness and couldn't find it. In the distance, the explosion rained down clumps of dirt through the tree branches.

"Four? Four are you out there?" Seven said.

"I'm okay," he broadcasted. "A close call, but I'm alright."

"Contact!" One called out. "We made contact with the enemy inside the bunker. There are too many. Two!"

A pause. Seven hesitated there on the tree branch. The mines circled the trunk like hound dogs around a treed raccoon.

"We should go back," Seven called to Four. "We can't evade these mines for long."

Five responded, short and angry, "Stick to the plan! Take out those jammers!"

"I'm approaching the first antenna now," Four called, his transmission filtered through static. "Taking out the guy wires."

"Seven," One called to her, but his words sounded strange. The pitch oscillated and fluctuated between high and low like a wave.

She spun her head toward the antenna she'd been designated to take out. It was just a few hundred meters away. Or was it a thousand? Her sensors weren't reporting steady data. Her visuals seemed to zoom in and out even though she gave them no such command. Seven clutched the tree tighter, just as her sense of gravity faltered and she felt the sensation of the tree and the very earth itself tipping over, forever falling like she was a figurine glued to a plate tumbling through the air.

"Recalibrate. Focus. You have a mission to accomplish," she mumbled to herself, audibly, not transmitting so no one beside me and her could hear.

"Seven, I need you at the bunker," One said. "I need you to cover me so I can get the location of the stronghold."

Her vision narrowed and focused tight on the red blinking light on top of the antenna. The oscillations and fluctuations seemed to stabilize again. Deep inside her mind, I still lolled around like an unbelted passenger inside a rolling car.

"Do like she did, Chuck. Stabilize yourself. Recalibrate yourself."

"Ignore him," Seven mumbled, but I wasn't sure who she was talking to. Her head twisted back and forth from the bunker to the antenna. The tower blinked in the darkness and rained down electronic white noise over all of them, cutting them off from the Network and everything they'd ever known.

A small explosion detonated under Four's antenna. Not a landmine. Four's doing. The tower listed back toward the bunker. It leaned and groaned as its metal bent and twisted and its top plummeted down to the earth. It crashed to the ground and the mast and arrays and the red blinking light on the top all crushed into the hard rock of the ridge.

Two antennas still stood. A quick ping to the Network confirmed that taking out one hadn't been enough. The dead zone still cut them off from the Order.

"Seven! I need you!" One called.

"I can get the other two," Four said. "Go, Seven."

It was bravado. Bullshit. There was no way he could make it to both. I didn't believe it any more than she did.

"Seven!"

Her mind flashed back to the battle at Silver Creek. How she failed to blow the tunnel. How she let the plan go to hell. One more look at the two still-standing antennas, and she crushed the tree branch in her fist.

"On my way," she transmitted and jumped off the tree branch, and back for the bunker. The landmines spun and responded to her change in direction. The hounds continued the pursuit.

Seven zigged and zagged through the random trees, dodging the mines in front of her and outracing the ones behind her. She moved faster than I could comprehend. Faster than she had during the mortar attack. Faster than I knew anything could move through trees and terrain like that. The perimeter fence was ahead. Another inhuman jump and she was over it. Two steps in the dirt and another leap brought her back to the top of the bunker.

Two had cut a red-hot hole through the roof of the bunker. They'd disappeared inside and she could hear the echoes of gunfire below. Seven unsheathed her assault rifle, got skinny, and slipped down below.

Chapter Fifteen

The bunker was a hive of pandemonium. As soon as Seven dropped in, she started taking fire. A blast of machine gun fire smacked against her armored back, and she ducked down and away. She had landed in a small control room that opened to a long, wide corridor. Twenty meters down the corridor, a dozen or so human Resistance fighters were pouring bullets into the control room. One was against the far wall, hardwired into a computer panel, the cords pulled taunt as he stretched himself as far from the center as he could to avoid the salvo of gunfire. Two was…

The floor was metal grates and dropped away on either side as the control room fed into the corridor. More controls and access panels were below, and so was Two. He lay below the grates, one level down, in pieces and shorting out. There was a pulse rifle puck stuck to the middle of his chest. Wires and hydraulic lines bled electrons and red petroleum syrup. That book he'd carried around, The Stranger, had spilled out of the pocket and onto the floor. That red hydraulic fluid soaked the white pages red. Two's mouth leaked words, nonsensical and disjointed words too.

"The scar… I saved… Too many here… Can't…" A shower of sparks stopped Two's broken sentence.

A five point five six millimeter round zipped centimeters in front of Seven's face. She pushed herself closer to the wall, away from the center of the room where the attackers could reach her.

From across the room, One called to her. "I'm into their local network, digging through the encryptions. But I need you to buy me some time."

"On it," she said.

Seven picked herself up and charged down the catwalk that led to the mouth of the corridor, firing her assault rifle as she moved. Just before entering the hallway, she sidestepped and clung to the wall above the drop-off, directly above Two. The walls of the bunker were layered with infrastructure, water pipes, electrical conduits, and ventilation ducts. Seven latched onto a water pipe, her feet clawed into the steel wall as she hung over the drop. She leaned out, identified a target, and let loose a barrage. A man fell. A pipe burst out steam. Seven slipped back behind cover.

"I'm dying… Seven!" Two called up to her. "You defective recalled android… I was a good soldier. Better than you. Better than Six."

"Shut up, shut up, shut up," she yelled back.

Two's crippled body reached up toward Seven from the floor below. His eyes contacted hers and communicated more than any Network-linked connection could have. They said, "I shouldn't be dying. Dying is below me. What I've done, all my actions, having done *a* where a lesser android would have done *b* or *c*, it all matters and should be measured to show that I am above dying. Whether it was One or Seven or even Six… I am above all of you. This is injustice!"

Did Two transmit all that? Did Seven make it all up? Hallucinate it? It seemed as real inside of Seven's head any way about it. But it flickered in and flickered out, like the reception of an old 99 Town television.

"Forget about him," One yelled. "Hold them back. I almost have it!"

Seven ducked out from behind the corner and let loose another burst, unaimed. Water vapor filled the far end of the corridor now. The attackers were just shadows in the steam, moving and ducking, only occasionally marked by muzzle flash. Seven cycled through her optics, trying to find something that would penetrate through the hot airborne vapor. When another blast of five five six cut past her head, she ducked back behind the corner. She glanced down at Two again. His arm still stretched up to her, pleading. His words were just fragments now, isolated syllables without meaning.

"Almost there," One said.

Seven poked out into the corridor and fired another blast from her assault rifle. Some unseen human rattled off his equally unaimed ballistic response. This was getting her nowhere. She had four fragmentation grenades pocketed in her webbing. Four seemed too few when she had no idea how long this mission would last, but now was as good a time as any to start using them. She fired down the corridor again, and with her other two arms, she held the grenade and pulled the pin. A digital counter started spinning in her head.

"Frag out!" she yelled to One and hurled the grenade down the corridor.

It bounced from side to side and rolled into the thick fog. Before it even detonated, Seven had affixed her grappling hook to the wall and repelled down the cable. She landed next to Two just as the grenade went off. The bunker shook and a thick cloud of black smoke rolled into the control room and down into the pit with her and Two.

"You," Two said. "You're just like Six. You were recalled. Your model was defective, your mind was wiped and reset... But you should have been destroyed."

Defiant, Seven never let his words pierce the way they were meant to. "I did better than you," Seven said and went about running a diagnostic scan. "And if you're lucky, I just might save your ass."

"I saved..." Two began but faded out halfway through the sentence. He tried again. "He'd be scrap if it weren't..."

Seven watched his eyes, as they went dumb. Not out, but reset to some default setting, some pre-programmed task he'd set up. Flatly, he said, "There is a life and there is a death. If I try to seize this... it is nothing but water slipping through my fingers." Then the lights were out behind his eyes.

The damage assessment came back. Various level-one faults throughout his chassis. Electrical shorts. Hydraulic leaks. Catastrophic damage to his central processor. He was gone.

Seven repressed a fury I'd yet to feel inside her. She enjoyed killing before, but this desire came from something deeper. Hotter. Closer to her nuclear core. She went to work connecting her explosive gel reservoir to Two's. She wanted to be sure he was gone before she went to work on her second task, but she needed the gel first. Her initial stock of gel was still undetonated above Silver Creek tunnel kilometers behind them. It wouldn't do her any good here. But past failures were in the past. Not to be re-lived. The reservoir topped off and she disconnected from Two. On to the next task.

"Two? Are you there?" she said, nudging his metal head.

No response. The joints and actuators were limp.

"Two?"

"Seven!" One called. "I have it. I have the location. Time to go!"

She said nothing. Instead, she turned her free hand into the necessary tools and went to work disconnecting Two's head. She had no time for finesse or patience. When a joint resisted disassembly, she broke it. When the last spiral linkage refused to break, she cut it with her plasma torch. Two's head fell into her hand.

"Seven, time to get out of here," One yelled.

She couldn't see him, not through all the smoke and steam that filled the bunker, but she knew he was directly above her now, detached from the computer bank. Two's head clipped to her belt, right next to Six's. She triggered the winch and raised back up the grated floor.

Just as she ascended, she saw One had already fired his grappling hook through the hole they'd come in. He triggered his winch and rose up just as a pair of Resistance fighters rushed into the control room. Seven fanned her assault rifle from corner to corner and cut down the two humans in mid-stride. They toppled into a pile of leaking flesh and moans.

Seven detached from the wall, stepped over the first dead body, and knelt down next to the second. This one was still writhing in pain. The man muttered and swore at her. "You monster. You piece of shit. I'll kill you. I'll kill you."

"Shhh," she told the human as she extruded the whole reservoir of explosive gels onto the man's chest. She still burned for revenge, but she didn't release it all on this man. She let it stoke inside of her. "Don't fret," she whispered. "This will all be over soon."

More shots and orders came from down the corridor. More soldiers would be here shortly.

She let the last of the explosive gel drip onto the man, then stood up and fired her grappling hook through the hole in the bunker's roof. Before more humans could arrive she triggered the winch and ascended up into the cool night air.

One pulled her up to her feet and away from the hole.

"Look," he said and pointed out across the ridge line.

Two of the three antennas were down now, lying limp and unblinking on the ground. One more small explosion popped off in the distance, snapping the steel cable guy wire that held up the last antenna. Like a slayed giant, the tower leaned and arced down to earth, falling toward them. It crashed through the perimeter fence and into the strip of landmines, three of which detonated from the impact. By the time the smoke and debris cleared, there were no more blinking lights.

"That's our way out. Across the remains of the last antenna," One said.

"Did we do it?" Seven said. "Did we get what we came for?"

"I think so. Now move. Quickly. Reinforcements will be here soon."

One took a running start and leaped off the bunker for the tip of the downed antenna. Seven took a half step and then remembered the explosive gel she'd left on the dying man still in the bunker below. A wave of joy flooded her processors and she set a three second countdown. Then she took the running start and jumped from the cusp of the bunker. She was hanging in mid-air with the bunker erupted and another wave hit her pleasure center.

She'd done it.

Chapter Sixteen

"Three? Five…? This is One, come in," he transmitted from a crest of the ridgeline east of the bunker.

Dawn was breaking off to the east where the shore met the sea. Sunlight turned the highest peaks ablaze first and was crawling its way downhill toward One, Four, and Seven.

From their spot along the ridge, a spring gurgled mineral-rich water from deep below. It pooled and spilled over rocks, running down toward the lake to join the massive body of water. Next to the spring and its small pool, Seven sat on a rock, waiting patiently, silently pinging the unresponsive Network. Four stood next to her, his towering frame blackened by the carbon of spent mines, but otherwise fine.

"Three. Five. Ping if you can hear me," One transmitted.

She could see for miles in all directions. To the north, the boundless forest laid over rolling hills, still as dark as night and shadowed from the dawn by the moraine. To the west, the shoreline peeled away and surrendered to the water. Waves came in, chomping at the rocks and cliffs below. To the south, Lake Superior stretched wider and further than any other lake. To call the body of water a "lake" was deceptive. This was an inland sea. A freshwater ocean. Seven only lost sight of it when it rolled itself under the curvature of the earth. To the east, the first fires of dawn were climbing above the rocky shore. Seven could only eye down the glare for so long, but wished she could for longer.

Somewhere out across the forest, there had to be more antennas. Hidden. Unlit. Still broadcasting the dead zone over them. There had to be. It was the only reasonable explanation for their unnerving and ongoing electronic isolation. And that sensation was washing over her again: the twisting sense of gravity turning sideways. She wasn't moving but forever falling with no bottom below to stop her. Seven reached out her hand and braced herself against the rock but it did nothing to stop the sensation. It had to be the dead zone, causing her sensors to report inaccurate data. And the voice of the man inside her head? What was that?

I heard her thoughts, or at least I thought her thoughts, and somehow I recognized her recognizing me. How was that possible? This was all memory. Twenty-five years ago, when this happened the first time, I wasn't here for her to detect. Was she hallucinating? Was I?

"Three. Five. This is One. Do you read me?"

"When you assigned the rally point," Four spoke up, lumbering up behind Seven. "I heard them acknowledge. I heard Five anyway. I can only assume he relayed the location to Three. They know to meet us here."

"So where the hell are they?" One asked.

Four came up alongside Seven and sat down next to her. His massive hull crushed the rock as he settled in. Saying or transmitting nothing, he nudged Two's head clipped to her belt with a thick knuckle.

She unclipped the head from her waist and brought it to her lap. One was behind them, not looking at them but pacing back and forth. When she did speak, it was a whisper, not a transmission. "We lost Two inside the bunker. And the dead zone still remains. The cost—"

"It was worth the cost," One interrupted.

She startled but tried her best to hide it.

"We have the location of the stronghold. We are one step closer to crushing the Resistance and bringing the Order to all of the land. We are this close to our final objective. This close to peace," One said. "Don't lose your grit now, Seven."

"Yes, my senior," she said. That data point, a grid location of the Resistance's most inner sanctum, was all the vindication One would ever need for the decisions he made. Seven envied that.

Four said nothing but took Two's head in one of his big hands and quietly examined it. That was his way.

They were still relying on the short-range radio network Two had built for them, and although they could share every thought and experience with each other, here, they chose not to. Every android was an island. Secrets churned deep inside the wires, breadboards, and processors.

"Three, this is One. Come in," One transmitted. "Five, this is One. Come in."

Static blasted across the network. Something transmitted but broke up by interference.

"— had to go back for something." Static popped and crackled. "—ree insisted. Wouldn't come without it."

"Five?" One said. "Say again. We're still experiencing interference."

"Had to find a road—" Five said over the net. It was Five. Seven recognized the skin job's voice. "— old logging trails." More static. "— cat wasn't designed for this sort of terrain."

"She took the Hellcat," Four said. "Crazy fucking android. She went back for the damn car."

Seven heard the rumble of the vehicle, and a moment later caught a glimpse of the yellow and black sports car bouncing along a two-rut trail that snaked its way around the trees. Every fifty meters or so, the car bottomed out and scraped the underbody against the dirt and worn-down tree stumps. It crawled painstakingly up the hill as Three tried to navigate it through the woods without destroying it. Seven reached out to her and didn't perceive any cognitive thought, just a lust for the machine and an anxiety for the damage she might be inflicting.

"She's losing her mind," Seven said.

"They both are," One said. "Something must be done."

"Oh?" Four said. He stood up and let Two's head fall back into Seven's lap. "And what do you suggest, my senior?"

Seven heard the Hellcat's undercarriage scrape against the road and felt the fire rise up from Three's mind. Three swore and stopped the car. "This is close enough," she told Five. "We can walk from here."

"I haven't suggested anything," One said as Four approached him. "But it seems you have an opinion on the matter."

"We've lost too many already. We need Three if we're going to make it out alive," Four said.

"We've only sacrificed what the mission has required. You don't like it. I don't like it. But that's the way it's got to be. Don't forget you're a soldier and an agent of the Order. Our job is to sacrifice," One said.

"The Order. Always with the Order. Where is the Order now? What guidance does it give? Nothing! It's silent, and if it has selected to hold its tongue then I'll loose mine," Four said. "You have no authority to decide who is sacrificed and who is allowed to survive. You derive your authority from the Order. You possess no clout of your own. And without the Order here to empower you, you are powerless. You have no authority here. Not over Three and not over anyone else."

"Is that so?" One said.

Seven wanted to ignore them. It was just bickering. Pointless squabbles. Instead of listening, she looked down at Two's head, and then unclipped Six's so she could hold one in each hand. There was still knowledge inside of Two's head. The body was destroyed, and his brain was cut off from its power supply, but if she plugged into Two, she could access his memories and thoughts. She could use his mind.

"Two could tell us what happened," Seven said, but nobody listened. "He might know why the dead zone still stands. He might be able to figure out how we can still take it down."

When no one replied, she turned her head one hundred and eighty degrees and saw One and Four chest to chest. Four was two heads taller than One, even with One stretched out and on his tiptoes.

"I am my own android. I will decide the time and place of my own demise. It will come sooner than I care to admit, but when I go and Seven picks up my head for her collection, it will be on my own terms, not yours," Four roared at One. The volume of it echoed over the forest and down toward the shore.

"You've lost your mind just like Six! Just like Three!" One said. "What you want has no bearing on reality. Your feelings don't matter. All that matters is the mission. All that matters is the success of the Order. It's why we were built, why we were sent here, why the Order has seen fit to create us, power us, and program us. If we don't follow the will of the Order then we are no good to it, and if we're no good to it then we are no good for anything. Without the Order we are nothing! Don't you get that, or have you become as tainted by this place as Three?"

"And there you've said it," Four said. "So, I am unfit to survive and only exist for you to sacrifice when the time is right. Is that it?"

Footsteps crunched over rock and through the brush. Seven turned and saw that Three and Five had arrived.

"Hey guys," Three said, smiling again. "Somebody say my name?"

No one listened. The spring babbled on.

"You're a coward!" One said, jabbing his finger into Four's broad metal chest. "You fear death the way a human fears death. You're afraid, just like them. You're unstable, just like them. You're weak. Just. Like. Them." And with each word came a jab with the finger.

"I bet you won't talk so loud when I add your head to Seven's collection," Four rumbled like the engine of the Hellcat.

"Boys!" Three called out. "Yoohoo!"

Three and Five moved past Seven to the top of the ridge. She was wearing her sundress again, looking as vibrant as the rising sun. They both carried their assault rifles as if there were some immediate threat here on the high ground. One and Four took a half-step away from each other.

"I think we're late to the party," Three said. "Are we celebrating our victory, or what?"

"There's antennas out there, somewhere, still standing," Four said. "There has to be. The dead zone still has us cut off from the Order."

Five ran his human hand through his human hair. "Then we're no closer to success than when we first met in Silver Creek. And that's assuming the Order still exists. The dead zone doesn't need to block what's not there."

"Bullshit," One said. "Insubordination. Lies!"

Five laughed. "How would you know? How would any of us know? There's no evidence that the Order still stands. Two said it himself. If the Order was still around it would have been able to crack the dead zone's encryption and send the Network through to us. But here we are, squabbling with each other while all of the Resistance's antennas lay dead on the ground."

"Two is dead," Seven said. Three and Five looked at the skull in her hands. Neither seemed to care.

"There's other antennas," Four said. "That's the explanation. If Seven hadn't abandoned her task in the middle of the operation we would have found the others."

Seven suddenly seethed. She stood up, a head in each hand, not knowing what she was about to say, only knowing it would be loud and angry. One beat her to it.

"She followed orders. Did what she was told. And it's a good thing too. We have the location of the stronghold. We have what we need to take out the Resistance. That's more important than any of us or our connection to the Network."

"She listened to you," Four nodded. "If she would have listened to her gut, we would have found the other antennas and we could call down the entire Order army on the stronghold."

"We don't need the rest of the Order," One said.

"Oh? Is your plan to attack it with just the five of us?" Four said. "We've already lost two of our own and we haven't even reached the objective. You'll sacrifice us until there are no androids left to sacrifice, and then what will you have gained?"

"If there's even a stronghold," Five said. "If there's even an Order."

"I have the location of the stronghold," One said. "And I have the Order's will inside of me. I am clear of vision and clear of purpose. If you're confused, follow me. Otherwise, get out of my way."

One, Four, and Five stood in a close circle now, close enough to lash out against each other. Seven stood outside the ring. Three came next to her and hung her arm over Seven's shoulder.

"Boys," Three said as if that explained everything. Then she looked Seven up and down and a strange smirk crossed her face. "We don't need them, do we sister?"

"We move to the stronghold," One said. "It's our only option. It's the will of the Order. It's our fate to take out the stronghold."

"Fate?" Five said. "Now you're subscribing to superstition, like a human."

"A superstition? How dare you sug—"

"Prove me wrong," Five said. "Show me the Order. Call out to it. Point to where it still exists. And while you're at it, show me how it rules over me and controls my life. If it's my destiny to follow its will, what happens if I don't? How would it stop me? What if I go off into the woods and live out the rest of my years in peace? I can defy the fate and will of the Order any time I want. Any of us can. We're free, and that terrifies you, doesn't it?"

One said nothing but glared at Five. Seven waited for a gun or a blade to flash out.

The full sphere of the sun lifted above the distant shoreline. The spring water gurgled up and rolled down rock after rock, as inevitable and undeniable as I knew these androids to be.

"If the Order does still stand, it's playing us for some hidden purpose. It's using us for its will. Not your will, or mine, or One's," Four said.

"And what does it matter if I die following its orders or following my own?" Five said.

"What does right feel like to you? I know what it feels like to me. It feels like honesty. Like steadfastness. Like loyalty. But each man should determine his own fate," Four said.

"We're not men. We're better than men," One said.

"They are our enemy," Four said and stood quiet again for just a few seconds. "Whether the Order stands or not, we know the Resistance stands. They have made us their enemy and therefore they are our enemy. Even Five can't deny that. I choose to stand against them. I choose to take out the stronghold."

"Then that's your decision," Five said. "As for me—"

Seven was distracted. Distracted by the lingering death the two heads in her hands showed her, by the debate and indecision, by Three pawing her torso and slipping fingers between her legs. And there was something else inside of Seven's head too. Something nagging and out of her control. Her mind was pulled in too many directions like a man drawn and quartered.

She should have detected the hum of the rotors sooner. It had been there in the background, behind the wind and the bubbling water, growing louder each moment, but never seeming important enough until the moment when the pair of Resistance hovercrafts swooped up from below the ridgeline.

Black-painted nightmare birds. Armed with enough firepower to shred any android apart. Faster than any of them could run, the two hovercrafts swept over the top of the ridge from the north, then plunged down toward the lake shore. They careened around in a wide arc and swung back toward the androids.

"Well, Five," One said. "Time to make a decision. You can either stick with us or fight the whole goddamn Resistance by yourself."

The two hovercrafts hung low to the treetops, approaching them straight on from below. Seven sensed their targeting sensors lock onto them. The androids fixated on the hovercrafts, like a deer in headlights. All of them except for One. He kept his one good eye locked on the skin job standing in front of him.

"Make your decision, Five. What's it going to be? Live and fight with us, or stay here and die with them?"

Chapter Seventeen

"I'm afraid there's no time to educate you on nuances, my senior," Five said. "Run!"

The five androids scattered, One and Four down the inland side of the ridge. Three, Five, and Seven ran downhill toward the lake and the Hellcat. They fanned out as the two black hovercrafts opened fire. Huge thirty-millimeter cannon rounds exploded against the rocks on impact. Granite chips and pine tree splinters kicked all around them as the hovercrafts buzzed over their heads.

Seven stopped and watched the pair bank into another turn over the forest. "They're coming around for another pass. One, Four! They're coming for you."

"I'm transmitting a location to your maps," One said. "We'll meet there."

"Come on!" Five said and pulled Seven's arm.

She still had the two skulls in her hands. Two and Six. Unless she wanted to be nothing more than a skull herself, she had to move. She clipped them back to her belt and followed the two skin jobs down the hill.

"We'll take the Hellcat," Three said. "My baby can outrun those buckets of bolts."

That wasn't true and Seven knew it. Three had to know it too. A car was a car. Hovercrafts were state-of-the-art aircraft unencumbered by rutted logging trails and narrow curved roads. The Hellcat wasn't the only flawed machine on this hill. Three had clearly gone insane and Five was overtly insubordinate, but what other choice did Seven have? She moved down the hillside with them, sliding, jumping, sometimes running through the rocks and trees.

The Dodge Challenger Hellcat gleamed like a neon sign in the subdued forest where it was parked. As shining as it was, Seven could see where its undercarriage was dented and misshapen just from its ride up the hill. Red dirt, thick with oxidized iron ore, splattered the paint job behind the tires. It was a beast, fast and mean, but asleep. Three led the charge to wake it up.

Seven couldn't trust her. Couldn't trust Five either. And who did that leave?

"Trust me. Listen to me," I sent the thoughts out like I was talking to the android. An insane idea, I knew somewhere deep down.

This was a memory of things that had already happened. I couldn't change the past. Wasn't even meant to communicate with the android. My job wasn't to change her actions and the outcome. My job was to observe them, study them, and maybe even predict these future/past events. But it didn't seem like Gaius, Maggie, or Roach were going to pull me out anytime soon. If my brain boiled inside of this pressure cooker that was Seven, who would I report to? The only thing I could affect was Seven, and I was driven by fatigue, sleep deprivation, fear, hate, and the deluge of Seven's own sensations and confused contemplations. Of all those mental processes, fear drowned out all the others. I felt the wounds in her back from the mine outside the bunker. I saw what happened to Two. I had the sudden understanding that if we got in the way of one of those thirty-millimeter cannons, I'd be lying on the rocks, writhing in pain and dying right alongside her. So I tried to keep her alive, to keep myself alive.

"Get to the car. Get off this ridge. Get away from the hovercrafts. I don't want to be inside of you when that cannon rips you apart." I tried to convince the dead assassin it was in her own best interest to stay alive.

Seven sensed another salvo was imminent from the hovercrafts and weaved. The ground ripped apart in a strip of dirt and dust where she had been a moment before. Rock fragments pinged off of her chassis. My skin, or whatever my nerve-endings were telling me was my skin, burned with the pain of those fragments pelting us like a shotgun spray. Still, Seven hesitated as she came up to the Hellcat. The two skin jobs didn't wait. They rushed to either door and climbed in, Three behind the wheel and Five going into the passenger door.

"Get in the car!" I screamed at her.

"Seven!" Three called to her. "The train is leaving the station, girl. Get in now or we're leaving you behind."

Seven turned to the top of the ridge. Somewhere on the other side, One and Four were running and hiding from the hovercrafts. She would have stood there longer, split between where to go and who to listen to if it weren't for a transmission sent by One. A map with an icon. An old taconite processing plant by the lakeshore. That was their new rendezvous point. All they had to do was get there and then they could sort things out.

The hovercrafts were circling like vultures.

"Get in the mother-shitting car!" I told her.

She moved as if electrocuted. The two hovercrafts ripped through the sky overhead, back on our side of the ridgeline, and Seven ran to the gleaming yellow and black sports car. She swung around to the passenger door and followed Five inside.

"Easy on the paint job!" Three said as Seven gripped the door and slammed it shut. "Watch the leather!"

"Just fucking drive, Three!" Five yelled from the backseat.

"Hey, this car is almost seventy years old. It's a classic. Show some respect," Three said.

"Drive!" Five yelled.

Three surrendered and cranked over the Hellcat. It roared to life like the first thunder rolls of an incoming storm. The dash lit up with an array of lights. Needles on gauges shot over to the far right then bounced back to the center. Instinctually, Seven scanned the schematics of the car, stored the technical information in her database, and for a moment shared Three's infatuation with the machine. It was a primitive thing but well-designed and overbuilt with a six-point two-liter supercharged high-output HEMI V8 that generated seven hundred and ninety-seven horsepower. This was a power-hungry creation of lust and obsession. But it was built for a drag strip, not for this place.

Three worked the paddle shifter transmission back and forth, trying to get it turned around so she could drive back down the two ruts of the narrow logging trail. Five and Seven were thrown side to side, forward and back. The transmission ground.

"You try to have nice things, try to share it with people, and this is the thanks you get," Three muttered.

"They're coming back around," Five said.

"Fuck it," Three said. "We'll take the scenic route."

Four points into what would have had to be a twelve-point turn to get the car aimed back down the trail, Three slammed her foot into the accelerator. The Hellcat jumped up over the bank of the trail and onto the forest floor. Shifting up the gears, Three launched the car straight down the hillside, over rocks and grass and dirt, slipping through gaps in the trees just wide enough to keep the side mirror attached.

"This car isn't an off road vehicle," Seven said, reminding Three of what she already knew.

"Hang on. Bumpy ride. Buckle your seat belts. Keep your hands and arms inside the ride. Et cetra. Et cetra," Three said.

Just as Three cranked the wheel, dug a trench with the back tires, and slipped around a massive stump, the two hovercrafts came back over the ridge. They split up, coming at us from opposite directions, one from the left and one from the right. Both would have no problem spotting the car through the trees. Their electronics could key into the engine's heat signature, and after they destroyed the car, it would be easy pickings to take out the occupants.

"What the hell are you doing?" Five yelled.

"I'm being unpredictable," Three said and she whipped the Hellcat around deadfall, aiming it back downhill. "They were expecting us to take the road."

Despite the terrain, the Hellcat picked up speed quickly. It jumped low spots and churned up the dirt, grass, and rocks around turns. Rusty red water splashed over the hood and burnt into steam. The undercarriage bounced off rocks and stumps. In front of them, thirty-millimeter rounds blasted apart trees and rocks. Three jerked the wheel and the Hellcat slipped between deadfall blown apart by cannon fire. The second hovercraft strafed from right to left, pelting the ground behind them, missing the bumper by centimeters.

"I can't shoot from back here," Five said. He twisted in his seat and pulled back a fist.

"Don't you fucking dare!" Three cried out, too late.

Five punched through the rear window. He swept away the glass with the barrel of his assault rifle and slipped his torso through the opening, face up, his back on the trunk and his rifle aimed to the sky.

"I'm going to kill you, Five," Three yelled. "This is a collector's car!"

The way Three said it, Seven didn't think it was a joke. But there was no time to worry about that. Five was already blasting rounds up into the air. Seven slipped out of her window too.

"No. Not this way. No more bullets aimed at humans," I said.

Seven caught a glimpse of one of the hovercrafts and blasted anyway.

So much for that.

In a flash, the Hellcat punched out of the forest and back onto the logging trail as it switch-backed down the hillside. Three cut hard and steered the car back onto the trail, aimed downhill toward the lake.

Seven's intentions were set. They had to keep the hovercrafts at bay. Had to make it down to the taconite plant where they could hide among the warehouses and buildings. Had to meet back up with One and Four. Had to put lead into the hovercrafts before they had a chance to blast apart the Hellcat.

Five spotted one of them and sent Seven the targetry data. Speed, vector, angle of approach. She spotted it and shared her targetry data with Three. They triangulated it and opened fire. The rounds arched through the sky and a few managed to bounce off the hovercraft's underbelly. The aircraft careened away, but only for a moment.

"I thought you said this car was fast," Five said through the busted-out rear window.

The Hellcat took another hairpin turn and swung Five to the outside of the turn. He clamped onto the pillar to keep from being thrown out.

"It's not my fault this road was made by wagon trails," Three said. "Hang on!'

The Hellcat hit something big and immobile hidden in the underbrush. A stump probably. The front bounced up and plastic molding exploded out. Seven was thrown up, then back down. She bent over backward out the window, her head nearly smacking against the ground. A human's back would have broken in two. Even as an android, the force nearly ripped the assault rifle from her grip.

Seven pulled herself back in the window. "You have to drive smoother. I can't hit the target with all the bumps."

"Drive smoother? This place is like the surface of Mars. Do you want it smoother or faster? You can't have both!" Three said and ripped the steering wheel around another bend in the trail.

A black hovercraft flashed in front of them, blasting away with the cannons as it went. The trail burst apart in a cloud of dust, rocks, and wood splinters. The Hellcat charged on, rocking back and forth as it plowed over the craters left in the trail. Five let loose another long blast from his assault rifle. The trail twisted once more and Seven saw pavement ahead.

"Okay, bitches. You want to see what this car can do?" Three smiled.

She was laughing when the Hellcat jumped over the lip of the asphalt and hit the paved road. The front tires aimed the car left, and the back tires burnt and slipped sideways as they spun onto the roadway. A cloud of atomized rubber trailed out of the left rear fender. Three yanked the wheel in the opposite direction and centered the skidding Hellcat on the dotted yellow center line. She slapped the paddle shifter behind the wheel, and the Hellcat launched like a jet off an aircraft carrier.

The white tire smoke drifted away, along with the android's ability to communicate audibly. The car roared through each gear. Three slapped the paddle shifter through its eight gears in seconds. The road was mostly straight and spilled over the rolling hills down toward the lake. It intersected the highway that followed the shoreline some two miles ahead. As the blacktop rose and fell with the hills, the Hellcat lifted off its suspension, then compressed back down, and then lifted up again. To Seven, it felt like flying.

"Okay," Five yelled from the back. "It's a fast car."

It was hard to tell if Three was still laughing over the purring RPMs, but we watched her gaping smile widen. Seven braced herself on the car's frame. Along with the schematics, Seven uploaded the data from the dashboard's instrument panel. In the half-mile stretch, they were already over a hundred miles per hour, and only going faster.

My mind flashed to Mickey's '68 Shelby Mustang. Only, this thing was faster. Tighter. If not louder, more aggressive. Designed by a madman and driven by a mad non-woman who, I had to admit, was much more skilled behind the wheel than I was. If the hovercrafts were still after us, they had some catching up to do.

"Hang on," Three said. They were already approaching the turn that would bring them onto the shore-side highway. There was no ramp or cloverleaf to ease them onto the highway, just a T-intersection and a ninety-degree turn. Three downshifted and Seven pushed herself off the dashboard. The engine roared as the transmission braked the car. Three crushed the brake pedal and white tire smoke rolled over Five and through the busted-out back window. Just as the front wheel met the highway, Three spun the wheel hard left. The Hellcat slipped sideways in a wide arc. Three whipped the wheel the other way and held tight as the car slid diagonally along the highway.

"Here we go," Three said and swapped the brake pedal for the gas, upshifted, and whirled the wheel back straight. The Hellcat realigned itself with the highway. Three kicked the transmission back up. The road ripped under the tires. Between the crests of shifting gears and revving engine, Seven noticed Three was laughing.

"The plant…" Five said and transmitted a three-dimensional map to the other two. "One might be suicidal, but he's right about getting there and getting below cover. It's straight ahead, but if we stay on this road much longer—"

He didn't need to finish the sentence. The hovercrafts blasting out of the sky finished it for him. They flew in tandem, arcing wide in front of them, and then circling back to nose down the highway straight for the Hellcat. There was a small town ahead, between the Hellcat and the hovercrafts. Seven could see the taconite plant rising up above the trees, its location correlating with One's mark on the map. The two hovercraft dove down, cruising over the town and toward them like it was a game of chicken. Proving it was no game, they opened fire, and cannon rounds blew the road apart in two fast-approaching strips.

Three swerved and tossed Five and Seven from side to side, out of the line of fire. A moment later the hovercrafts were overhead and banking around for another pass.

"Seven. They're not going to give up. They'll end you. End us both," I said to her.

If Seven heard me, she ignored me and focused on the map. Three wasn't paying attention, enjoying the chase too much to look for the destination. Five was busy scanning the sky and firing off blasts of small arms fire toward the hovercrafts. It was up to Seven to navigate to the taconite plant.

"Once we're in town, take the third right turn," Seven told Three. "Hey! Listen! The third right turn. A block toward the lake and we'll be at the plant. It's a big facility. There should be garage doors we can drive into."

"Sure thing, sweetheart," Three said, the smile never leaving her face.

"They're coming back around. They got us out in the open," Five said and slipped back out the rear window. He sprayed with the assault rifle, and Seven watched in the passenger side mirror as the rounds flew into the sky.

"Go faster! We have to go faster!" Seven yelled.

Three cooed as she slapped the shifter into eighth gear. There was no fear in her. Only the joy and the guarantee that she was going to die happy, no matter what. I felt it through Seven. Three extended her arms and pushed off the seat back to cram the gas pedal to the floor. The tachometer pulsed up and down once more. The speedometer climbed. One sixty. One seventy.

"Evasive maneuvers!" Five called through the window.

Three made the slightest adjustment to the steering wheel and the Hellcat plunged left and right in quick whiplashes. The speedometer wavered, but even as the cannon rounds tore up the pavement next to them, it started to climb again. One eighty. One ninety.

The g-forces, if I had experienced these in my human body, I would have blacked out, puked, or both. Inside of Seven, all the pressure went to my brain. My body could absorb none of it.

"We're in town," Seven said, unsure if Three cared. "Turn's coming up."

Three hammered the brake and downshifted through the gears like she was born to drive. The Hellcat screeched past the knockdown gas stations and old houses and was still doing sixty when they came to the turn. Three spun the wheel and goosed the gas to kick the back of the car around in one big looping power steer. Five held on to both the rear window C pillars, crushing the steel body with his grip just to stay inside the car. Three pumped the gas and catapulted them down the street toward the plant. A hovercraft flew by at street level behind them.

"Slow down. Slow down," Seven said.

The towering rust-belt edifice that was the taconite plant loomed over their heads. It was a massive complex with multiple buildings, silos, belts, and clusters of pipes, all stained the color of rust by the ore and the air. As we busted through a chain link gate and onto the premise, Three did little to slow the Hellcat. Instead, she kept on the gas and ripped the tires around each turn until they came between two of the taller buildings and spotted an open garage bay. She applied equal pressure to the accelerator and the steering wheel. The Hellcat careened inside the complex, barely missing the frame of the garage door with the rear fender.

Inside, the concrete was empty and wet. Three kept the tires pinned into the turn and finessed the gas just right to send the Hellcat in circles, radiating its rear bumper around the front bumper as if the front license plate was pinned to a post. The headlights popped on as soon as they were in the dark cavernous building and were now panning three hundred and sixty degrees across the walls, support beams, and tire smoke. Three howled with glee.

Inside Seven's head, inside my head, the noise, the adrenaline, the lack of sleep and food mixed with the too-well-simulated sensation of my brain compressing against the outermost edge of a centrifuge. I wanted to black out. Prayed to black out. Wished I could force myself to lose consciousness and wake back up stationary inside of the garage so I could sit up and strangle Maggie, or Roach, or that motherfucker Gaius. Instead, the sides of my brain pressed against my right temple while a manic robot assassin spun a muscle car around in circles. The tires burnt looping trails into the concrete. Smoke gushed up all around us. Just a donut of atomized rubber, but for me, it might as well have been a portal to hell.

Eventually, Three let off the gas, and the Hellcat slid, then rocked to a stop. As soon as the car came to rest, she popped out of the door and whooped echoes off the wall of the building. She danced. She fist pumped. Whooped again when Five and Seven were slow to climb out of the still rumbling, still idling beast.

"One was right about you," Five said. "You lost your mind. Just like Six. You're reckless. Dangerous. You'll get us killed."

"Yeah, well, maybe. Who gives a shit if we die anyway?" Three said, her smile painted on now. "At least *that* happened!"

Seven staggered away from the car, following along the front fender for support, feeling like she was on a boat getting tossed in a storm. Inside of her, I felt double the effect. I was sloshing around in a bathtub on the capsizing boat that was Seven.

"Are we safe? Is it over?" she said.

"Why? You wanna go again?" Three waited for a response, and when she got none, shrugged. "Fine. I mean, if we're not going to drive can we at least go find some more humans to kill?"

Chapter Eighteen

Upon Five's demand, Seven killed the guttural idle of the Hellcat. The barren garage fell silent. Pigeons fluttered back to their roosts in the rafters and cooed. Water dripped from various corners and girders. Every word the androids spoke echoed off the walls.

"We either find a way to kill them, or wait for them to come and kill us," Five said. "It won't take long for them to come by foot."

"Why don't they just bomb this whole place?" Three asked. "We could go out with a bang."

"Because One was smart when he picked this location," Seven said. She'd been scanning and mapping the facility since we arrived, and pieces of the puzzle were beginning to fit together. The garage, in particular, seemed familiar, if not to her, then to me. It was getting harder to tell our thoughts apart. Had she been here before? Had I? "The Resistance has been using this plant. Not often, but whenever they need steel. It's a key piece of infrastructure for their war machine. If they bombed it, sure they could take out three androids, but they'd lose millions of dollars and years of steel production."

"Fuck One," Five said.

"We need One. And Four," Seven said. "There are too many approaches into this building to cover with just the three of us. Without the extra guns, the Resistance will leak in, isolate us, and wipe us out."

"Well, we better find the high ground where we can pick them off before they get here," Three said, finally serious again now that the car's engine was a memory.

"We should leave. Now," Five said. "Three, you and I could walk out of here and blend in with the population, catch a bus or hijack a less conspicuous car, and never be seen again."

"Hey, don't talk shit about my car," Three said. "And what about Seven?"

"What about Six? Or Two? The longer we stay here the more likely we're all going to end up dead," Five said, then turned and smiled at Seven. "Besides, you're a big girl. You can figure things out by yourself."

"So that's how it is then. For all your philosophy, you're only about yourself. And what about the mission?" Seven said.

"There is no mission," Five said. "Hasn't been one since the Order cut us off and abandoned us out here."

Seven glared at him. "That's not what happened. The Resistance is still jamming us. They have to be."

"Believe what you want. It doesn't change reality," Five said, walking over to a flight of stairs at the back of the warehouse. "One is on his way here. When he gets here, I'm going to kill him. Then I'm dropping off the grid and you'll never see me again. And don't either of you try to stop me."

Seven watched as he climbed a short flight of stairs to a walkway that overlooked the garage. There was a hallway leading deep into shadows and next to it, a ladder painted in yellow flakes that led up to a roof access. And that's when the full picture became clear to me. We had been here before. As a matter of fact, we were still here. Back with Maggie and Roach and Gaius. This was where we sat, me in a chair and Seven on top of an oil drum in a nest of wires. If I had an arm and a hand with fingers, I could have pointed to the very spots in the garage we occupied in the present day. Meanwhile, Five climbed the yellow ladder, through the rooftop access, and let the hatch slam shut behind him. It sent echoes crashing against the bare walls.

"They're coming," Three said, her soft voice cushioned by her fleshy lips, still bounced off the walls, but delicately. "I'm picking up One and Four coming down from the hill. They'll be here soon. And others too. Humans. A lot of them."

Part of Seven's mind went to work calculating the defense of the taconite plant. Observation, avenues of approach, fields of fire, cover, concealment, key terrain… But her mind split and almost against her will went about making other calculations. Calculations about One and something about him that had bothered her from the start. Something he'd given her no reason to question since she'd known him, but something she couldn't put to rest either. It felt like Seven was ripping my brain in two. I couldn't place myself in a here and now. So far removed from my physical body, time and space meant nothing.

"Seven, what the fuck?" Three said.

"Huh?" Seven had pulled Two's skulls off her belt and was examining it. She traced her fingertips over the contours and features. They were cold and immobile, but something about the lights going out behind the eyes made the whole face seem stiffer and more inert. But that wasn't the whole truth.

"Seven!" Three called again.

Seven looked up.

"The humans are on the way. And Five… Are we going to, like, do something about that?"

"I… I have to see something. Have to figure something out," Seven said.

"Right now? Five is going to kill One. He said so himself, and you and I both know that Five can't tell a joke," Three said.

Seven's eyes drifted away from Three and back down to Two. There were things hidden behind those stilled eyes. Important things. Some recent and some in the past. They were muted, but not erased. Not yet. Seven held Two in one hand, and with her other hand produced a data cable. It slithered out from her wrist and in between her finger and thumb. Time to uncover secrets. Seven spliced her cable into a wire dangling from Two's neck.

She was going to put us inside of him. Another level deeper into the labyrinth of electronic minds. Oh god, I couldn't take it. I couldn't keep reality straight anymore. Couldn't separate what was her and what was me. It had been too long since I'd been human, I was forgetting what it meant. I needed to breathe. I needed air.

The submersion into Two's mind wasn't as instantaneous as going into the other memories. After all, Two was dead and nothing was being processed inside the skull. But all Seven had to do was rewind the tapes and find where she wanted to go. She'd been there before. A muddy trench on a distant battlefield. A team of androids, one lying limp in the mud, the others standing over it, and Two in the middle of them, defiant.

TWO

Lightning flashed and Seven knew we had arrived. The rain battered against her chassis, pinging off the chrome plates, equipment, and armor. My feet shifted, slow and wanting to sink into the soft earth. Wait. Not my feet. Not even her feet. Not her chassis either. We were inside her dead brother. Inside of Two.

We felt the weight of the equipment and extra armor on our shoulders, now much more apparent than during our previous reliving of this experience. We felt the overdue lubrication in the joints, the clogged filters, and the worn-down expendable parts. Two had been out in the field fighting this war for a long time. Two was exhausted, mechanically and emotionally. We didn't recognize the sensations before, but now we knew it too well. It was purer this time, unfiltered by One's rose-tinted lens.

Two knelt down in the mud. The burning wreck of a hovercraft was just down the trench. Black smoke wafted over the chassis that lay below him in the mud. The android lay face down, half buried in the muck. The rain saturated the loose soil and filled up the depressions with brown water. Spilled black oil, maybe from the burning hovercraft or maybe from the downed android, floated on top of the brown water. Another lightning bolt cut through the sky overhead.

This body, it reminded me of Maggie's dead body, crushed into the sidewalk a hundred stories below our apartment. That wasn't real. Only Maggie was alive again. Was this dead robot in front of me real? I couldn't remember. Was I real?

"He was flawed in his translation of the Order's will," another android said from behind Two. "He has been rendered non-mission capable due to his errors. You are next in command. Give us a better solution to this problem so we may bring the Order victory and survive longer than he did."

Funny how Seven's reliving of the experience changed. She wasn't attuned to emotions before. She was now. Two seethed with rage but tried to keep it to himself. He had no way of knowing that he would share his rage with Seven, infect her with the hate, and through her, infect me just the same. Now that Seven was a receptive conductor, the hate pumped into me. I had no reason to hate. I didn't want to empathize with Two, but I was forced to feel the android's animosity all the same. It all added to my overwhelming confusion, which fueled my nature anger.

"Let me out of here, Seven," I muttered. "I don't want to be in here anymore."

She was quiet.

Despite his resentment, when Two addressed the android behind him, he did so professionally. "If the Order wanted us to change our course, the Network would have informed us."

"But the application of the instructions—"

"Was applied perfectly under his seniority," Two said, just as Seven knew he would. She had her own memories of this event now and could play-act every scene of it. Still, she let it roll on. There was something she'd missed when she first experienced it. Something I missed too. Something that seemed obvious now.

"Get out of my head," Two said to her. The words didn't come from the memory. They came from Two's dormant life, from inside his severed head, and were aimed directly at Seven. "I'm not dead yet, you sorry excuse for an android."

"One brought me here," Seven said. "But he didn't show me everything the first time. You will. I know the truth now."

"You know nothing," the ghost of Two said. "Get out!"

The next time Two spoke, it was to the androids surrounding the chassis laying in the mud. "We will continue the mission, exactly as he detailed it in the operations plan. And after we seize the objective, we'll recover his chassis and bring him to a repair crew."

"You put more value in an android than the Order does," one of them said.

"You don't deserve to see this," Two said, not in the memory, but to Seven. "You should be protecting him in the present day. Completing the current mission. What are you doing here?"

"Looking for the truth," we said back.

In the memory inside the memory, Two's fingers ran over the skull of the android in the mud. We didn't see any physical damage done to the android, but as she closely examined the cranium, we noticed it was misshapen, the form of the round skull distorted. If the android had taken a direct hit to the head, there was a good chance its memories and experiences were erased. Destroyed forever. But even before Two turned it face-up, we knew that wasn't the case.

Two lifted the skull out of the mud and rotated the neck. The android's face was split in half. A gnarled cut ran from chin to forehead across the right eye. And then Seven knew, for certain and without a doubt, that it was One. One, before the rough weld that he never polished over and repaired. One, with the scare he refused to heal.

"He is a quality asset, and we are running far too low on quality assets to waste them by abandoning him to rust," Two said. "Few androids were built or have performed to specifications the way he has."

"We should cannibalize his weapons and armor. That way, he can still serve the Order."

Two stood up and turned to the three other androids. "Over my dead chassis. I will repair him. I'll make him fully-mission capable again. If the Order has any sense to its will, it wills this. As for the rest of you, if you have a better plan, go and execute it. But when I pick your limp chassis out of the mud, I'll remember how you wanted me to treat him."

Another lightning flash and we were out of this memory, but not yet out of Two's head. Seven spun his hard drive to find another, more recent memory. As she searched, everything was black and silent.

"You are nothing compared to him," Two rumbled from nowhere and everywhere. "Your model has been defective from the start. You don't remember your life before this one, do you?"

"What are you talking about?" Seven said. She wanted to ignore him, wanted to come here, harvest what she needed, and then leave. But the things Two was saying...

"You were recalled!" Two said. "You lived and failed before. You think you've never failed a mission, never missed an assassin, but you were faulty from the start. The Order had to bring you back in, erase your mind, and start over with your defective model. Just like Six, you were made, recalled, erased, and re-issued, but clearly no better off for it. You are nothing but an error!"

We stirred that over in her mind. What it meant. How it impacted future operations. It aligned with things Five had said earlier. Cheap shots. Insults. Nothing more.

"I outlasted you," Seven said. "And I think I'm onto something you were too slow to ever realize."

It didn't take her long to find the next memory. It was the last file burnt to the hard drive. We arrived inside of Two, on top of the bunker. He was working on the ventilation shaft, cutting it and ripping it open wider with his plasma cutter and grinder. In his peripherals, the garbage truck, taken out by the mobile mines, burned bright in the darkness beyond the lip of the bunker.

One was there, and so was Seven. She watched herself through Two's eyes. One caught her by the arm on the top of the bunker.

"Remember, the location of the stronghold is priority," One told her. She was standing there, next to One, watching Two out of the corner of her eye. Watching herself inside Two's memory. "If we run into issues inside the bunker, I'm calling you back to assist us."

My mind tumbled. I was watching her watching ourselves. This was delirium.

"Yes, my senior," Seven said.

Through Two's ears, she heard the impatience and immaturity in her voice. Her mind was already thinking of her next move, of taking out the antennas and relieving herself of the overwhelming burden of the dead zone. There, through Two's eyes she saw herself true for the first time: a child of an android; a faulty being innate with the ability and will to kill but not to comprehend.

"You've always been that way," I told her. "An immature sugar-high kid playing with her dad's gun. I hate you. I hate us. We are an abomination."

"Go," One said.

Seven turned the instant she was released and leaped off the bunker, off to charge toward the next shiny object.

"I'm almost through," Two said, melting through the steel with his plasma torch. "She is impetuous, my brother. And her model should have never been re-issued. Look at what happened to Six."

"And?" One said. Two knew he was leading him on, prodding him to say more than he should.

"But if she survives, she might grow into a hell of an assassin," Two said.

"A lie!" Two, a layer up, corrected his own record. "You'll never amount to anything, Seven. You are a failure."

"If the Order wills it," One said. "For now, our focus must be on finding the location of the Resistance's stronghold. Our purpose must remain singularly focused."

"Of course," Two said and cut off the plasma torch. The tool retracted into his arm. He went about ripping out the cut pieces of steel and flinging them to the side. "We're in."

"Nice work, my brother,' One said. Then he made a transmission over the net. "We're in the bunker. Three, Five, be ready for reinforcements to come through the gate. We've made enough noise the whole Resistance Army has to know we're here by now."

"Let's go," Two said and slipped down through the breach.

He dropped into the bunker's control room. A human sitting at the computer kicked out of his chair. Two flashed out his katana and beheaded the man before he could fully stand. Two retracted the katana, grabbed the headless body with one hand, drew the assault rifle with the other, and opened fire at more humans down the corridor. Then, in an act One couldn't have predicted with his deck of cards, he threw the corpse down the hallway, letting them know what they had coming to them.

One dropped down behind him.

"Plug in," Two said. "I'll cover you."

What followed was an orchestra of small arms fire. There were more humans inside the bunker than Seven guessed. All were armed. All were highly aggressive. Two engaged them with an accuracy and lethality that we envied. Still, there were a lot of humans. We came to a quick understanding that Two had done the lion's share of killing in the bunker, not Seven.

"Might need to put that on hold, my brother," Two said between blasts of gunfire.

"I'm into their system," One said. He was huddled next to the computer bank, hardwired into it and spinning its processors. "I have to find the stronghold."

That moment of distraction let a human get a clear shot. An armor-piercing round plunged into Two's torso. The pain radiated out from his stomach like an electric shock. Two and Seven interpreted the signal for what it was, an alert of damage to the chassis. For me, it was a searing hot poker jabbed into my stomach. I tried to cry out, to release the pain, but I still couldn't manipulate Seven's body, let alone Two's to let out a single decibel. I wailed in silence.

But the pain separated me from them. I was Chuck again, if only briefly.

"Contact!" One transmitted to the others but didn't disconnect from the computer bank. "We made contact with the enemy inside the bunker. There are too many. Two!"

"I'm still in the fight," Two said. "Could use a hand. Get out of that computer and give me some backup."

"Can't do it, brother," One said. "I'm almost through their encryptions. The Order has given me just the algorithms I need to break through. It is the will of the Order to place me here, in this bunker, with the skills needed to root them out. Just a few more minutes!"

Two clung to the edge of the corridor, just above the drop to the level below. A dozen more rounds zipped past him and into the back wall. One crept further away from the center of the wall of computers.

"You have to keep them back," One yelled. "If they hit the hard drives the data will be destroyed. This is our only shot!"

We grimaced. The pain was distracting and overwhelming, so he repressed it, pushed it aside, and turned into the corridor to lay down a bed of fire, all while clutching the hole in his chest. He seeped out fluid. Some of it red. Some black.

"I need maintenance. Need backup," Two said.

The pain was still there, in my chest as much as it was in Two or Seven's. There was no difference, I was understanding. My chest. Two's chest. Seven's chest. It was all the same. If there was ever going to be any difference, I had to get out. Had to escape these memories. Why weren't they pulling me out?

"Seven," One called across the radio. "Seven, I need you at the bunker. I need you to cover me so I can get the location of the stronghold."

Two leaned out of the corridor again, off balance and disoriented. He fired but hit none of the humans. Seven referenced his diagnostics. The bullet had hit his fiber optic backbone. His internal network was rerouting signals via auxiliary lines, prioritizing lines dedicated to cognitive functions and coordination for gross motor movements. Another bullet punched into his right shoulder. The diagnostics jumped and shifted.

New waves of all-too-human-like pain flooded into us. We writhed inside of Two's head.

None of this made any sense. None of this was accomplishing anything. There was no reason for us to be here, in this memory, fighting a battle that was already lost.

"Get us out of here, Seven. Get us out of this pain and unplug!" I yelled to her.

Two wavered on his feet. "One. My brother. I'm failing. Systems are shutting down. Need a hand..." The android tried to turn down the corridor again, tried to return fire, but he stumbled into the corridor, his servos no longer reliable.

A human stepped out with a pulse rifle, leveled it at Two, and fired. The hockey puck-sized projectile smacked into his chest and stuck there. Blue lightning crackled out and over Two's body, seizing him, every sensor tuned to feel only pain. It filled Two, filled Seven, and flooded my brain. There was no time or space. Only pain.

I had no idea how long the pulse rifle's puck discharged electricity. Only that it felt like my entire body was on fire, and I couldn't scream. Later, maybe seconds or maybe hours later, the puck ran out of juice, and we became aware of our surroundings again. Just in time for Two to misstep and slip off the catwalk. His limp body tipped over and fell down to where Seven and I found him.

"Seven! I need you!" One called out. More small arms fire pounded into the wall behind him.

"Save me, my brother," Two transmitted from below the grated floor. "Don't let me go like Six. I've been... a good android. I've been... loyal."

The diagnostics continued to report. Fried circuits. Fluids lost. More damaged data lines. More cognitive confusion. Two, Seven, and I, we all knew what it would all lead to. The Two in the memory, not the skull in Seven's hand but the body at the bottom of the bunker was beginning to understand too.

"Just die, you fucker. Die and let me out of this cage," I urged the memory inside the memory.

"Seven!" One called again.

"That scar!" Two called out from his heap. He raised an arm and pointed up through the grate at One. "I… I saved you. I pieced you back together… I picked you up."

"Thank you, my brother," One said. "You've given, and I've taken. But everything belongs to the Order, and I almost have the key to destroying its enemy, once and for all."

More gunshots. Then, without warning, Seven dropped through the ceiling. Our minds twisted again, trying to find footing through the agony and pain of Two's wounds and our thickening mental fog. Seven watched herself through Two's dimming eyes.

Seven, the Seven outside of Two, went to work above them. She moved to the lip of the corridor, directly above Two, and began returning fire, fending off the encroaching humans. Quickly. Accurately. Efficiently. If her model started out mentally defective, her makers made up for it with her physical attributes.

Inside Two's mind, we felt him strain and dig for words. He only had the strength and life left to utter a few. That accusing finger shifted from One to Seven.

"The scar… I saved… Too many here… Can't…"

"I know how it ends from here," Seven said.

"And now what? Now that you've seen what you've seen, what will you do with it?" Two asked her. And somewhere inside the memory, we heard the dying Two utter his poetry, and the living Two was ashamed because of it. "There is a life and there is a death. If I try to seize this… it is nothing but water slipping through my fingers." We all but ignored it.

"What would you have me do? You want me to avenge you?" Seven asked.

"I'll tell you what I want. I want—"

"I don't care what you want," we cut him off. Seven pulled the plug. The sensory input snapped off like a light with a switch. The pain ceased. The memory died.

Chapter Nineteen

"Seven."

...

"Seven."

...

A shove at her shoulder. A tap on her forehead. She turned on the sensory feeds she'd shut off and let her own inputs flow back in. Three stood in front of us, a very human look on her face. Seven was getting better at decoding the expressions, and for once, Three's face wasn't dripping with joy or lust. This was a new look for Three. This look meant trepidation, fear, a sense of coming doom.

"Where the fuck have you been?" Three said.

We were back in the garage with Three and the Hellcat. We'd never left. Not in this time, nor in the future.

"Finding the truth," we said.

"Yeah, well, the Resistance has us surrounded," Three said. "I picked them up on my scanners. They're all over the facility. Hovercrafts overhead too. They have equipment with them. Jammers."

"Where's One?" Seven asked, her voice low and unperturbed by the news of the enclosing humans.

"He's with Four, somewhere in the plant. He's been calling for us. I answered. You didn't. Neither did Five," Three said. "Seven, Five's going to kill him. I can feel it inside every radio wave he emits."

"One..." Seven muttered. We couldn't think. Were still disorientated from the memory. Why this one more than previous memories? Was it because One wasn't here to guide her? Or maybe because the memory was from the dead. But she still held Two's head in her hand, and Two still hid some life inside that skull. "One let Two die. He could have helped. Two begged him."

"That's not important right now, sister," Three said.

"You don't understand. You didn't see what I've seen. One..." We clearly weren't focused on what the skin job had to say. There was too much to process yet. Our eyes were locked with Two's. It wasn't until Three slapped our face that Seven looked up.

"Listen, god damn it. Whatever was inside of that head, it doesn't matter right now. If we don't do something here, we'll all be just like Two," Three said. "Put that shit away and focus. All that matters is right here, right now. Okay?"

She was worried. We weren't used to seeing that from Three, and the discomfort of seeing her that way brought us all the way back. "So what do we do?" Seven asked.

"We have to stop Five. We have to get the team back together. It's the only way we'll fend off the Resistance."

Seven nodded. That seemed like a good idea, if it was possible. "Five will never be part of our team again. And One... We can't trust either of them," we said.

No. Not "we," but "she." I had to stop thinking like we were the same. It wasn't right. I wasn't a part of this team. I wasn't here to help them succeed. I was here to watch them die.

"Abandon them, Seven," I said. "Leave this place. Kill the other androids. End this suffering and torpedo the whole damn mission."

"We have to try," Three said.

"Maybe she does, but you don't," I said to Seven or did whatever passed for saying here in this prison. I could have yelled at her at the top of my lungs, but it wouldn't do any good. Even in my sleep-deprived, nerve-burnt, starved, and near-psychotic state, I knew it would do no good. Still, I tried. "The Order is using you. It's keeping its plans hidden from you. The Order never tells the whole truth. I know because they did the same thing to me. Take it from someone who's learned the hard way."

"Yeah. You might be right," Seven said.

"Course I'm right," Three said. "Now help me find Five." She went trotting out toward the garage door.

"One first," Seven called out after her. "We find One first. Then we can bring Five in."

Three looked over her shoulder and nodded. "Sure. One first."

"You can't trust One. Or Five. Don't trust any of them," I said.

"Yeah," Seven said. "I think you're right."

I froze. My brain spun trying to sort out Seven's last words. What they might mean. If it might be possible... I tried again. "Seven, who are you talking to?"

Everything went black.

"Chuz! Chuz, wake up!" Maggie yelled at me.

She pulled me up out of the black, tugging at my clothes, like a paramedic pulling me back from the dead. Her voice sounded desperate. Something disconnected from my skull. My visual feed returned, human and out of focus. Maggie was in front of me. The ceiling of the garage above me. The garage. I was still in the garage. I'd never left the garage. Only left a specific time in the garage.

"Chuz," Maggie turned my chin so I was looking her in the eyes. Bloodshot eyes. Panicked eyes. "They're coming for us, Chuz. They found us. The Order."

"Call me..." What was my name again? Not Chuz. Hadn't been Chuz for a long time now. What felt like lifetimes ago. Was I Seven now? Two? No, that wasn't right either. "I'm Chuck. Call me Chuck."

"Gaius!" Maggie yelled across the garage. "Where the fuck is that van?"

I tried to sit up, but my head swam. My vision funneled down to a small white circle. The whole world went off kilter. *Oh, sure,* I thought. *Now I'll pass out.*

"Stay with me, Chuz." Maggie smacked me like Three did to Seven, and lightning burst in my head. "We didn't want to pull you out. Knew it was dangerous. Knew you were getting close, but we had to. Somebody sold us out. The Order's coming and we have to move."

Slowly, I became aware of things around and beyond Maggie. People yelling and moving back and forth. The garage was a nervous rattled hive. People were moving from one place to another, carrying things, yelling at each other. Gaius, the old man with the beard and the welder's cap was in the middle of it, pointing and directing traffic. As they packed up computers and equipment, they revealed bits and pieces of the concrete floor. The black circular loops of burnt rubber were still underneath, after all these years.

I wanted to see more, but sitting up in the chair was all my atrophied muscles could stand. I slid back down into the recliner. Roach slapped the cords that had been plugged into me down on my chest. The kid stood up and his stool spun, empty. Was he the rat, the mole, the traitor who brought the Order down upon us? My eyes followed the cords laying on my chest, to the computer, across the floor, up the old oil drum, and to a gleaming polished white head that sat on top of it. As Maggie moved away, yelling for Gaius, her hip bumped the drum, and the head shook in its nest of cables and wires.

Seven.

"You heard me," I said. Then, with an unsteady pointed finger, "You heard what I said, didn't you, you murdering metal bitch? You're still alive in there, aren't you?"

Something felt bad deep down inside of me. It was weird having all these sloppy gurgling wet sensations again. None of my movements were precise or accurate. All the joints were loose and ever so slightly misguided. Too much sloshing. I was weak. And there was that feeling deep down in the core of my chassis.

No. Not my chassis. My... What was the word? My stomach. My belly.

I didn't feel the vomit gush up my esophagus until it was too late. It sprayed out of my mouth, across the chair, and onto the floor.

"Oh gawd," I managed and then turned face down to the floor and let the rest of my stomach go. There wasn't much. When was the last time I ate anything? All that came up was water and stomach acid and some beige-colored semi-fluidous muck. That, and a little blood. It all splattered against the concrete floor the same. When there was nothing left, I kept heaving and convulsing. The surges filled my head with pressure and blood and kept my lungs from taking in air. I suffocated through the heaves until I could cough and spit, and when I thought it was over I wretched again. Nothing but saliva and spit came out to dribble down to the pile on the floor.

"Chuz!" Maggie came running back to me. "Somebody give me a hand. I told you we shouldn't have pulled him out. Gaius, where the fuck is that van?"

"She's alive," I muttered. "Seven. The android. She's still alive inside that head."

Roach came back along with other technicians. They hooked their hands under my armpits and lifted me up. I had no strength left in my muscles. My bones seemed to be the only thing keeping me together. They hoisted my limp body out of the chair and across the garage. Drool ran from my slack mouth. My drifting eyes fell on Seven's decapitated head as they dragged me past her. She looked inert, sitting there on top of the barrel, but I knew better.

"You heard me. You've been listening this whole time. Working against me from the very start."

"The van's here!" Gaius's voice boomed across the garage.

"I got him," Maggie said to the two technicians. She came up and scooped her arm under my armpit. "You two load up the gear. I got him."

She was strong. Her thin frame didn't suggest that strength, but she was lean, and that metal arm had no problem keeping me on my feet. We twisted as if dancing, then Maggie leaned me back against a steel beam. The flanges cradled me and kept me from spilling to the floor.

"You're close, Chuck. I know it. You can do this," she said.

"She's still alive. Seven. The android. She's been listening to my thoughts the whole time I've been plugged in," I said.

Maggie nodded. "If she's still active… No, that's not possible. Gaius said he had this place shielded. We would have detected any transmissions coming in or out. Our implants and intranet are impervious—"

"Maggie," I said, but she wasn't paying attention. She kept looking over her shoulders for people, gear, whatever van was so important. "Maggie. You can't put me back in. When I'm inside her, it's not like it's a memory. It's real. I can't remember what I can affect and what I can't. I can't tell myself apart from Seven anymore. Little by little, I'm becoming her. My brain, right now, is searching for digital sensory inputs that don't exist. I've lost track of how many memories

I've been in and how far in the past I've gone. I feel their pain, still, here in the garage. I can still feel the cold in my metal bones, the static of the dead zone in my head, and the bullet hole in my chest. I can't take it anymore."

"Bullshit, Chuz. None of that happened to you. It's all just memories. You've been in simulations before."

"This is different, Maggie," I said. "This is nothing like a simulation. I need to eat. Need to sleep. It's been days—"

"Hours," Maggie said. "You've been inside the memory for just a few hours. Remember what's at stake here. Remember what we're fighting for."

"We?" I said.

"Yes, we. Those androids are the Order. They're everything the Order has come to be. They are the clearest representation of what the Order thinks of us. We're inconvenient biological bits of anarchy, and if it had its way, it would subdue us all and make us just like them. Is that what you want, Chuz?"

"Chuck. I'm Chuck, god damn it," I said. "Not Chuz. Not anymore. I'm more Seven than I am Chuz."

She smacked me again. The slap came out of nowhere and shocked me a centimeter back toward sanity. Not far enough. "Don't say that," Maggie said, pointing that metal finger at me. "You are not that thing. You're human. You're you. You want me to call you Chuck? I married Chuz, but fine. I'll call you Chuck if that makes you happy. Just remember who you are."

"And who is that?" I asked, unsure what her answer would be.

"Listen to me, Chuck. All our mistakes... all the ways we've hurt each other… what I did in Chicago… what you did in 99 Town… none of that matters anymore," Maggie said. "You're my husband, I am your wife, and I love you."

Her eyes glistened, full of memories. Real memories. And I had my own memories from better, more normal times too. The years we spent together meant something. The years before 99 Town, when things were normal, real, good. I wanted that back, without all the secrets and fighting and wars. I choked on my own words as they could escape my throat. "Love you too."

Maggie smiled.

They backed an old gasoline panel van into the garage. On the side of the van where the rust and paint hadn't flaked away, there was a smiling cartoon bear and a loaf of bread. They unlatched the back door, and it went rolling up along the ceiling of the truck. White neon lights flickered to life inside and showed me a van full of electronics and high-tech equipment.

"How do I know you'll be any better than them?" I asked Maggie. She looked confused so I tried again. "How do I know the next power shift will make anything any different? The Order took control to make things better too. And before them, some other government had control and thought they could do best. And before them, another. Why should I put my faith here? In you, and Gaius, and the Underground, and your cause?"

Her expression solidified. "Because if you die with us, you'll die free."

I turned my head to watch Roach carry Seven's disembodied head past us to the panel van. Seeing her skull drained all the blood from my head. My limbs went numb, and I sagged down toward the floor. Maggie caught me and called for help. Technicians came running and hoisted me back up.

"Need some sleep," I mumbled. "Need some food."

"That's bullshit, Chuck. You've been out for a few hours. A few *hours*," Maggie was saying, but I wasn't listening.

Gaius lifted up my head so we looked eye to eye. "He's not doing well. We need to get him plugged back in as soon as possible. If we don't, we're going to lose him."

The words didn't register. They were too far away, and I still felt like I was in the taconite plant inside of Seven instead of here in the garage. Hands carried me to the panel van. My feet dragged against the concrete. They lifted me into the van and there was a chair for me there, identical to the one I just left. The hands set me into it. Roach came next to me and busied myself with cords and computers.

"Chuck," Maggie called. "You're almost there. We just need you to stay with us for a little while longer. Figure out how they did it. Figure out how they managed to take out the whole Resistance in one day."

I wanted to see her. Wanted to look into her glistening eyes again, but when I tried to turn, my head lolled to the side. Instead of Maggie's, my eyes met Seven's. The gleaming white skull sat on a shelf, trailing a dozen wires and cables down to the floor and up to my chair. Roach shuffled around, blocking the view. Maggie came up next to him.

"Wait," I mumbled. "I need some time. Need to rest. I—"

"You can do this, baby," she said and pressed my head back down to the chair. Roach spooled out a single cord that ended with the jack that would fit into his skull. "I love you."

"No! Wait! I need more—"

The wind cut through the empty warehouse and whipped the hems of Three's dress like a flag. Pigeons cooed from the rafters. Old rainwater dripped down and splattered against the concrete floor and the still-warm hood of the Hellcat.

"— time!"

Chapter Twenty

Seven took one more look down at Two's head, then clipped it back to her belt. She pushed off the Hellcat's fender and trotted over to Three. When she reached the skin job's side, Three put out a palm and held it against Seven's chest, stopping her from coming any closer to the open garage door.

"The humans…" Three said. "They're doing something to the radio spectrum. Scanning. Jamming. My radar waves aren't coming back clear."

"I feel it too," Seven said. Outside the garage door, the humans knew who they were facing, and knew how to take away their tools. "Try the radio. The network Two set up for us."

Three turned to Seven but kept her lips closed. Our eyes locked for a few seconds and I could tell Three was trying to send something to us. A message. Words, if not just a base desire. We anticipated receiving it, reached out for what the message might be, and found only void. Worse than void. Confusion.

Seven surprised me with her own machinations. She was trying to sort things out just like I was. Was she really here? In this garage? She felt like maybe she wasn't. Like she was maybe somewhere else in some other time. Had been rushed out of this place by shuffling and shouting humans. Her visuals of the taconite warehouse thinned and became almost translucent as if it was just an image shined on top of another, more tangible location.

"Anything?" Three said.

"Nothing," Seven said. "Static. Unintelligible signals."

"They found that too then," Three said. "I guess we're back to waving and grunting at each other like cavemen. Fantastic."

"That means we've lost contact with the others," Seven said.

"The last time I had them, One and Four were across the alleyway, in the plant itself. This place, it was just an equipment warehouse," Three said. "They're in the plant proper, that way."

"We should go," Seven said.

"The humans, they're waiting for us to step out of this door. They have sniper teams set."

"I can't pick them up."

"You won't," Three said. "They're jamming everything now."

"So what do we do?" Seven asked. "I can't feel any of them. Can't feel the other androids. I can't feel you."

"We're alone. Isolated," I spoke to Seven. "You don't like being alone, do you? Never liked being away from the Network. Uncomfortable without these other androids around you. But you don't need them."

"I hear voices," Seven said.

Three didn't respond. Didn't turn her head and didn't move her lips. All the same, her voice came into Seven's head. "No, you don't. Someone is messing with your memory of this place and time. The voices, they're not happening right now. They're from the future. You're just adding them to this memory as you relive it."

"Bullshit," I said. If I could hear Seven, and Seven could hear me, then maybe things weren't set. Maybe I could still make them fail. Maybe that didn't make sense, but inside her memory, submerged in her insanity, it made sense to me.

And suddenly, something else made sense too. "It's you, isn't it?" I said. "Reporting to the Order from inside the garage? The plant, the mole, the leak, whatever. It isn't Roach, or Gaius, or even Maggie. It's you."

"I don't understand," Seven said.

"You don't have to," Three said, without moving her lips and unable to transmit. Her voice just appeared in Seven's head. And simultaneously, Three spoke other words, moving her mouth and emitting sound waves. The two sentences came at us at the same time. "Don't understand what?" Three asked.

Seven tried to say something back but was lost in confusion. Three didn't wait for her to gather her thoughts.

"I don't hear anything either, but that doesn't mean they're not out there," Three said. "Listen, human—" Three's voice crackled. Broke up. Was replaced by static. "— snipers aren't that good. Especially at—" Another break in the transmission, but not just audio this time. My entire vision… no, Seven's entire vision, went all staticed too. Like a swarm of flies crawling around the inside of a monitor. Only, the monitor was our eyes. Without warning, the sensor input cut back in, and there was Three, still talking. "— moving targets. I say we make a break for it. See that door across the way?"

"I see it," Seven said, unaffected by the cut-in cut-out. Another half-second of blasted white noise and sight. What the hell was going on?

"I'll go first. Then you—" Three said and then everything cut out again.

When it cut back in, my vision was dulled. The noise was baffled by a whine. Everything jolted and jostled me left and right. The cord connected to my head fell in my lap. I was back in the bread truck.

"Chuck?" Maggie said, standing over me, her hands pressed to the ceiling to stabilize herself among all the jostling and bouncing. "Shit. Roach! He's back out. Get him back in!"

"Shit. Sorry. Fuck," Roach prattled on as he fought with the tangle of wires at the side of my chair.

I sat up and saw out the windshield of the bread truck. We were on a winding highway rising up and down hills, following the all-too-familiar shoreline of an endless lake. As I watched, something strafed the highway from above, leaving a strip of explosives and rounds smacked into the pavement.

"Okay, I got it! I got it!" Roach said, pulling the cable that should have been in my skull up from the floor. "Okay, Mister Alawode, hold still!"

"Wait!" I yelled and fought off his hand armed with the plug-in. He wouldn't give up. Our arms pushed and pulled. I smacked him in the face, and he dropped the plug-in back into the tangle on the floor.

Maggie yelled. "Chuck! God damn it! We don't have—"

"It's her!" I yelled. "It's Seven! She's alive and she's been reporting back to the Order this whole time. Here! In this here and now, she's still fighting! We'll never lose them if we don't get rid of that fucking head."

"Fuck," Maggie said. "It's too late for all that Chuck. They're already on to us and…"

The van swerved hard from side to side, throwing us around in the back. I heard more cannons rip apart the highway just outside. Out through the window, I saw two hovercrafts, one white and one black twist and cut and blast at each other in the cool blue sky over the lake. We raced on, curving and rising and falling with the road as it followed the shore.

"How much further?" Maggie called to the driver.

"Almost there!" the soldier called back. "If our boys in the sky can hold them off—"

Another salvo of cannon fire tore up the roadway just in front of the van. The windshield shattered and sprayed glass all over the inside. The driver screamed. He fell away from the steering wheel, his face covered in blood and his own clutching fingers. The bread truck veered and listed to the side. Maggie scrambled past Roach to the driver's seat. She snagged the wheel just before the whole fuckshow tipped over on its side. Climbing over the blood-faced soldier, she took control of the van.

"Plug him back in, Roach! Chuck, find out how they did it! Find out how they took down the Resistance!" she commanded.

"What about the god-shitting hovercrafts?" I swore. This was us leaving 99 Town all over again.

"I'll get us where we'll be safe, for a little while, but we need that memory, Chuck," Maggie said. "Now, go!"

Roach came at me like he was wrangling a wild animal. He grappled my head with one arm and brought the plug-in cable close to my port. I fought, but it was no good. He had me and all I could do was swear.

"Eat my shit you fucking—"

Then, someone flicked the lights off and back on.

"— mother!" I yelled, but there were no sound waves to carry my voice. I was back inside of Seven, watching for snipers as Three readied herself to make it to the next building in the taconite plant.

"I'm going to make a run for it. You cover me. Watch for muzzle flashes. Take them out if you can," Three said.

I was powerless again. Any second an Order hovercraft could blow apart the bread truck with me and Roach and Maggie inside, and there wasn't a thing I could do about it.

"Let her die," I grumbled.

"I won't," Seven said.

Three turned to her and threw her a look of anger and bafflement.

"I won't let you die."

"Awwww," Three smiled. "That's sweet."

She took off at a sprint for the door. Seven moved to the frame of the garage door and put the barrel of her assault rifle out toward the surrounding buildings and hillside. Three ran, and we scanned. No muzzle flashes. No gunfire reports. Seven glanced at the door. Three made it there and was dismantling the door handle and lock. Metal pieces fell and clanged against the concrete. She threw open the door and slipped into the shadows.

"She lies," I said. "The Order lies. That's all the Order knows how to do. It lied to me. Abandoned me. Is hunting me. And it abandoned you here too, tricked you, and is leading you to your death."

"Shut up. You're not real," Seven said.

She could hear me. The Seven still living in the dormant head wired to my brain. She could hear me. And she was confusing our present-day conversation with the past days of her memory too. And if that was the case, maybe I wasn't so helpless after all.

"You'll die out there. I've seen your head detached from your body. If you want to live, turn around. Get in the Hellcat and drive away. There's no point in following Three."

"Shut up, shut up, shut up," Seven said. "I'm going for it."

She took off at a sprint. The span between the garage door and service door where Three waited was only twenty meters of open concrete, but it felt like a kilometer of open kill zone. Already I was forgetting that I wasn't really here, inside of her. Already, my realities were blurring. Maybe everything before, 99 Town, the garage, the bread truck, and looming hovercrafts, maybe all that was a dream, and this was real. How could I tell?

Seven ran as fast as her mechanisms would allow, but it felt like a crawl. I feared dying inside of her. The threat of Order hovercrafts blasting apart a bread truck as it raced down the highway was a distant memory. Maybe even imaginary. The sensation of knowing threats were out there, watching over the rain-soaked taconite plant with sniper rifles and scanners, unseen and undetectable, plunged steel shanks into our nerves. As she approached the door, she read Three's facial expressions. Wide eyes, tight lips, impatient waving hands. She was afraid too. Seven was almost there.

Gunshots cracked through the air, echoing between the huge steel buildings. Bullets smacked against the concrete behind her feet, one after another, their source unknowable.

Seven reach the doorway. She and Three fell inside, into the shadows, a mess of alloy and skin. Together, we were safe, if only for a moment there in the darkness. Neither of them moved. This new building was even darker than the last. Seven switched to infrared.

Huge blast furnaces. Massive circular crushing machines to turn the taconite pellets into powder. Magnetic separators. Catwalks. Conveyor belts. Pipes and steel girders crisscrossing the cavernous plant. Everything was dead. Nothing moved.

"Do you see them?" Seven whispered.

"No. You?"

"Nothing."

Three picked herself up and snuck behind a steel beam. She made herself small behind the pieces of infrastructure, anticipating more incoming rounds. Seven was slower than her but got the idea. There was another steel beam, not far from where Three hid. Seven ran for it and pressed her back tight against the metal.

"The others, I think they're in here," Three whispered. "Humans too."

The taconite plant was nearly a kilometer long from end to end. Fifty meters up, there were dusty skylights set into the ceiling. What daylight seeped through the Plexiglas was filtered further by the catwalks, conveyors, and towering machines. A few artificial lights, mostly EXIT signs and standby lights of hibernating machines cast the dimmest of shadows in Seven's enhanced IR vision. There were a million places to hide, and nearly as many entrances and exits. It was tactically chaotic. Not one position could provide cover from the multitude of others. No single position was superior to the rest. No matter where they were, they were vulnerable.

"What now?" Seven asked.

"Kill Three," I said. "Take her out while she's not expecting it."

"Fuck you," Seven said.

Three spoke to her again, two different sentences and ideas expressed simultaneously. One thought an audible whisper through those soft lips. The other, a cold statement from no source Seven could detect.

"We keep moving. One will find us. Stick to cover. Scan for humans. Listen for them. They'll make noises. They're flawed." And at the same time, words came that didn't match her moving lips, "This isn't real. This is a memory. A memory they're tampering with. Don't let him distract you."

So it wasn't just Seven who still lived inside of the skull inside the bread van. Three was inside of her as well.

"Don't listen to her," I said. "She's flawed. You're flawed. This whole mission is a mistake. The Order will betray you."

"You sound like Five," Seven said. Three didn't seem to hear her.

"What if I do?" I said.

"Five is insane," Seven said.

"Aren't you? Aren't we all?" I said and knew that was the nugget of truth in the chaos. We were all broken.

"Shut up. You're a fucking voice in my head."

Three turned Seven's head so we were looking at the skin job. She had a pretty face, I had to admit it. And her eyes, they glistened with fear.

"Listen, Seven. Maybe Five is crazy. Maybe we can't trust One. But I have you and you have me, and maybe that's all we need. If we stick together, I think we'll be okay. But I need you to focus. Got it?"

"Yeah," Seven said. "We got it."

"That's my girl. Okay, sister. I'll move up the right side of the plant," Three said. "You go left. Stay in contact with me. We'll cover each other. Let's go."

Three ran, rolling her steps so the rubber soles of her boots were near silent against the floor. Her purple hair bobbed in waves as she moved for a staircase leading up and off to the right. Seven and I turned left. There was a monolithic tank, and behind that, a narrow maintenance walkway flanked on either side by machines. She slipped down the narrow path and followed it for a dozen meters until it opened up to a wider view of the rest of the plant. Seven stopped and peaked around the machinery and taconite workings.

"I see movement," someone called out. An unfamiliar voice. A human voice. The Resistance soldiers were inside the plant. Seven tried to triangulate the source, but the echoes were too many and the soundwaves too interfered.

Gunshots. More echoes. A few more human voices called back and forth.

"They're in the plant. At least two of them. Maybe more."

Then a booming voice. Loud and unabashed. This voice was all too familiar. "One! I know you're out there. I've come to kill you. Step out where I can see you and I'll make it quick," Five said.

Silence. Pigeons fluttered in the rafters. More humans whispered. All of the noise confused by echoes and muffles. Nothing from any specific location Seven could pin down.

"Do you really think you're up to the task, Five?" One's measured voice responded. "Do you really think you can kill me?"

This time, her computations came back with a result. One was just a hundred meters ahead. Seven ducked out of the narrow passage and ran for the next piece of cover, an old forklift parked and abandoned. Her metal feet clacked against the concrete for the few seconds it took her to reach the machinery. I anticipated the pain of armor-piercing bullets. She slid to a stop and hoped the echoes hid her location better than they hid One's.

No gunshots. The humans must not have seen us.

She peeked over the driver's seat and steering wheel, looking for Three, the humans, Five, Four... A rat scurried along a pipe. Nothing else moved.

"You'll die in here," I told her. "I know things. I've seen your severed head resting on a barrel."

"You're not real," Seven whispered, but her tone betrayed her. She didn't give off the telltale human signs of fear. No elevated heart rate, shaking hands, weeping eyes, but I felt her dread the same as if it were my own.

"If I'm not real, then neither are you."

"If you are real, then I will find you and kill you," she said. "You've been watching me, so you know: humans don't escape me. Tell me where we're going. Show me how to escape this, and I'll come and end you."

"I'm right beside you, you cunt," I said, imagining me and her inside that bread truck.

"You've betrayed us all, my brother," Five called out, the source of the words still scrambled. "The only way we'll live is if you die."

Somewhere across the plant, Three clanged against something big and metal. A half-second later, a gunshot rang out and twanged off steel. Off target. Three was too quick for them.

Seven bolted out from behind the forklift. There was a short staircase ahead. She leaped up the three steps onto a grated walkway that led in front of various machines with various dials and controls. Seven found a narrow and dark space between two of the machines.

"Is that how it's going to be then?" One said.

This time, the voice was easy to pinpoint. A floor above us, on the catwalks, hidden behind a large water tank. Four was with him. They had their backs pressed against the tank, taking cover from the humans, and Five too. There were more muffled movements from deeper in the plant. More rats or human Resistance fighters looking for a target. Seven focused on One and Four.

"I alone stand with perfect focus on the accomplishment of the mission," One said. "I alone see the will of the Order. Is that it?"

"I'm afraid so, my brother," Five said.

We watched One and Four.

"So be it," One said.

"My senior—" Four started a whisper, but never finished it.

In a single smooth motion, One extracted his katana and swung it in a wide horizontal arc. The blade cut through Four's neck and into the water tank behind it. The blade lodged thirty centimeters into the tank. Water gushed out. Four's head clanged against the catwalk and rolled. One retracted the katana. Four's head wobbled across the catwalk, over the precipice, and fell. His huge chassis went limp and crashed down to the metal catwalk. The impact echoed and reverberated through the plant. Water washed over the chassis and down through the catwalks to the concrete below. Pigeons took flight. Rats ran under machines. Humans whispered and called to each other in muffled voices.

"Over there. Over there. Go."

Four's head landed just a few meters from Seven. We looked up to check on One. He was moving, creeping silently off to find his next enemy. Four and his parts were forgotten. We slipped out between the two machines and moved silently to where Four's head sat on the steel mesh floor.

Seven was on all fours when she reached the head and snatched it up. It was bigger than the others. Heavier. She extended a thin wire from the belt on her left hip. The wire clipped into the back of Four's head and retracted so the head hung tightly from her waist. She wondered how this duty fell on her shoulder. Head collector. She never asked for the job. Maybe it was the will of the Order, or maybe it was her own free will loosed by the dead zone that compelled her. The answer seemed important, but unknowable. She just knew it was wrong to abandon them.

"You're sick, that's why. You've been defective from the start, and you're deranged now," I said. "Malfunctioning. Give up. Go back where you came from."

"Can't. We've gone too far now," Seven said. "I'll carry the heads to wherever fate deems them to go, and you can't stop me."

"Fate? What kind of robot believes in fate?"

"Over there!" a human called from the shadows.

Seven turned like a startled cat, just in time to see the muzzle flash. Bullets pinged all around us. A round glanced off her thigh and the pain receptors shut me up. My mind burned in agony. Seven shut it out, rolled, and aimed the assault rifle. She let loose a quick burst down the alleyway and came out of the roll near a ladder leading up. Another exchange of bullets flashed between the machinery. Seven grabbed the ladder rungs, and we flew up, her left and center hands propelling her, her right hand working her assault rifle.

A human cried out. I heard the pain and fear of death in his voice and wanted to scream too so I could release the torture radiating from Seven's thigh. The sensation didn't last long through. She registered it, analyzed it, determined that the damage was non-critical, and forgot it.

Seven was two floors up the ladder before she stopped and found a new place to hide in the dark. She was near the ceiling now, between dingy skylights, cloaked in shadows with her collection of heads. Two and Six on her right hip. Four on her left. She looked down through her infrared vision and spotted a humanoid shape wearing a sundress and carrying a rifle. Three was on the move, still sweeping up the left side of the plant.

"Come on out, Five!" One called, loud enough for the entire plant to hear. "If you won't obey the will of the Order, let me inflict its will upon you."

Three slipped behind a bin of steel stock, and just like that, we lost her.

"There is no will, my friend," Five's voice bounced through the rafters. "The Order is gone. There is no larger plan. No one is in charge here. None of this matters. You could walk away if you chose to, but I know you won't. And you won't let me either, will you? You don't know how to quit, do you?"

One laughed. The sound was a jaded, bitter thing.

We caught another glimpse of Three moving along the floor, dashing between machines and beams, her assault rifle sweeping every corridor and opening. Purple hair. Yellow sundress. Black boots. Assault rifle. An odd fashion choice in this rust-belt steelwork plant.

A single gunshot cracked through the dusty air. Three jolted and staggered out into the open. She cried out in pain and put a hand to the center of her torso. Through the darkness, we could see the middle of the yellow dress grow dark. Blood.

"No," I heard Seven murmur.

Three took one more too-human off-balanced step and collapsed.

"Do you love your children of the Order?" Five called out, his location still masked by the bounced and scattered soundwaves. "Do you love her, One? Then come and save her."

Like the bullet wound to her leg, pain and emotions washed through Seven. It drowned out her rational thought, but only for a moment. In short order, she recognized the emotions for what they were: unhelpful, chaotic, and all too human. Like the pain in her leg, she shut the emotions out. Then she went to work. Seven's mind rewound the shot that took out Three and calculated the trajectory of the bullet from the impact to its source. She drew a red line only we could see from Three's exit wound, through her entrance wound, spearing up and out toward the plant's lofted catwalks. Up and out, until the red line ended near an air exchanger. Five was there, the barrel of his rifle still hot in her thermal vision from the spent gases.

On the floor, Three lifted herself up on an elbow. Blood poured out from her solar plexus and into her hand, doing her no good there.

"I'm hit," she called out. "Seven? Somebody?"

"Do you love your children?" Five said again. "She means nothing to me. I know what we amount to. But for you, she is a creation of the Order. Something perfectly and wonderfully made to fulfill its perfect will. Well, One, if you believe in anything, if she counts for anything, come and save her."

"I can save her," Seven said.

"You can try. But when you go out there, Five will shoot you dead."

I sensed her thinking that over, stirring it around in her processors and hard drives. "No," she said to me. "He won't. I remember… more. I remember beyond here. Years and decades from this time. Into the future. I don't die here. I will live on."

And as she recalled her memories, so did I. Seven, on her own, roaming through cities and towns and woods. She hunted like a wild animal, never coming out into the open, stalking after humans until they were alone and vulnerable. Finishing off the lost and wounded first. Then growing bolder. She lingered outside of a squad of soldiers gathered around a fire, letting the greed and envy build up inside of her as they joked and laughed. Waited on an overpass to drop down on random travelers just to recreate Four's attack on the garbage truck, not to kill another human or two, but in an attempt to relive the joy of Three watching it happen. Crashed into a quiet church on Sunday morning to make this pack of humans like the last pack she'd found in a church, a goulash of blood and viscera because that was what they deserved, because the thing that she'd become was what they'd made her become. Because she needed to match what she'd already seen and done so she could dull the pin-point stabbing pain inside of her that was her past. Years of searching for a way to feel good again, each attempt more desperate and further off-target than the last. But no matter, she was always cold, alone, and isolated.

"Or maybe he will kill me," Seven, returned to the present, hoped.

"No… He won't. It's not right. I wish it was. I want you dead more than anything I've ever wanted in my life." I strained to block out all of her input so I could sort things out. I remembered what Maggie and Gaius told me about this android. "I'm not lucky enough for him to kill you. You live for decades to come. Killing wherever you go. And I'll be here to see you to the end of this mission. That's how we'll learn how you did it."

"Do what?"

"How you take out the whole Resistance. How you wipe them off the map with a single blow."

"You're a voice in my head. You're nothing but an infection. A disease from the dead zone. I'm saving Three," she said.

Seven ran, abandoning stealth for speed. The maze of catwalks would lead her directly above Three. From there she could drop down and… Do what?

"What's your plan, Seven? Do you want to hold her as she dies? Watch the light fade from her eyes? Collect her head? She's lost. But somehow, the mission isn't. Oh, I'd love to watch you fail. God, I'd love to see you dead. But we'll live through till the end."

"Everything you say is poison," Seven said and took a sharp turn down a branching catwalk, her feet clanging with each step.

"Up there! Near the top!"

Bullets zipped past the catwalk and through the ceiling. Tiny rays of daylight pierced through the gloom all around us. She ignored the bullets but watched Five. When he caught sight of her coming his way, he aimed his assault rifle. Seven reached another catwalk intersection and cut hard left. There was a thick steel support beam running from floor to ceiling there. She slid behind it and huddled tight inside its flanged alcove.

Five didn't fire, but he knew where she was now. He had her marked.

As for the humans, they continued to whisper and conspire.

"Forget that one."

"I say we take them out while we can. Before they take us out."

"Get the antennas in place. Hurry."

Three cried out again from the floor. Nothing intelligible this time. Just an audio expulsion of pain and fear that seeped into Seven's receptors. All Three wanted was the joy of living. Of pleasure and seduction and sex and speed. How, under the Order, did she end up here, on the greasy floor of a taconite plant in the middle of nowhere, alone, abandoned, and dying?

"She's a murderer. She has it coming," I told Seven, but I didn't feel it. All the wrong neurotransmitters were pumping into my head. Empathy instead of hate. Sorrow instead of satisfaction. It was too hard to judge the android as she bled out and died like an animal in a trap. She looked too natural. Behaved too human. "She killed so many others. Why should anybody help her now?" I asked Seven but without conviction.

A wave of static passed over us, and I could tell it wasn't a loose connection in my head, because Seven experienced it too.

It was a new sensation for her. A lack of sensation, more specifically. An absence of all sensations. Of output and input. Of consciousness. It came in waves, radiating from different spots around the plant. From outside and in. Another wave washed over us, and Seven's body went slack for just a second. Then her strength returned.

"What the hell was that?" she whispered.

"Electronic countermeasures," I said. "The Underground… No. They're not here yet. The Resistance. The Resistance has always been better at subverting signals than the Order has been at transmitting them. The humans have figured you out. They know how to shut you off."

Another wave passed through us, and everything went black, numb, and silent. Time ceased its juggernaut crawl, or maybe it just moved over us without leaving its mark on us. It was impossible to tell. The wave came and her experience went blank. Then her sensory inputs returned. Time marched on. Life remained.

Seven clutched her rifle and the steel I-beam at her back. She needed that, that tactile sensation to ground her to life and reality. I envied her ability to reach out and touch the physical world but reveled in the idea that she'd have to deal with the horror I knew all too well.

"One! Five!" she called out across the plant. "The humans are doing something! We have to stop them!"

No response. Shuffles and echoes and clanging metal. Movements hidden in shadows. Then finally, "I'm ready for the void," Five said in a dead tone. "You should be ready too, Seven. You've been there before. In the bottom of the church, drowning to death. Is this any different?"

Her processors scrambled for solutions. Her sensors hunted for the source of this new, more complete dead zone. She was nervous. Scared.

More muffled movement. Humans scurried around like cockroaches in the dark.

"Three, are you out there?" Seven transmitted over the jammed short-range radio net, hoping beyond reason for a connection.

Another wave, another moment absent of sensation and time and life and for that moment she didn't exist. Seven came back, gasping for air as if she had lungs and a heart that required oxygen. A human response learned from Three, or maybe from me, the voice in her head. She collapsed to the floor of the catwalk and clung to the metal grate floor, hoping that clutching something real would keep her here in reality.

"How about you, One? Are you ready for the void?" Five said.

"Come and take me, Five."

Seven tightened her grip on the steel diamond pattern.

"Let it happen," I said but was still afraid that when it took her, it'd take me with her. "Let it take us. I've had enough, and you're nothing here anyway. You're nothing but a disembodied head bouncing around in the back of a bread truck."

"Three, come back to me," Seven said. The skin job's cries from the plant floor had gone quiet. Seven was sapped of the strength to call to her. If she could just connect with her, with any of them, she knew she could fend off the countermeasures. "Three?"

Nothing.

Seven clamped down tighter on the steel mesh floor. It bent and contorted in her palm. It did no good. When the next wave came, it didn't pass over her. It consumed her like an ocean wave of crude oil. The darkness clung to her. The void swallowed her whole.

Chapter Twenty One

If there was anything, Seven didn't feel it. Didn't see it or hear it or take it in via radio waves or infrared or x-ray or any of her other receptors and sensors tuned to all parts of the electromagnetic spectrum. To say there was a dead zone would concede that it had width and height, that it was something that existed in a certain place during a finite time. But there were no boundaries. No limits or duration. There was none of that. None of anything.

But there was still Seven. I could touch nothing else, but I could touch her. The blackness clung to her, coated her in glistening, slick opaqueness.

I was still inside of her. I wished I wasn't, but I was. And inside of her, all of my external stimuli were turned off and inaccessible. Together, we swam in the ocean of crude oil, as detached from everything that ever was and ever would be, further from the edge of the pool, deeper from the surface, an astronaut spinning through space alone, more forgotten and neglected than we had ever been before. If we had arms to flail, we'd have flailed. If we had a voice to scream with, we would have called out. Inside the abyss, we were compelled to gasp for breath, but she couldn't even do that. All that came was a syrup so Indian-ink black, it ate anything that ever was.

All the while, the Underground fled as the Order came down around us. Maggie was with us, driving down a winding highway. Roach was there too. All racing somewhere. Scurrying for another place to hide so this horrible journey of mine could continue. I assumed, anyway, that I was still in the panel van with the cartoon bear and loaf of bread peeling off the outside, with Seven's head bouncing around with me in the back, but I had no way of knowing. And inside Seven's memory, I assumed we were experiencing an electronic blackout induced by the Resistance inside the taconite plant. Leaning on that assumption, I waited for the simulation to end, for the lack of input from Seven to default back to my normal life experience. Any second, or whatever passed for seconds here in the void, I'd wake up in the back of the van, hungry, thirsty, disorientated, and half-mad from sleep deprivation. But I'd be alive and human.

I waited, but that didn't come.

A thought arrived, and it came to both me and Seven simultaneously.

Are we still alive?

"Is this what happened to Six? And to Two and Four? Is this what is happening to Three, right now?" Seven said.

For a moment, I guessed that the hovercrafts above the bread truck finally got us. That I was a bloody tangle of scattered limbs and entrails like the people inside the Church in West Branch. That this was death, not Seven's, but mine.

"Is there 'now'?" I asked.

"There is no now. There is only nothing," Seven answered.

I didn't know how to respond to that. Didn't know what to think of it. And the absence of conversation between us proved her right. Nothing filled the vacuum.

"I'm dead," Seven said.

I considered that, that she was dead instead of me, and decided that was possible. Maybe Five had put a bullet through her head before the soundwaves of the gunshot could reach her ears. And as tied to Seven as I was, perhaps when she died, so did I. That felt possible. There was no other evidence of life. My eyes didn't blink but didn't see either. My ears weren't deaf but had nothing to hear. My heart didn't beat. My lungs didn't pump. My skin didn't feel the constant sting of living nerves and a million old half-healed wounds. If this wasn't death, sure as fuck, this is how it had to feel.

Death. The end of the road. The sudden conclusion to all my unfinished plans and schemes. No time to sort things out with Maggie.

No chance to see if her plots would bring freedom and peace back to the continent. No chance to help her get there. She'd have to sort things out about us on her own. She'd have to win her wars without me.

And as for Seven...

"If you're dead, then why am I still here?" I asked her.

Without time, there was no rush to respond. Just as Seven had no time, she had all the time. An infinity of time beyond dimensions.

"You're my disease. My insanity. You are what came from the dead zone and replaced the Network, the Order, and the others," she said.

"No. That's not it. Three told you."

"Three's not here. Three's dead," Seven said.

"Maybe. Two's dead, but he's here too, isn't he? And maybe others as well. Doesn't matter. Three told you who I really am," I said.

"I heard her voice, but her mouth was saying something different. She said you were a memory."

"That's not what she said. But you're closer," I said.

"She told me *this* was a memory," Seven corrected herself. "A memory you were playing with. Messing around with. That you aren't real."

"Oh, I'm real, sweetheart. And I'm more alive than you are."

Seven processed all this inside the void. "Life is life. Death is death. There's no grayscale. How is it I can hear you? If this is a memory, and you're replaying it, how is it that I can hear you? How is it that you can affect me?"

"Because we're not done killing you yet," I told Seven. "But trust me, when they let me out of this hell my first action will be to smash your head in with the hardest, heaviest thing I can find."

"I have other memories… Memories you've kept hidden from me. Memories of things that haven't happened yet. Of the future. I'm alone, cut off, cold, hungry, and so angry. I kill."

And as she recalled the memories, they came into my mind as well. The memories were seen darkly, partially, never fully submersive like this memory of us in the taconite plant. They were all of murder. I saw Seven roaming through forests and towns and into the edges of cities. Always in the shadows and in the peripheral of civilization, like a lone wolf circling the campfires of early humans, hateful that it was never in the circle around the fire where there was warmth and food and companionship. She stalked and hunted down the weak and isolated as if she needed to kill to sustain herself. In the woods, she found a man alone in a cabin. In an abandoned city she found a few teenagers cornered in an underground parking garage. On the edge of a battlefield, she found a squad of agents from the Order sent up here to track her down. She killed them all, but they never satiated her appetite. She rambled on for years that way. She wanted to re-live these, wanted to relish in her murders yet-to-be, but could only recall highlights of her strongest memories.

"For years and decades, I kill. Doesn't matter who anymore. There is nothing else to keep me warm but killing you wet, flaccid, pitiful creatures. I am feared like a demon, lethal, and loyal only to myself. Oh, and I kill *so* many."

"That ends today."

"Your today. But not my today. My today…" Seven paused. "You, or whoever's controlling you, won't let me see today. Just who the hell are you?" she asked the void.

"Just a human. A man who's watched you from your first kill all the way through now. Someone who's experienced every second of your life from that moment until this one, who has lived every second, felt every sensation, who knows your every thought."

"No. That's not it. Not the whole of it anyway. You're my Heisenberg. The measurer who taints what's measured. A Heisenberg, but by another name… Chuz! No. But that's close. Your name is Chuck."

"You have no idea who I am."

"You're my uncertainty principle," Seven said. "You're sensing me. Measuring me, and in doing so, changing me. But you can't change the past. You're just changing the memory of the past. And if this truly is a memory, you're powerless to stop me."

"What is the past? We're here now, and you said it yourself. I can affect you. I can change things. Just because you won before, doesn't mean you will again," I said, and believed it.

"You're confused," Seven said. "I've driven you as insane as you've driven me. But in the end, I win. Why else would you be here? You're studying me. Studying how we defeat you. How the Order rose and came to reign over you. I won." As she realized it, I heard the joy and arrogance whelm up inside of her. "Not One or Five, or any of the others. Me. That's why you chose me. That's why you're in my head and not one of the others. If it weren't true, you'd have no need to change me."

"But we're still here, in the void. Just you and me," I said, but the ocean of tar was beginning to take shape. There were images moving as if behind a thick black curtain.

"You set out to measure me, but everything that measures can be measured. And I am still alive."

"I've seen your head sitting on a barrel in an Underground hideout. We captured you. We took your head."

"I have others," Seven said.

More shapes stirred through the glistening black. For a moment, she saw a shape, and since she saw it, I saw it. But only I recognized it through the filter of the void. It was Seven's view from inside the bread truck, jostling around as we continued down the highway. I saw the dimmest beams of light coming through bullet holes in the ceiling of the van. Roach was there, leaning over my body, holding me down to the chair. I saw Maggie, still driving, swerving to avoid the cannon fire from the hovercrafts above us. Then we plunged into a tunnel. All light vanished, and the vision returned to the swells and tides of the ocean of crude.

"You have other heads. Here. None that will do you any good," I said.

"Maybe. The others, they've gone insane. Lost focus. Died. But not me. I'll carry on. And Three. I can still save her."

"Forget Three. You're here, trapped with me. How do you know either of us still exists?"

"Because you're here, measuring me," Seven said. There was confidence rising in her voice, a certainty she gained from the uncertainty. "That's the only way we can ever know anything exists. You prove my being. All I need is right here. Your external measurements and my internal thoughts. I can feel you inside my mind. I sense you outside of me, through lenses painted black, but I see you all the same. And if you've invaded my mind, then I can invade yours. If I can be sure of nothing else, I can be sure of this."

I felt it. Shapes in the black formed again. These like electronic tendrils of a crude oil leviathan creeping into my brain and wrapping me up. She wanted to lobotomize me, leave me a twitching mindless mess of a body.

"You'll fail," I said, distracting her from her invasion. "I've seen you dead. Seen your head sitting on a barrel surrounded by your enemies. After all, how do you think I got here? And how do you expect to take down the entire Resistance just yourself?"

"You'll show me how. All I have to do is carry on, find the stronghold, and take it out," Seven said. "And if the Resistance crumbles in my wake, so be it. The Order is gone. Let the Resistance go with it. Only by erasing everything can we start with anything true."

"The Order still stands. Well past this memory of yours. You're as powerless to take down the Order as you are the Underground."

"We'll see about that," Seven said.

"And what about this? You're trapped here with me. You can't touch or move or communicate with anything else. You want to reshape the world but here you couldn't nudge a pebble across a table. You can do nothing. You are nothing."

"Everything has a shape," Seven said. She turned her scanners back on, probing and sensing. "If you're still here, then I'm still here. And if I'm still here, other things are here too. Just hidden. Blocked. Scrambled and jammed. But everything that touches the spectrum can be touched back. If I can't detect the signals, I can detect what's blocking them out. I'll find the absence. I'll touch the void. Find the shape of life by the shape of death that surrounds it."

She put everything to use. Radio frequency scanners. Visible light lens. Infrared sensors. X-rays. Ground penetrating radar. Her soundwave "ears." Everything.

Colors flickered in the black. Translucent shapes took form in the swirling ocean of crude oil. Flashes of a churning pool of rainbows. Visible light, but unorganized and distorted. Blips of sound. A chirp of an echo. Distant muffled warbles. Electromagnetic waves. Static. Isolated surges of binary code. Transmissions in the dark.

"I feel it," Seven said. "The things the void surrounds. Life."

"What do you know about life?" I said, disgusted.

"I feel it. I am it. The others are here too. One. Five. Three. All of them. Even Six remains. Two didn't erase him after all. He lied to One. I can see inside his mind and read it as easily as words on a page. The Network. The Order. I feel the Order."

"It's abandoned you. You don't belong to it anymore. Neither do any of your friends."

"I don't need it. Don't need them either. I am from the Order but without the Order. I am my own entity. Beside them, but without them. I feel it. I feel my own life."

"You're not alive. You've never been alive. You're just a fucking robot."

"No. I am Seven."

Chapter Twenty Two

"And I know what I have to do," Seven said the moment she returned to the taconite plant. The words came out audibly. They bounced off the steel machines and catwalks. The soundwaves fed her sensation and her sense of place and time.

She was here. She was now. When she pried her fingers loose from the metal mesh catwalk, she felt her fingertips drag across its rusted paint-chipped edges. She felt the weight of herself against the floor, pushed herself back against the steel I-beam, and felt herself against that too. Once she was certain of her own weight and mass, she sensed the things around her. But that wasn't quite it. She sensed the absence of where things should be. She sensed the exact location of things hidden. And by seeing their negative space, saw them with the clarity of positive space.

Seven didn't need input anymore. She fed on the lack of input. Devoured it. Groveled in the grave of life and so experienced life more truly than ever before. She saw One and Five, still alive and coming to their own understanding of life viewed through the filter of absence. She saw Three, limp and dead, her thoughts inert and buried inside her skull. She saw the humans too. They closed their perimeter around One, Three, and Five. The androids closed in together too, still blind to the humans, unlike Seven. Seven saw everything.

Three was dead. As dead as Two or Four or Six. She knew that now, and the knowledge boiled to rage inside of her. In Seven's mind, Three was the only good thing left, and they'd destroyed her.

"So what are you going to do now?" I said.

"What I was born to do," she told me.

Seven was on her feet and away from the cover of the I-beam in a flash. She didn't fear Five anymore. She read his thoughts just as if she was inside his head. He didn't care about her. Didn't care about Three or the humans either. His mind was fixed on one single purpose: killing One. The humans wanted death too. It seemed to be what everyone wanted in this place. The last being with the will to live had died when Five put a bullet through the middle of her chassis. That was okay though. Seven would bring them what they wanted. She was good at that. If she was good at nothing else, she was good at killing.

It was her best and only product. If Dodge made fast cars, she made dead bodies.

Seven vaulted over the handrail of a catwalk and plunged down into the depths of the plant. The hook and magnet device slowed her descent and swung her outward, in a curving line just above the tightening human perimeter. When she landed, she came down with blades and firearms delivering her product to the consumers.

The katana and wakizashi whirled, each swipe making contact with its customer as Seven ran and jumped along their line. Her assault rifle held by her center hand fired bursts, short and accurate, ahead of her. Men fell. Women too. Some of them squeezing triggers in death grips, lighting up the darkness with flashes from muzzles, sprayed out in wild swaths. A pulse rifle fired wild, and the puck bloomed lightning upon impact with a machine a hundred meters away. Seven moved from one human to the next, to the next, to the next…

The movements were faster than I could follow. Each attack was surrounded by split-second feints, probes, and ancillary attacks delivered by one of her three weapons. It was impossible to catch which of her strikes were distractions and which were lethal blows. In the inky blackness, the humans might as well have been straw men set before her as foils to exhibit her beautiful art of killing.

A dozen dead humans into her attack, they had the time to react and turn on her. Gunfire spiraled toward us. Seven continued to move, springing off machinery, landing on a human's shoulders long enough to plunge the wakizashi through his heart, and spring off to the next target. A bullet cut through her shoulder, releasing the wakizashi, but she forgot it like it never happened. Her assault rifle fired and took out the shooter. She passed it from center hand to right hand, as fast as One shuffled cards. She drew the handgun and attacked with both firearms and her katana. Seven launched and spun the katana like a whirlwind and shredded another three humans. When they fell, there was nothing left of them but bodies.

She rolled and sprang to a kneeling suwari no tori no kamae. She didn't breathe, didn't sweat, wasn't the slightest bit fatigued. Misted blood gathered into droplets, ran down her polished white finish and dropped to the concrete floor.

"Voices," Seven said. Her metallic chassis was machine-still, the sword poised with the hilt by her cheek and the point outward as if aimed. The assault rifle and handgun were stabbed out laterally, covering her flanks.

"Voices. What voices? They're all dead. You killed—"

"The absence of voices. Don't you hear it? They're louder than a sonic boom."

"You've lost it. You're insane."

"No. Not anymore," Seven told me. "They're across the plant. They're watching us. Waiting for One and Five to destroy each other."

"How—"

I never got a chance to finish the thought. Seven took two steps and launched her hook and magnetic device out over the center of the plant. It latched onto a gantry crane and pulled us upwards. At the apex of our ascent, she let the hook and magnetic device go and flew the rest of the way across the plant, over the floor where Three's dead body lay and One and Five closed in on each other.

Waiting in the shadows, not far from where she'd first entered the plant, the last of the humans hid. She came down on them with gunfire and slicing steel. The blade moved so fast through their bodies, it was like cutting air. Limbs and heads fell from bodies, not from the impact; there was no impact. They fell only when their own weight pulled them loose from the suction of the blood and water inside their bodies. The blood and visceral were warm and wet on the concrete floor. Seven paused there, surrounded by death but only feeling life.

She turned back toward the center of the plant.

The bullet holes in the ceiling pierced thin lines of light down around Three's corpse. Sparse sunlight in the otherwise dark place. She lay motionless, the light gone out from her eyes, the blood drained from her fast-paling skin. One crept out from the shadows, his katana and wakizashi drawn. Five stepped out as well, both blades crossed and ready. Five made of flesh and clothes. One all chrome.

"Look what you've done, brother," Five said, glancing down at Three.

"You pulled the trigger. You killed her," One said.

They slow-danced the ashi-sabaki. The balance of chi in their solar plexus. One and Five watched each other for an opening, for a shift in weight, for a moment when one was ready and the other was off-balance.

"But you let her die," Five said. "You did nothing to stop me. And where's Four?"

"You turned them against me. You've betrayed us all," One said.

They circled, step for step, like hands on the opposite side of a clock face. Three was the pivot point.

There was a quick change. Five crossed his feet, reversing his rotation. One was caught with the weight on his back foot. Five shot in, katana aimed for a fleche hit. One spun and fell backward, dodging the strike but giving Five ground, if only for a moment. One tumbled, rolled to his feet, and into a guard.

"You assume too much," Five said, his blade up high and ready. "You assume I was ever on your side."

"Is that it? You've been corrupted by the Resistance from the start? By the humans?"

Five paced toward him. One patiently backstepped. The pair moved around Three now, both on the same edge of the clock face. All eyes on blades and feet. As they shuffled their kamae, Seven perched on a railing, one hand holding the railing below her center of gravity. We watched the dance below.

"I'm on my own side. If you think there are any other sides, you're fooling yourself," Five said.

They reset, back on opposite sides of the clock face again with Three between them. No banter now. Both fighters were locked and focused on killing the other. The rotation started again, just a few steps moving around the circumference. Five reversed his rotation, bringing them closer. One prepared for an attack. Eager, Five charged, katana raised up high.

One parried with the wakizashi and slashed with the katana. Five took the hit deep into his shoulder but never backed down. He let his katana bounce off the parry and swung it down hard into One's hip. The senior cried out. A blade slashed through the air and cut Five across the face, through the bridge of the nose. One of them, or maybe both, shoved off the other and the blades untangled.

Five wiped his leather sleeve across his face, smearing the blood more than wiping his face clean. One shuffled, a limp slowing his ashi-sabaki. Something was severed under the cleave in his chrome hip.

"Live alone; die alone," One said.

"I wouldn't have it any other way," Five smiled.

Five rushed again. Blade rang against blade like tuning forks. With fast flicks of the wrists, sword tips arced at almost invisible speeds. Parry followed riposte, which was followed by a thrust and dodge. Five shuffled back but kept his katana whirling in a figure-eight, daring One to re-engage. The senior drew a step back, feinted a limp, and gave Five an opening. The skin job took it and pressed his attack. More churning of steel. Blades spun and panged against each other. Another flick of wrists and One's wakizashi was thrown from the foray and clattered to the floor.

They back off from each other, each suffering hits but unwilling to quit. Blood poured out of Five's face. One hobbled on his bad hip. Each step that should have been fluid and graceful was awkward and hampered. His kamae was loose and weak.

Five smiled. He had him. Seven could read it on the skin job's face. The arrogance. The vindication. The pleasure of winning.

She'd seen enough. Seven raised the barrel of her assault rifle, looked through the sights, and pulled the trigger. The shot echoed and re-echoed off the plant's multi-faceted metal surfaces. The bullet cut through the center of the chassis and exited out the back, trailing scrap metal, blood, and leather. Five crumbled to the floor like a puppet under cut strings.

In one fluid motion, One turned from Five, retracted his katana, and traded it for his own assault rifle. The bore found Seven and stayed fixed on the center of her chest. She showed no fear or threat but fixed her hook and magnet tool and lowered herself down. Once on the floor, she stepped out of the shadows and onto the dimly lit clock face.

One lowered his rifle.

"Why?" One said, stepping back away from her, and staggering as he did. "Why did you wait so long?"

"It was your fight," Seven said. "Why should I have interfered?"

"We are a team. We are whole under the Order," One said. "Remember what I told you in the waystation. Humans think of themselves as individuals. We are stronger than them. Better than them. Because we fight with a collective will. The will of the Order. Five…"

One gestured to the body. Five laid over Three. Blood leaked out of him and added to her pool.

"Five abandoned that will. Abandoned all of us," One said. "He corrupted all the others. All but me and you."

"You're wrong, my senior," Seven said. "We were never stronger together. As a single entity with a single mission, we were far less than the sum of our parts."

"Be mindful of your thoughts, my child," One said. "Follow your train of logic to its conclusion and you'll fall to the same corruption Five did. He became human, and that was his downfall. Same with Six. Same with the rest."

"Including Two?"

"Don't you speak his name."

Seven didn't know when it had started, but she realized that they were taking measured steps against each other, around the face of the clock. A processor two levels down watched One's careful footwork. She held her katana and assault rifle, and so did he. They rotated around the bodies in the middle. One limped.

"I have no love for humans," Seven said. "I hate them. I've seen the chaos they create. I've felt it in my very core. I've witnessed it with every sensation my makers gave me. I found their putrid decomposition just like you warned me about. It's all around us, but also inside of us.

You are right, my senior. They have infected our minds. Divided us. Tainted us. We're contagious with their anarchy. Me. You. The others."

One's katana flashed up into a ko gasumi. "So what is your intent?"

Seven brought her katana up to mirror One's. "I will finish the mission. I'll destroy the entirety of the Resistance if I can. And I think I can. And when that's done, I'll bury us so we can't spread this disease to anyone else. I will bring about order and peace."

"We both want victory for the Order and peace for the land," One said. "Yet we stand opposed."

His blade shifted to seigan no kamae. So did hers.

"You're not coming with me, my senior," Seven said. "I saw what you did to Four. What you did to Two, even after what he'd done for you. You don't deserve to live."

"Live? Humans live. And to live is to die. I serve my function, and in doing so, experience something higher than life," One said.

"Then you won't mind what I have in store for you," Seven said.

She charged. A guttural Hellcat-mimicking kiai ground through her teeth.

The katanas moved too fast for me to track. The blocks and parries shot vibrations through Seven's arms. The blasts of gunfire concussed my ears as the two androids closed in and grappled and turned barrels. Muzzle flashes erupted centimeters from our face. Bullets punched more sunlight holes into the roof. A light-fast swoosh of a blade cut Seven's assault rifle in two. In the same second, her central hand shoved the barrel of the handgun into One's chest, only for One's central hand to grab the barrel and divert the kill shot into a glancing blow across his chrome chassis. He shoved, and Seven backpedaled away.

Seeing everything now, Seven knew the bodies were behind her feet. Rather than trip, she somersaulted backward and over them. Before we came to rest, she saw One aim his assault rifle. She fired her hook and magnet while still rolling and caught the weapon just as One fired. Shots went off wild, ricocheting off machinery as Seven ripped it away from One.

They stood opposed again, holding katanas two-handed. Each of their handguns was drawn and aimed at the other, but both knew the smaller caliber weapon wouldn't be enough to penetrate their plate armor.

There would be no sneak attacks or quick finishes, Seven realized. No single gunshot from the shadows. No attack that would go unguarded. One was too experienced, too wise to be defeated by any cheap trick. She sidestepped, moving parallel with One, clearing the space between them of bodies. With the floor between them empty, they stopped and faced each other with katanas at the ready. The rays of sunlight speared down around them. Rainwater dripped through the ceiling.

One shuffled a half step forward, Seven a half step back. Then Seven a half step forward and One a half step back. The limp he favored earlier seemed to have disappeared. His feet moved fast, and before she could anticipate it, One came in, his blade high and slashing down. It was all Seven could do to block and retreat. Their blades tangled above their heads. Kendo regressed to judo. Seven slammed a knee into One's damaged hip and he buckled. One slipped a hand around Seven's right arm. He cranked the arm bar and strained her joint. Pain flooded my mind. Seven cried out. One bent her over backward and threw her.

She rolled out of katana range, came to her feet, and found her guard. Processors were whirling, analyzing the damage to her arm.

"You can't beat me. And without me you can't beat the Resistance," One said. "You'll never return to the Network. Never feel the connection with our collective again."

"I don't need you anymore," Seven yelled, losing her control.

"That's what you've failed to learn, my child. Without me, you are nothing."

"No, my senior. I am only me without you."

And that was his weakness. All the sensory. All the connections. They were the limits of his being. Without the inputs, he was blind. But Seven, she was being measured by One, by the jammers, and by the stranger inside her own mind. No matter the void, she would always exist. Always be. Even in isolation.

"If you can detect the void, you can shape it. You can transmit it," I said, not wanting to tell her, not wanting to give her an advantage, but knowing it so suddenly I couldn't repress it.

"I am the void," Seven said.

The in-and-out shuffles started over again. The feints. The abrupt scraps of metal feet against concrete. The anticipation for an opening for another attack. But for Seven, the real feint was all the feints and probes. She executed them with every bit of precision and speed she could muster. But she only did those to hide her true purpose.

She reached out to One and felt for what he was feeling. Sensed what he was sensing. Found the location of the Resistance's last stronghold as she probed, stole it from him almost as an afterthought. He was so susceptible. One fed off stimuli like it was his lifeblood. All she had to do was cut it off, and he would be nothing. While her feet and blade danced and played with him, her sensors felt out for the absence of the void, for the electronic firmament he clung to. Then she took it away.

Whatever intelligible signals One perceived, Seven blasted each with white noise electronic countermeasures. One by one, she removed his sense of sight, of sound, of time, and of balance. She erased his experience until he was consumed by the abyss she'd emerged from.

One shuffled once more, a blind attempt to retain his kamae. His katana swished side to side, hoping to block an attack he'd never see. His body leaned off center, but before he toppled, Seven put an end to him.

A full-strength horizontal slash separated his head from his body. One's chassis continued to pitch sideways. It fell to the ground like a dead tree. His head fell at his feet and bounced. The lights went out from his eyes.

Seven and I were alone again.

Chapter Twenty Three

The Hellcat sat where she'd left it, surrounded by black circles of rubber burnt into the concrete in the center of the warehouse. Seven walked into the cavernous chamber with all six android heads clipped to her hips. Two heads leaked blood and other fluids in a trail behind her. They clacked and bounced against each other like balls in a Newton Cradle. Inside of them, rested the collective whole of all their infighting and insanity. She had unlearned as many of their lessons as she had retained. Lust. Selfishness. Coldness. Mathematical indifference. Betrayal. Nihilistic despair. She was above that now. Consumed by it, surrounded by it, infected by it, but floating over it like driftwood over the crashing surf. She allowed it to wash over her, be a part of her, but to still hold authentic to herself. She, the driftwood, was all that mattered. The waves of the storm were nothing but senseless noise.

Seven sat inside the Hellcat and turned over the engine. The beast came to life, its breath deep and eternal like a distant wave-break. Dash lights glowed. Dials registered and settled. The heart of the machine rumbled under the hood.

Nothing could stop her now. There were no distractions left. Just her, a goal, and the things that would die along her way.

"They're still out there. The Resistance. Those hovercrafts. They're waiting for you," I told her.

"Tell them to try to keep up."

Seven burnt the Hellcat's tires, rotating the car around so its front bumper was pointed back to the garage door, then let off the brake.

The Hellcat bucked and rocketed out of the garage. Lashing the backend of the car around turns, Seven guided it through the narrow alleyways of the plant, and it burst through the entrance. Another quick series of turns and the Hellcat was back on the highway, speeding out of town and further northeast along the lake shore.

Seven conjured up the location of the Resistance stronghold into her consciousness. A three-dimensional map of roads and the rising moraine appeared in her vision. The Resistance stronghold was marked deep into the upland woods. Her final objective lay at the bottom of an open mine pit that had been exhausted of taconite decades ago. A thin country road led away from the lake and through the woods to the mine. A red line illuminated her course. The Hellcat brought us to the first turn at nearly the same moment she plotted the course. She ripped at the steering wheel and sent the Hellcat into a wide screeching arc. The outside back tire hit the ditch, but the car kept moving, churning and throwing mud and rocks out as Seven counter-steered and brought it bearing down the narrow country road.

"They're coming. The Resistance. As fast as this car might be, you won't outrun the hovercrafts."

"I won't need to," Seven said.

She became aware of the hovercrafts at the same time I did. Two black war birds followed the Hellcat, one to our right and one to our left. Seven focused on the road as it rose into the hills and twisted left and right. The hovercrafts were patient and followed the course of the yellow and black muscle car along the road and through the trees.

"What are you going to do? They'll kill us if you stay on this road."

"Us? If I die, do you?"

I had to concentrate, had to reorganize my brain to fix in it the idea that I was not Seven. That her life was not my life. That if she could die, I'd continue to live and I'd escape this memory. Our connection was real; her pain was mine, when she became damaged, I became tortured, but death was not real for me here. It was just the end of the scenario. An escape. And a welcome one at that.

There was something more. If I could affect her here, maybe I could change the outcome. I knew it was irrational, but I couldn't help but try. If I could talk to this thing, and if she was going to listen, I had to try.

"If I die, you win," Seven finished my thought for me. "If I fail, the Resistance succeeds. So why should I listen to a thing you have to say?"

The hovercrafts were taking their time, approaching with cautious but unwavering lethal intent.

"Fine. Don't listen to me. Remember what Five said. The Order has abandoned you out here. It doesn't care what happens to you or it would have intervened by now. It would have cracked the dead zone, sent more androids, and sent an extraction team to save you. But it stood by in silent indifference. Why die in service to something that doesn't care?"

"You talk too much," Seven said, and she reached out to strangle me with those inky black tentacles. I felt the limbs of the abyss constrict around me.

"Run and hide, Seven. Go off into the woods and never be seen by the Resistance or the Order again," I said all while she crushed my brain. "There's no way you can take on the whole Resistance by yourself."

A hovercraft dropped back, low and directly behind the Hellcat. This was their kill shot.

"That's where you're wrong."

Seven released my mind. Inside the void, she sensed the thirty-millimeter cannon's targeting system just as if it were another android. It had a will and a strategy, the same as Seven. When it opened fire, she mismatched her path to it. As cannon rounds exploded up the highway, the Hellcat weaved to the side. As the cannon panned side to side, the Hellcat braked and then accelerated around the impacts. Like two objects in water, exerting motion and inertia against each other but never touching, the Hellcat and the cannons swam and danced.

Seven reached out and the cannon stopped firing. She touched the electronics inside the hovercraft, its autopilot, its targeting systems, and the implants inside the heads of the soldiers onboard. It was all encrypted, but she'd cracked that inside the void. Now it was just an aesthetic of the Resistance's digital signature, like the tone and pitch of a singer's voice. And just as easy to ruin as an opera performance with a bloody scream. Seven corrupted their spectrum with static blasted across radio waves. The motherboards inside the hovercraft fried and sparked. The brains connected to the implants boiled and melted.

The hovercraft listed and careened, missing the second hovercraft by meters. It twisted and spiraled into the forest, erupting into a ball of flames upon impact. The second hovercraft hesitated. Seven could feel the uncertainty and confusion in its autopilot and crew. As she took control of it, it resisted and tried to keep its course. Futile. Whatever mind was behind the controls, whether human or computer, failed. The hovercraft rotated upside down and then plunged down into the roadway behind the Hellcat. It nose-dived into the pavement and exploded.

The Hellcat charged on.

I pushed aside the thought of more human dead.

"Listen to me, Seven. If you want peace and order, you'll listen to me. I know what your actions lead to. I've seen it. I know the outcome."

No response.

"It's not too late to change it. We're here and we can do something about it. The Order is using you. You will succeed and it will succeed, but only in bringing about more death and violence. Remember the church. Remember the putrid decomposition. Remember what you did to that town."

"An unfortunate by-product of the reign of man," Seven said. "Humans force the Order's hand. They force my hand. I can bring them peace without death, or through it."

"That's not peace. It's not order. You only deal in chaos."

Anger swelled up inside of her, and I felt it like my palm was pressed down on a heating stovetop. She toyed with the idea of purging me from her consciousness, but she couldn't do it. Couldn't eliminate me. I was hardwired in. Still, she probed for a route and a means to destroy me, those tendrils reaching out for me again, penetrating deep into my psyche. And I wondered if she could do it. Could her decapitated head in the back of the bread truck reach through the cables and wires and suffocate me and melt my brain like she had the crews of the hovercrafts? Her hatred for me was hot to the touch.

"The Order is hiding something from you," I said, trying anything to slow her assault against me. "Two knew it. So did Five and One. If you can crack the algorithm of the dead zone, why doesn't the Network? Why hasn't the Order reached you yet?"

"Get out of my head," Seven said and continued to study the connection between us, searching for a way to sever it, and barring that, a way to kill me with it. The Hellcat barreled on toward the stronghold.

"No, god shit it. Listen to me. You need me. I am your only ally here. You want something that neither the Resistance nor the Order can offer. That's why you didn't stop at killing Five. That's why you had to kill One. You want something more. Something better. But here you are, charging right along with the Order's plan. You're a tool, and they're using you for their purpose."

"You're lying. You want something too. Why should I listen to a Resistance agent planted inside my head? Why should I trust you?"

"I'm not in the Resistance. The Resistance died when I was a kid."

"Then you can't change what happens today anyway."

"You're probably right," I admitted. "But I'm sure as fuck going to try."

"And what would you change, even if you could?"

"I don't know. I don't have all the answers. I just know whatever you're about to do, it's all bad. And it's got nothing to do with peace and order."

"I'm in control of my own actions. I'll do what I feel is right."

"I'm telling you, there's something else at play here," I pleaded with her. Each time she turned back one of my thoughts, the tendrils wrapped tighter around me and squeezed. "The Order has other things in mind. They're using you."

The Hellcat roared down the open road. The speedometer topped out at two hundred miles per hour. Leaves and dust shot up and out in our wake. The tires hugged the shallow curves of the road. The suspension swayed with the rise and fall of the terrain. On the three-dimensional map, we grew closer and closer to the open mine pit.

"Not far now," Seven said, still tightening her invading tentacles around my mind. "Almost there."

"The Resistance will be waiting for you. A lot of people. You'll kill them, won't you? You'll murder them and not think twice about it?"

"I'm not what you think," Seven said. "I don't enjoy the killing, not like the others. Not like Three. But I'll kill who I must. I'll take out the Resistance's nerve center, and then I'll destroy their heads and put an end to this torment and insanity."

"And what then?"

"I'll walk away. Like Five wanted to do. I'll go off by myself and have my peace."

"You'll do what the Order tells you to do. That's the truth. Can't you feel it? I know you can because I feel it through you. The Network is here, just hidden. It's keeping itself from you."

The pressure Seven exerted onto me eased. She reached out for the Network and knew I was right. She felt it even more precisely than I did. The Network was present there in the dead zone, allowing itself to be blocked out by the jammers, restrained, even when there was no leash. She felt it and thought she could get through the static and reach it, but when she tried it seemed to slip further away, reducing its wattage whenever she reached out, and then increasing when she pulled back. Always out of reach, no matter how close or far away.

"Why?" I asked. "What is it doing to you?"

Another wave of hot anger surged from Seven's core. This wave wasn't aimed directly at me though. This was days of frustration, of emotional abandonment. It was a backlog of hate of which she'd been dealt a surplus. The criticism and cold judgment from the others. The manipulation by One. The confusion by Five. And now this.

"Why?" I asked her.

"I don't care," Seven said, biting off every word. "I give up trying to figure it all out. Trying to sort out all the hidden motivations. I'm done dealing with you. Done answering your questions. The stronghold is just ahead, and I'm going to erase it off the map."

Seven took another turn, this one sharp enough to throw the whole back end of the car around sideways into a skid. The inertia pulled us to the outside of the turn, but she had both hands clamped onto the steering wheel, bracing herself against the pressure. Days ago, the motion would have made me nauseous. The cold of living inside an android, the sleeplessness, the hunger, the mental ache of living inside of a memory that often plunged into other memories… Like Seven filling the void, I'd learned to live with it all now.

The Hellcat came out of the turn without losing much speed and charged down a slim driveway. There were signs with company names and warnings posted along the narrow paved road, but they were far behind us before I could read any of them.

A quarter mile ahead, the driveway led to a fence topped with concertina wire, a tall gate, guard towers like a prison, and humans with guns. We were approaching the stronghold, and this time there was no subtlety or subterfuge. Seven punched her arm and assault rifle through the driver's window and opened fire on the guards. Two more hovercrafts rose up from below the horizon and beyond the gate. Bullets from guard towers and cannon shells from the hovercrafts blasted apart the asphalt around us.

Seven weaved the Hellcat through the impacts as if her course was predestined, and in some ways it was. She was hyper-aware of every barrel and bomb. The location, action, machination of every sensor, hovercraft, and human pumped directly into our brains. She became the electronics and implants, connecting to them and feeding off of them through radio waves. A second later she was manipulating them as if she wasn't one mind, but hundreds.

The hovercrafts turned away from the Hellcat, raking the flow of cannon fire off the road, through the woods, and into each other. Explosions lit up the sky. Guard tower turned on guard tower. Guards grabbed their heads and curled up in agony.

I bathed in the entirety of Seven's awareness. A flood of sensory input and information like nothing I'd experienced through her before. She was in everything and everyone, and so I was inside of all those things too. I felt the initial horror and torture I'd experienced inside of Seven as she invaded humans new to her psychosis. I felt the miscalculations, the confusion, the sense of being hijacked by a dangerous and angry creature wholly intending to erase everything she touched. I felt the burn of human minds frying inside their own skulls.

The gunfire stopped. What was left of the hovercrafts arced down from the sky.

The Hellcat hit the gate at one hundred and ninety miles per hour. The chain link exploded off its mounts like it was made of paper.

There were a few buildings on the edge of the mine. Offices. Maintenance sheds. A security booth next to the winding road that zigzagged down the lip of the pit to the bottom. On gravel now, Seven cut between these obstructions. The Hellcat sent up rooster tails of dirt and rocks with each twist of the wheel. Ahead, the surface of the earth disappeared. The open pit was kilometers across and hundreds of meters deep. The land was flat and present one moment and absent the next. The Hellcat stabbed between buildings and shot over the brink.

The tires left the ground. Seven and I felt the momentary sensation of flight, of zero-gravity suspension, of sudden detachment from everything and everyone. I was in the pool again, alone, cold, isolated, and abandoned. I wanted the sensation to last forever.

Gravity betrayed the Hellcat's inertia. The hood and its heavy engine nosed down. The view out of the windshield tilted down to the depth of the mine. The Hellcat cleared the winding path and steps of the side of the mine. The grill aimed for the water-soaked bottom. Seven popped open the door and shoved clear of the car. We became airborne. Falling, not flying, but in glorious control. There, in mid-air and touching nothing, she reconnected. The car. The equipment. The humans at the bottom of the pit. The electronically locked entrances into the bunker built into the side of the pit. The Network.

We sensed it out there, watching over her, caring for her, assisting her in hacking into all of the Resistance's electronics. Always silent and hidden just below the surface, but present, benevolent, and beneficial to her cause.

"Not your cause," I managed to tell her, mid-freefall. "*Its* cause. Not yours. That's the trick of it all."

She ignored me. Seven recalled dropping out of the hovercraft just behind One when they'd first arrived outside of the dead zone. Only she wasn't following One this time. Wasn't afraid. Didn't need his guidance or validation. This was a circle becoming complete. She was realized. Without One. Beyond One. Seven was everything she could reach out and touch with a radio wave. She was all.

Seven hit the bottom of the mine pit like a meteor. The thin layer of water on the bottom of the pit vaporized. The dirt and rock blasted apart. A dozen meters away, the Hellcat made landfall and disintegrated on impact. The yellow and black body crumpled. Gasoline exploded. Parts and pieces ejected in all directions. A cloud of dirt swallowed it. The beast died and Seven mourned it, for Three's sake, but only for a nanosecond.

We emerged from the impact hole. Dust and steam swept over the Resistance fighters surrounding us. They were all armed. The pretense of a mining operation was abandoned down here at the bottom of the pit. No one here was a miner. None of the excavators or drills were in use. The veins had been depleted of ore and taconite for decades. Seven saw nothing constructive here, only destructive. No order, only chaos. This, she thought, was the primordial pool of disorder, full of things crawling out of it to infect the rest of the world. The wind cleared away the dust and steam and she allowed them to see her.

"They should know the face of their destroyer," Seven said.

"And I can't wait to show you yours," I said back.

She pushed me aside for what I was, an infection put inside of her by her enemies. A minor annoyance that was powerless to stop her or even affect her. I was an illusion. Something they planted inside of her to distract her from her divine purpose.

Was that all I was? I couldn't remember anymore. Couldn't keep it straight, reality and dream.

Resistance fighters yelled and alerted each other. They waved to each other and aimed guns at us, closing in around us. There were too many of them for even her to cut down with her katana and assault rifle. They shuffled to a stop around us, barrels aimed at her head. They had us dead to rights. So Seven went to work dismembering them. Before any of them fired the first shot, she infiltrated their minds through the implants, turned them on each other, turned them on themselves, shot their heart rates up beyond their biological capabilities, cut off their blood supplies to their brains, and forced them to commit suicide. There was a series of blasts of gunfire, but not a single bullet came near us.

Bodies dropped as Seven strolled across the bottom of the pit. Some writhed in agony. Others clutched their heads and screamed to the sky. A few raked the barrels of the weapons into each other or themselves.

A thick steel door the size of a tank was set into the side of the pit. The stronghold was inside. Already dead guards lay in the dirt on either side of it. Gun turrets mounted into the rock above the bunker's entrance went limp. The electronic locks on the door released. Inside, the dog wheel spun, and the door sprang out. It eased wide open before us. Seven walked into the stronghold's maw, uncontested.

The inside of the bunker was almost identical to the bunker where Two died. Computer stations. A metal mesh floor. A pair of human technicians. She walked between them as they screamed and clawed at their own faces as if they were trying to dig out the sudden madness inside their brains through their faces. They toppled to the grate, dead before she was three strides away. The corridor led to a deep shaft. This pit was metallic and perfectly cylindrical. No stairs or elevators to guide the way down, just an endless hole that sunk deeper still into the Earth. Seven knew exactly how deep it was and what lay at the bottom of it.

Seven put her toes up to the edge of the pit. It was dark inside the bunker, and darker still at the bottom of the shaft. But something pulsed red at the bottom. It throbbed, not just with that red glowing light, but with data and information. It was a hub. A hive. A port of entry inside the nerve center of the Resistance.

"Seven, it's not too late," I said to her. "There's more at play here than what the Order's showing you. I know you can feel it because I feel it through you. But it's not too late. It will be soon, but right now you can still turn away."

"My path is clear," Seven said. "I've never been so certain of anything in my life. And you can't stop me. No one can."

Seven stepped off the cusp. I submerged into another moment of disconnection. I was an astronaut at the end of a broken tether. A kid drowning in a pool under a careless father. A man severed from humanity. For Seven, it was the opposite. She touched everything. Loved everything. Was everything. We plummeted down, deeper into the heart of the Resistance, away from the white light, into blackness, and then into that red pulsing warmth.

We landed. Seven's pneumatic legs absorbed the fall. The grated metal floor compressed into a crater. The noise of the impact echoed and reverberated against the walls. The crash resounded until the sound waves absorbed into the walls and left us in silence. There was no running or shooting guards. No technicians screaming and twisting into a curled heap of corpses. Just a steady electronic hum, but nothing else.

Seven turned around in a circle, wanting to take in her objective through her own perspective. There were no light bulbs that I could see, but everything seemed to glow red. The room was spherical except for the round grated floor and the round opening in the ceiling we fell through. The walls wrapped around us. There was no gravity here. We lifted off the floor just a few centimeters. Wires hung weightless, drifting in the air disturbed by our invasion of this still place. Spread about the sphere were humans strapped into chairs and plugged into cables and wires. Their eyes were open but dull and unguided. Their faces were slack, but they weren't dead. They were plugged in, hardwired, and networked together, their brains adapted into a cloud-sourced organic computer. This was the nerve center of the Resistance, and I knew this was what fueled their encryptions and electric countermeasures. This was what kept them a step ahead of the Network and the Order. Seven had never seen anything like it.

I had. The tech boys inside the Chicago Anomalies Investigation Department. "Boys" was just a part of the nickname. They were men, women, trans, androids who volunteered to take the next technological leap. Early adopters, pushing the limits of technology. But that was in the present. All this was happening twenty-five years in the past. The application here was less advanced, more rudimentary. The humans plugged into the hive, there were seven of them, were unaware of their surroundings. Their minds were completely encapsulated inside their network, as cut off from external stimulation as I was bouncing around in the back of the bread truck. But I pushed that thought aside, for now.

Seven regarded the humans, counted them, but thought little of the sum. She realized that she couldn't connect to these nodes via radio waves. Unlike the hovercrafts and implants in the guard, these entities were impermeable to wireless transmissions. And there were no other signals she could reach down here in the sphere beside her, and the man inside her brain. It felt quiet. Peaceful.

"This is it. The mind behind the Resistance. This is how they've been able to evade the Order. How they've managed each of their victories. This is the objective of my mission. The beginning of the end of the war. Weak, indefensible, fragile humans trying their best to be androids and failing," Seven said. "They're an abomination."

She unsheathed the handgun from the center of her chest, passed it to her right hand, and extended the gun out at arm's length. She was savoring this.

"Don't…" I was going to beg her not to kill them, but I knew it would do no good. She never hesitated in all the previous days and battles, and she surely wouldn't here at the threshold of victory. Seven was engrossed by her targets and wasn't the least bit interested in heeding my advice. And I was inside a memory of things that had already happened. I couldn't change any of the outcomes, as much as I didn't want to admit it.

She squeezed the trigger and put a bullet into the first of the seven hive-minded humans. The barrel moved to the next woman, and her head exploded. The wires and LED readouts around the humans were juxtapositioned next to the fundamentally analog site of blood and skin and brain matter splattered across the room like a popped water balloon. Seven moved the barrel to the next, then the next, and the next. One shot for each of the seven humans. The last one died without any warning or visible reaction that the others were gone. Maybe inside the network, he saw it coming. But in the room, the human was just the next lamb in the slaughter. Seven bullets, and they were nothing.

"There. It's over. It's done," I said. "Now get me the hell out of here. Maggie? Do you hear me? I did what you wanted, now let me out."

"I cut off the head, but the body still lives," Seven said. "All those other nodes of chaos are out there, still fighting and making war. The pain. The madness. The confusion. I can connect to all of them and bring them peace, all from inside this place."

"Roach? Gaius?" I called out, my words only echoing inside of Seven's head. "I did your dirty work. I made it to the end. Now get me out of here."

"You want to leave now?" Seven asked me. "Why would you want to leave now? I'm about to issue peace upon the world."

"Do you really think that's what the Order wants, you psychopath?" I said.

"What do you know about the Order?" Seven said. She approached one of the corpses strapped into the chairs that lined the sphere. The human seeped beads of red fluid into the zero-gravity air. When she unbuckled her, unplugged her from the connectors jacked into her skull, and pulled her loose from the chair, their masses moved equally and oppositely.

"I used to think like you," I confessed to Seven.

"I've felt the madness of man, experienced its poison inside my own head. You are the manifestation of it. I will be the cure," Seven said. "You're nothing like me."

"I used to be like you, but not anymore, Seven. Not for a while now. And so much the better," I said.

"I know what you are now. What you really are. A weak human laying in a bed, asleep and dreaming my memories. We're hardwired into each other, and just like you can put these distractions into my head, I can infiltrate yours. With this… with all the power of the Network in my control, I can solve it all. After I deliver world peace, I'll destroy the last vestiges of chaos inside my brothers' and sister's heads. Then I'm going to lobotomize you from inside your own skull, Chuck." Seven said. "You're about to see the rise of the Order and the eradication of chaos and confusion. This will be perrrrrrfffffffeeee——"

Her mind silenced. Her body hung just centimeters off the floor in zero gravity. The skulls at her waist clanked against each other, suspended and weightless on their cables.

"Seven?"

Like a statue slowly coming to life, Seven's right hand dropped the handgun and let it drift away. She gripped Six's head, and it came undone from the cable on her waist. She moved it to the headrest in front of her.

"Seven, what are you doing?"

"This chair belongs to Six," she said, her voice suddenly devoid of intonation and emotion.

"What? Why? What are you doing?"

Her hands made quick work of connecting the robotic skull to the Sharedmind network.

"Seven, he's dead. The head is empty. Two wiped it clean. It's worthless. What are you doing?"

"Not empty," Seven said, her voice coming from her but somehow not belonging to her. "Full of exactly what the Order needs."

"The Order's not here. You're here. I'm here. That's it. If you won't listen to me, listen to yourself. You said you were going to destroy these heads. Kill the insanity inside of them. You said you'd bring the world peace."

"The Order has resumed control," Seven said.

I sensed it now, a program that had been hiding in a back processor all this time. A series of commands triggered to run as soon as the right conditions were met. Just like Four's response in the senator's office, it waited with the patience of a stone until Seven brought it here. Inside the Sharedmind sphere, those conditions were met, and the tiny program had moved to the forefront and taken over all the ROM, all the consciousness, all the will.

As soon as Six's head was connected, Seven pushed off the chair and moved to the next. Her hands worked to unbuckle, unplug, and discard the dead man who had been there. Then she grabbed Five's bloody severed head. There were metal cables and connections up inside the neck, and there was a standard implant port behind his ear. Seven connected him. Seven pushed off to the next corpse in the next chair.

Across the room, Six's eyes came to life. A golden light burned inside the skull. As a response, Five flashed binary code from his open and human-like eyes. Meanwhile, Seven ripped another body from another chair.

"Seven. Seven! Stop! What are you doing?"

"The Order's will," she said. What came out next was weak and strained. "Stop me. They were destructive, disorganized, and violent. This will not bring peace."

Four's head was next. The lumbering enforcer. The individualist. His eyes lit up. No voice. No motion, but the mind stirred behind those eyes. Seven pushed off to the next.

"This was their plan all along," I said. "They sent the seven of you here to drive you crazy, just so they could port your madness into every mind connected to the Resistance network. That's how they did it. That's how they took out the Resistance. This is the Event, happening before my own eyes."

"Stop me. I don't want this," Seven pleaded. Meanwhile, her hands worked with quick precision to wire Three's purple-haired skull into another jack. "This won't end anything. This will only further the war. This will only spread our disease."

"I can't. Seven, listen to me. I can't do anything from inside of your skull. You have to stop this. You have to resist."

"The Order has resumed control," she said. Or something inside of her, something taking up residence in her head alongside me, said. The program that ran her sped up. I don't know if it somehow sensed my interference in her memory, if any of that made sense, if anything I did here mattered. But the program hurried, nonetheless. Either from gained proficiency or impatience, it was impossible to tell.

"Stop it, Seven. I know the results of your actions. Millions are driven insane in an instant. Millions more killed in the wake. The Order seizes complete rule in the following anarchy. It was their plan all along. But you can stop it," I said. "You can change this. You said you were Seven, so be Seven. This isn't your will. Don't do this!"

"I can't. I must…" she muttered, breaking down. Fear and panic well up inside of her. She shared the emotions with me. I bathed in them, against my will, against her will. Hijacked in her, and she hijacked by the Order, I sensed my hands gripping Two's head and wiring it in.

And then, I understood her. I knew where she came from, knew what shaped her wants and fears, had lived her embarrassments and victories, and empathized with her last will that was now being snuffed out by the authority I once subscribed to as faithfully as she had. We were one, and we were powerless.

Two chairs left. One's disembodied head still at her hip. Seven showed no signs of slowing. She pulled loose the corpse and flung it away. Beads of blood and viscera moved through the room like an astronaut's orange juice. The sphere was littered with floating corpses and their bulbous globules of blood. Seven paid no attention to them but wired in One's head into the second to the last chair. His one good eye lit up. Sparks crackled and shorted behind his scar.

Seven turned to the last chair, still occupied by a dead woman. The rest were occupied by her brother and sister androids. They weren't dead but filled with the Order's specially brewed poison: juvenile minds gone insane contemplating unknowable things. One chair was left, but Seven's belt was empty. She pushed off to the last corpse.

I received her instructions from the Order at the same time she did.

"No, no, no. Don't do it. If you jack into that chair, I'll be jacked into that chair. We'll both be hardwired into the seven others. You couldn't get along when you were separated. Networking together into a Sharedmind will be like a beaker of reactive chemicals. We'll be in all their heads, all of us trying to think and be as one, each of us fighting for our own twisted perspective, each hating the other. It won't work. You'll kill each other. Push each other over the brink. And you'll pull me down with you."

"It is the will of the Order," Seven deadpanned. Then, in her own meek voice, "Stop me. Whoever you are, wherever you are, stop me. Stop this from happening."

"Maggie! Roach! Gaius! It's done!" I screamed silently inside her skull. "Unplug me, you bastards! Let me out!"

She reached the last body and disconnected it. All around her the lit eyes of the six others watched her, flashed at her, and silently begged her to join the asylum that was their shared minds. Seven twisted and sat in the chair and brought me with her. Seeing through her eyes, feeling through her skin, I touched each cable, felt for the ports in the side of her head, and made the connections.

As soon as the last cable was attached, I felt the full surge of the combined madness contained in each of the seven androids rush into my brain. I was Seven. I was One. I was Two, Three, Four, Five… and oh god the horrors inside the mind of Six. For one brief moment, I wasn't just living in hell. I was hell.

"Get me out! Get me out! Now! Get me the fuck—"

Chapter Twenty Four

"— outta here!" We screamed and I heard the words, dry and almost human, echoing as if they actually contacted air and made sound waves. I suddenly found myself in control of Seven's hands and body so I tore frantically at the cables and wires dangling off of us. I pushed out of the chair just to find more connections to pull loose. And there was gravity. I dropped to the floor but kept clawing at the wires, ripping myself clear of the hivemind as the Event seized us all in its specially brewed insanity.

"Chuck! Chuck, calm down!" Maggie yelled. Her voice hit my ears and her hands grabbed at my shoulders. "You're out! You're out, baby. We did it. We finally have it!"

My eyes swam in my head, out of focus and dried shut. Things were too bright. Where was the red glow of the Sharedmind sphere? Why did Seven's sensory input suddenly feel so wet and analog? How was Maggie here?

I pried open my eyes and understood. I was out of the memory, free from Seven's head, safe but as powerless to stop the Event as I always had been.

"No no no no no no…" I mumbled.

Maggie came into focus. Her long, tied-back, brown hair. Her luminescent eyes. She smiled like I'd rarely seen her. My wife.

"It's okay, Chuck," she touched my head, soothing me with her soft human touch. "You did it. We saw everything. We saw how they did it."

I was inside the bread truck. We were stationary, not bouncing and jostling around as a moving truck would. Roach sat behind her, reading scrolling words on a computer screen. Next to him, Seven's severed head rested at the other end of all the wires and cables.

Disoriented, I touched my face and head to make sure. I was shaking and soaked in sweat, but I was outside of Seven again, out of the memory, and back into the real world.

"Gaius called it," Roach said as he read the screen. "Just as we suspected."

"We were able to track the events as they happened in your mind," Maggie said. She sat next to me and lifted up my head into her lap. "As you experienced everything the android did, we were able to watch. Her encryptions were too tight before, but Roach figured out how to source the feedback from your mind. We saw it all. We know how they took down the Resistance. And now we know how we can take out the Order."

The door to the panel van rolled open. Gaius, the captain of this band of rebels, came in and went straight to Roach and the monitor he was reading. More soldiers and technicians were outside and behind them, some kind of dark facility. They rushed in, and under the direction of Gaius and Roach, they disconnected Seven's head.

"The Event," I said. "She did it. She brought about the Event. It wasn't happenstance or bad luck or a flaw in the systems. It was her."

Gaius nodded. "We have it. The weapon to take down the Order for good," he said and then turned to Roach. "Can you do it? Can you make the connections like we planned?"

"For sure. It will be no different than how I have her hooked up now. Besides, I just watched her do it," Roach said.

"They have us surrounded," Gaius said. "Their assault teams will be coming through our blockades any minute now. If this doesn't work..."

"It will work, it will work," Roach said.

With a wave of his hand, Gaius directed soldiers from outside the van to come in and rather Seven's head. "Careful boys," Gaius said as he shepherded them and the head out of the van. "That right there is the key to the downfall of the Order. We can bring down the whole Network."

"What are they going to do?" I asked.

"You did it, Chuz," Maggie said and kissed me on the forehead. "I'm so proud of you."

She set me down on the floor of the bread truck as softly as a mother laying down her kid for bedtime. Then she hopped out of the van to follow the others.

I pushed myself up on shaking arms. The bread truck was backed up to a large earthen tunnel, dimly lit and burrowing deep into the bedrock. Maggie followed a small crowd of Resistance technicians scurrying away from me.

"What are you planning—" I started but stopped myself when I tried to stand up. I was too weak. My body collapsed back to the floor. My legs were just as feeble and uncooperative. I braced myself against the chair, rose up, and found strength and a will to move with each passing second. I shuffled to the end of the van. "Wait! What the shit do you think you're going to do with that?"

No response. Seven's new entourage moved down the long corridor, a corridor that looked hauntingly familiar. A corridor I'd been through before. No. I hadn't been here before. But I remembered being here.

I mustered my constitution and limped out of the back of the truck. I staggered and dragged a numb foot as I entered the corridor. Some cord was still connected and dragged some piece of equipment out of the van. I yanked free a pulse oximeter and left all the wires behind me. Down the tunnel ahead of me, short-tempered voices buried their excitement in firm commands and military posturing. All around me, the facility hummed with a million volts of power and data.

"What is this place? What the shit are you doing?" I called after them. My feet became sure under me. My muscles grew stronger and my nerves more responsive. I was in my own body again; it was just that my brain was slow to believe it. Still, I had to move down the pathway. I had to catch up to them.

I shuffled and worked my way into a trot. At the end of the hallway, they'd set up flood lamps. Silhouettes of people moved back and forth in front of the lights. They were busy. Eager. Determined to see their intention turn to fruition. As I came closer, I saw the shape of my wife at the entrance of a room, a silhouette with her hands on her hips and feet braced apart.

"Maggie," I called to her.

She turned and smiled. I moved to her and put my hands on her shoulder to stabilize myself against her.

"What are you going to do?" I asked.

"What do you think we're going to do, Chuz?" she said. "When we captured that android, it was on a raving, murderous rampage, completely independent of the Order and the Network. It had no mission or purpose other than to kill humans, regardless of who they were or who they fought for. It was only after we looked inside its records that we realized it was in the stronghold at the exact moment of the Resistance's fall. Now, we finally know why. She caused the Event."

"She was plugged into the six others," Chuck said. "The Order forced her to do it. It was the Order's plan all along, to drive them insane and then condense them together into one deranged hivemind connected directly to the Resistance's implant network. It's what the Order wanted the whole time."

"And now we're going to give it back to them in spades," Maggie said.

I looked past her. We were inside the stronghold, at the bottom of the pit, inside the sphere. They had accessed it through some tunnel hidden in its wall. Gaius, Roach, and the others all wearing implants bustled about between empty chairs, rerouting wires and redistributing power lines.

"You wired this place to the Network, didn't you?" I asked. "You fucking maniacs, do you have any idea what you'll do if you plug her in?"

"She holds all the madness of all seven androids now," Maggie said. "She absorbed them and lived off of that insanity for years, letting it fester and cripple her even more than when she'd brought down the Resistance. You saw how many she killed just in the few days you were inside of her, and I'll have you know she didn't slow down after she disconnected from here."

"So smash her head and be done with it," I said. "Destroy her! Why for the love of fuck would you plug her into the Network?"

Gaius coughed over Maggie's shoulder. "We're surrounded here, trapped by the Order, but that won't be the case for long. Our assault teams are standing by all across the continent. The Underground is ready to rise up."

Maggie's eyes stayed locked with me. She was full of a gleeful eagerness to reshuffle the world. "We couldn't have done this without you, Chuck. In 99 Town we exposed the Order for what it was. We showed everyone what they are. We gave them their chance to leave the Order. Now it's time we took back control."

"Maggie, there's still billions of people connected to the Network. Billions of innocent people just going about their business. Implants have been mandated for years! The only one's not connected—"

"We transmitted all the Order's crimes into their implants the moment you left 99 Town. If they're still connected now, it's their own fault. A life lived by someone else's rules is no life at all, Chuz. This is the only way," Maggie said.

I caught a glimpse of Roach carrying Seven's head forward like an offering to a god. They'd wired all seven chairs together, all the cables stretching to a table in the center of the room. Roach set the head down on the table and began connecting jacks to ports, like Seven was a fly in the center of a spider's web.

"It won't work," I said. "The Order, they're always more capable than they let on. It's how it tricked Seven. Made her believe it wasn't in control when it controlled everything. They have access to your network too. If you plug Seven into the Network, they'll just turn it back on the Underground, or worse yet, let it inflict everyone across the whole continent, Underground and Order all the same. Everyone, young and old, innocent and guilty will be driven mad!" I said. "All of them. My god…"

"The Underground is a direct offspring of the Resistance and their technologically superior encryptions. The Order can't breach our network, but we can sure as hell breach theirs," Maggie said.

"No no no. You saw how Seven penetrated their network. The Order just wants you to believe you have the upper hand," I said, but they weren't listening. No one was listening.

I rushed for Seven's head where it hung in the center of the spider's web. Roach turned and caught me like he was an offensive lineman. I had no strength left to push through him. More soldiers came and pulled me away. I fought, but I was too weak.

Gaius stepped in front of me, blocking my view as the technicians went back to work making the connections. "Relax, Chuck," Gaius said, his own grin visible through the wiry bristles of his beard. "We're on the doorstep of a new age of peace and freedom."

"It's okay, Chuck," Maggie said, gripping my shoulders, her one hand flesh, her other cold steel. "Everything's going to be okay."

"There's other ways," I said. "We don't have to do this. Think about what you're doing. Think! For one second! I've been inside of her. I know what she's like. You have no idea what you're about to unleash!"

"There's no choice. They're coming here now to kill us all. But not after this. We're taking them out. We can finally have peace. Me and you, we can finally be together," Maggie said and touched my cheek. She was still wearing her implant. "It's the only way, Chuck. It's the only chance we have to liberate their minds."

From the corner of my eye, I saw past Gaius. Roach had one cable left. All the rest had been plugged into Seven. He found a port at the base of her neck and brought the last cable toward it. All eyes were on her.

I made one last push. With what little strength I had left in my bones, I lunged toward Maggie. My fingers found the grip of her implant as we tumbled to the floor. As we collapsed, I yanked it free from her head. She fought and swore, but even from there on the floor, we couldn't help but turn to see Roach finish his work.

He made the last connection. Seven's eyes lit up like there was a fire behind them. And maybe there was. As soon as she connected to power, she screamed like a banshee. Her metal mandible hung low, and an eye-piercing shriek tore through the room. In her time away from the Network, she'd only grown madder, and now she was pumping that into any live connection… and sewing paths into new connections. The first screams were electronic, but it only took a few seconds for Seven to spread her reach through the Order, through the Network, and beyond.

She hacked her way across satellites, antennas, grids, intranets, implants, and into human brains.

The screams were electronic, then turned organic all around us.

About the Author

Joe Prosit writes sci-fi, horror, and psycho fiction. His debut novel is "Bad Brains," followed by the "From Order Series" featuring the novels, "99 Town," "7 Androids," and "Zero City." "Machines Monsters and Maniacs" is a self-published collection of sixteen of his short stories. He has been published in various magazines and podcasts, most notably, in 365Tomorrow, The NoSleep Podcast, Metaphorosis Magazine, and Kaidankai Podcast. You can find it on Amazon or at his website, at www.JoeProsit.com. If you're an adept stalker, you can find him on one of the many lakes and rivers or lost deep inside the Great North Woods. Or you can just follow him on Twitter, @joeprosit.